# Ruin Creek

*Also by David Payne*

CONFESSIONS OF A TAOIST ON WALL STREET

EARLY FROM THE DANCE

# Ruin Creek

DAVID PAYNE

DOUBLEDAY
NEW YORK  LONDON  TORONTO  SYDNEY  AUCKLAND

PUBLISHED BY DOUBLEDAY
*a division of Bantam Doubleday Dell Publishing Group, Inc.*
*1540 Broadway, New York, New York 10036*

DOUBLEDAY *and the portrayal of an anchor with a dolphin are trademarks of*
*Doubleday, a division of Bantam Doubleday Dell Publishing Group, Inc.*

*Every effort has been made to locate current copyright holders for the lines from both*
*"The Wabash Cannonball" and "The Big Rock Candy Mountain" (lyrics and music by*
*Roger Truhart), both of which are excerpted in this book. Please send any information*
*regarding copyrighted material to the publisher.*

*We gratefully acknowledge permission from the following:*

*Lines from* Our Town *by Thornton Wilder, published by HarperCollins. Copyright*
*1938, © 1957, 1966 by Thornton Wilder, copyright renewed 1985 by Union Trust*
*Company. Reprinted by special permission of the Estate of Thornton Wilder. Lines from*
*"Respect," lyrics and music by Otis Redding. Copyright © 1965 East/Memphis Music*
*Corp. & Time Music. Copyright assigned to Irving Music, Inc. (BMI), 1982. All*
*Rights Reserved. International Copyright Secured. Excerpt from "Burnt Norton" in*
Four Quartets, *copyright 1943 by T. S. Eliot, and renewed 1971 by Esme Valerie*
*Eliot. Reprinted by permission of Harcourt Brace & Company. Excerpts from "The*
*Waste Land" in* Collected Poems *1909–1962 by T. S. Eliot. Copyright 1936 by*
*Harcourt Brace & Company, copyright © 1964, 1963 by T. S. Eliot. Reprinted by*
*permission of the publisher.*

*Interior photo courtesy of the New York Public Library Picture Collection*

*Library of Congress Cataloging-in-Publication Data*

Payne, David (William David)
  Ruin Creek / David Payne. — 1st ed.
    p.   cm.
  I. Title.
PS3566.A9366R8   1993
813'.54—dc20                        92-42476
                                         CIP

*ISBN 0-385-26418-6*
*Copyright © 1993 by David Payne*
*All Rights Reserved*

*Book Design by Gretchen Achilles*

*Printed in the United States of America*
*October 1993*
*First Edition*

1   3   5   7   9   10   8   6   4   2

*This book is dedicated to the memory of George A. Rose,*
*and to my father, for giving*
*me a wilderness*

*I had learned long ago, but had forgotten in my frenzied love, that there is a draught that we must drink or not be fully human . . . I knew that one must know the truth. I knew quite well that when one is adult one must raise to one's lips the wine of the truth, heedless that it is not sweet like milk but draws the mouth with its strength, and celebrate communion with reality, or else walk for ever queer and small like a dwarf.*

—REBECCA WEST
*The Return of the Soldier*


*"I'm beginning to believe all this I hear, about how young folks learn all the things in order to get married, that we had to get married in order to learn."*

—WILLIAM FAULKNER
*Sanctuary*

# PROLOGUE

I stumbled on the photographs by accident some years ago, a cache of secret treasure lying underneath a film of dust at the bottom of a drawer. It was a cold, wet late fall afternoon on the Outer Banks, the barometer falling and a northeast gale whistling through the screens and whipping spindrift off the ocean. Though it was some hours shy of cocktail time, I'd poured a glass of whiskey, lit a fire and set off wandering through our drafty old summer house into what had been, once upon a time, my parents' bedroom—I still thought of it as theirs, though "they," in any sense of mutual enterprise, had long since ceased to exist except in my imagination. I was looking, as well as I recall, for a deck of cards, thinking I might play some solitaire.

Sitting at the desk, I tried the banked drawers one by one. Swelled at the joints, the bottom one creaked open with a musty whiff of rust and woolens. Inside I discovered a worn jigsaw puzzle that had belonged to my grandmother, Nanny Tilley. She, who never visited Europe, had struggled every summer with this scene, the Champs Élysées under snow, coal smoke in the air and horse-drawn wagons. In the years since Nanny's death, the picture on the box had begun to blister, delaminating from the cardboard. As I lifted it out to take a closer look, my eye fell on a yellowed folder with a deckle edge and a double border of gold piping. *"Candid" by Byron Wells, State Line, South Carolina* was embossed in the bottom right-hand corner.

Flipping it open, I found myself staring at a black-and-white eight-by-ten of a young couple. Though college age, they seemed hardly more than college-age children, a well-dressed boy and girl standing at the curb before the open door of a white Chevrolet, a 'fifty-five Bel Air from the first shipment of the model year. We still owned that Chevy when I started school and I remember winter mornings rolling down our steep-pitched drive in silence till the heater and the radio kicked in as my father popped the clutch . . . It was curious to realize there'd been a time that car was new.

Behind the posing couple, a series of low steps rises to the open door of a small brick chapel. Standing there is Nanny Tilley, younger than I ever knew her, still fat—as she was not toward the end—her eyes narrowed in the smoke of a cigarette that dangles, Bogart-style, from the corner of her mouth. One hand holds a box on which the words "Mahatma Rice" are clearly legible as the other cocks to throw. On the back of the print a stamp reads: *Please credit to B. Wells*, together with the date, *September 21, 1954*.

The first day of fall—my parents' anniversary was always easy to remember. That is who the children are and what the pictures show, their wedding . . .

I had finished college by that time and never seen these photographs or known they existed. They had not been on our mantelpiece at Ruin Creek or among the thickets of family memorabilia on Nanny's piano on Country Club Drive in Killdeer. My mother was not represented at that stage, though there were others—I recalled a chubby twelve-year-old in a shapeless white dress, awkward and embarrassed at her confirmation, who turned suddenly and without warning, one picture farther to the left, into a startling slim-waisted beauty in an off-the-shoulder cocktail dress with pearls and elbow-length gloves. You had to check twice to be certain she was the same person.

Nanny's gallery ranged back to my great- and great-great-grand-parents' generation, sepia portraits of a bearded man with two fin-gers slipped into his waistcoat pocket beside his watch chain and fob, his wife standing behind his chair with tight-drawn hair and lips and a high collar pinned with a cameo brooch—severe, primitive-look-ing people grave with troubles difficult to imagine now. Weddings, christenings, birthdays, Christmases, school pictures of my younger brother Reed and me and our two cousins sporting crewcuts and missing our front teeth . . . In that whole extensive gallery my par-ents' marriage was not included.

If it had ever occurred to me to ask the reason—and, truthfully, it hadn't—I could have come up with an answer. I'd heard the story many times—Mama creeping barefoot down the back staircase with her shoes in her hand . . . Daddy parked off on a side road with his headlights off, smoking a Lucky Strike, ducking in the seat every time a car passed . . . the midnight ride across the border to South Carolina . . . the rushed wedding in State Line, a town that spe-cialized in rushed weddings . . .

It was Nanny Tilley's presence on the steps that triggered the alarm; turning the photograph into a puzzle, she became the piece that didn't fit. She was not alone either. As I leafed through, my other grandparents made their appearances one by one, smiling un-accountably festive smiles for the camera on the occasion of their childrens' secret elopement, which they'd supposedly protested. As-sembled for a group shot, they stand on the next higher step above my mother and father, an invisible line of demarcation dividing the shot into two neat halves, Tilley versus Madden, three and three, as cleanly as with scissors.

Below them, my mother stands facing Daddy, one hand fiddling with the sprig of baby's breath in his buttonhole, the other clutching her white gloves. Her bag rests in the crook of her elbow and she's wearing a wide-brimmed hat with a shallow crown that looks some-how otherworldly, like Saturn surrounded by its rings. In black and white you can't make out the color of her dress except that it's not white, and you can tell it's after Labor Day from her dark shoes.

She's turning for the snap and the camera has caught her laughing and a little unprepared; she wears a coy expression with something about it of the clever little girl who knows full well her misbehavior is adorable, especially to Pa, her daddy. She's eighteen.

But even here, already, there's something in her eyes that does not participate in the general festivity of her expression. They are black-dark eyes, like a grove of evergreens where even on the brightest summer day it's always shaded, and there's something not quite innocent in them that trusts itself to the judgment of the camera as though expecting in advance to be found wanting. This is apparent—to my eyes, at least—even as she lifts her heel behind to touch her hem, parodying the infatuated secretaries in 1950s' movies, swept off their feet by the men they love—half swept off, I should say, for her other foot remains firmly planted.

My father towers over her at six foot six, his pale summer suit hanging loose on his thin frame and a pimple on his chin. I've never seen him as slim and young as he is here—the man I remember was sixty pounds heavier—and perhaps it's the contrast that gives the younger one in the photograph something of the gaunt aspect of a concentration camp survivor. It's hard to imagine him as an athlete, though in his senior year at Killdeer High he was the highest scorer in North Carolina in 2-A basketball and made two cuts on the freshman team at Chapel Hill before he blew his knee out in a Sunday pickup game at his fraternity.

Where my mother's expression varies from shot to shot, his is essentially the same in all of them, and his face is far more troubling to me. When I look, everything goes toward it like the vortex in a tub of water spinning toward the drain. He gazes straight into the lens with his hands clasped in front of him, composed and dignified, the only one of the party who isn't smiling.

His eyes are large and bright with clear intelligence, but the animation and playfulness I prefer to remember are absent. His expression makes me think of our neighbor Mr. Poe, my friend Stevie's father, on an afternoon in what must have been 'sixty-three or 'sixty-four, when he turned onto Ruin Creek Road on his way home from work to find a group of neighborhood kids standing around the concrete birdbath on his lawn, watching, while our mothers watched more discreetly from their windows or porches, as his house burned down, the flames roaring above the roof as high as the old oak trees in his yard. My father looks as if he's gazing back from a great distance at a world in ruins—it's difficult for me to hold his eyes, particularly when I recall that he was only twenty-one. A part of me still wants him to look happy about what is happening here, starting his marriage and our family, as though it could make any difference now, as though the past were still negotiable.

Even the incidentals in this picture possess a curious weight, which they've accumulated, bit by bit, with time and repeated study. For instance, over the roof of the Bel Air, a white Greek Revival house stands across the street. It has two separate entrances, one finely detailed, with dentiling and leaded sidelights, the other a plain screen door that appears to have been added later when the house was cut up to accommodate a second family. On this side a ladder leans against the wall for no apparent reason, extending to the sill of a second-story window. Following it up, you notice a pale blur in the window, standing out against the dark interior like a dogwood petal in deep twilight. Someone is there—man, woman or child, it's impossible to say for sure, though measuring by the sash height a child seems most likely.

In any case, that's what I decided long ago, that it was a boy. I didn't notice his presence the first time I examined these photos, perhaps not even the first fifty or a hundred times, but one day, or night, I looked and there he was, staring back at me through the sunburst on the pane. Long after I had memorized every inflection in my parents' faces, his presence continued to draw me. I wondered what the view was like through his window in the second story of this divided house, where the photographer has accidentally captured and frozen him in time as he gazes from the dark interior into the bright, flat, end-of-summer sunlight, across the street, at my parents' backs.

# ONE

## Joey

At night the east wind off the ocean spreads a silver dew across the porch at Pa and Nanny's cottage in Nags Head—that was where the footprints were. The first morning after we got to the beach that summer, as soon as I woke up, I found them trampled in the dew. They looked like stencil maple leaves you make in school to show the change of seasons, only these were all dark green, the color of the porch paint, like they'd fallen off the tree too soon. There were thousands upon thousands of them, and me and Reed could not tell whose they were. Looking at them, though, I got that funny feeling in my stomach I'd had pretty much the whole fifth grade, especially since I turned eleven back in April. I felt like one more thing I didn't want to change was going to anyway, and sure enough, that Thursday night when Pa came for the weekend, Daddy wasn't with him. I wanted something to hold still.

Till then they rode down together every week, Pa and Daddy,

after closing the Bonanza, Pa's tobacco warehouse on Commerce Street, the biggest one in Killdeer and the five surrounding counties. After the last auction Thursday afternoon—they never sold on Friday, not at Pa's—they packed the Cadillac and set their watches and took off, and if they caught the lights in Roanoke Rapids they could make it to the beach in three hours and ten minutes. Reed would get to stay up past his bedtime, and by eight o'clock he'd be bouncing off the walls and yelling, "when will Daddy *get* here, Mama? Which town is he in now?" and Mama would say, "Jackson, sugar," or "Murfreesboro, baby lamb," or "Reed Madden, I don't know—what do *you* think?" and Reed would grin to get her goat and say, " 'Liz'bef City," because that was the closest and the one he wished.

And finally, just as dusk was bluing into night somewhere toward nine o'clock, there'd be headlights turning in and the sound of tires crunching over loose sand in the driveway. Before the car had even stopped we'd all be running down the steps, Reed shouting, "Daddy! Daddy!" while Tawny, our Chesapeake retriever, whined and wagged her tail, just dying to jump someone and not real particular who, though Daddy was her favorite.

By the time the Cadillac pulled in, we'd have things all set to go upstairs. There'd be starched linen napkins on the table and new white candles burning in the chimneys of the hurricane lamps, which were all sparkly from Dee Lou going after them with vinegar and water, which she swore beat Windex any day. The water for corn on the cob would be at a slow boil on the stove, fogging up the kitchen windows, and Dee would keep cutting it off while Nanny went behind her cutting it back on and saying, in that froggy voice which came from smoking Old Gold cigarettes, "damnit to hell, Dee Lou, they'll be here any minute—don't you mess with it again, hemme?" and Dee Lou would say, "yes, ma'am, Miss Zelle," and do just how she liked.

My job was setting up the grill for Pa, who brought the T-bones down from home, cut that afternoon by Mr. Foley, the butcher at the Piggly Wiggly, who always took Pa in the back and let him pick his cuts and trimmed them just the way Will Tilley liked, which was none too lean. The way Pa ate a steak, you'd cut away the fat and save it for dessert. He'd slice those curly grayish strips in bite-sized

pieces and slap one on a buttered saltine, shaking his head and going, "umph, umph, umph," like it was just about the limit you could
ask for.

Reed would want to help me stack the charcoals in a pyramid the
way Pa liked, with no strays, but he'd always mess it up and I'd tell
him to go find Mister Rex, his stuffed tyrannosaurus, only Reed had
got to where he wouldn't fall for that so much.

Mama and Nanny would be wearing dresses instead of Bermuda
shorts or bathing suits and had their hair done and their make-up
and jewelry on. They'd be peeling shrimp boiled in beer and Old
Bay spice, blowing their noses and patting their eyes with balled-up
Kleenex from Nanny's cocktail sauce, which was the only thing I
ever saw her make except milk toast, where all she did was pour the
milk on it when Dee Lou brought the toast. Every fifteen minutes
Nanny would decide the sauce wasn't hot enough and add another
tablespoon of horseradish till Mama said that it would give you
ecstasy and visions.

There'd be music playing on the Dumont Balladier, Tommy
Dorsey if Nanny chose, and she'd be sitting in her chair, one fat leg
across the other, her shoe dangling off her heel as she worked out
the beat. If Mama picked, it would more likely be the Coasters or
the Drifters or perhaps the Kingston Trio, and if it was Reed you
could bet money it would be "Puff, the Magic Dragon," which he'd
listen to over and over, a hundred times in a row if you let him,
sucking his thumb with a face as sober as Abe Lincoln and holding
Mister Rex, who didn't look much like a Magic Dragon if you want
my opinion.

Mama and Nanny would be on their second cocktails, which
sometimes they'd let me mix for practice, making a fuss of it when I
brought them over, careful, from the bar, trying not to forget the
cocktail napkins. "Thank you, *sir!*" Mama would say, and Nanny
would swirl the bourbon on the cubes and stare at it and sniff and sip
and say, "Lawdamercy, that ain't half shabby, but heah"—and she
would hand it back—"hit me with another splash and never mind
the jigger." She'd be warming up and starting to get funny then,
Nanny would, and Mama would be laughing as she stirred her drink
and sucked it off her finger. "Mama, she did *not!* You're simply

awful! That's a lie and God is listening!" She'd egg Nanny on to top her worst, and you could tell they got along and liked each other when they drank, which wasn't always certain when they didn't.

As much as Nanny liked to misbehave herself, when it came to Mama or Aunt June—especially Mama—Nanny's favorite saying was *"Remember who you are,"* which meant her daddy was rich and didn't have to work but sat at home all day at Seven Oaks reading *Idylls of the King* and *Ivanhoe* and such, while Nanny's mama spent her time doing good works for the Killdeer poor. They sounded fairly cool, if you ask me, Nanny's parents did, though they died before I ever got to meet them. But when Nanny said *"Remember who you are"* it made our mama cross-eyed mad. "Mother," she would say—not "Mama"—*"Mother*, I'm almost thirty damn years old, and I'd appreciate it *greatly* if you wouldn't treat me like a child." Nanny would say, "pshaw, May Tilley, you ain't a minute old to me," and Mama would get so ticked off she'd forget and turn around not half an hour later and use *Remember who you are* on Reed and me.

But not on Thursday nights. On Thursday nights the weekend started and everybody could forget who they were supposed to be and just cut loose and there we'd be, eating shrimp and listening to records and talking too loud all at once, when suddenly lights would flash across the wall and you'd hear tires crunching up the sandy drive. Mama would jump up and run downstairs and throw her arms around Daddy's neck and he'd swing her in a circle with her feet a foot up off the ground and they'd kiss with their mouths open and wouldn't care who looked, which everybody would but Pa, who'd stare down at his wingtips like he'd better shine them soon. Nanny was the worst—she'd hawk straight out like "shame" was not in any dictionary she had read, and Reed would tug at Daddy's khakis, wanting them to stop and lift him up. Me, I'd feel a little queasy watching them do that, but mainly glad because they weren't like anybody else's parents.

They were both still pretty young and won the dancing contest at the country club and I heard people say I don't know how many times how May Tilley was the best-looking girl who ever came from

Killdeer—only Mama was May Madden now; sometimes they'd act like they forgot. And at the high school gym on Saturdays they still picked Daddy first or second when they split up teams who was once the highest scorer in our state in basketball. If he hadn't hurt his knee he probably could of played for Frank McGuire when UNC beat Kansas and Wilt Chamberlain in triple overtime and won the national title. If you're from North Carolina you've heard of that.

So I was proud to have them for my parents and didn't mind it when they kissed that way. They'd usually leave their shoes and walk off barefoot up the dune toward the gazebo, holding hands, so Daddy could tell the ocean hi. Pa would say, "come on, you buzzards, let's go start that fire," and I'd say, "I get to throw the match" before Reed thought of it, and Pa would say, "I'm thinking what we got here is a *two*-match fire." Nanny would say, "now, Will, don't encourage them to play with fire," and he'd say, "yes, ma'am," and wink at us so we knew we'd get to just as soon as she had gone upstairs.

Then, plop, plop, plop, the corn would go into the boiling water on the stove, and the Big Boy tomatoes Pa grew back home along the garden wall on Country Club Drive would get sliced up in the kitchen by Dee Lou, who'd float them in a china bowl with ice and watered vinegar, and a touch of sugar, and black pepper, lots of that.

Downstairs me and Pa and Reed would be tending to the sizzling steaks, and Daddy with us sometimes, though usually it was either Pa or Daddy grilling, not both at once, because they had competing theories about when to flip the meat and whether you should sear over a flame to seal the juice or wait till the coals died down and cook it slow, which to them was either all right or all wrong but ended tasting just about the same if you ask me.

It would be full dark by then, and Pa would be squinting down to try to see the color of the meat as he cut into it with the Barlow pocketknife he kept handy at all times for cutting twine or fishing line or whatever might come up. I wanted one real bad myself but Mama said I had to wait till I turned twelve. There'd be a Chester-field dangling from Pa's lip and he was still wearing his felt hat but with his tie pulled down and his jacket off and the sleeves of his white shirt rolled up to the elbow, which you wouldn't see too much in Killdeer.

Not counting his pajamas, Pa had four sets of clothes to cover every situation you could meet in life. The first one was a business suit with a dark tie and a felt hat; the second was his fishing clothes: white cotton ducks, a white short-sleeved shirt splayed open at the neck so you could see his undershirt, and a Panama hat with a dark band; third, his beachcombing outfit, a Ban-lon sport shirt and ma-dras Bermudas he wore with black stretch socks that came up to his knees and a brimmed cap with a leaping marlin, gold on a black patch; and, last, his bathing suit, which he would only wear three times a summer, Memorial Day, July the Fourth and Labor Day, when he went in the ocean and floated on his back squirting water through the space in his front teeth and drawing his knees up toward his chest, his big toes and his index fingers sticking up above the water. That was called the Midget in a Bathtub because it made him look like he was only four feet long.

When Pa performed the Midget for us, you could see this one long piece of side hair he would usually wind around and pat down with Vitalis to try to cover up the bald spot on his head, which was the whole top part, and it would float out on the waves about as long as someone's arm. Mama and Nanny called that piece of hair the "two-mile strand," laughing till you thought they might choke from meanness, and that was why he always wore a hat, I think.

When the meat was finally done to everybody's order Pa would let me run the platter upstairs like Jim Brown, straight-arming the screen door and letting it slam behind me. "Joey . . . Joey Mad-den," you could count on Mama saying, "I won't have you running through this house like a wild Indian. March right back out that door and try again, and this time I better *not* hear it slam," and I'd say, "Mom—the steaks!" like I was on a higher mission, and Daddy would say, "look, Ma, no hands!" which would distract her long enough for me to make a getaway into the kitchen and hand off to Dee Lou.

Then on the stroke of ten o'clock we'd sit down at the table and Pa would say the blessing, taking his hat off first, and looking real serious, except that his eyes behind his gold-framed spectacles were a little red and blurry, which made you know that aside from the one cocktail he was legally entitled to on Thursday nights, he'd maybe had another nip or three out of the pint bottle of Seagrams 7 he kept in the glove compartment of the Cadillac or the other one in the bottom tray of his tackle box beneath the sinkers and packages of Eagle Claw hooks. I knew Pa's secret hiding places, some at least, and wouldn't ever tell on him, just like I knew he never would on me when I did something I wasn't supposed to like drinking from the water bottle in the refrigerator, which would give Mama or Dee Lou or Nanny either one a fit, but me and Pa would do it every chance we'd get because, no lie, it's not as good when you pour it in a glass.

Then, everybody holding hands, Pa would sigh like he was going to preach a psalm, except he'd aim this little wink at me and say,

> *Good bread, good meat.*
> *Goddamn, let's eat!*

Nanny would roar laughing, and Mama would say, "Daddy!" acting shocked, though Pa did the same thing every week, grinning just like Reed when he was bad and felt especially pleased about himself.

After dinner they'd all reach for their cigarettes and fire up—Pa a Chesterfield, a Old Gold for Nanny, a Pall Mall for Mama, and for Daddy a Lucky Strike, L.S.M.F.T.—and we'd push back from the table to digest and listen to the breakers cracking out there in the dark. At certain times there'd be plankton in the water that would make the waves light up like sparklers up and down the beach as far as you could see.

Reed would be nodding off in Daddy's lap with Mister Rex, saying, no, he wasn't tired and didn't want to go to bed, posed to pitch a fit if someone tried to make him and just daring them to try. Finally Daddy would pick him up and tiptoe to the bedroom with Mama bringing up the rear to sing him "Baa, baa, black sheep, have you any wool" if he woke up, which was another song he liked except she'd sung it first to me.

I'd kiss Nanny first, and then my pa, whose cheeks were blue and stubbly by then and had a smell like whiskey, smoke and Aqua Velva on them. "Can we go fishing in the morning, Pa?" I'd ask him every time, and every time he'd smile at me and say, "youbetcha, if the weather holds," and it did for a long time, the weather held for us. I guess I believed it always would.

# TWO

## Joey

But even before the footprints showed up on the porch, there were signs of it, that change. I'd had that funny feeling in my stomach going on a year, ever since my second week in Mrs. Wilson's fifth-grade class, when Mama picked me up one day with a red nose and Kleenex balls all over the front seat.

"What is it, Mama?" I asked, and she said, "honey, I don't want you to worry, but your nanny's sick." She had hypertension, Mama said, which meant high blood pressure plus something else to do with nerves. Our family doctor, Walter Pound—everyone in Killdeer called him Dr. Watt—had given her a check-up as soon as we came home from the beach, and said she had to go away—not next week either, but right now, today.

We drove over to Country Club Drive to say goodbye, and Bobby, Dee Lou's husband, had the Cadillac already packed. Pa was out in the driveway with Dr. Watt, who was our cousin, and Nanny came out on the steps with her Old Gold smoking like a furnace, looking mad enough to bite the head off a live rattlesnake. "So he'p me, Watt," she said, "I don't see why I cain't take a week to sit down and collect my thoughts . . . If I had good sense, I'd fire you and git me a real doctor. I always knew that diploma in yo' office was for horses." "Now, Zelle," he said, "don't take it out on me. I didn't make you eat those Hershey bars . . . your diastolic is one-ten, and even a vet knows what that means—you could have a stroke to-night."

"If I don't have one now it won't be any thanks to you," Nanny said, "listen how he talks to me." Her eyes got kind of misty. "I use to change yo' diapers, Walter Pound." "It's about time someone gave you a dose of your own medicine, Zelle," he said, "I'm sorry I have to be the one to do it," and she said, "pshaw, you never had more fun in yo' whole life—that's what it is, revenge." He just shook his head like he knew better than to try to get the last word in on her.

"Come here and kiss me, sugah pie," she said, and when I pulled back from hugging her she winked and whispered, "it ain't Hershey bars either, is it? It's Reese's cups, and I want you to bring me up some frozen ones when you come visit." That was what we liked to do, leave them in the freezer chest in her garage till they got hard, then gnaw them like a termite does a board. It made my face turn red when everybody in the driveway heard her say it, especially when I noticed Dr. Watt frowning like he might have doubts about my diastolic, too.

Not that I was fat, because I wasn't. I was only big. Mainly big was what I was, and strong. Big and fairly strong. And anyway, being fat was just a stage that you outgrow. That's what Mama said, and you would think she ought to know, since she was fat when she was little, too, and turned out pretty good. So every year when school began and I would say I didn't want to go, she'd tell me, "Joey, honey, it's a stage." I believed her, too—every single year I did.

So anyway, they shipped Nanny off to Durham to the Rice House and kept her there till Christmastime and sent us home a skeleton—I'm not kidding you; she was no thicker than a playing card and almost disappeared when she turned sideways so you were afraid that any breeze might blow her off. And there was some new look in Nanny's eyes when she got out that wasn't there when she went in.

The first time I saw that look was when we went to visit—I only got to see her once. It was when *The Sound of Music* came, which was too big for the Ambassador Theater in Killdeer. Mama and a bunch of other mothers got together and drove us up to see it so our education wouldn't be neglected. I sat in the balcony with A. Jenrette, my cousin, dropping popcorn bombs, and we could hear the whole row of moms sniffing and heaving sighs below, especially when they sang "Edelweiss" on the guitar. Mama had to fix her make-up in the rearview mirror before we went to visit Nanny, who was upstairs in her room still wearing her nightgown in the middle of the afternoon. She started crying the minute we walked in and said she wanted to come home, smoking one cigarette after another and stabbing them out in a full ashtray. We sat on either side and held her hands for a long time, but she just cried and cried and couldn't stop, till Mama finally said, "now, Mama, that's enough— remember who you are," which seemed a little mean if you ask me, except it worked.

Nanny blew her nose and cheered right up, starting in on imitating the director of the Rice House, a German man she called "Herr Doktor" and "the Fuehrer." You had to salute and say, "Sieg Heil!" when he came down the hall, Nanny said, and everywhere you went you had to march in line and do the goose step, like the Krauts on "Combat" with Vic Morrow, my favorite TV show. She was pretty funny on the subject, just like her old self, only you could tell she really hated that director underneath. It was a war between those two, and Nanny had a pretty good idea she wasn't winning.

On our way home we stopped at Shoney's, which was my favorite restaurant back then, but A. said, "hey, look, y'all, there's Joey!" pointing out the window to the statue of the Big Boy on the lawn, holding a tray over his head and wearing red checkered overalls and a ducktail Elvis hairdo. Everybody laughed, and I just ordered cottage cheese and tuna on a bed of lettuce and sat there picking at it, feeling mad at them and sorry for myself. I noticed that if you looked really close he wasn't fat, the Big Boy. Mainly what he was

was big, or husky, as you might prefer to say, and in those comic books they handed out he was the one who always put the crooks in jail and saved the day. That's what I told myself at any rate, but saying it didn't make me feel a whole lot better. To tell the honest truth I guess it sort of shook me up, that visit to the Rice House.

When Nanny came home things were different. Her hypertension was all gone, and she bought a polka-dotted two-piece, which looked more like it was meant for someone Mama's age, and go-to-hell sunglasses, but there were no more frozen Reese's cups for her. She couldn't even eat a steak with us on Thursday night, but just a tiny portion of white rice and a boneless chicken breast with no skin, no butter and no salt—not *ever* any salt—the same thing every night, cooked in her own little pot separate on the stove from ours in different water, distilled from copper tubes into a big green bottle, one drop at a time. And there was no more bourbon either, but just a single glass of sherry every night at cocktail hour, though sometimes Nanny cheated and had two.

The whole thing was a little like when you're out driving somewhere with your family in the car, singing songs or playing cowpoke, and suddenly a wheel slips off the edge and you hear gravel plinking up and everybody's face turns white. Even after you get off the shoulder back into the lane it takes a while for everyone to get their spirit back. Seeing Nanny in the Rice House felt a little bit like that—the first wheel slipping off.

# THREE

## Joey

If I could of picked who I'd grow up to be, Pa would of been the one—well, next to Daddy—only I would of liked to keep my hair and not have a big spare tire like Pa's. Only it was *hard*, Pa's stomach, and if you didn't think so he would let you punch it just to see, and I can vouch for him—your fist would bounce right back like off a trampoline. Even if I told Archie different, Pa was my best friend, and I would of rather spent the day with him at the Bonanza than with Archie.

When I was off from school, I went to work with Pa sometimes. He'd stop by the house and pick me up at seven and take me out to breakfast at the Scuppernong Hotel, which was across the street from the railroad station in downtown Killdeer. Uncle John Landis would be there, who was the president of Carolina Fidelity bank, and Uncle Herbert Kincannon, who owned the Dixie Bagging Mill —they were Pa's best friends. There'd be buyers down from Reynolds and American and Philip Morris up in Richmond for the sales at the Bonanza and Top Dollar, which was our competition, and you knew they were important, the buyers, because they all looked like the president or king of something. There were traveling salesmen, too, which you could tell by the different kind of suits they wore, which wouldn't hang just right and looked a little shiny. They might have a gold tooth or a gent's diamond or a tattoo peeking out from under a cuff, and they'd think they could pull a swift one on us, like that time they tried to sell Pa some timberland in the middle of the Dismal Swamp. Pa said they figured we were simple country boys who came from a hick burg, but if they messed with us, especially Pa or Uncle Johnny, boy, they'd wish the Seaboard Railroad never let them off in Killdeer, North Carolina.

Breakfast at the Scuppernong was a kind of happy feast, and anything you wanted or could think of, Beulah Pye could fix it who was cook. Pa was partial to a pork chop, fried green tomatoes, hash browns with onions, a sliced Big Boy daubed with Beulah's home-made mayonnaise, which was orange from all the paprika in it, grits, shad roe and maybe a small piece of catfish fried in cornmeal on the side if it was fresh. Me, I tended to prefer the hot country sausage with soft scrambled all thrown together in the middle of a steaming soft bread biscuit with a smear of grape preserves—not those purple Yankee grapes either, but green-gold summer scuppernongs right off the arbor vine out back, which is what they named the hotel for —and you'd have to eat it with your fingers like you do fried chicken or else it wouldn't be as good.

After breakfast we'd head down the corridor to wash up in the first-floor bathroom which was about the same size or a little bigger than the ballroom where they held cotillion dances, and if you ever happened to stop in between seven-thirty and eight o'clock on a weekday morning you wouldn't have to wonder why. There'd be cigar and cigarette smoke swirling up above a dozen stalls and news-papers rattling behind the doors—the *News & Observer*, or the *Dur-ham Morning Herald*. They'd all be quiet and respectful of their neighbors' privacy, except maybe you'd hear someone clear his throat, and then you'd hear a *bbbbbplffftt* and a *ffffffpluttt* and a short sharp one like a cap gun, and someone would sigh, and someone else would say, "Lord, Lord," and let out a slow wheezer. I'd be bending over double, holding my sides to keep from laughing, while Wallace, the attendant, would look at me kind of patient and forgiving like I was a fool or else too young to respect the holy nature of the place I was in. His eye whites were the color of old Scotch tape, Wallace's, which my daddy said was from exposure to the fumes.

Then somebody would read out a headline, and Pa would call out, " 'zat you, Herbut?" and Uncle Herbert would say, "yessuh, Willie, and ain't this mess in Congress the sorriest yet?" and Uncle John would say, "don't know what we're coming to," and Pa would throw in a "umph, umph, umph." They'd blow a couple more and before you knew it they'd be talking business, pinning down a deal, only they'd wait till they'd washed up with one of Wallace's warm lemon-scented towels before they shook on it. And on your way out you could slap you on some aftershave, Aqua Velva or Old Spice, and leave a nickel tip in the cigar box, which was the price of a Co-Cola at the warehouse, except I don't think that's what Wallace drank to make his eyeballs look that way.

After that breakfast I was ready to lie down in the shade some-where and sleep till nine or ten o'clock at night, but not Pa, no sir. He'd stroll out on the verandah with his hands in his pockets and a peppermint-flavored toothpick in the space between his two front teeth, looking fit and satisfied. His eyes would have this kind of shine to them like some old hound dog lifting his muzzle to the breeze, grateful to Almighty God for the gift of a whole day to do the one thing next to fishing Pa loved best: some *bid'ness*.

First off, we'd look in at the warehouse and see how things were shaping up. Otis would be out back at the scales weighing out the loads the farmers brought in on their dusty pickups wrapped in burlap sheets. Then Reb and Skeeter would hoist them on a dolly and wheel them out onto the auction floor and set them up in aisles. If they weren't real busy Reb might start telling me some tale about how the last time he went fishing out there by the Killdeer River Bridge, know what he caught? He'd stare at me, grinning like the devil that he was, and eventually he'd make me squirm and have to ask him, "what?" except I didn't want to.

"A muh-maid," Reb would tell me, "blond-headed, 'bout

twinny, twinny-five year old—yessuh, sho did—come up on my
trotline. Didn' have huh on no bathing suit neither—and titties on
huh? Umph, I'm telling you, son, like two Ridgeway can'aloupes,
sweahdaGod she did." I'd look disgusted at him but it would bounce
right off and Reb would keep on going, telling you the biggest lie
you ever heard, crossing his heart and hoping to die at every turn
and saying God could strike him dead, which I only wished he
would.

Then I'd go in the office and say hello to Mrs. Weems and Marie
and Tina and the other girls who did the checks and check stubs.
Daddy might be sitting at Pa's desk with his feet up, which he liked
to do, wearing white suede bucks and a red alligator shirt, which
didn't fit in so well at the warehouse as it did in the Nineteenth
Hole, which was the mens' lounge downstairs at the Killdeer Country Club. Daddy liked to play gin rummy or stud poker with Tommy
Janklow, the golf pro, who wasn't married and drove a cherry-red
Corvette, and some other men like him who Mama didn't like so
well when they came over to our house for poker night because they
kept up me and Reed with all their hooting and left a mess and
didn't compliment her cream cheese and olive finger sandwiches,
which was Nanny's mother's recipe.

Daddy would be talking on the telephone to some man down at
J. P. Taylor or RJR or Universal, telling him the check had not
arrived and how could we pay money to the farmer if we didn't get it
from the manufacturer, and while we would dearly love to go nonprofit and subsidize the county and were working toward that end,
we had not arrived quite yet, and so, yes, it would be fine if they
would cancel it and cut a new one and have somebody bring it over
as long as it was here by noon, because the deposit had to be
credited *today*, and please give his best to Linda, too.

Daddy would be on such a roll you could tell he almost hated it
when the man agreed to do what Daddy had called up to ask for in
the first place, but would rather go on for another thirty minutes or
a hour to see how many other good ones like "nonprofit" he could
come up with. He could talk a blue streak, my daddy could, and
loved to do it, and had this big deep speaking voice like Granddaddy

Madden, who was the high school principal and had to give a lot of speeches about "civic duty" and "Christian virtue" and "team spirit" to the Jaycees and the Rotary.

Whenever we ate Sunday dinner at Granddaddy and Grody Madden's house, Grody would get on me all the time about *e-nun-ci-at-ing* and using *proper diction*, and wouldn't let me get away with saying "ain't," or using "won't" for "wasn't"—like I won't even *thinking* about doing such-and-such a thing. Of course, I already knew that junk except that I *enjoyed* to talk that way the same as you would going barefoot in the summertime or drinking from the water bottle, which was the same for Pa, who could use good grammar when he had to, like at Saint Paul's Episcopal, where he was on the vestry. Only I don't think Grody approved of anyone enjoying themself too much at the expense of grammar, because she was a Methodist, see—which was in third place in our town behind the Episcopalians and Presbyterians, but above the Baptists—and used to be a schoolteacher besides, Grody did. Grody liked everything in a straight line like it was laid out with a ruler, and she had a formula for everything, like *Children should be seen and not heard* and *Children should only speak when spoken to*, and I heard Mama say to Nanny once that that was why Daddy loved to talk so much, because he never got a chance when he was small and had to make up for lost time. I wasn't supposed to hear her say that, but it wasn't the first time or the only either.

But I was telling you about my daddy and don't even know why I got off on her, except that at the warehouse sometimes I'd hear him talking to some farmer in brogans and a pair of overalls, and Daddy would be saying "yessuh" and "nosuh" and " 'spect so" and " 'preciate it" and "y'all come back and see us, heah?" like Pa. And you could tell that farmer didn't know quite what to make of Daddy, except he liked him.

Daddy had a certain way about him that made you feel good when he talked to you, like you were standing in a spotlight. Like when he teased old Mrs. Weems about her miniskirt and said we got more business at the auctions when she wore it. "If you'd just show a little knee from time to time, Miz Weems," he'd say, "we'd drive the

Top Dollar right on out of town." Mrs. Weems would blush and get all tongue-tied, but you could tell she liked it, which seemed right pitiful to me—because she had to be fifty years old at least, and might have been sixty or seventy. Once they got up that high it was a little hard to tell.

In back, Tina and Marie would be giggling and whispering behind their hands so you could tell they thought Daddy was pretty cute and didn't know too many fellas who wore alligator shirts and would go out of their way to flirt with a old lady to cheer her up. They liked him, too, and that's what I mean—everybody did. He was wired up some way different, Daddy was, and everybody knew it, even me.

Except I don't think Daddy knew, or maybe he did and just wanted to fit in more like someone who'd come up on the farm, where they aren't on you all the time about your grammar, more like Pa, who was just naturally that way and fit inside himself like you would fit in some old favorite broke-down pair of shoes, because that was the only way Pa knew to be. But with Daddy it was like there was two or three different people all mixed up inside him—a professor and a farmer and a hotshot at the country club—and he had to choose but couldn't make up his mind which one.

So about the time he hung the phone up, Pa would come in from out back with Otis, and Daddy would take his feet off the desk and get up quick. Pa would say, "keep yo' seat, son, keep yo' seat . . . Otis, what did Billie Thomas weigh out when he came?" and Otis would say, " 'leb'm hund'ud 'n seb'm'ty-fo' pounds, Mr. Willie, I *b'lieve* is what it was." "Miz Weems, how much is that at fifty-six and a half cents a pound, subtracting our commission?" Pa would say, and Mrs. Weems, meek and little-bitty and soft-spoken as she was, would fire that answer at him like a pistol and never even blink. She was the fastest adder at the warehouse, where anybody, even Skeeter, who was a brick shy of a full load, could figure faster than a adding machine, and in their heads, too—you never ever saw a pad and pencil, which if you even brought one in the door would be about like going out to football practice with rubbers on your cleats. Pa would laugh and shake his head and say, "she's somp'm, ain't she, boys? We wouldn't last a week without Miz Weems," and, old as she was, she'd blush like a debutante whose beau has paid a compliment.

If there was nothing special Pa had to tend to, he'd leave Daddy to run the auction with Otis looking on over his shoulder to make sure it all came out, and we'd hop in the Cadillac and take a drive out in the country someplace. Because, like Pa would always tell you, at a tobacco warehouse it's twenty-five per cent *doin'* business and seventy-five per cent *gittin'* it, and that's where we would go, the two of us, to get some.

The day would just be starting to warm up as we headed out Route 1 or 319—different days, different ways—then turned off on some dirt county road that might have oil on it to lay the dust but sometimes wouldn't. Then it would fly behind you like a comet's tail and keep on going if you stopped, a big white-yellow cloud rolling over you so you couldn't see the fins or the hood ornament till it passed.

The towns out there wouldn't be more than two houses, a Baptist church and a rundown country store with a bubble-headed Esso pump out front and dusty tins of pork and beans and sardines in the windows. Inside on the counter there'd be a sweaty hunk of orange hoop cheese under a glass bell and two-gallon jars of Penrose sausages, pickled eggs in vinegar, dill pickles and pigs' feet, which Pa would buy sometimes when a hankering came on him, but to me they looked too much like what you'd see the mad scientists on "Sunrise Theater" growing down in their la-*bor*-a'try.

Instead, I'd get a Moon Pie and a Sun Drop Cola, and we'd stop outside and talk to the old men sitting on the bench that might be painted with our advertisement or maybe the Top Dollar's. When they'd see Pa, they'd all grin with half their teeth gone, which would make them look like six-year-olds whose grown-up teeth hadn't come in yet. "You boys gittin' on all right?" Pa'd ask, and they'd say, "fair to middlin', Mr. Will," or "cain't complain," and nod their heads at the same time like those wooden dolls you get for prizes at the county fair.

They'd talk about the weather, how it was going to be another scorcher and the tobacco was going to get all burned to cinders in the fields, or if the forecast was for rain it would either wash them out or send the crop into second growth and ruin it. Whichever way it went, the end was pretty near, and they'd all shake their heads at the same time and sigh out "umph, umph, umph," and Pa would cut a little wink at me so I'd know I shouldn't take the news too hard.

Then Pa would ask one of them which field his son was in, and when we got back in the car he'd say how it was a shame to see them all brought down, who used to be big strapping men who took pride in the crops they made and in providing for their families. Now all they had left was sitting there all day, counting cars go by, wanting back what they once had and mad as hell at life for taking it away. "It slips up on you from behind when you ain't looking, boy," Pa would say. "In the twinkling of an eye, it's gone." And I would try to understand what it was that did the slipping up, and what it was that got away, and if it was two things or only one, and also how Pa could understand what those old men were feeling just from some remark about the weather.

We'd fall in behind a tractor going to the fields and as we pulled around, Pa would lean over me in the shotgun seat and call out, "you're holding up the march of progress, Roy," and Roy, or whoever it might be, would shout back, "trying to, Mr. Will," and shoot us a big grin. All around us the fields spread to the tree line in the distance, and the silage corn and millet might still have a little of that bright spring green in it which made it look like it was glad to be alive but faded off as summer wore along till it looked fed up and ready to be done with it. And there would be tobacco, everywhere tobacco.

Pa would pull off on the shoulder and wait for the dust cloud to pass by, and then we'd get out at a field where some farmer and his boys might be cultivating or topping out, wading down the rows whacking off the spiky white tobacco flowers that would draw the sap off from the leaves if you let them grow. Up and down the rows the ground would be white with blossoms like a wedding, and it would be so pretty you almost hated to see those fellas out there stomping them to pieces with their boots.

Pa would put his foot up on the bottom fence rail and lean over on his elbows, studying the polish on his wingtip like he could of got a better shine, and gradually the men would come our way with the sweat trickles leaving clean tracks in the field dust on their faces and raccoon rings around their eyes. Their knives would be all wet with sap and they'd be carrying them in hands that didn't look like mine or Pa's or Daddy's or any man from town, but like something a carpenter had roughed out of a block of wood in a hurry without bothering to carve the details in.

"Some right pretty tobacco you got here, Buck," Pa would call out to the oldest one, "don't b'lieve I've seen a better-looking crop this year," and Buck would say, " 'preciate it, Mr. Will—so far anyhow." As Buck got up to the fence Pa would clap him on the shoulder and say, "how you been keeping, son?" and he'd say, "cain't complain too bad, Mr. Will, yo'self?" Pa would answer, " 'bout the same, I reckon—Buck, this is my grandson Joey Madden, Jimmy's boy."

When I first started going out there I'd say, "nice to meet you, sir," and stick out my hand to shake like you're supposed to, only that farmer man would look at it funny like I was some sort of little joker and then give me the limp fish. He wouldn't know about a good firm grip and looking straight into a fella's eyes like I was taught. So after once or twice of that I figured they just weren't as big on shaking out there in the country as we were in town, and the best thing was to keep my mouth shut and watch Pa.

Usually there'd be a boy about my age with his shirt off, itchy from tobacco sap and scratching up against the fence post. I'd see him sizing up whether he could whip me, which usually I would just as soon not put to the test, because those boys out there were not the sort that you could *reason* with, like Mama always said to do but which never worked one single time in my whole life. They'd just want to whup you first—not even mean but just sort of the same thing as me sticking out my hand to shake—to get to *know* you, and once you got it over with, if you didn't cry or shame yourself, they'd usually be your friend and let you hold their knife or show you the right way to spit or something fairly good.

Pa would take out his pack of Chesterfields and offer it around and they would thank him kindly but pull out some plug, or maybe roll one by hand, and everybody would fire up or take their chaw. The younger boys would climb on the top rail of the fence, and the older ones would lean, and everybody would listen as their daddy talked to Pa about the drought and whether it was finally going to break, and how many more days the crop could stand of it, and the high cost of water, and the problem they'd been having down in Granville County with the wilt or the mosaic, and how there'd been no sign of it up here, so far, but there was hail the week 'fore last.

Everybody would smoke out his cigarette and grind the butt out underfoot, and they'd say how they probably ought to be getting back to work, and Pa would say that we were running late ourselves, and they'd wade back out in the tobacco, and we'd drive on to the next field, or maybe it would be a farmhouse during the noon meal, or late afternoon out by a barn where they were feeding livestock or taking apart a disc harrow on the floor with grease up to their armpits.

Or it might be just as dark was falling, me with the kids out whooping barefoot in the yard, and Pa with the old folks rocking back on the screened porch, having another smoke and watching the lightning bugs light up and listening to the cicadas and the tree frogs and the bullfrogs sounding off as loud as pistol shots down in the pond. The air would be all soft and cool then, and there'd be bats veering up against the biggest moon you ever saw coming up over the fields as orange as that hoop cheese in the store, setting the soil to sparkling like there was a million tiny diamonds in it.

Pa knew all of them, the women as well as the men, and their children, too, how many there were, their names, and he could generally guess within a grade how old they were. If they had a dog, Pa would know his name and personality, whether he was a respectable yard dog who stayed and guarded things and wouldn't let you on the porch till he had looked you over, or else a red-eyed bowser who would disappear for days on end and come home with his fur in tatters and his tongue dragging in the dust and his eyes all muddy-looking, ready to curl up underneath the porch and sleep off whatever evilness he'd done.

If Pa knew a man's daddy, or if *his* daddy, Mr. Reed Tilley, had known that man's daddy, they'd talk about the old days before allotments, when a man could sell as much as he could stand to grow. "I tell you, Mr. Will, seems like the gub'mint has got a finger in every hole these days," they'd say, and how they'd all be lucky to hang on five more years, and Pa would just sit there listening, with his hands in his lap and that mild expression on his face and his gray eyes clear behind his glasses, and let them say whatever it was they needed to —you could tell they didn't get the chance that much.

The wife would keep filling up your ice tea or your lemonade and you would notice how she'd changed out of her house dress to a nicer one and brushed her hair and maybe even put on lipstick. She'd be all nervous about her pie, saying how her crust didn't turn out as flaky as she liked and it must be the humidity, and Pa would say, "Peggy"—or whatever her name was—"you're right, this is the worst blueberry pie I ever tasted, and I believe I'mohafta ask you fo' a second piece." She'd blush and just go all to pieces over that, she'd be so pleased. Then when she couldn't make you eat another bite, she'd settle down and listen to the conversation and half the time she'd turn out to have more to say than her husband and be smarter, too. Pa said women tended to have more common sense than men and didn't mix up what life ought to be with what it is.

And the whole time Pa would never say a word about business— asking them to sell with us—but 'most always there would come a point toward the end, after everyone had said their piece and they felt satisfied, when they would say, "wellsuh, I'mon come down'nah to see you, Mr. Will, Lord willing I make my crop, I sho am," and Pa would seem almost bashful as he said, "well, Tommy, I'mon try to do right by you and git you the bes' dollar I can." "You always treated me fair and square, Mr. Will," Tommy would say, "and that Red Poley down the road, Peggy and his wife are in the church together, and I'mon work on 'im fo' you, Mr. Will, I'mon git him down'nah to see you—if I cin, now. I ain't promising, but I'll sho talk to 'im."

And one time we were way out somewhere on the Townsville Road near this farm that Pa and Uncle Johnny owned and went to see a man named Shafter Roberson who was as old as Pa. Mr. Roberson wouldn't let us leave until he fed us supper; his wife fried chicken and made squash and corn chowder and wax beans and baked blackberry pie like it was Sunday. After we ate he told this story of how Pa's daddy, Mr. Reed Tilley, who they named my brother for, held the note on Mr. Roberson's daddy and several other families out that way, and in 1921 when cotton dropped below five cents a pound and folks were going under right and left, he could have called it in and took their farms, Pa's daddy, except he wouldn't. Mr. Roberson had this fierce look on his face like he was mad at something, only you could tell it wasn't that. "I won't much older than this here boy of yours," he said, "but I 'member just as clear as yesti'd'y the day we heard that Mr. Reed was dead. My daddy walked right around the corner of this house and dropped his hat down in the dirt and cried for twenty minutes, Mr. Will, just like a child, which I never saw him do but that one time. I don't b'lieve I ever tol' you that before, but, nosuh, long as I can make a crop or my boys either one, I 'spect I know where I'mon sell it at."

When we got back in the Cadillac Pa took out his pocket square and spent a while wiping clean the lenses of his glasses. He didn't say a word and I didn't either because I knew his daddy killed himself and that was when they lost Rose Hill, which was the Tilley homeplace, and Pa had to come back home from Chapel Hill and go to work in a dry goods store. Mama's eyes would get a shiny look to them and she would drop her voice down when she spoke of this. I don't think Pa ever did, or not to me, but I could sort of tell when he would think of it because he'd get real quiet and pop the glove box and sip his pint of Seagrams as we drove, and this seemed to happen more after Nanny went off to the Rice House.

Toward the end of that September—Nanny hadn't even been away a month—Pa had a heart attack. He didn't even call us, but walked across the yard and rang the Dades' doorbell and sat down on the steps to rest till they got out of bed. I think that scared me even worse than that new look in Nanny's eyes, but Mama told us not to worry because for a heart attack it was a pretty mild one. That's what *she* said, but I heard Dr. Watt tell Daddy in the buffet line that Sunday at the club it was a warning how Pa ate too much and drank too much and smoked too much and worked too much and did too much of everything except relax. Pa wasn't a young man anymore, Dr. Watt said, and had damn well better learn to slow down some or he was going to meet the bear and wouldn't like it much. 'Cause when the bear gets hold and puts a squeezing on you, that's all she wrote, boys—not even Mr. William Tilley *whatevuh he might think* could wrestle with that bear and come out in one piece, except I think Pa figured he could wrestle anything, and so did I.

But everyone ganged up on him and made him go in the hospital up at Duke where he could talk to Nanny over at the Rice House and not have to worry about long-distance charges, which always made Pa nervous—he'd keep a eye peeled on the second hand whenever we called Aunt June.

While he was there they found this blood clot in the calf of his left leg which was stuck down in the vein so that the blood was blocked from circulating. There was a name for it which Daddy told us from the year he spent in med school up in Chapel Hill when he and Mama were first married, but I can't remember it right now, only that was what would make Pa limp sometimes. The doctors were scared that clot would break away and shoot up to Pa's heart which is why they wanted to amputate below the knee, except Pa said a man would have to be a goddamn fool to cut his leg off to cure a charley horse.

I think the worst for him was this young doctor Daddy's age who said he should quit smoking and all the bad things cigarettes can do, like heart disease and cancer. I heard Pa telling Otis after he got back, "if tobacco's wrong then this whole town's wrong, Otis, 'cause every brick and board in the Bonanza and every store and house and church in Killdeer came from it . . . Every dollar was a leaf of bright tobacco first and grew right from the ground, and if I thought I made my living selling poison, Otis, if I thought that's how I fed my wife and girls and put the roof over our heads, if that's what I believed . . ." Pa didn't say what he'd do if he believed that, but Otis put his hand on Pa's shoulder—they were out back on the loading dock and I'd just come from the office and stood in the doorway watching—and he said, "don't you let it eat you none, Mr. Willie. A young fella like that—how much could he know?"

They put him on some medicine to thin his blood and made him buy this fancy bed that sat about five feet off the floor and had a motor in it. You climbed up a set of metal steps and flicked the switch at night when you got in and it would crank you up and down and turn you halfway in a circle and then back to where you started to get your blood to circulating right. Pa said every night he dreamed he was sailing on a ocean liner and would wake up seasick so he had to hold on to the furniture to cross the room when he got out of bed.

Sometime that October, when Pa had started feeling better, Little Will and Grant, our cousins, who were Aunt June's boys, came up from Edenton to visit so we could all help cheer Pa up, and we camped out in the garage. Pa didn't use his motor bed while they were there but slept on a Army surplus fold-out cot with us. We lined up five of them in a row, each one with a Army surplus mummy bag like Vic Morrow and the other GIs had on "Combat," which scratched the dog out of you, except we hardly cared it was so cool. Everybody had a Army surplus periscope-type flashlight that you could beam up any time you thought you heard a vampire bat or something flapping in the rafters, only usually it would just be a mosquito which would buzz right up beside your ear like a itty-bitty power saw and you would slap yourself half silly and think you got it but about five seconds later there it was again. We all had our own supply of candy bars for quick energy in case of a emergency, and Army surplus canteens, too, filled with warm Co-Cola that had lost the fizz.

And every once in a while Grant or Reed would call out, "Pa, I got to pee," and he'd say, "who else needs to go?" and we'd all say, "I do, Pa," because nobody was fool enough to get left in there where vampire bats might be nesting. Pa would pull the cord and the garage door would rattle up, and we'd all march out in a line to the edge of the driveway where you could feel the cold wet grass on your toes but not your heels. We'd stand there in a row from big to little and then we'd hear one little stream begin to trickle, and then another, and Pa would come in sounding like a horse, and the other two would join in, each one with a different note to it like a barbershop quartet except for five.

We'd all just stand listening to the quiet splashing sound and the tree frogs and cicadas—not as many as there'd been in August, but it was warm that year—and there would be this clean black smell to everything, and the air was soft. Off across the back yard we could see our oak tree, which was bigger than the one at Tanglewood in Winston-Salem which has a sign claiming it's the biggest in the state, except it's not. A few last lightning bugs were blinking in the branches, strung like Christmas lights, and overhead there were a million stars twinkling like the lights we saw out the window of the plane the time Mama took us to New York to visit Aunt Winnie and Uncle Mark. One of those nights we saw a satellite or shooting star streak by and everybody crossed his heart real fast and made a wish, except that it was hard for me to think of anything. All it was was standing with Reed and Pa and our two cousins taking a leak in the back yard, but if I got another chance I know what I would ask, to make it all hold still and stay the same forever.

In the morning we all put our pants on over our pajamas the same way Pa did and drove to the Scuppernong for breakfast, and Pa was pretty good that first time and only had a couple of soft scrambled and a few strips of bacon. But after Grant and Little Will went home to Edenton it seemed like every time we went back Pa would add on something, like the pork chop or the hash browns with onions or the fried green tomatoes or the catfish fried in cornmeal, till before long you couldn't tell the difference from the way he used to eat. And when he chewed you could sometimes see this forked vein stand out in his forehead kind of throbbing like a purple lightning bolt and he'd perspire a little across his upper lip and have to mop it with his pocket square. It was serious business for him, eating, you could tell.

Pa wasn't too good at sticking to a diet, but at least he took his medicine and Dr. Watt wouldn't let him go to work, which was good for Daddy because he got to run most of the auctions that fall, and good for me because I got to go back to the beach with Pa and Uncle Johnny for three days in November for the bluefish run. My first day out, I caught a fifteen-pounder in the surf who fielded my spoon like a pop fly before it hardly hit the water. When I finally got him to the beach I ran him back up to the house still wriggling on the pole and conked him in the head out in the driveway. I scaled him while Pa filleted another, cutting out that streak of oily dark meat which the big ones have. Uncle Johnny battered the fillets in corn meal and fried them up so fresh they were still turning back-flips in the Crisco. That and cold pork and beans out of the can was what we had for breakfast, and the same again for lunch.

The second day, we got up at the crack of dawn and took the boat down to the public launch at Oregon Inlet. I thought maybe they were finally going to let me go with them out to the ocean, only as we put the boat in, the wind blew off Pa's Panama, and, boy, I'm telling you, that thing hit the water heeling like a sloop and it was gone. Pa looked at me and frowned, and I knew I was sunk. He told me the same thing he'd said a hundred times before—the current was too strong, it could sweep a grown man into the Atlantic in the twinkling of an eye. I knew he was right—even Daddy, who used to be a lifeguard at Camp Blue Moon, was always careful there—but I can't say I liked it much.

So we just spent the morning anchored in the lee of some small island in the sound, bottom-fishing for flounder. Way off in the distance I could see the Bonner Bridge, which wasn't finished then —it looked like a brontosaurus skeleton the scientists had half put together in a museum. They quit biting in the afternoon and Pa showed me how to tie a sheepshank and a boatswain's hitch and tested me on the fisherman's knot, which is the one you need the most.

The last day of the trip, Pa and Uncle Johnny hired a guide and went ahead without me to the ocean, looking for red drum. They didn't catch one, though, which served them right if you ask me. That afternoon when they came in, Pa said maybe next summer he would take me trolling offshore, but he'd said that last year, too, and what it really was, I knew, was Mama, who whenever I asked, would say she thought *we* ought to wait another year, like she had anything to do with it.

After Thanksgiving, the weather got too cold to fish, though there were still a few nice days when me and Pa went after catfish in the Killdeer River. To tell the honest truth, it didn't seem that great after being at the beach. But even if we were just jerking bream over our shoulders with cane poles baited with hunks of balled-up Merita white bread, something there's hardly any sport to at all, I didn't mind. I liked just being there with Pa, way out in the country, sitting on the bank of some green pond a farmer let us use, drinking a Sun Drop and not saying much, keeping a eye peeled on the cork float for when it would begin to tingle as that bream or smallmouth came up and nosed the bait, deciding if it suited him. And then, oh, boy, the way it bobbed down under water and jerked your pole right over double and shot electric current up your arm . . .

It was about the limit, boy, and there were lots of times, that fall of fifth-grade year, when I wished I could stay with Pa and not go home to our house anymore to listen to Mama and Daddy arguing, which was getting pretty bad by Christmas. Once or twice a week, it seemed, Daddy would get mad and storm out, slamming the front door so hard it sounded like the wood was going to splinter. Then Mama would go cry upstairs in the bedroom and that would get Reed started, too, till she'd come out and look at us like we were poor abandoned orphan children and kneel down on the floor and want to hug us to her bosoms and all that.

Sometimes I wished I could go live with Pa, except I never asked because I was afraid it might upset him and do something to his heart, but I was always making plans about how I might run away. If I could get down to the beach, I knew there was a key buried in a jar beneath the cottage steps. I could live there and nobody would even know, except I wasn't sure exactly what the roads were that you go on.

And anyway, I couldn't just walk off and leave Reed by himself, even if we fought a lot and I was mean to him, like one time I hit him under the eye so hard it left a cut. He could of lost that eye, Daddy said, before he took out the glass belt, which wasn't really glass but shined like it, and made me take my pants down and lean across the bed before he tanned my hide, ten whacks, hard, which left red marks that later on turned blue. And there was this other thing Reed started doing right about that time—pounding his head over and over in the pillow till I had to reach down from the top bunk and wake him up to make him quit so I could sleep.

One Saturday morning real early when I was watching Boris

Karloff in some mummy picture on "Sunrise Theater," the mailman rang the doorbell and there was Reed, buck naked, one hand holding Mr. Thompson's and the other clutching Mister Rex. Mr. Thompson said, "is this your child, son?" and I said, "no, sir, he's my little brother, Reed, my parents' child," and Mr. Thompson said, "well, here, you better take him." He told me he found Reed just wandering the neighborhood several blocks away without a stitch of clothes and wouldn't say his name or where he lived, which made me think that maybe Reed would of liked to run away as well, only he was still too little, so we had to stay.

But that's why every time we had to haul up anchor in the sound, me and Pa, or leave the bank of that green pond out in the country, I would get that funny feeling in my stomach and ask Pa if I couldn't have another Moon Pie and a Sun Drop. He mostly always let me have it even if Mama said it spoiled my appetite, which I have to tell you honest I don't believe it ever did one time in my whole life. And I believe there was a part of Pa that would of liked to stay there, too, playing hooky with me, and not go home, even if he loved Nanny, and I know he did just like I loved Mama and Daddy but still sometimes wished that I could live another place but home.

I think that's why, the last day of that fishing trip, when it got dusk and all the reels had been rinsed off in fresh water and we both knew that it was time to think of heading back, Pa hesitated a minute and asked me to pop the glove compartment of the Cadillac and pass that pint of Seagrams. He sat there in the driver's seat with the door open and his bad leg stretched out on the ground and screwed the cap off and took a little nip, was what he called it, while I ate my Moon Pie. We were quiet then, watching the charter boats come in and the sun melt like a pat of butter running all down in the Albemarle. The wind came up tossing little whitecaps off the waves that trailed bridal veils of foam backward over the black water, and I felt goosebumps rising in my sunburn. Pa stared out through the windshield with a wet shine in his eyes, and I thought that maybe he was thinking of his daddy, Mr. Reed, who got so sad he didn't want to live. I was thinking of my daddy, too, who wasn't happy either, and by the time the fifth grade ended, that summer when the footprints came, I had a pretty good idea what does the slipping up and what it is that gets away from you and what Pa meant when he would say *The twinkling of an eye . . .*

I would of liked to put my arms around him and tell him everything was going to be all right like Mama said to me or Reed when we woke up from a bad dream, but me and Pa were both too old for that and wouldn't do it to the other one because of our respect—being men, we couldn't afford to let our hearts get broke too easy.

So what I did instead to shake Pa out of it was ask if I could have a little nip myself. He looked across the seat at me and got this great big grin and said, "nosireebob, you *may* not, I don't wawnchooda be picking up my habits." I promised him I wouldn't ever drink, though I kind of liked the way the whiskey smelled on him, all mixed up with his Chesterfields and Aqua Velva and the Vitalis that lingered in the lining of his hat. All of it was comforting to me some way, like when the wind came around onshore and brought that fresh smell off the ocean, or the way the ground smelled after rain.

That night Pa poured a thimbleful of Seagrams in my Sun Drop, which made me feel all warm and blurry so I wanted to sing along to the radio on the drive home. Later on, we turned it off and I sang the songs Daddy taught us on the ukulele. His favorite was "The Big Rock Candy Mountain," Daddy's was, but "The Wabash Cannon Ball" was mine.

> *From the calm Pacific waters*
> *To the rough Atlantic shore,*
> *Ever climbing hills and mountains*
> *Like no other did before.*
> *She's mighty tall and handsome,*
> *And she's known quite well by all,*
> *She's the Southern combination*
> *Called the Wabash Cannon Ball.*

When I finished singing the last verse—*Here's to Daddy Claxton, may his name forever stand*—Pa asked me to go back and start over, which made me think it was his favorite, too, and eased his mind, but by the end of that fall, he wasn't quite his old self anymore and I think what it was was not so much his heart as his worrying about the rest of us, not just Nanny, but Reed and me, and Mama and Daddy, too—especially them. I think Pa would of liked to hold it still for all of us, but even he could not.

# FOUR

## May

August 29, 1954—I remember the date exactly. It was the afternoon of Mama and Daddy's party, their thirtieth anniversary. That's
when I told Jimmy.

It was a Sunday, after church, hot. Lord, it was hot. The air
conditioning at Saint Paul's was out, or maybe they hadn't put it in
back then, but that was all anyone could talk about, the drought and
if it would ever break. Daddy and Uncle Johnny were worried sick
about the crop and drove out in the country every day to look, but of
course they liked to do that anyway; it was their way of playing
hooky. Personally, the whole subject of tobacco bored me half to
tears, but I suppose that was not a grateful or becoming thought—
considering the source of our advantages, I mean, though I don't
mean to brag.

Mama had a tent pitched in the back yard, the most wonderful
pink-and-white-striped tent, Lord knows where she found it. Every-

one in town was there—I bet the club didn't sell a single plate at the buffet. I'd just come back from the beach and stopped at Fannye's on the drive because I didn't have a thing to wear. The dress I bought was white organdie, light as a whisper—white was my color then—and I was the only one there without a hat. It seemed rather daring not to wear one, though I suppose that's silly, but I was tired of hats . . . hats filled me with intense ennui, which is how my Ascension friends and I liked to talk back then, thinking it was chic and cosmopolitan and all.

Was I vain about my looks? Oh, Lord, I don't know, I suppose I probably was . . . I don't think it can possibly count against me now, because I'm not that girl anymore—I hardly even recognize myself in pictures. I've often thought people who don't have it— looks, I mean—have a notion that if they did, it would make every- thing different and they'd be happy, but in my opinion it doesn't change that much. That's what I know *now*, of course. Back then I didn't and, see, for me it had come on all so sudden, right around fourteen, so it was like a new dress or something that feels magic the first time you put it on and maybe the second, but after while it just recedes into your closet and becomes part of all the other pretty things you had last year . . . the only pleasure you get out of it then is seeing, for a second here and there, the pleasure other people take in looking, but just try living off that and see how far you get. I guess I ought to know, but as I said, I'm not that girl anymore . . .

Well, anyhow, I hadn't seen Jimmy since July the Fourth, when he came down to Nags Head for the weekend. I was at the cottage with June and Malone—it was the first year they were married and they were supposed to be my chaperones, but what a joke that was. Malone hadn't quite made up his mind he'd graduated yet—he was a Zete at Chapel Hill; need I say more?—and June, well, don't get me started . . . Every morning for breakfast they made a pitcher of Bloody Marys and slept out on the beach till lunch. June was using motor oil for suntan lotion, something that crowd from Edenton brought down, and so help me she was blacker than Dee Lou until her skin peeled off in one big sheet. If I hadn't been there, I'm sure they would have burned the house down without a second thought. Those parties, Lord—four and five A.M. every night, and the boys

Malone invited over . . . I liked a good time as much as anyone, but I'm sorry, the Zetes were just degenerates. The Dekes were always more my speed—that's what Daddy was, of course, though he never got to finish Chapel Hill because of everything that happened with his father when they lost Rose Hill. Of course, Jimmy was only a KA, but he joined up not knowing any better.

Jimmy didn't have a wooden nickel to his name, of course, but that didn't bother me that much. If marrying money improved a person's character, I couldn't tell it from my sister, and Mama and Daddy, bless their hearts, didn't argue all that strongly for it either. Besides, Jimmy was going to be a doctor, not that either of us was bucking to get married right away—I was going to finish college first. Back then I was thinking maybe I would like to be a doctor, too —why shouldn't I?—though I knew better than to bring it up with Mama, who thought it was just one more way I meant to spite her. Not that Jimmy and I hadn't discussed marriage some the way you do—you know what I mean—but what we meant was we couldn't imagine not being together in the future, tomorrow or next week— at least I think that's what we meant. But what I was after was love and happiness, and the money just seemed what you settled for if you couldn't get it, and mainly what I wanted was a different life from what Mama and Daddy had, and, I don't know, I guess maybe a different one from mine, advantages and all, because advantages are similar to looks that way if you ask me—you pay a price. Well, Jimmy Madden was the most different boy I'd ever run across—I can say that just as much today as I could then, only back then *different* meant all good.

I'd thought I was in love with Sumner Dade, bless his heart, but a month after Jimmy and I started dating I couldn't imagine what I'd ever seen in him. It's hard to explain, but there was something in Jimmy that seemed more alive than anybody else, as though he had a fever, only not something *wrong* but something *more*. I remember just driving somewhere with him in the car, how he'd talk nonstop and wave those great big hands around and slam them on the steering wheel when he'd laugh and shake his head and punch the lighter for a cigarette and light mine first and reach out and pull me close against his shoulder and smile with a shine in those green eyes of his, fiddling with the radio the whole time. I'd sit and watch him sparkle through a dozen moods in half a minute, smiling to myself and thinking, *he's mine, he's mine*, thanking my lucky stars because it seemed to me my happiness had finally started and none too soon . . . What was looks and money compared to that? What can I say, I was eighteen, I thought that you could live inside the flame of love forever.

Of course, all I saw then was the light side of Jimmy's difference. There was a dark one, too, but that took a whole lot longer to show up, and when it did I guess it must have had a lot of lost time to make up for. Maybe my first glimpse was that afternoon at the party, as I started to tell you . . .

I hadn't seen him in six weeks and he strolled up the lawn with a new haircut and one hand in his pocket and a fifty-cent bouquet of daisies for Mama in the other and a grin from here to there. He had on that pair of white suede bucks I made him buy the spring before and white ducks and a double-breasted navy blazer with gold buttons. I think it was the only coat he owned but it was beautiful. He got that from his mother; I will give Lilith that, much as I hate to. Now Lilith, tight as she was with everybody else, was right up there in the same league with June when it came to her own clothes and probably spent more on her wardrobe than Mama and I did put together, where poor Daddy Madden, if he had three suits to his name I'll kiss a cow. Of course, Mama thought Jimmy dressed too flashy, but she was used to Daddy, who had probably fifty Hickey-Freeman suits in that big walk-in closet, all of them exactly the same, just slightly different colors. Not that Daddy didn't care, because he did, but he only cared so far, and according to Mama that's how far a man should care, anything more was suspicious. Clothes was the least of it, though—I expect my mama had it in for Jimmy Madden before the day he was ever born, and if you want to know the truth, that didn't exactly count against him in my book.

I kissed him dead on the lips right there in front of everybody and he blushed about a dozen shades of red and then I licked my fingertips and wiped the lipstick off the corner of his mouth. "Hey, bub," I said, "nice shoes." He looked down and said, "yeah, the salesgirl was real helpful," almost bashful. I said, "in your dreams."

"Especially in my dreams." "Did you miss me?" "Every single day," he said, and I said, "not at night?" He smiled. "Then, too—I thought about you right before I went to sleep." "When you said your prayers?" Jimmy laughed and his eyes said he wanted me so bad he could hardly stand it. I laughed, too, and didn't let my eyes say anything so he would only want me more and more, but inside I felt just the same and Jimmy knew and knew I knew he knew, and then I took his arm and said, "come on and take your medicine," and he said, "I'm prepared," and even that seemed priceless.

"Mama, look who's here," I called, leading him over, and she cut her eyes right to that bouquet. "Well, look-a-here," she said, "are those for me? Ain't you sweet, and daisies, too—just what my asthma needs." I made my eyes wide at her. "Mama, you be nice now." She addressed the group: "He's trying to kill me off already, y'all," and Jimmy said, "happy birthday, Miz Tilley," and I thought, *oh, God!* "You're four months late," said Mama, "but thank you just the same." "Isn't it your thirtieth birthday?" Jimmy asked, "I thought that's what the invitation said." Everybody laughed but Mama, who just narrowed her eyes to slits, though you could tell he got some points however much she grudged it. I was so proud I would have busted my buttons if I'd had some.

At the luncheon Daddy had too much to drink and started telling jokes and cutting winks around the table at everyone but Mama, who had bloody purple murder in her eye. In spite of everything he did for her and us, she was unforgiving of his failings, and if you ask me, part of why he drank was just to get a rise from her. All things considered, I was on Daddy's side of it, the same way June and Mama were a team. Daddy, bless his heart, was the only one who didn't realize there were any sides, but there's certain information men aren't strong enough to take. At least he didn't drink that often, but I still hated for Jimmy to see it, it embarrassed me so much.

As soon as people started leaving we slipped away across the road and followed the path down through the woods to Collie Pond, and Jimmy went skinny-dipping and asked me did I want to, but I couldn't think of it that close to home, not in broad day anyhow. But I admired that sort of loose and easy way he had about his body . . . I guess it's different for them, not growing up with all that guff about how it's your treasure and you have to guard it with your life and all. Not that we put too much stock in that, even back then in the dark ages—if nothing else, watching June cured me of any such ideas quite young—though at the same time you couldn't help but half believe it. Anyway, I was feeling just a little nauseated after lunch and fretting whether I should mention it, because I figured it was probably nothing, Malone and June had both had summer colds, and I'd been late before. Mainly I was just so scared to mess things up, I guess, though I told myself that was silly because I knew he was crazy about me and would take it how he was supposed to if it came to that, only I just didn't want it to . . .

So I'm sitting on the bank with my arms around my knees, grinding my bare toes into the dirt and feeling that things are closing in on me, and out he comes with a big grin, slicking his hair back with both hands and dripping water everywhere and his . . . I'm a big girl, I can say it, *penis*. I just don't like that word, it seems too scientific or something, and all the other ones, dick and cock and peter, are just coarse and ugly and none of them really seems like what it *is* . . . Right that second I wasn't in the mood to pay attention and of course that's exactly what he wanted, swinging it around that way, to be admired, however casual he tried to act.

"Hey," he said, and I said, "hey, yourself." "You really should come in." "We won't ever be like them, will we, Jimmy?" "Like who?" he asked, and it annoyed me that he didn't get it right away. "You mean the people at the party?" "I don't know," I said, "I guess," and he said, "what's the matter, darling?" and suddenly it sounded corny, that "darling." I said, "nothing," and he knelt down in the pine straw. "How about a kiss?" he said, and didn't bother waiting for an answer. When I gave him my cheek, he looked surprised and then a little hurt. "I'm just scared I'm coming down with something," I told him, "June and Malone both had this bug," and he said, "a June bug?" and smiled so nice it pulled me right up out of where I was. "I don't want you to catch it," I said, stroking his cheek with the back of my hand. "I'll take my chances," Jimmy said, and then I felt his arm curve around my lower back and lift me into him and the wet coming through my dress, and, God, I didn't care, it felt like such a relief to have his mouth.

The next minute I was crying and he said, "what is it, May? What's wrong?" "I don't know, I feel like such a dope . . . maybe it's just my period. I hope it is." It just slipped out, and then there was no stopping. "You're late?" he asked. "I don't know . . . well, yes, I am, but not that much." He took a beat and stared, his face as empty as a house the people have moved out of overnight and stuck you for the rent. "I thought you said it was okay," he said. "I thought it was." "*Thought?* Jesus, May—you didn't know?" I was just about too shocked for words. "Listen, Jimmy, who forgot to bring the you-know-what?" I said, which was another word I couldn't stand. I never would have brought it up, if he hadn't been acting like a shit. "I didn't *forget*, May. The pharmacy was closed when I got there, I told you that." "Is that supposed to be my fault?" I asked, and he said, "no, but I asked you if it was okay," harping on that point. I didn't know what else to say.

When he came down that weekend of the Fourth we hadn't seen each other in a month, Malone and June had gone to bed, we had the cottage to ourselves . . . what were we going to do? Yes, I said it was all right, but I didn't *know* . . . I said it was all right because I wanted to go to bed with him and couldn't stand to wait another minute, and, don't kid yourself, he believed me for the exact same reason. Only *now* he starts in quizzing me how many days it's been and all, as if I were some sort of scientist and kept count in my head or if I didn't, then I *should have.* That's the implication; it's my fault, but I didn't bring it up to make it his, so why did he blame me?

It was the first time since we'd been going out that I saw something in him I didn't like, but then he caught himself and changed his tack. "I'm, sorry, May. It's just that I wasn't expecting this, you know?" "You think I was?" I asked, and he said, "no, I don't think that, I know you weren't," real big and generous of him. He slipped closer on the pine straw and put his arm around my shoulder. "Listen, May, it's going to be all right, okay? Whatever happens." He lifted my chin and made me look at him. "I love you," he said, "hear me?" I nodded and felt my eyes fill up because that's what I'd wanted him to say at first. He kissed me again and smiled and I sniffed and said, "it's probably nothing anyway, but maybe when you go to Chapel Hill to see about your house, you could, you know, ask around—they might know something at the med school . . . and I will, too."

Deciding we'd finished with the subject, Jimmy said, "goddamn, I can't believe how beautiful you are," which is sort of what I mean about it doesn't do you any good . . . and you want to know something else? We did it then, too, right there by the pond with no more protection than the first time. I told myself, well, either my period's coming any minute now or I'm already pregnant, so why not? That's what I was thinking till I wasn't thinking anymore.

It was after dark when I came in by the back door, and there was Mama on the hall phone, fielding thank-yous for the party in her robe, the receiver tucked into her neck as she lit an Old Gold.

The minute she heard the door she turned around and hit me with *the look*, her eyes all wise and slitty as if she knew damn well what I'd been up to and didn't trust me as far as she could throw an elephant. I felt it was so unfair, because even if I was guilty now, she'd treated me the same when I was innocent, before I ever thought about a boy, and June was twice as bad, but did Mama ever look at *her* that way? "Just a minute, Annabel," she said and put her hand across the mouthpiece. "So you decided to come home . . ."

"Hi, Mama," I said, "it was such a nice party. Jimmy said to tell you how much he enjoyed it."

Mama didn't say a word, not one, she just let her eyes drift over me head to toe and toe to head, and, Lord . . . Lord, Lord, Lord, that look just sent me all to pieces. For her to suspect was one thing, but it was something else again for her to *know*, to look and see the evidence on me, and I was so sure she could, though I'd been careful, Lord, how careful I had been . . . I'd picked the blades of pine straw from my hair and washed off my ruined make-up in the pond and reapplied my lipstick. I'd smoothed the wrinkles in my dress the best I could and made Jimmy watch as I turned all the way around two times—he acted as if the whole thing was a joke: "no trace of incriminating evidence that I can see." But in spite of everything I did there are certain signs you just can't hide, that flush and kind of dreamy look you get, which in the mirror afterward would make my face look strange to me, as though I could see it clear for once and like it more than any other time. That face was the one I couldn't let my mama see, not ever. All she ever wanted was our happiness—that's what Mama always told us—only now it seems I spent more time protecting her from it than anything.

Brushing by her in the hall to reach the stairs, I caught a trace of her perfume, Guerlain, and I could only pray that Mama didn't catch a whiff of mine—*please, God, don't let her smell it on me*—that was the worst thought of all, however much I liked the way Jimmy would sniff at me afterward sometimes like a great big grinning dog which seemed so rude and wonderful and made me laugh too hard . . . It excited me for us to be two animals to one another and forget the rest of it. That's what I was thinking as I took my shower, soaping out my panties and hanging them on the shower rod to dry before I put them in the hamper for Dee Lou.

When I sat down at my dressing table to comb out my hair, the girl in the mirror didn't have such dreamy eyes . . . I was scared, and I hadn't been till then. I guess I must have been naive, because I'd expected to feel better after telling him. I was none too pleased to find it worked the other way . . .

Later, when I went downstairs, Daddy was reading the Sunday paper in the den, repenting. I sat down on the arm of his chair and read the headlines with him over his shoulder till he rattled it and put it in his lap, smiling up at me. "Hey, sugar." "Hey," I said, "what's the forecast?" "More of same." He shook his head. "You okay?" "Fine," he said, "took me a nice long nap," aware what I was asking him and telling me in his own way.

Most times I would have got up then and gone about my business, but instead I stayed a minute longer as his eye scanned back down the column. I looked at his bald spot and that piece of hair he tried to hide it with and smelled his Aqua Velva and thought about the hundred bottles of cologne I'd given him which he'd wear for a week, and then, as soon as he figured I'd forgotten, back would come the Aqua Velva; truth to tell, I guess deep down I loved it more than any other one. I sat there feeling the sort of tenderness that seems to come sometimes right out of nowhere, washing over you like a wave, and I thought of telling him, *Daddy, I'm pregnant,* and the way his face would change, how it would strike him some-place deep he didn't have any defenses for, and just to think of it brought something to my throat so I could hardly swallow.

"You all right, sugar?" he asked, looking back up, "something on your mind?" I smiled for him and shook my head and kissed him and got up.

I went straight to the library then, which is where I'd started out to go. Closing the door behind me, I stared at Mama's portrait for a minute, which that man from Richmond did, who came down to Seven Oaks, her daddy's house, and stayed six weeks and finished six or seven times and drank up all her daddy's whiskey. She was a flapper with bobbed hair then around the time she first met Daddy, who was still thin and had his hair and was the horse to bet on in our town. It scared me to think they'd once felt the same as Jimmy and I did and had forgotten or changed their minds on love . . . because what if it wasn't as big and wonderful as it felt now, or didn't last forever the way it was supposed to? No, we were different, Jimmy and I; we weren't like them. That's what I decided, and I went to the *Britannica* and took out P and sat down in the window seat and turned to "pregnancy" to see if there was anything to help me there or tell me if I was. It was just a bunch of scientific words like "zy-gote" and "placenta" and these colored pictures of the stages where the closest one to where I was was this sort of tadpole thing with gills and a long tail. No, I could not be pregnant—I decided, as though my wish were a decree—not May Tilley. I was going to be the May Queen at Ascension in the spring, all my girlfriends said so.

The plan I hit on hinged around Dee Lou, and I thought I was just so clever I could hardly stand myself. After everyone had gone to bed I went up the back staircase to her room the way I used to when I was a little girl and I'd get scared at night—I would no more have dreamed of going downstairs to Mama and Daddy's room than flying to the moon; no, it was always Deely, and she never said a word, just lifted up the covers and let me climb right in.

She was sitting in her rocking chair that night with that funny little cap thing on to help keep her hair straight—it made her look like an old Pilgrim woman—and so little bitty, her feet hardly touched the floor. She was sewing a button on her uniform with her reading glasses on, which she was too vain to wear in public.

"Hi, Deely, you asleep?" "What it look like, girl?" she said, and I saw right then she had an axe to grind with me. "You gone be the death a yo' po' mama yet, May Tilley, running off all day and don't say a word to no one where you going." So that was it—it wasn't hard to tell Mama had been tearing me up one side and down the other. "You coming in or just gone stand there?"

I sat down on the bench before her little dressing table and watched as she wrapped her thread and bit it off. "Well, I'm sorry everybody's mad at me," I said, "it was a lovely party, everything was all so nice, and I know you must be half dead on your feet, so I probably shouldn't stay." She looked me over like she was wise to all my tricks, but Dee could never resist that sort of compliment be- cause to her it was her party, she did the work, the only part Mama played was taking all the credit. "I bet I walked a hundred miles though," she said. "Did Mama drive you crazy?" "Don't you try me, girl," she warned. "She was on the warpath, though." "She just want things nice," Dee said, "it gits her nervous." "Mama? Nervous?" The idea struck me as a hoot. "That's just how she shows it," Dee said, "some one way, some the other . . . Reach me that brush." "That's okay, Dee, you don't have to." "Hush," she said, and turned me toward the mirror and started tugging the bristles through my hair. "You got some pretty locks, Maybelle." I smiled up at her. "Remember how I used to come and sleep with you?" She said, "I remember," and her face had softened up by then.

"Can I ask you something, Dee?" "What, baby?" "There's this friend of mine at school," I said, "you haven't met her and I can't tell you her name, but she was at the beach while I was there, and she told me something but you have to promise not to tell, okay?" Dee frowned. "Uh-huh." "Well, she isn't sure," I said, "but she thinks she may be, you know, in trouble." She quit brushing. "She's late and doesn't know what to do," I said, talking way too fast. "She can't tell her parents, and she asked me if I knew anything . . . you know, like how you could get it fixed? if there was anybody? and of course I didn't know, but, Dee, she's scared, so I said I'd try to find out something, and I wonder if you know."

"Look at me, May Tilley," Dee said, and I thought my heart would just collapse. "What, Dee?" I batted my lashes as innocent as you please as she turned my chin up to her face.

"Oh, Dee, don't be silly," I said, laughing a whole opera scale. "It isn't me, really it isn't. I'm just asking because I want to help her," and Dee said, "well, you want to he'p her, you tell her tell her mamindaddy right doggone quick." "Then you don't know anything?" Dee said, "I know plenty mo'n you think I do or's fit fuh you to hear."

"Well, I just asked," I said, pouting, "you can't be mad at me for that," and she said, "I cain't? Why cain't I? If I didn' love you all to pieces I'd turn you on my knee and wah you out, messin' in such business. You stay out the middle, hemme?" "Yes, ma'am," I said, "but please don't stop, okay?" And she kind of snorted like she was satisfied.

Then I leaned back into her and closed my eyes as she began to brush again, my heart going ninety miles an hour but sure I'd saved the day. Oh, I was such a clever girl.

# FIVE

## Jimmy

*You know you love her, stay and be a man,* said the little white adviser perched on my right shoulder. The little red one squatting on my left said, *run like hell.*

You know how it is at twenty-one—you have a future all mapped out in front of you, a folder full of travel brochures about exotic ports of call like George Bailey in what used to be my favorite movie, *It's a Wonderful Life*. I guess that's who I thought I was back then, or who I'd have liked to be. Only I was going to take May with me in the role of Donna Reed. After I became a doctor, we'd open a clinic somewhere in darkest Africa, where I'd write poetry like Pasternak or William Carlos Williams, and stumble on the cures to some diseases on the side. If May's view was more along the lines of New York City, a penthouse on Park Avenue and galas at the Met, never mind, why not do both? As long as it was free. You're never going to stay in Bedford Falls, but then you do, we weren't the only ones. Who knows why it happens?

I guess there's really just one reason—Capra nailed it, which is why you'll never find a dry eye in the house after the lights come up. There are more George Baileys out there than you think, but fewer angels to come down and pull them from the river when it all blows up. I guess that's why I couldn't watch that movie for a long time after May and I split up.

You won't get rich or popular pointing out such sentiments to a room that's primed to sing and weep. I'm a case in point. But if you're a student of life—and I like to think I've remained that, whatever else has fallen by the way—it's not a wise thing to omit.

But, yes, I loved May. I loved her that special way it is when you first stumble into love like King Tut's golden tomb and think nobody in the history of the world has ever visited the place before or felt this thing the two of you are in. You go bumping into walls and breaking china and forgetting where you're driving in the car, and everything is going to change forever—it already has. It's absolutely true, love changes everything, only it takes time for the true nature of the change to dawn on you.

May and I both bought the advertisement in the travel folder—love as a permanent vacation in a tropical paradise where no one fails or ages and the drinks are on the house. The difference was, she had a harder time accepting the mosquitoes and the snakes and shotgun shacks and hurricanes, the things the ad leaves out. Even back then I knew that whatever dreams and hopes you bring with you to the contest, if life pays you fifty cents on the dollar you should count yourself a lucky man and run to cash the check. I don't know how I knew—basketball, I guess, the best and hardest school I ever went to. When my knee went out my freshman year at Chapel Hill it taught me there's a magic you can take for granted, and then one day, going up to make the same shot you've made twenty thousand times, you come down in a slightly different way, and just that fast, in a split second, it's all taken from you. You crash down into the world where everybody else has been living all that time, and having been an astronaut, set apart and special for so long, you don't easily acquire a taste for flying tourist class. No, we don't own the magic, and it's a big mistake to trust whoever does.

I certainly knew that by the time I left the Tilleys' party that August afternoon in 1954. After May had dropped the bomb—at that point it wasn't much more than a smoke grenade—I stopped at Lonnie Ruffin's Shell station on Raleigh Road and bought a pack of Lucky Strikes. I remember the occasion because it was the first pack I'd ever purchased for my personal use, though my whole senior year at Chapel Hill I'd been mooching them at parties. Lonnie smoked so much he had those little yellow calluses between his knuckle joints, but he gave me this worried look and said, "hey, Jimbo, playing any ball?" as if he was watching his idol teetering on the shelf, about to fall. You'd think my parents had recruited him to disapprove for them by proxy. Sometimes it felt that way—as though I had to drive twenty miles outside town and go down in a soundproof concrete bunker to cut a fart.

I sat there in the lot and stripped the cellophane and fired one up. As Lonnie switched the sign on in the dusk it struck me, looking at that bloody shell, that it's a scallop, and I remembered from someplace, Chaucer maybe, how the scallop was the badge of Saint James, patron saint of pilgrims and wanderers. I had a feeling the journey I was tempted to make that minute in the car—out of town at a high rate of speed—was not one George Bailey would approve of.

At home, I parked at the curb and climbed the steps to the side door and turned the knob and stopped. Instead of going in, I walked around to the back yard and stood in the shadows near the garbage cans and watched through the kitchen window like a prowler. It was dark enough by then for Mother to have switched on the electric lights, one more sacrifice God imposed to help her keep her muscle tone for suffering intact and live a Christian life. Every day was more than she could stand and she was stronger than a bull rhinoceros from standing every one. She was in her apron at the range, stirring something in a pot that looked a lot like trouble.

Beside her, Sam was sitting on the countertop with his back to me. His hair was wet from his shower after football practice and he had his usual glass of milk. He was chatting on in that loud elated voice of his which hadn't finished changing yet—Sammy seemed to think he had to put as much mileage as possible on that new baritone before the repossession company took it back, but probably I'd been that way, too. I could tell he'd made the cut and I was pleased, because he'd finally get his letter jacket even if he rode the bench— that stuff never came as easily for Sam. His heel was banging against the lower cabinet as he talked till Mother stared at him with that little crease between her eyebrows. He stopped everything then, swinging his leg and talking, too, and when he picked back up it was in a softer tone. That's training for you.

Behind them in the nook, Dolly was writing at the breakfast table with her schoolbooks open—algebra, the subject Daddy used to teach before they made him principal. She had on that old cardigan of his that I kept telling her made her look like a spinster librarian of fifty, but she'd just say, "it's *cashmere*, Jimmy," as if simple ugliness could not stand up to such a fact. Killdeer High didn't start for two more weeks, but you could count on it: she'd taken the books Daddy brought home from the storeroom and knocked out the first six weeks of lessons.

As I watched, Daddy strode in from the den and stood behind her chair, batting the rolled newspaper in his hand, frowning over Dolly's shoulder with that expression of severe probity I think they stamped on in the assembly line. Never more than once or twice in his whole life, I expect, did he betray the secret he was most ashamed of—that he had a tender heart. I'm not sure Daddy even knew, but compared to him, Mother, for all her sighs and languors, was a stevedore, Stanley Kowalski in disguise as Blanche DuBois. Leaning over Dolly's shoulder, he pointed with the paper, and the hanging lamp lit up the dull gleam of his scalp through his hair. Also frowning, Dolly erased her mistake, wrote something new, then looked up hopefully. Daddy nodded and patted her shoulder that awkward way of his, as if touching was a foreign custom, and then he went back toward the den.

Standing outside, I had a sense of looking back from a great distance at some old family photograph I'd once been part of, only someone, probably me, had taken scissors to it, leaving an empty outline in my place. It was hard to sort out pain from love in the dumb ache I felt, and there was still a part of me that would have liked to stay and fight their fights for them until that distant day of victory when we could all drop our chains and greet the sunrise, holding hands and singing opera. Another part was ready to abandon the pilgrims on the ship and save myself, just like my namesake in Joseph Conrad's book. My red and white advisers were with me out there in the back yard, too—they're never far away, and make it hard sometimes for me to come to a decision. Not this one, though —it was already made. No, Lord Jimmy was out of there on the first lifeboat, and none too soon.

Mother had been on my case all summer, ever since I graduated and came home. I never remembered it that bad growing up. I don't know what it was—maybe I'd gotten used to different ways living at the KA house, or maybe she was punishing me in advance for leaving and exacting as much severance pay as possible. I was trying to save money for school working the job Daddy got me with Bill Hughes on the grounds crew at the high school. Mother made me pay half of what I made in rent and seemed to feel it was little enough to ask that I do all her errands, too, in exchange for the privilege of sharing my old room with Sam. If you get down to it, I guess the real debt was her bearing me and suffering me to live for twenty-one whole years—I'd worked it out to pay on the installment plan.

That summer made being on a riverboat in the Belgian Congo headed upstream for the heart of darkness seem attractive—I hadn't realized back then that you don't have to go so far from home. As far as I was concerned, med school couldn't start soon enough, and I wasn't even sure I wanted to be a doctor. The esteem May held it in, the pride that lit her eyes whenever we discussed my future—meaning ours—enhanced medicine's appeal. To be honest, though, it was never more than a fall-back position. My first love had been acting, my second poetry. Becoming an M.D. had never once occurred to me till four years before. I came home one afternoon from rehearsals—I'd been cast as the Stage Manager in the senior production of

*Our Town* at Killdeer High—and announced at dinner that I was going to be an actor. The line did not play to the house; it went down flaming like the *Hindenburg*.

Daddy and I had the most extended conversation of our lives that night—every bit of fifteen minutes—and he did all the talking. Acting wasn't respectable or solid, he told me. Actors were a bare step up from barkers in the carnival (I liked them, too). He didn't want to influence me, of course, but he'd always dreamed I'd be a doctor, like his father—the father Daddy never knew—who practiced in Front Royal, Virginia, in the Shenandoah Valley, and died young, leaving his wife seven children and a mortgaged house. If Daddy had asked me to be a knight errant I expect I would have bolted on a chain-mail suit and set out looking for a charger, and it wasn't so much because I loved him as because I wanted to so badly. Here, my senior year in high school, a way appeared that I might finally penetrate his own formidable armor—I thought it was a gift and scraped acting from my shoes like so much dirt. But the dream had been sweet for that one afternoon—oysters on the half-shell and champagne for breakfast, lighting my cigars with hundred-dollar bills—wasn't that what actors got to do?

So there I was, standing by the garbage cans in our back yard, spying on my family through the window, thinking *freedom* on the one hand, and on the other thinking *May*, and the thing about it was that up until that very moment on that very night I'd been thinking *May and freedom* both on the same hand.

Too shaky to go in, I climbed back in the car and headed off, not knowing where I meant to go until I found myself downtown, passing the Bonanza warehouse, a square brick fortress occupying the whole block at the corner of Commerce Street and Church, leaking tobacco smell at every pore and seam, a sweet, rich, heavy smell like bourbon-sex and darkness, like forbidden fruit in heavy syrup . . . Up above the door the sign read WILLIAM G. TILLEY followed by a blank where he never got to write & SONS. Wouldn't that be something if he got to now, I thought. *Oh, shit.* Across the way at Dixie Bag two fat smoke clouds hung over the twin stacks, pale in the blue dark, like comic strip balloons without the writing. I looked at them and thought, that's right, you get the picture long before you get the joke. It can take years, but count on it, it's generally on you.

I dipped beneath the underpass and entered Bagtown—identical tin-roofed boxes set back by a strip of lawn, and not a tree or bush in sight. One house to the next, the only difference was whether it was painted and the grass was cut, and on every block of a dozen houses —some statistic fundamental to the human race—the one with the rusted Chevy up on blocks in a front yard of tire-rutted yellow clay and trash littered where they ate or drank or smoked and a broken-down couch sitting cockeyed on the porch where you could see the mean gleam of an orange coal as some man sat smoking in his undershirt, watching you drive past and deciding what to hate about you and what he'd like to do to you if you gave him the chance. KILLDEER, A NICE PLACE TO VISIT. I don't think Will Tilley and John Landis and Kincannon and the rest of the rich men who ran the chamber and the school board and my father's life had Bagtown in mind when they placed the order for that sign. I could never pass it without wanting to stop and write, *But you wouldn't want to live here.*

As I drove through, I was thinking of Red Wells, the point guard on the Killdeer team, who came from out that way. *Wells and Madden, the Pirates' one-two punch* . . . that's how the paper used to write of us in 'forty-nine and 'fifty, the dark-horse year when we knocked out Durham in the conference final and took the title . . . seven seconds on the clock when Red hit me down low in the paint with so much sizzle on the pass it almost caromed out of bounds. I faked right and went left, tossing a hook meant for the glass that hit the back rim instead and bounced up higher than the backboard. It was still hanging way up near the rafters when the buzzer sounded. Then it dropped through so clean the net splashed up and hung— Killdeer 52, Durham 51—and then everybody screaming, *Jimbo! Jimbo!* and storming down out of the stands. Nineteen-fifty, that was our big year, mine and Red's. We saw each other every day and had the kind of crush you get in sports when two of you make something magic happen that neither one could do alone. I could count on Red's hard straight passes in the lane, and he could count on me to take them to the hoop. We were best friends for a whole year based on that, no more, no less, and since I'd left for Chapel Hill I'd seen him once at Earl's with a gut and a scraggly new mustache and a sullen-looking wife and a screaming kid that probably wasn't his and bags beneath his eyes and a grin on his good face. He told me he'd just gotten on the line at Dixie Bag, the graveyard shift, and acted like the world was his own oyster.

Red was the one who told me about Cassie Grimes, and remembering that as I drove through Bagtown I realized why I'd come and where I meant to go. Of course, I'd known who she was before . . . any kid over eight years old, any boy at least, knew who she was and had probably rung her doorbell and hidden in the bushes across the street and watched to catch a glimpse of her, a thin black-haired woman with one of those pinched country faces, wearing a robe and a man's white tube socks crumpled over at the ankles and no slippers, talking to herself—"halle-*loo*-yuh, puh-*raise* his name"—or singing Christian battle hymns. Her house was famous, fire-engine red with crude white crosses hand-painted on the shutters and a tree in the front yard she'd also painted white as high as she could reach. What Red had told me senior year was that his older brother, Billy, took his wife to Cassie Grimes with fifty dollars and a fifth of whiskey and two clean sheets—they couldn't feed another mouth—and Cassie Grimes had fixed what ailed her.

Halfway down the block I sidled to the curb and cased the joint. There was one light burning in the window. My heart was going like a hammer in an empty fifty-five-gallon drum. *See, Miss Grimes, this is about my sister.* Dolly wouldn't mind; her life could use the spice.

I reached in the glove box and lit another Lucky to calm my nerves and think it through. *What are you doing here, Madden?* my white adviser was asking, and his counterpart replied, *I'll tell you what* . . .

The Friday before I set out for the beach to visit May over the Fourth, Bill Hughes and I had made a run out to the dump and come back late. By the time I pulled up to the pharmacy, old man Eller was nowhere in sight, the blinds were drawn on the front door. His sign said 8–5, my watch said two minutes till, his other sign said CLOSED. And there you go—I mean, a man's whole life could not be long enough to expiate a sin like that.

At the beach, June did everything but wink as she said, "come on, Jimmy, let me show you to *your* room." Those Episcopalian girls weren't like the Methodists I knew—wine compared to grape juice, or maybe I should say blood compared to wine—either way, the transubstantiation had occurred long before I came on the scene. Across the candles, May and I made eyes at each other all through dinner while June beamed and joked about "the lovebirds."

"Well, we old married folks are plumb exhausted," she said at ten o'clock, "I think we'll retire early . . . I can trust you with my baby sister, can't I, Jimmy?" Malone had an irritated look as he followed her into the bedroom, probably because he'd had to swill his drink a little faster than he liked, and when I stood up from the table to say good night, I had to hold the napkin in my lap to hide where May had slipped her stocking foot—just say I'd been giving her a little foot massage beneath the table. On the porch, she called out, "night, Jimmy, see you in the morning," loud enough for them to hear, smiling like a little girl whose ruse is meant not to deceive but just to charm the victim.

I went downstairs, and not five minutes later May appeared at the door, and we fell on one another like two starved animals. We had to put our hands over each other's mouths to keep from waking up the neighborhood. She left toothprints in my palm I could still see the morning after, and I can't say I didn't bite her, too. The bed began to walk across the floor, beating a tattoo like a peglegged madman with Saint Vitus's dance. I held her silky cheek in one hand and with the other gripped the windowsill to try to steady us, the box springs going like a runaway stagecoach—I wouldn't be surprised if I added six inches to my reach.

We were up half the night, and afterward we lay in the sopped sheets, exhausted, laughing every time we looked at each other, passing one of May's Pall Malls, listening as the wind began to rise outside, banging a shutter against the house. Two cats were keening somewhere. My knees and knuckles were rubbed raw, but I didn't feel it then—not till the next morning at breakfast when May showed up with her cheeks and one side of her neck bright red from my stubble. She seemed less eager to be obvious as she offered some excuse about a sunburn. "Oh, did the sun come out last night?" said June, "I thought you'd had a facial"—her mother's patent wit.

Did I love her? I couldn't even start to count the ways . . . I loved the way she clambered out to meet me through the hole in the back fence at Ascension with her heels in one hand and dirt smudges on her pretty knees. I loved the somber way she listened when I read to her from the dog-eared Eliot I kept in the back seat of the ancient Chrysler I'd inherited from Dad. Sometimes I snuck her up the fire escape at the KA house, and I loved how she took the rubbers from my dresser, pinching them between her thumb and finger with a wrinkled nose, calling them my "galoshers," putting an *r* into the word and making fun of me when I corrected her—*excuse me, Professor.* I loved the way she danced, May Tilley in white silk and pearls with the natural wave in her black hair and little white gloves that buttoned at the wrist, and those beautiful black eyes, so deep and grave, searching into you for something you were suddenly afraid you might not have. Take her into Earl's some Friday night when they had a roadhouse band and before you knew it she'd kick her shoes across the room and go for broke—she taught me how to do the down-and-dirty shag, but I was never in her league. Those Episcopalian girls, I'd thought they were all stuck-up prudes, but what did I know? Most of all I loved the chemistry we made in bed.

It wasn't something we ever had to learn or practice—God bestowed it as a gift. It was like that from the first time we made love, at Homecoming the year before she went off to Ascension. I came home for the game wearing my fraternity pin and carrying an umbrella, feeling like a college man. Afterward we went parking. I wasn't really sure we should go all the way—not that I didn't want to, only May Tilley wasn't the type you fooled around with lightly. She didn't seem to share my qualms. She lay back with her eyes squinched closed and let me finger her, twisting her head this way and that with a little grimace on her face. I thought maybe I was doing it too hard and hurting her, but that wasn't it. I watched her face in secret, surprised, interested, yes, but a little afraid of what I might be getting into—because I didn't love her then. May was way down deep inside of something, way down in another world.

"Do you think we should stop?" I asked, and she moaned and said, *"come on,"* almost as if she was angry at me, then pulled me down on top of her. And it was different for me, too. I felt her pull me down into that far world where she was, and for a few seconds as I came I forgot where we were, that we were in the back seat of my dad's old car out at the quarry. I opened my eyes afterward and felt that I'd been *somewhere else.* I didn't know where, but no other girl had ever taken me there before, not even close. The others had all been stiff and disapproving in some way. Even if they said they liked it, it was more as if they agreed to get some hold on you, and when it got down to it, they just wanted it over with as quickly and hygieni-cally as possible. I'd always been pretty much ready to take sex how I found it, but after May I wasn't interested in going back to the old way.

I'd never encountered an abandonment like hers, and I mean sex, but not just sex. May didn't hedge her bets on many things. When she committed, that was it. I don't believe she heard the double voices arguing yes and no from opposite shoulders—if she did, she knew how to shut them out much better than I did. I envied that and wanted to be close to it. Probably I romanticized it, too, something love and being twenty-one are both known to contribute to, not to mention an undergraduate degree in English lit. Sometimes I thought of her in almost mythic terms, Salome dancing the Seven Veils, but there was something in May that never took off more than six. She gave me everything except the *last* thing—something even deeper than sex, some part of her soul—and I'd be lying if I said I didn't like that, too, her withholding it. Because in my experience when someone gave you that—I'd loved girls before and seen it happen—they died for you somehow, the glow passed off them. I liked that May kept something for herself so I could keep on want-ing it, looking forward to the time when it would finally be deliv-ered. The mistake I made at twenty-one was thinking the withhold-ing was deliberate, some exercise of female wiles. I know better now. May no more knew what was behind that veil than I did, or how to take it off, or even that there was a veil. It was as much a part of her as her own skin, and maybe that's what she was trying to shed and what love was for her, the shedding of it.

But there comes a point where the enticement of a withheld thing turns to frustration, and I guess from the very start a part of me resented what I also loved in her . . . because I hadn't forgotten those summers as a boy, caddying at the country club, holding some M.D.'s bag, my shirt soaked through with sweat, as the girls around the pool—not May, but girls like May—sat on the chaises in their bathing suits, drinking lemonade or cherry Cokes in highball glasses, looking cool in their dark glasses, whispering together and sending pointed looks in my direction, taunting me to join them while perfectly aware that I could not.

All these troubled and conflicting currents were playing through my mind that night as I sat at the curb at Cassie Grimes's, trying to summon up the nerve to knock. The tobacco smell was sweet and heavy over the whole town, as if they owned that, too, the air. Fifty dollars and a fifth of whiskey and two sheets, as though it could really be that simple or that cheap—no, this was not where you brought Donna Reed. I didn't even bother knocking, I just flicked my cigarette away, shoved the stick in gear and scratched away, home.

When I told May about that night years later—I don't know how long it was, but things were already on the slippery downhill slope—she just gave me a frustrated look with those heartbreaking black eyes. "You couldn't even act on that, could you?" she said. Maybe she was right. As Prufrock said, I was never meant to be Prince Hamlet. Or even George Bailey. I just made a long, illustrious career of pissing off everybody who thought I was. It never seemed to dawn on them that the outcome was a little disappointing to me, too.

# SIX

## May

Out the window I could see the workmen in the back yard taking down Mama's pink-and-white-striped tent.

It was the day after the anniversary party and I was upstairs in my room, packing my trunk for school. As I wrapped my shoes in tissue, I was thinking where I'd worn each pair, saving till last the ones I'd worn as a Maid of Honor in the May Court at Ascension. When I kissed Genevieve congratulations at the crowning, she whispered in my ear, "well, sugar, next year's your turn." Strange how happy that thought made me, as though if only I could stand where she was standing and have everyone's eyes on me, if just one time that could be me, then it would be like—I don't know—a magic wand that touched my life and turned it into fairy dust and gold forever. Amazing, isn't it? I was singing as I packed, I do remember that, singing when Daddy called from the bottom of the stairs,

"May, sugar, would you step down here a minute? Yo' mama and I got something to discuss with you."

I walked out on the landing. He was standing below me in the foyer with one hand on the newel post and a ripe tomato in the other. I don't think Daddy even knew he had it, but I took one look at that ripe Big Boy and got what I believe they call a sinking feeling . . .

When I walked into the living room, there was Mama by the mantelpiece with her mascara ruined and a face like death. She cut a look at me so help me like General Sherman watching as they set the torches to Atlanta. Before anybody said a word I knew they knew and how they'd found out, too—Dee Lou. It was over before it even started. Oh, I was too damn smart for my own good.

"Honey," Daddy said, "there's no point beating around the bush. If you're in trouble, we want to he'p you, but we cain't 'less you talk to us."

I dropped down on the sofa and stared at my hands—they seemed like someone else's—and I couldn't think; each thought weighed a thousand pounds. I looked up at Mama, who stared hard at me and then away. Her eyes were filling, too.

"I don't know," I said, "I don't know if I'm . . ." I simply couldn't say the word—*pregnant*. Daddy—God, I could see how it just killed him—Daddy said, "but could you be?" not using the word either, being discreet to try to spare my feelings. I didn't answer, just dropped my head and started sobbing—I suppose that answered it right enough.

Daddy sat beside me on the couch and took my hand and patted it. He was struggling so hard to be kind, but the look on his face— oh, it was the one, the terrible one just as I'd imagined it, and I couldn't help him. "I'm so ashamed," I said, "I'm so ashamed," and Daddy just kept patting my hand. "If it's done, it's done," he said, "y'all ain't the first, honey, and if it comes down to it, yo' mama and I were young once, too."

I was so upset I hardly even heard that then, though later it stood out as clear as anything. "Mama?" I wanted so bad for her to show me something, just some little sign. Tears were rolling down her cheeks, leaving dark streaks in her base, but she didn't give an inch, as tough as nails. I gave up hope, and right that very instant she held out her arms and I ran across the room to her, I ran so fast. For that one minute in her arms it felt as though we were the family I'd always wanted us to be, the family we were supposed to be, only day in and day out there's something that comes in and separates you from it, and the separation is where the unhappiness comes from.

"Well, I expect we better call Watt Pound and set up an appointment," Daddy said. They offered to go with me downtown to the office, but I said no. I don't know why . . . I guess I was determined to make it just as hard as possible on myself.

As if I needed any help, who should I run into at the bottom of the drive but Sumner, pulling into his parents' house next door. He'd stopped to pick up Catherine's mail, and I tooted and waved my I'm-running-we'll-talk-later wave, but he ran out in the street, oaring his arm for me to roll the window down.

"What gives?" he asked with a big grin, "you ducking me or what?" He had on madras slacks and a pink cotton sweater with a monogram, which made me wonder suddenly what had happened to that black leather jacket with zippered wrists he used to have—it was bound to happen, I suppose.

"Hi, Sum, when did you get home?" I asked. "Just this very minute—is this fate, or what? Let's pop up to the club and get a bite." "Can't," I said, "wish I could, but I've got to run some errands," and he said, "errands?" in that teasing way of his, like how could that compare with him. "Why don't you come over this afternoon and have a drink?" I said, "I know Mama would love to see you." He said, "Mama?" and his eyes said, *how about you?*—I ignored his eyes.

"Anyway, I can't," he said, "after lunch I'm headed to the Hill." "Jimmy's up there now," I said, "he and Whit are looking for a house." "Ah, Jimmy . . . you're still an item then." I smiled and Sumner said, "alas," which made me feel a little pang—for him, though, not for me.

"I hear you're dating Molly Windsor now," I said, doing what I could for him, and he said, "ye olde grapevine?" I smiled. "Ye olde grapevine." "The four of us should get together sometime up in Chapel Hill," he said, and I said, "we'd like that—I expect to be up there a lot this fall." I saw him wince a little at that "we," but it seemed necessary to be clear. "I wish I could chat, Sum," I reminded him. "Oh, sorry, I'll let you go." He stood up from the window. "Good to see you," I said, and he said, "yeah, you, too—be good, May B.," which was what he used to call me back when "maybe" was my answer.

Watching him in the rearview mirror with his arm raised goodbye, I felt even sadder than before. I'd had a crush on him for years while he loved June, who strung him along playing sister, telling him all her hurtful secrets about the other boys she loved and never caring how he felt. On autumn nights after the football games the bell would ring at the back door and I'd answer it and have to tell him June was out. Sometimes he'd come in and we'd play gin or watch TV; eventually he'd ask those little questions he didn't really want the answers to, trying to be casual—it was written all over him.

He still wore that leather jacket then, which possessed a meaning I could deeply understand, the opposite of madras slacks and monograms. I was sixteen when he looked at me one afternoon in the back yard and said, "I never realized you were more beautiful than June—when did that happen?" I was thrilled, but I did not believe him. Sumner was my first—a special thing. And all that remained of it was that joke he'd made about my name, May B., and everything we'd shared had somehow left us more distant than if our lives had never touched at all.

As for the appointment, all I remember is Dr. Watt telling me it was no use worrying over what hadn't even happened yet, the bunny would decide. I wanted to tell Jimmy, but I didn't. It seemed better to wait until the test came back and not worry him. I can't remember how long it took—three days, maybe four, it seemed longer. I do remember praying. I prayed as I'd never prayed before.

Not counting Christmas, I doubt I'd been to evening service at Saint Paul's more than half a dozen times in my whole life, but after that appointment I did go. I don't know exactly what I wanted that night. Yes, I do—I wanted to gaze at the flowers and the altar linens and the candles winking in the brass, I wanted to listen to the liturgy, not the words, but just the rhythm of the words—to me it was the same as sleeping with the window open at the beach, letting the waves shush me to sleep. That's mainly what church was for me and that was what I wanted, to be soothed and lifted up and lost inside the Holy Service.

Taylor Hale, our new rector—"new" meant he'd been at Saint Paul's only three years—came in from the vestry and nodded greetings all around. He held my eyes a moment and his smile seemed bashful, as though he was self-conscious of that new mustache. He lifted his arms, there was a rustling, creaking sound as we stood up, and then he said, "O God, make speed to save us," which was not the same as morning service—I didn't know the right response. And from that moment, I was thinking.

Part of it was seeing Catherine Dade, Sumner's mother. They'd lived next door for years and she'd intrigued me all my life—I guess because she seemed so different from Mama. Where Mama made a style of being crude and off-the-cuff, Catherine was poised and elegant and deliberate in everything she did, as though she planned her smallest gestures with an audience in mind. She moved like a queen, perfect in some way, and when I was a little girl I used to pretend sometimes that Annie Dade was Mama's daughter and I was Catherine's, and when she smiled at me, that was our secret sign. Yet those startling blue eyes of Catherine's always considered first before she spoke—they hardly ever laughed or cried or flashed the way Mama's would. Yet those two were best friends, their backgrounds no more different than two bricks in a wall. What made them turn out the way they had? Which one was I going to be? That was exactly the sort of thing I didn't want to think about.

As we stood for the Apostles' Creed, those words I must have said a thousand times before stood out some way they never had, like italics in a book: "I believe in the Holy Ghost, the holy catholic church, the communion of saints, the forgiveness of sins, the resurrection of the body, and the life everlasting. World without end. Amen." What did it even mean? I don't believe I'd ever stopped to ask what I was promising, and I guess that's what I was really thinking of that night—promises.

"On the night he was handed over to suffering and death, our Lord Jesus Christ took bread"—Taylor raised the wafer and broke it, beginning consecration—"and when he had given thanks to you, he broke it, and gave it to his disciples, saying, 'Take, eat: This is my Body, which is given for you. Do this for the remembrance of me.'

"After supper he likewise took the cup of wine; and when he had given thanks, he gave it to them, saying, 'Drink this, all of you: This is my Blood of the new Covenant, which is shed for you and for many for the forgiveness of sins. Whenever you drink it, do this for the remembrance of me.'

"And now, as our Savior Christ has taught us, we make bold to say . . .

"Our Father, who art in heaven . . ." We all joined in.

At the rail, I knelt and cupped my palms, right over left, looking up into Taylor's gentle eyes as he pressed the Host into my hand.

"The Body of our Lord Jesus Christ preserve you in everlasting life."

I closed my eyes and put it on my tongue, thinking for some reason of his new mustache, his white MG. I remembered the Reverend Mophet, our old pastor, who told us once in confirmation class that it's a sin to take the Bread of Faith without belief. Did I believe? I'd always thought so, but suddenly I wondered. I was careful not to chew.

"The Blood of Our Lord Jesus Christ preserve you in everlasting life," Taylor said, wiping the lip of the cup with a white napkin before he raised it to my lips.

I closed my eyes and bowed my head, wondering why it's called the holy *catholic* church when we were Episcopalians and didn't even like the Catholics, and what was meant by "the communion of the saints" . . . yet even if I didn't know those answers, somewhere deep inside I was still sure that I believed. I knew it as the wine went down, in that sweet burning. I knew the promise wasn't all those things, but simpler, just a vow you made to God to love and serve him through a good and honest life. And if you did that, God made you a promise back. He made things happen for a reason, even if you couldn't understand the reason at the time, even if it seemed too hard. I believed that, and I believed that Jimmy and I had made a promise, too.

It was trusting to that promise which made it possible for me to take my clothes off in front of him without shyness and share his bed and to break all the other promises I had to break each time we made love. It was that promise which made it bright down where we went in sex, like water in a shining whirlpool that spun us round and round so fast until we disappeared into the eye of it and were gone. We were lost, but in that lostness I was not afraid and not alone. That was loving someone, and I did not believe it was at odds with loving God—if there was a promise. Jimmy and I had one: he loved me, and I loved him. I knew it in my body. It was crystal, hard as rock.

Even if at first I hadn't cared, or thought I hadn't cared. Now I cared. Even if we hadn't waited. I'd done my painful waiting with Sumner and that was part of what had poisoned things for us. Sumner and I had had a promise, too, but it was not the same. Only the words "I love you" were the same, the outward husk of it.

That night I think my mind was learning what my body knew already, and that's why I was thinking. Sumner and I had made our promise not as who we really were but who we wished to be or thought we were supposed to be. We'd promised as adults, thinking love would make us so, but it had not, and we were not. We were still two children, and it had been a bitter thing to learn. With Jimmy, it was different. I knew it in my body as I knew the wine.

Kneeling there with my eyes closed, I suddenly saw that tiny tadpole thing with gills from the encyclopedia swimming up at me out of the dark, thrashing its small tail. And what about the child, if there was a child? Was it part of our promise to each other, mine and Jimmy's? And, leaving us aside, what promise had we made to it?

I suddenly felt as if I were drowning and opened my eyes. I didn't want to think—that thought was the reason—but I was thinking, thinking hard.

When I looked up, someone was waiting to take my place at the communion rail. As I stood, I felt lightheaded and could taste the port still on my lips. I wondered if I'd been praying. I wasn't sure.

"Keep watch, dear Lord," said Taylor, sending us back out where we all had to go, "with those who work or watch or weep this night, and give thine angels charge over those who sleep. Tend the sick, Lord Christ; give rest to the weary, bless the dying, pity the afflicted, shield the joyous; and all for thy love's sake."

"Amen."

Outside, as the other women walked off toward their cars, I sat on the stone wall and smoked a cigarette. I thought of Catherine and Big Sumner at the dinner table, sharing the day's news and gossip. I thought of what my pregnancy would mean, not just to me but to Mama and Daddy. It was as if I could hear all those women's voices rising up above the town, rumbling like thunder: "May Tilley, Will and Zelle's little girl—did you hear? . . ." I thought of Jimmy—what would it mean for him? What was my promise to him —was it to spare him? And what about the promise he'd made me?

*Oh, God, please*, I prayed, *don't let me be pregnant.*

And if I was, wouldn't it be best to—I couldn't say the word, not even in my thoughts. Our lives wouldn't be disrupted then. I could go back to Ascension, Jimmy back to Chapel Hill. We'd continue dating. Maybe there'd be some discomfort in the beginning, but it would pass. He'd become a doctor, and I'd finish my own studies— who knows, maybe I'd become a doctor, too. In the coming spring I'd be elected May Queen, and later on I'd transfer to Chapel Hill. We'd be together. And later, much later, we'd come back to this same place, this door, and choose to open it of our free will.

We'd keep our promise then, some other time.

It was so clean and simple—it could all just go away.

But what about the child?

This was my new thought.

Grinding out my Pall Mall, I left a black smudge on the stones and started home through dark back streets.

The day of the appointment the forecast called for rain. Daddy was waiting for me on the front steps of the house when I came down, studying the sky—it was that sort of plum-blue color it gets before a storm. The air was dead and heavy.

We didn't talk much on the drive, not till we pulled up outside the office, when Daddy turned to me and squeezed my hand. "I'm not pregnant, Daddy," I told him, "I'm sure I'm not—I've just got this feeling." He looked at me as though that was the saddest thing he'd ever heard: "Even if you are, sugar—" But I said, "no, don't say it, you'll see," because I didn't want anything to break my concentration, as though if I willed it hard enough it was bound to be.

Dr. Watt was with another patient, but Lucy showed us straight into the office, where I sat down in the leather chair beside the desk, noticing it was the nicest in the room, the one you sat in when you got the news—that's why it was the nicest. Daddy walked over to the window and stared out, his hands in his pockets.

We heard Watt coming up the hall, speaking in a cheery voice. "Just keep off it, Tom. Lucy'll call the prescription in at Eller's and it'll be waiting at the counter . . . Lord, look at that—we're in for a blow."

Then the door opened behind us. "Morning, Will. Coffee?" he asked, brushing down his cowlick, which was steely gray and stiff as a wire brush. You could see the little broken veins in his cheeks. "No, thanks, Watt," Daddy said, and Dr. Watt said, "May?" I just shook my head and tracked him as he walked around the desk, trying to read something, but I couldn't, not till he squeezed Daddy's elbow and looked at me and pressed his lips.

"I'm sorry, honey, the test was positive," he said, and suddenly out of nowhere it popped into my mind, *the bunny died, the bunny died*, and it was as if all the air was sucked out of the room. Suddenly it was like a thousand hateful voices, Catherine Dade and the women at Saint Paul's and all my Ascension friends, whispering, *May Tilley—did you hear? Knocked up, a bun in the oven, poor thing, she seemed like such a nice girl, too* . . . And I would never get to be the May Queen now—that was the first consequence that dawned on me. I had a picture of myself on stage, a pregnant Queen in a rabbit stole holding a bouquet of weeds . . .

The next thing I knew Daddy was in the chair beside mine, clutching my hand and patting my back as if I were a child in a high chair choking on her portion. "There, now, there," he said, "it's going to be all right, honey, hear me? It's going to be just fine." "Here, Will, get her to drink this," Watt said, taking a bottle and a glass from his desk drawer. When I finished it they led me into the examination room and told me to lie down on the table and rest, and then they talked together in the office for a long time.

I remember listening to the thunder rumbling closer and the first sharp lightning crack. There was a hush and then that queer fresh smell came through the screen as I heard the first drops patter down, streaking the dusty panes. I closed my eyes and tried not to think of anything, and I remember reaching down and touching my stomach to see if it felt different. It was the first time.

As Daddy dropped into the driver's seat, I could smell the rain on his suit—his shoulders and his hat were black—and there was bourbon on his breath, though he wasn't drunk, just at that first stage where everything is crystal clear as long as everyone agrees with you.

"Daddy," I said, and he turned toward me in the seat. "Now listen, honey, lemme say something first, all right? Watt knows a doctor up in Philade'phia. We called him on the phone. You can be up there on the train one day, in the second, back home the third night. I'll be right there with you, and yo' mama, too. Course it's yo' decision, but I think it might be the best thing all the way around— for you and Jimmy, too." "But it is my decision, Daddy," I said, resisting the temptation to put a question mark on it. I watched that bourbon confidence evaporate and Daddy's eyes turn sad behind his glasses. "Yes, yes it is, May." "Jimmy loves me, Daddy, he really does," I told him, and he said, "May . . ." and put his hand on my arm.

"Honey," he said, "I've always liked Jimmy, and you know I have, but he's awful young, May, awful young, and so are you to have all this come down on you. It changes everything, May—take my word for it. Most of yo' life is gonna be 'bout family and children and responsibility, honey, but you're only young one time, and in the twinkling of an eye it's gone. You hadn' had yo' full share yet. You may regret it, if not now then later on. That's all I'mon say. The rest is up to you and Jimmy. I just want you to know"—and his voice quavered when he said it—"you're the most precious thing in my life, May, and this don't change it, not one hair. Now, you reach and open up that glove box."

Inside, together with two packs of Chesterfields and a pint of Seagrams, was a long blue velvet box with a watch in it, one with a window in the face that opened to a dark blue sky with tiny golden stars and the fingernail of a new moon.

"Oh, Daddy, what have you done." My eyes filled up. He was sitting there polishing his lenses with his pocket handkerchief. "You knew, didn't you? You did this on purpose," I said, but he gave me his best poker face and said, "no, ma'am, I did not." "Where did you get it?" I asked, and he said, "found it in a mule's track," the way he always would. "I was gonna put it in yo' Christmas stocking, but, way I figure, you might as well know what time it is right now."

The rain was over by the time we reached the house, and Daddy stopped at the bottom of the drive and leaned out for the paper, which struck me odd somehow—everything was supposed to stop, I guess is what I thought.

We weren't halfway up the hill before the front door opened and Mama came out in her robe, tossing down her cigarette and grinding it on the slate beneath her slipper toe. I remember thinking, *she'd have my hide if I did that*, and I was steeled for it.

She looked at Daddy first and her face dropped like one of those big safes in the movies, crashing floor by floor. Then she looked at me—the news was already as old as the headlines in the paper Daddy held.

"I thought you were going to call me," she said to him, as though that's what she was furious about, and I said, "I wanted to tell you myself, Mama," which was the last thing on earth I wanted. Mama shook her head as though denying it was true, and her eyes had that hot look of tears. "I'm sorry, Mama," I said, the only thing that I could think of. "Honey, I am, too," she said, and, because I wasn't expecting any sympathy, it stabbed me like a knife.

"Tell us what we can do for you," she said. "There's nothing, Mama, thank you. I'm going to take a walk, if it's okay." I saw her bite back what came to her lips—all the pressing business we had to attend to now. "Go on then," she said. "I won't be long, I promise." I glanced at my new watch and then at Daddy. "The umbrella's on the seat, honey," he said, but I didn't bother, not afraid of rain.

All the way down the drive I felt their eyes like sober spotlights tracking me, and at the bottom I stepped out of my flats and put them in the mailbox not to ruin them, the way I used to do when I went out to play, defying Mama, who said, "ladies don't go barefoot." One day the mailman brought them to the house and when she gave them back to me she said, "next time use a stamp." The beach was about the only place where I went barefoot anymore. Somewhere along the way I'd decided I didn't like my feet, size nine like Mama's—she called hers "boats."

The rain was running in a twisty stream along the curb, the color of butterscotch, making a gurgling noise as it fell through the grate. It seemed strange to set out barefoot down the middle of the road in broad day, like cutting class. The rain had rinsed away the dust so everything had that green shine again as though it was back to early summer. The tree trunks were black with wet and I could see each wrinkle in the bark some way I'd rarely ever noticed, and this dank green smell was rising off the ground. There seemed to be more oxygen. A gust of wind swept through the leaves, turning up the ashy underbellies, sprinkling me all over, and I heard a jaybird cry across the road and thought about the way we used to shout when we ran through the sprinkler on the lawn. I don't know what it was, but the street seemed different, not the same one I saw every day, another I could barely remember.

At the bottom of the hill where Country Club turned up toward the gates, the road was flooded curb to curb with yellow pollen dusted on the surface and a rainbow skim of oil. When I stepped in I noticed an earthworm flushed out by the rain. It was wriggling feebly in the pool, its pink color blanching in the water. It made me think of fishing trips with Daddy when I was little, the smell on my hands and the dark green gook that spurted when the hook went in. I always had to force myself to do it, but Daddy was so proud. Leaning over watching as it drowned, I suddenly thought, *smaller than that*, and jerked up straight so fast the blood rushed to my head.

I didn't hear the car till the tires sloshed in the pool behind me and came to a stop. In the glare of the windshield I could see my own reflection and another woman's face behind it, peering through.

Ellie Sims—Ellie Williams, by that time, a friend of June's—stuck her head out the side window. "May? You all right, honey? I didn't want to blow my horn at you." I could tell it struck her odd, me standing in the road like that. "Hi, Ellie, I just dropped an earring," I said, unclipping one as though brushing back my hair.

"Want some help?" she asked, and I said, "found it," showing her my hand as I leaned in. Her little girl, Lisa, was in the car. I hadn't seen her since I baby-sat for her before I went off to Ascension. She was only three months then, and almost overnight, it seemed, she'd turned into a pretty child of four with the most exquisite hazel eyes. "That's not Lisa," I said. Ellie smiled. "Say hi to Miss Tilley." Lisa piped right up, "hi, Miss Tilley," so mature it made me smile. "I bet you don't remember me, do you?" I asked. "Miss Tilley used to baby-sit for you, Lisa," Ellie said, and I said, "when you were just about this big," and made an inch between my thumb and finger, suddenly remembering the way she'd nuzzled me, trying to nurse, and the strange way it made me feel, awkward and tender all at once.

"We have a swimming lesson this morning," Ellie said in a sing-song voice, "I just hope we aren't rained out."

"No, Ellie, she can't be old enough," I said, exaggerating my surprise. Ellie smiled. "I can hardly believe it myself. You'll find out though, just wait. Can we drop you at the club?" "Thanks, no," I said, "I'm just walking."

Ellie put the car in drive and leaned back out. "When you see June, *please* give her my love," she said with a heartfelt look that turned her face into a mask, "will you do that, sugar?" "I will, Ellie." "Say 'bye to Miss Tilley, Lisa." " 'Bye," Lisa said, and I waved as the station wagon sloshed on through the pool. There was a stroller in the back with a Raggedy Ann slumped over in the seat.

*Will you do that, sugar?* I don't know what it was, but there was something in the way she'd said it that reminded me so much of Mama. Sometimes June would try it on for size, that tone, but she just seemed pretentious, where Ellie pulled it off somehow. Yet they were exactly the same age, June and she. They'd run together and shared clothes and jewelry . . . I'd always thought of them as two like items, both popular and pretty and conceited, and they never took me anywhere with them, though I sometimes begged to go. But Ellie had changed in a way June hadn't—she seemed almost a different person now. And it wasn't their personalities, it wasn't being married—they both were. The only thing I could think was that it must be Lisa. Lisa was the difference. June had kept her selfish sparkle, while Ellie Sims wore an old lady's bathing suit and sat with the other young mothers around the wading pool in a clutter of diapers and bottles and bright plastic toys. My group occupied the chaises near the rail, looking over the eighteenth green, where we could see, and be seen by, the men as they played home. And it suddenly struck me how it was two different countries, ours still at war, theirs at peace or neutral, with the deep end between like a frontier.

What would it be like, crossing to the other side? I tried to imagine . . . for Ellie, it was all settled. She didn't have to worry anymore who would call for dates or where she'd spend the weekend. And yet, that bathing suit, her heavy thighs . . . she'd lost her shine. It had passed somehow to Lisa, and I didn't know if I was ready to give up my shine.

I stared back at my reflection pitching in the pool, where that earthworm was still struggling. Careful not to touch it with my foot, I splashed it up on a dry patch of road. Was that my decision?

Somewhere deep inside a voice said, *yes, there really is no choice,* and for a fraction of a second I felt calm. Across the wall I heard someone spring the diving board and splash, and then the lifeguard's whistle. Just as suddenly as the calmness came, it vanished. What was I thinking? It wasn't that simple. This was the worst thing that could ever happen. The worst.

Three days in Philadelphia, and no one ever had to know. Daddy said he thought it was best. He'd never lie or wrongly counsel me. But what about the child? How could it be right to kill it? Because that's what it meant, Philadelphia—to kill the life we'd made.

And what about Jimmy? Had he meant it all those times he'd said he'd marry me? Would he want to now? Would a decision for the child be one against Jimmy? But what about the promise? What about me?

*There really is no choice.* That voice kept saying it, and it was frightening and hateful because it seemed like someone else's voice, not mine. I started running, something else I rarely did—not any-more—but after a few yards I had to stop because it hurt my breasts.

Winded and starting to perspire, I realized where I was. Off to my right, an old footpath led down to the far side of Collie Pond. Through the shifting trees, I could see mist rising off the rain-cooled water as the humidity returned. When I started down, some-thing went crashing through the brush. I stood a moment, thinking of a little boy who'd drowned the second summer after we had moved from Montague Street. My heart was punching me.

The near end was shallow and filled with cattails, head-high and velvety brown, so full they put a slight bend in the stems. I held the hem of my skirt and stepped into the water, cringing as I sank ankle-deep in the black muck on the bottom. As I waded out, the mud sucked at my feet, bubbles of trapped gas bursting with a smell like rotten eggs. The water was teeming with things I didn't like, those little skater bugs with pontoon feet darting everywhere, and a pod of frog eggs with the baby tadpoles like itty-bitty black commas squirming in the cells. I don't know why I kept going. It grew deeper and, sinking on one knee, I lost hold of my hem, grabbing a stand of cattails as I pitched forward. One burst, leaking golden threads like eider, which drifted down in the dead air.

At the edge of the stand, I held my sopping skirt, peering into deeper water, where it was dark as brewed tea. The water looked appealing, but my blouse was white, and I couldn't walk home wet. And just like the other time, I felt shy of undressing there, though there was no one to see.

I didn't notice it at first, but something queer stole over me and I realized I was not alone . . . something was out there after all. I felt its eyes on me, and in the stillness as I held my breath I could almost hear it breathe. I couldn't tell what it was, except that it was not a person, not a human thing at all, and not an animal. I won-dered suddenly whether it was God. But I don't think it was.

I stared at the pond, and it did not seem separate anymore. It was as though something like my skin but not my skin had dissolved and mingled me with it, with the cool green water on the surface and with the black muck rotting on the bottom. I felt part of that as well, the mud and insects and the tadpoles squirming in their cells. I'd never seen the pond or anything that way before, as though its skin had been removed and I could see the organs quivering underneath, absorbing nutrients, excreting waste, death feeding life and life feeding death, and they were equal in the pond. That was what I saw, or didn't see but felt in my body, raw—life didn't win. It was not preferred.

And wasn't that really why Mama had told us not to play there? A little boy was seized and devoured by the pond and the trees and earth and sky looked down. All nature watched and didn't care. It wasn't fair, it was against the rule of goodness, it wasn't kind or moral, there wasn't even any shame. And it could happen to anyone at any time—in the end it happened to everyone. No one had ever told me it was like that. Daddy and Mama hadn't, it was never mentioned at church or in the lessons I was taught in school. Young girls weren't supposed to belch or fart—I was embarrassed even when my stomach growled—and I was sure I wasn't supposed to see this. That was why I didn't go barefoot anymore, or run, or leave the house without my make-up on—all those rules were part of the protection. But I'd had sex—I'd broken the one great rule—and suddenly all *this* wasn't at a distance anymore, it wasn't something I could take or leave. Nature wasn't part of me, I was part of *it*. This was my body. I was pregnant.

*Ellie did it*, that voice inside me said, *just jump, plunge into it, be brave*. Something in me knew that it was right and that I had to do it. *There really is no choice*, it said. My life seemed to hang in the balance, and then I couldn't. I dissolved in tears because I couldn't jump into the pond and wasn't brave. I wasn't going to have the baby, and that seemed such a disappointment—not to have a baby I wasn't even sure I wanted felt like a lack of courage. That had been the test, and I had failed.

I waded out and climbed the bank and lay down in the pine straw. I could feel tears dripping down my temples, but they had no meaning. I wasn't sad, just drained and overwhelmed. Suddenly I felt so sleepy I could barely keep my eyes open. That just seemed another failure, so I failed and went to sleep.

The next thing I knew something plopped into the pond and startled me awake. I heard children's voices and sat up. Three little blond boys who looked like brothers were standing on the far side, undressing. I peered through the reeds at their slim hips and tiny penises. The youngest one ran into the water, splashing and laughing till the tallest one called out, "watch out for the alligator." The child stopped dead where he was and I could see terror in his face together with a brooding stubbornness. "There aren't any alligators here," I called, and they all turned as I stood up. I felt I should know these children—they were all singularly beautiful—but I could not think who their parents were.

And then it came to me—*this is a dream*. I realized it the second right before I woke. I sat up gazing through the cattails to be sure— there was no one there.

I got up slowly, stiff and sore as though I'd been through a battle. *I should go home*, I thought, *Mama and Daddy will be worried*. Instead, I skirted the cattails and headed east around the shore. The bank was caved and plunged off steeply into clear deep water there. I stopped a minute, and now the pond revealed another face, green and pristine as a jewel. Dragonflies were darting and hovering, their wings blurs of shimmery blue. A fish breached toward the middle, stirring rings. The reflection of the trees around me, the tangled roots beneath me on the bank, my own image mirrored in the water —you could hardly tell the difference or which was real. I had the sense of standing outside myself, gazing back into my own eyes and seeing myself more clearly than I ever had. *There is a choice*. It was her voice that seemed to tell me, the other May, gazing up at me out of the water. The choice was to accept or not accept, and it meant choosing sides in life—I never had till then.

A gust of wind sprang up, breaking through the trees like surf, and everything that I saw written in the pond was quickly erased. I dove in, forgetting my white blouse and the walk home.

The water was a cool surprise and swallowed me, waking my senses, cell by tingling cell. I opened my eyes and swam under water, feeling my hair tug backward with each stroke. Near the middle, I came up gasping.

In the east a patch of deep blue appeared through the tattered overcast the storm had left. In that blue I saw the new moon riding like a little boat, carrying the dim shape of the full cargo in its hold. I'd forgotten my new watch and when I looked, there it was again, the little image on my wrist mirroring the big one overhead. A breeze rippled the surface, spangling it with gold, and seeds as bright as sparks turned cartwheels in the air. I was filled with awe, as though an angel had brushed me with its wings, and then it hit me— *the children in the dream were ours.* They were mine and Jimmy's, and it was like an arrow through my heart. He was going to be my husband. I knew it, and the knowledge was like a brilliant light bursting inside me, obliterating everything that came before. He was going to be my husband and we were going to have the child, not a tadpole thing with gills but the child who'd come to me in my dream. That was the moment when it happened, when I first knew my son, and in that moment nothing, not even God himself, could have taken him from me.

The things that had seemed to matter so much only an hour before—returning to Ascension, becoming May Queen, all the scandal and disrupted plans—all of it dissolved like ghostly images from someone else's dream and someone else's life inside that brilliant light. The worst that could ever happen had happened, and it was the first thing in my life that had ever really mattered, the only thing, and it wasn't because of looks or money or being Will and Zelle Tilley's daughter—it was because of me, and it was mine.

It was all so clear. We'd make a life together, Jimmy and I, different from our parents' lives. The prospect filled me with a devastating happiness unlike anything I'd ever known. My whole life before sank down in the mud at Collie Pond, and I didn't care. I didn't need it anymore. The future seemed clear and final. All I had to do was show Jimmy what was now so clear to me—there was one choice, and only one: life. And he would see it, too. My confidence in him was like a diamond. He'd see because it was the truth. And there was only one, or so it seemed to me that day at Collie Pond, and nothing that has happened since has made me change my mind.

# SEVEN

## Jimmy

September, med school about to start . . . I'd just come back from Chapel Hill with Whit Thomas, who was in my class. We'd found a great house in the country, a little run-down, but it had a pond in back with a swimming float, and a brick barbecue pit in the side yard. My first day back at work at Killdeer High I went out to the parking lot to get my lunch and found a note beneath my wiper blade—*May Tilley called.*

At first I thought it was from Mother. It was on a sheet from one of Daddy's memo pads, the kind Mother used to list our calls and chores—at breakfast every morning you'd find a sheet under your orange juice. The thought of her driving all the way out to the high school to deliver it had me sweating marbles, let me tell you.

But it wasn't from Mother; it was from the office secretary, Mrs. Raines.

*From the desk of Thurston Madden.* I stared at it, remembering how when I was eight or nine I once took a pack of pencils from a gross box in Daddy's office—Number 2 Ticonderogas. Daddy found them in my desk and lectured me that they were school property and it was "tantamount to stealing" as I stripped my pants and leaned across the bed. He always gave us ten and made us count them out, throwing in a lesson in arithmetic. After my whipping, we drove down to Rose's five-and-ten and Daddy gave me a nickel to buy a pack of my own. I could never read one of Mother's notes at breakfast or pass that six-inch stack of hoarded memo pads by the hall phone without getting a bad taste in my mouth. I guess the lesson I learned was different from the one he meant to teach me: first, that he secretly went through my things behind my back, and, second and more important, that there were two laws in our house, one for Mother and another for everybody else.

I was relieved when May—not her mother or Dee Lou—answered the door. Her hair was wet, as if she'd just come from the shower. "I'm glad you came," she said, seeming calm enough. *Maybe it's okay*, I thought. But there was something in her face, some kind of openness I'd never seen before, not even when we made love. She didn't have on any veils that day. She took my hand and led me around the house toward the back yard. The minute we turned the corner, she stopped and, without a word, put her arms around me. Her bare shoulders were still cool from the air conditioning inside, and it was suddenly hard to swallow.

"I'm pregnant, Jimmy."

I already knew—by then I did—but something wallowed in my gut when I heard the words out loud.

She pulled back to look at me. She was smiling and her eyes were wet. "Your parents know?" I asked, and she just nodded, as though that detail was minor. *Shit*, I'm thinking, *shit*. I had no idea what to say. "I'm sorry, May," I told her, choosing that. She shook her head. "No, don't be. I'm not." Her smile, her calmness, that almost happy expression on her face—it struck me as incomprehensibly askew, even sinister. How could she be pleased? To tell the truth, it seemed a little crazy. I just stared and blinked, thinking, *wait a minute here, wait just a minute . . .*

In the back yard, she dropped my hand and sat down in the swing. "I had a whole speech made up to say to you," she said. "I've been going over and over it in my mind all day, but now it seems beside the point. Mainly it was just to say I know how miserable this has been—for both of us, you too—worrying and not knowing. I've been sick about it, and when the test came back I was just crushed, but it's a relief to have it all out in the open—in a way, it is. I was ashamed before, but now I'm not. I don't see why we should be ashamed of loving each other. I hope you aren't . . ."

"I'm not ashamed," I said, and she said, "I'm glad, because I don't want you to be. I don't want you to regret it, Jimmy, because I don't." "What are you saying, May?" I asked, "you act as if you're happy." "I don't know if happy's the right word. I feel . . . sure, I guess, sure and calm inside. I don't think I knew how much I really loved you till today."

Her eyes filled, and I said, "May"—my heart was in my mouth—but she shook her head. "No, let me say it. For the first time in my life I feel there's something important for me to do, and it's not like being a deb . . . all that was for everybody else, but this belongs to us, Jimmy, it's ours, and I've never had anything like it before, that was just mine. It's like a treasure, but for me to have it, you have to want it, too. Maybe it sounds selfish, but I want you to want it, not just for me, but because I think it'll make you happy, too. Can't you see it? Our own little house with our own bed where we don't have to hide or answer to anybody anymore? You'll be such a wonderful father . . . oh, Jimmy, I feel I've been waiting my whole life for this. It floors me to say it, but I want the baby, Jimmy. I really do. So much. I think we should get married, don't you?"

*Don't you?* That question was like a stone dropped down a mile-deep well, and I stood waiting for the splash to tell me what the answer was. I could see the picture May was painting—it wasn't that I'd never thought of it before. Far clearer to me, though, was the different picture of the life I'd planned—med school, my new house in Chapel Hill, not to mention that clinic out in Africa, the one where I was going to write poetry like Pasternak and May would be my Lara. There'd been babies in that picture, but none of them was mine. All the exotic places in the travel brochures I'd collected started flashing by, like landscape through the window of a train, as I stood there, going, *wait a minute, we just passed my stop.*

And May seemed so happy, too, like someone in the middle of a beautiful dream whom you don't want to wake. Her face was radiant, and it's not an easy thing to say the words you know are going to make the lights go out. "I can see that, too, May, I really can." I was trying to tread lightly. "It's only"—I lit a cigarette—"I'm not sure it's quite that simple, now. I mean, what made you change your mind?"

As I waved out the match, May blinked like someone coming out of a trance. "What do you mean?" she asked, and I said, "I thought we agreed abortion was the best thing." She looked surprised. "When?" "The other day after the party," I reminded her, "you asked me to see if I could find out anything, remember?" "But nothing had even been decided then," she said, "how could I change my mind if I'd never made it up?" "But still," I said.

"Still what?" Her face now was dark and wide awake. "What I remember is you telling me you loved me and you'd see me through, whatever happened. I assumed that meant you'd marry me, and if it didn't, then what about the hundred other times? Or did I make up all that, too?"

And there we were, suddenly in court. I hadn't realized it till she began to cross-examine me. "No, you didn't make it up. I said it, but, May—"

"What?" she said, "but what?" From her face I knew I couldn't tell her what was true, that I'd said it in the way I think most people do, in a happy moment to express a future hope, not as a commitment in the present. Suddenly my Lucky tasted bitter—I threw it down. "Come on, May, be fair. I do love you, but is that the same as wanting to marry you right now and have a kid and turn my whole life upside down? Is that what I have to do to prove it?"

From the way she looked at me I could tell I'd devastated her. "You don't want to, do you?" she asked, as if the possibility were so far-fetched it had never crossed her mind. Tears stood in her eyes, and I said, "don't cry, May . . . please don't cry, okay?" My heart was in my mouth—I was eating it.

I knelt in front of her and took her hands. "I always saw us getting married, May. I still do. But, Jesus, honey—like this? What about school? How on earth am I supposed to support you?"

The vulnerability in her expression was hard to take. "Daddy would help us," she said, and I said, "did you ask?" and she said, "I don't have to ask."

The knee I was on, my bad one, had started aching, so I stood up and walked over to the big white oak and gazed across the field. There was a brown depression in the grass where her mother's tent had been. I remember noticing that and listening to the swing's rusty chains creaking as she twisted back and forth. "Jesus, May," I said, and when I turned, I noticed she had on my KA pin—she'd worn it on purpose. That just stabbed me.

I remembered the night I'd given it to her. We'd stayed up dancing at a party, and in the morning we drove to the arboretum, the only place where we could be alone. Flowers were blooming all along the walk and I picked one for her, not knowing what it was. May said it was a hyacinth.

> "Yet when we came back, late, from the Hyacinth garden,
>  Your arms full, your hair wet, I could not
>  Speak, and my eyes failed, I was neither
>  Living nor dead, and I knew nothing,
>  Looking into the heart of light, the silence."

I read the lines to her out of my dog-eared Eliot and we lay on my coat in the wet grass, passing a cigarette and watching the sun come up through the trees. Afterward, as we walked to breakfast down Franklin Street, people stared at us as though some strange light emanated from our bodies. I had the sense that morning that May and I were the only people on that street who were alive.

"The Hyacinth Girl," I said. "Remember how I called you that?" May didn't answer; she just stared at me forever and finally said, "tell me what you want to do, Jimmy," in a firm, quiet voice. "I don't want to lose you," I said, hoping, I suppose, that she'd say, *you won't, Jimmy, you won't ever lose me.* What she said instead was, "you don't have to," and the girl in the swing, whoever she was, wasn't the Hyacinth Girl.

"So there's a price," I said, and she said, "did you think there wasn't?" "I don't know," I answered, "I guess I did. I guess I thought this one thing, at least, was free."

"Anything worth having has a price, Jimmy," she pointed out, "this too, whether we knew or not." "You aren't leaving me much choice," I said, and she said, "I didn't know you'd want one. I didn't realize marrying me was such a sacrifice." She was holding herself straight, on the verge of tears—that pride tore me up and made me love her more.

"Don't put words in my mouth, May," I said, "it doesn't help the situation. All I'm saying is, I'm not sure I can do this now." "You mean *won't*," she said, defiantly ignoring my advice. "Don't strain yourself rushing to deny it," she added after leaving me a pause. "I'm not sure there's any point in my saying anything here," I said, "you seem to know all my answers in advance." "All right," she said, "I'm sorry, you tell me."

"I need some time to think. Is that okay?"

The way she regarded me made clear it wasn't, those fine black eyes of hers filled with somberness and disappointed judgment. It was the first time I ever saw that look. "Christ, I haven't even told my parents, May. It's going to kill them." If I expected sympathy, I didn't get it there.

"You think it over and decide what you want to do, Jimmy. When you make up your mind you know where I'll be." Then she got up and started walking toward the house and never looked back once.

I stared after her, feeling like Judas with the kiss still stinging on my lips. What I felt guilty for I hardly knew . . . for having had a different life and a different future when I drove up the driveway twenty minutes earlier, I suppose, a life and future I was less than thrilled about exchanging for this different one she'd worked out for me in the meantime. The part of me I'd always taken as the angel of my better nature sounded like a tyrant and a shaming bully, shouting, *damnit, be a man*. Was that what manhood was, acting for her happiness at the probable expense of mine? Was that the sacrifice love required? And if it was, did May love me? What seemed clear—one of the few things—was that it had not occurred to May, even as an afterthought, to offer me what she was asking, to be put first. The voice that pointed this out sounded far more sane and reasonable than the angel's, like a concerned adviser and a friend. It raised a host of questions, but they all boiled down to one—did I own my life or not?

Strange how clear and unequivocal the answer seemed to me at twenty-one in 1954—a terrible resounding *no*, clanging shut like the door of an iron cage.

Yet even as she walked away, a part of me admired her leap of faith. Whether it was brave or merely reckless, whether it was truly the right choice for her any more than for me, I didn't know, but I respected her decisiveness and clarity, her willingness to risk so much. Watching her, I felt the weight and substance of what I stood to lose, and it was no small thing to me. Not a day had gone by that summer in her absence, hardly an hour that I hadn't spent fifty minutes thinking of her, missing her with an ache, thanking my luck for what we had. After my injury in basketball, things had gone flat for a long time till she came into my life and brought back something golden I'd missed and didn't want to live without. No, I loved May—that was the bottom of the bottom.

And however real the impulse to run, it wasn't really an option. You could do that in a book, but what was I going to do? Drive to the docks—what docks?—ship aboard a tramp steamer, grow a beard, become a salty dog, jump ship off some South Sea isle, swim ashore and live in a grass hammock eating coconuts, fondling the native girls? That was the movies, and the other option was no option either: letting May carry the whole weight alone.

What was going to happen was already a foregone conclusion. It had been since May made up her mind; I just didn't know it yet. I stood there torn apart, unsure which scared me more, having her or losing her. What if some other, truer life lay ahead of me like a highway I might miss if I turned onto this side road? What do you do when you don't know what direction your life is meant to take, when you don't know what you want or believe in, but you have to choose right now?

I'll tell you what I did. For that moment I simply held the ball and listened to the clock tick down, unable to shoot or pass. I stood there wanting back the life I'd had when I got out of bed that morning, hating old man Eller because he'd closed the drug store two minutes early one Friday afternoon and fucked up my life for me.

At the bottom of the Tilleys' drive, I hesitated. Left led home; right, back to the high school. It didn't take me long to make my mind up. I drove straight ahead.

I hardly remember where I went, just passing by the freight yard and staring at the empty boxcars on the sidings—Burlington Northern, Santa Fe, Canadian Pacific, Seaboard. The platform was lined with hogsheads of tobacco headed north to the factories in Richmond. I pulled off on the shoulder, lit a Lucky and as I watched the workers on the loading dock, a snatch of song drifted through my head.

> *On a summer's day, in the month of May*
> *A burly bum come a-hikin',*
> *Down a shady lane, through the sugar cane,*
> *He was lookin' for his likin'.*

"The Big Rock Candy Mountain." I'd heard it first not fifty yards from where I sat. Walking home one night after baseball practice—I was nine or ten—a group of us had passed the freight yard and run across a man named Bones, a hobo in a tattered overcoat and laceless shoes whose body odor was past anything I'd ever experienced, fermented in his filthy clothes like juice hardened into cider. He asked us for money, and because we knew no better, we turned out our pockets, giving him what change we had. By way of payment, I suppose, he showed us his switchblade, hinting he'd killed men with it, his grin growing brighter as our somberness increased. Sipping a bottle of sweet wine, he told us we were little hicks and Killdeer was a shit hole, the worst he'd been in on the line. He spoke about the city where there were hundred-dollar whores, and so at last hit on the subject we'd been waiting for.

"You boys know what fucking is?" he asked, casually taking an apple from his pocket.

There were nervous snickers as we dropped our eyes and pushed sticks into the fire.

"I do," someone said and then grew shy. Bones looked from eye to eye and nodded, then plunged his knife into the apple's meat. The white juice dribbled through his fingers, and we sat mesmerized. He popped a section in his mouth.

"Let me tell you, boys," he said, "fucking's what your parents do —now there's a thought for you . . . Your sweet suffering mothers and your honest dads—that's what they do every night behind that bedroom door. You'd never guess it, would you? That dear woman who cooks your breakfast every morning, who's embarrassed if her slip is showing or if anybody sees her knee—well, behind that door she's not embarrassed. She begs for it, she puts her tongue into your daddy's ear and says, 'fuck me, Daddy, I'm bad and I want it.' "

"You're a liar," someone said. Another added, "come on, we should go." No one budged.

Bones smiled. "That's how they made you, every bastard son of you," he said with quiet relish. "There's all sorts of fucking, boys, and it's all fucking. Everything. The Bible calls it giving and receiving—I'm sure you know that, being good lads like you are. In other places it's called other things. But here, boys, in the freight yard, it's called giving it or getting it, it's called doing or being done. It's all simple when you see that key. There are two types of people—the fuckers and the fucked. The secret—and listen close, I'm only going to say it once—the secret's knowing which you are."

Bones threw the apple core into the fire and took a long slow sip of wine. That was when he sang.

I hadn't thought of him in years, but sitting in my car that afternoon after May dropped the news, Mr. Bones came back to me.

I stubbed out my Lucky and scratched away, suddenly furious at him and at his song, suddenly furious at everything.

Back at school I told Bill to go on to the dump without me and climbed the stairs to Daddy's office. *Going to see the principal*—the idea didn't seem as funny as it should have. He was in a budget meeting but was expected any moment, Mrs. Raines informed me. "We're all so proud of you—a doctor!" She wanted to chat, but I told her I had to make a call and escaped into the office, sitting in the visitor's chair, pumping my leg. I got up and paced to the window, lifting a slat of the Venetian blinds. Outside it was still the brilliant summer day I'd just left; in Dad's office everything was shadowy and dim, less cool than stale. I felt a brief claustrophobia, the panicked sense that I might never get back where the sun was shining.

Turning away, I noticed the rows of metal shelves on the wall crammed with boxes of letterhead and school supplies. *This is it*, I thought, *this is where he lives*. At home my father seemed more like a boarder, there from suppertime to morning and always restless till it was time to come back here—to what? A banged-up institutional metal desk and a few framed commendations on the wall from the Rotarians and the Jaycees with THURSTON MADDEN handwritten in the blank in ballpoint. There was nothing personal except the family pictures, and they all pointed home.

I sat in Daddy's chair and examined them. Mine was from junior high, a school picture in my JV letter jacket with a flattop and a pimple on my chin. Sam was eight or nine, and Dolly had on those old pointy glasses that made us call her Catlady—the nickname always made her cry. Mother had the largest frame, and she was someone different, too, a young unmarried girl with long hair, still dark, and some strange bit of fur around her neck. She was gazing over her shoulder with a demure expression in which there was a trace of unease, a girl who conned the fads of cities she'd never visited from the pages of magazines that had now become extinct. That girl had wanted something the woman I knew had learned to live without.

It was bittersweet to realize that was how Daddy thought of us, not as who we presently were, but as who we'd been in former times. But why those times? I wondered. Maybe things were simpler then, or seemed that way to him. Or maybe this was where he stopped, the place and time where he'd withdrawn from each of us and left the field to Mother and become the boarder in our house. It was too sad to think about. Probably he'd just neglected to update them, preoccupied with other business. That's what I decided.

Suddenly I was dying for a cigarette and knew I didn't have the nerve to smoke one there. Here I'd come to tell him I'd gotten May Tilley pregnant and I was afraid to light up in his office, even when he wasn't there. Glancing at the door, I opened the top desk drawer and scanned the contents—a box of paper clips, a pot of yellow glue, a ruler: schoolboy supplies. Along with them was a memo pad— *From the desk of Thurston Madden*—and some pencils, Number 2 Ticonderogas. I stared at them for a long time and suddenly realized that's what he'd been doing when he went through my desk, trying to find me, the same thing I was doing now. Was that love?

Cocking my ear, I listened for footsteps in the hall, then opened the deep bottom drawer on the left-hand side. Under an empty file folder, as though hidden, was a flimsy box of grayish cardboard. I opened it and saw a glint of cellophane—and took out a Moon Pie. Moon Pies in my father's drawer? Principal Madden, with his steel-rimmed glasses and his ramrod spine? My dad had a secret stash of Moon Pies! A case! Where did you buy a case? I could picture it— Daddy entering the store, fidgeting and avoiding the clerk's eyes, asking—*ahem*—for Moon Pies, "in bulk." I was cracking up, covering my mouth and putting my head down on the blotter so that Mrs. Raines wouldn't hear and think I'd lost my mind, which I probably had.

"Jimmy?"

I looked up and there he was, taking it all in from the doorway— his open drawer, the disarray among his pictures, his mad son's touseled hair and feverish eyes.

My laugh trailed off into a quaver. "Dad . . ."

It was there in his eyes, too, I'm almost sure it was—those Number 2 Ticonderogas. Our roles suddenly reversed, and it was as if our whole relationship had caught on that hook and come up bleeding from the water into daylight. I could see before a word was ever spoken that this was going to go wrong, too, the same as everything before, because that moment in Daddy's office was a continuation of all the others that had gone to make it.

"What is it, Jimmy? Are you sick?" I just hung my head and shook it. "No, Dad, I'm in trouble." I almost lost it for a second before something slammed down hard on the emotion. "It's May, Daddy—May Tilley?" I said, not sure he'd paid enough attention to remember who I dated.

Outside I heard the typewriter stop before he stepped inside and shut the door. He didn't speak or move, just stood there like a great beast in the cross hairs of a telescopic site.

"She's pregnant, Dad," I said, apologizing as I pulled the trigger.

He stood like a statue and for a second his features seemed to desolidify like something glimpsed through heated air. "Dear God," he said as his jaw clamped hard. "Dear God in heaven." There wasn't only anger in his tone—I heard disgust.

I flinched at his sudden movement as he started toward the window, remembering his speed when he'd grabbed my arm and pulled me down the hallway to the bedroom, kicking the door shut and whipping out his belt with a violent flourish.

Looking across the lawn, Daddy clenched and unclenched his fists. "Do the Tilleys know?" he finally asked, and I said, "yes, sir." He turned back. "What did they say?"

"I haven't talked to them yet, just May." He waited. "I think she wants to have the baby, Dad. I think she wants to get married" . . . I *think*—as though there was still some question on the point.

Dad's jaw was twanging like a bow string; he kept nodding, not as a response to anything, but in pure nervous tension. He sat on the windowsill, took his glasses off and pressed the bridge of his nose. His eyes looked watery and sunken without them.

"Have you told your mother yet?" he asked. "No, sir, I wanted to tell you first." "She'll have to know, Jimmy," he said, as if maybe I wasn't aware of that.

"Yes, sir, I know," I told him, and he said, "what did you tell her, son?" and I said, "May? I didn't tell her anything yet. I wanted to talk to you."

Daddy glanced at me directly for a moment; then his eyes flicked away. "Well, we'll have to tell your mother," he repeated, and I wanted to say, *forget her, can you? Once? I came to you.*

"I don't know what to do, Dad," I told him, having trouble keeping my voice steady, and he said, "I'd say that's fairly evident."

I had to choke the anger down. "But, Dad—" I said.

"What?"

"What would you do if you were me?"

I should have guessed his answer. "I wouldn't have gotten myself into the situation, Jimmy." His voice was not unkind.

"But I am into it, Dad. I mean, *now.*"

As he bent his wire frames back around his ears, Daddy didn't even look at me. "If she's pregnant and it's yours, you'll have to marry her."

A perfect syllogism: if all men are human, and if Socrates is a man, then Socrates is human. I wanted to point this out to him and offer my congratulations. I didn't know if I should laugh or cry.

*Am I the owner of my life?* My father certainly knew the answer. In the end I guess our answers were the same—the difference was, I asked the question. I don't think he ever had; or if he did, he'd stopped long before I ever knew him.

"I'm sorry, son," he said, and I said, "yeah, Dad, so am I."

"We'd better call your mother now and make sure she's at home. Wait in the car."

*If the professor is wise, and if the professor eats Moon Pies, then Moon Pies make you wise.* I felt real wised-up as I sat in the Chrysler, looking across the grass I was supposed to mow that afternoon. Tears were streaming down my face—that's right, they were. But when Dad finally came, my eyes were dry.

Mother was waiting for us on the porch. One look was all it took to see that the damage far outran my estimate. I'd already played the whole thing in my mind—either she'd be silent with a wounded, icy calm, or she'd be beside herself. She did not look calm.

Apparently, Dad's call had caught her in the middle of her nap; her hair was pressed flat from the pillow on one side. She was doing something odd with her hands—wringing them, I realized, a phrase I'd read in books but never seen or even clearly visualized till then. That was the sole thought in my mind, which had floated up about a quarter mile above the ground. I felt as if I were sleepwalking.

"Oh, Jimmy, Jimmy"—the first words from her mouth, and tears were flowing, too—"Jimmy, how could you? How could you? Tell me it's not true." She reached for me and I recoiled, and Mother said, "what did we do, son? Tell me what we did. We gave you everything."

"Now, Lilith," Dad said, the closest he could come to a rebuke. Even that arrived stillborn as Mother flashed a look at him, her eyes glittering like the edges of a broken bottle. A sob caught in her throat, and then she said, "oh, Thurston," and reached for him. I shut my mouth and followed them inside.

Mother sat down on the couch and started straightening the magazines on the coffee table, half distracted, putting things in order. Daddy took his armchair. Me, no way was I sitting down. I took up a position by the mantel, studying the still life over Mother's head, so dark you could barely make out what was in it. I don't believe I'd ever looked.

"Mother—" I said, but she impaled me with a look. "I've known something was wrong," she said. "You haven't been yourself all summer, and I thought, 'that isn't Jimmy, not my sweet boy.' I knew there was something on you, and, oh, Lord, how I've worried, how I've prayed. I knew you'd tell me when you were ready. You can't keep things from your mother—you never wanted to before."

She reached for her Raleighs on the table and fumblingly lit one, smoke pouring from her nose. "I won't say anything against her, Jimmy, but all these months you've dated her you never brought her home except that once, to dinner. She's never made an effort, and I've tried to overlook it for your sake. I didn't want to think badly of her. I wanted to see May through your eyes, but I've seen you change, son, I've seen you start to question things you never did before, and I've had my suspicions. It had to come from somewhere, because you were never like that, you were always sweet and glad to help. You know what I have on me in this house." Her eyes burned on that.

"I've never had a girl to help out the way she's used to. Of course, we did at Papa's—one to cook and one to clean and do the ironing. Not that I mean to blame your daddy; I know how hard he works. He's done the best he could for me and for you children. But,

Jimmy, honey, that's all May understands. Her parents raised her differently. I don't say we're better—I don't judge—live and let live, I always say, and I know Will Tilley's done well, if you measure success by what you've got, which I was not brought up to do. But, son, if you ask me, it isn't right to make a living off other people's vices. Even though I smoke, I say so. And a parent's sins show in a child; they can't escape it. Maybe it's not May's fault. But that night when she came over here and lit that cigarette at the supper table, right in front of me—it just made my blood boil. *In my house.* Why, when I was her age I'd no more have dreamed of smoking in our parlor than in the choir at church, and I never did, not till Papa was in the ground."

Mother paused to pick a flake of tobacco off her tongue and I stood at attention like a soldier at court-martial, wondering what had made her worship my grandfather so, a man of cold demeanor whom I remembered with a drooping eyelid from a stroke and noxious breath. For some reason I felt almost sorry for her.

"That's how I was raised," she said, "to respect my parents and my elders, and I've tried so hard to raise you children that way. If I've failed, I ask God for forgiveness. I know she's pretty, Jimmy, and she must have her good qualities, but from that night I knew she wasn't the right sort for our son. I won't say anything against her— you know how I feel about gossip, I just *despise* it—but Jimmy, son, when I came to your father I was a virgin. I told him on our wedding night—you ask him if I didn't—it was the greatest gift I had to give, the greatest one that any woman ever has, her only treasure, and that I never wanted to be possessed by any other man. My dream for you has always been that the girl you married could say the same to you. And if she can't, if she gave it up to you, Jimmy, however wrong you were to ask, if she isn't right and solid in that place, how will you ever know? How will you ever trust her? Do you even know it's yours? Can you be absolutely sure?"

For a moment a pure fury burned in me like current through a wire, and then the circuit broke. "I'm sure, Mother," I said, looking not at her but at the painting. In the murk I'd discerned a pale green curl of apple peel, a silver glint of knife.

"How? How can you be?" she said, and then I looked at her and

said, "why do you hate her, Mother? Because she smoked a cigarette?"

"I don't hate her, Jimmy, I only want what's best for you. That's
all I've ever wanted, and it breaks my heart to hear you take her part
against me. Oh, son, you're so young. You don't know life yet, and
you won't know either, not for years to come, till it's too late. All I
want is to save you from a terrible mistake. She's not your family,
Jimmy, and even if you marry her she won't ever be, not blood
family—that's what you don't know—in the end that's all you ever
really have, your blood. We're the only ones who'll ever know you
and love you no matter what. If I haven't taught you anything else, I
thought I'd taught you that."

So that was it—love was a house with no windows and no doors,
a house you were born into and could never leave . . . It wasn't so
much that she believed it—deep down I knew that anyway—but that
she said it with Daddy sitting right there in the room: that a husband and wife could never be to each other what a child and parent
were. It made my eyes sting with the insult, not to me, but to my
father. I looked over my shoulder to see if it had even registered on
Daddy, and so help me, he was sound asleep, head back, mouth
open, his brow knitted like a child having a bad dream.

"Dad?" I said. "Dad?"

"Don't wake him," Mother snapped, "poor thing, he can't help
himself. His heart is broken." With that, he stirred, staring around
with a guilty look and pulling himself straight. I almost wanted to
laugh, but a trembling in my chest prevented it.

"So let me get this straight," I said, turning back to Mother,
"you're telling me I shouldn't marry May?" She actually seemed
taken aback, as though only an idiot could have drawn the inference.

"Shouldn't marry her?" she repeated, "of course you'll have to
marry her. If May's made up her mind that's what she wants, there's
no question," and I said, "I see. So you're just accentuating the
positive here to help me make the best of a bad situation."

"You have no idea how that tone diminishes you," she said. "I
can't imagine where you get it—not from my side—but it breaks my
heart to hear you speak that way."

"I'm sorry your heart is broken, Mother," I told her, "I'm sorry this whole thing is such a tragedy for you," and Daddy said, "don't speak to your mother that way," as her eyes filled with tears.

"All I ever wanted was what was best for you," she said. "From the day you were born, I put you first in everything. I loved the others just as much—Lord knows, I did—but, you, Jimmy, you were my first, my pride. And now, to hear you talk like this, to hear you throw it in my face, makes me think God is punishing me by bringing down this shame on me and on our house. I don't know how your father and I will hold our heads up in church when this gets out, but I don't think about us, even now. It's you, son. How could you have shamed yourself this way? What were you thinking? Didn't you even know enough to use protection?"

Afraid of my answer, she forestalled it. "No, of course you didn't. How could you know? Tell me it was only once, honey, an accident. No, don't, I know it was. I know that in my heart. Oh, Jimmy, what's going to happen to you? Your life hasn't even started, and already this black strike against you."

"I'm going to marry her," I said, realizing it was true, "I'm going to marry May."

"Jimmy," Mother called, as I walked toward the door, "*Jimmy . . .*"

Outside on the porch the sudden brightness made me blink. In the trees across the street a bird cried—one long sad note followed by three shorter ones.

*Go, go, go, said the bird.* What was that line?

Behind me, the door opened. Daddy stood beside me and neither of us spoke.

I had the distinct impression he wanted to touch me—to put a hand on my shoulder, squeeze my elbow, something—and was agonizing over it, unable finally to grant himself permission. Maybe it was just my wanting to touch him and feeling equally constrained, perhaps by the same force whose name I think neither of us knew.

"She's just upset," he said finally, "she'll calm down . . . I think it was the suddenness," and I said, "I know, I know that, Dad," and out of nowhere my eyes turned hot. "I want to do the right thing, Dad," I told him with a quaver in my voice. "Of course you do, of course you do," he said with sympathy and something else that made me risk a look.

His expression was one I'd seen before, not many times, but on the few occasions when he'd tried to talk to me in an intimate way, as a friend, on a footing of equality. I'd interpreted that look in many ways—as disapproval, dislike, discomfort—but only that moment on the porch did its true nature dawn on me. It was fear, his fear that he wasn't good enough and didn't give enough. The level of his sacrifice had still not made him worthy . . . far back in his eyes there was a frightened little boy standing all alone, covering his nakedness. I wanted to say, *you are enough, no one has given more than you, I respect and honor you,* even as another part of me said, *who is this man? what is his meaning?* and was appalled.

"Are you happy, Dad?" I asked. He didn't answer right away.

"Yes, I think so," he finally said, retreating to his public voice. "I take satisfaction in my work . . . and in you children, of course. I'm certainly not unhappy."

"But they aren't the same thing, are they?" I asked, "not being unhappy and being happy?"

"I'm not sure we're put here to be happy, Jimmy."

"What are we put here for?"

He hesitated, frowned and cleared his throat. "To do a little good according to our capacities, to reach a hand to others . . ."

"To serve," I said, and he agreed, "yes, to serve."

"Is that enough?" I asked, and he said, "I think so, yes, for me . . . people have to arrive at their own answers."

Inside me one voice was screaming *No. No. No.* The other was saying, *he's right, damnit, be a man.*

I suddenly realized who Daddy was—my father was George Bailey, not me. He'd given so much to everybody else—to Mother, to the school, the town, the Rotary—there was nothing left. Had he ever wanted something different? Had he ever asked, *what about me?* I didn't know and now it didn't matter. For me, the choice was made, and it boiled down to attitude: I could take it like a man or take it like a boy. At least I loved May. We had that. Maybe love would be enough.

A sad calm stole over me, but deep inside there was a sense of uplift, too.

I took out my cigarettes and lit one. "I'm going to the Tilleys' now," I said, "so long, Dad."

As I got into the car I heard the sparrow cry again, and it came back to me:

> *Go, go, go, said the bird: human kind*
> *Cannot bear very much reality.*

# EIGHT

## Joey

On Christmas Eve that year, Pa and Nanny threw a party on Country Club Drive to celebrate what Nanny called her liberation from the Rice House. Everybody in the whole town was invited—well, almost everyone. In the rush, Nanny forgot to mail a invitation to Granddaddy and Grody Madden. At least, that's what she claimed. Daddy said that it was accidentally on purpose, but Mama said it most certainly was not and why did he assume the worst of everyone, particularly her mother? Granddaddy and Grody would probably be uncomfortable anyway, Mama said, since they didn't drink and disapproved of anyone who did, which would be everybody at the party, including *them*, meaning him and Mama.

But she got mad at Nanny, too, Mama did, and made her call Grody up in person and stood right by the phone. Only by then Grody had her feelings hurt and said thank you just the same but she and Granddaddy had a previous engagement, choir practice at the Methodist church—I think it was more the principle.

The afternoon before the party when we were delivering presents, Grody took Mama aside on the porch and said she appreciated Mama's efforts and did not blame *her*, but that her heart was simply broken, though she wouldn't complain. Of course her mother—meaning Nanny—had a lot on her mind with preparations and so forth, though she had help, which Grody didn't, but still and all, perhaps it *was* an oversight. Grody would try to regard it in the most charitable light, like a good Christian . . . not that she was one, mind you, for to say so would be boastful, but she did try her honest best, which was all she asked of others—to do unto Grody as she would unto them. Mama stood there, trying to keep her smile as her face turned red. I could tell she wanted to spit nails except she couldn't bring herself to talk back to Daddy's mama and couldn't find a crack to wedge a word in sideways anyhow.

So they didn't come, Grody and Granddaddy, and to tell the truth I don't think Nanny took it all that hard to get stood up. We were the first to get there, and she opened the front door and waved, all decked out in a red velvet dress with curlers in her hair and that new diamond ring from Tiffany's on her finger with a stone in it about the size to knock a buck deer cockeyed if you shot it from a slingshot. Pa'd had to fork out quite a bit to pay Nanny back for all her sufferings at the Rice House. The house was lit up like a ocean liner and "The Little Drummer Boy" was *rum-pa-pum-pumming* on the Dumont Balladier, which was like the one down at the beach— Pa tended to buy everything in twos.

"Lawdamercy, y'all git *in* this house before you freeze," Nanny yelled off the porch, flicking her Old Gold in the boxwood hedge, as we climbed from the Country Squire. "*Mother*, I wish you wouldn't do that," Mama said, "Bobby is just going to have to come behind you and pick up, *if* you don't burn the house down first," and Nanny said, "well, it's mine, ain't it. I reckon I can burn it down if I feel like it," which was just a joke except I don't think Mama saw the humor.

Bobby had hung a hunk of mistletoe off the chandelier and Nanny made us stand beneath it while she laid one on us. Nanny made Mama and Daddy kiss, too, but they were still mad about the invitation and it was just a peck. By then, even on the best days they weren't having any problems running out of air. But Nanny's eyes still teared up a little. "Look, Will, ain't they cute?" Pa strolled into the foyer in a tuxedo and a red bow tie, a sprig of holly in his buttonhole. "Yes, ma'am, they sho are and that's a fact." He cut a little wink at Reed and me and said, "and here come the buzzard brothers bringing up the rear." "*You're* a buzzit, Pa!" Reed shouted, and Pa rocked back on his heels with his hands in his pockets and just grinned.

"Mama, did you find those papers for me like I asked?" Mama said, and Nanny answered, "when do you suppose I had the time? They're right there in the bottom of the serpentine chest—he'p yo'self." Mama knelt with her skirt spread around her on the floor, opening the drawer and taking out a yellow scrolled-up paper that looked like something from the olden days. "What is it, Mama?" Reed asked.

"Come look, both you boys," she said, unrolling it real careful. "Mama is joining the Colonial Dames," she said, "which is a club for ladies from nice families, and these papers are about who our people were and where they came from." Pa winked at us and said, "they got to make sure we ain't got too many horsethieves in our clan."

"Mrs. Lane is in the DAR," I said, "she came and talked to us at school," and Mama said, "sweetheart, India Lane is as lovely a person as I know, but there's a big difference between the Dames and DAR, which you should know."

"That's right, bud," Daddy said, "if the DAR is stock car racing at Talladega, the Colonial Dames is Formula One at Indy." Mama looked at him all mad and sorrowful at once. "I don't find that comparison very useful, Jimmy." "No?" he said, "I thought the revving engines caught it rather well." He was smiling like it was a joke, but no one else smiled—let me tell you. It made something hitch up in my stomach to hear them talk that way.

Ignoring him, Mama turned to us. "To be a Dame, boys, you have to have an ancestor who was someone of importance before the Revolution. In the DAR you can be descended from anybody who was in the Army." "That's right," said Nanny, "even some buck private without two nickels to rub together in his pocket, or a rapscallion they only let out of the jailhouse to go fight." She looked at Daddy squinty-eyed, daring him to make another wisecrack. When he didn't, she said, "now y'all come see my tree."

We had to hold hands and close our eyes while she led us in, and when we opened them it was like a wonderland in there. The mantelpiece was garlanded with running cedar wrapped in wide red velvet ribbon like a candy cane and there were holly wreaths up on both corners of the big gold mirror. There were nests of giant pine cones everywhere and Nanny's crèche was out, together with this old-timey Santa Claus she had, with a cape made out of rabbit fur, who looked like he came down from caveman days. Then there was the tree . . .

"Mother, how on *earth* did you get it in here?" Mama asked, and Nanny grinned ear to ear like that question pleased her no end. "I thought we were gonna have to cut a new hole in this house to do it, so he'p me I did—I said that very thing to Bobby, didn't I, Bobby?" "Yes, ma'am, Miss Zelle," said Bobby, who was setting up the bar, and she said, "Reb and Skeeter had to truss the damn thing with tobacco twine to get it through the door, didn't they?" and Bobby said, "uh-huh, yes, ma'am, sho did." "And how many a them boxes of red and white satin balls did we put on?" Bobby shook his head. "Seems like it was fifteen at least." "It was not either," Nanny said, "it was twenty, and twenty balls to the box—how many 's'at make, Will?" "Fo' hundred, sugar," Pa said, and Nanny said, "fo' hundred . . . And every single one that Dee Lou hung I had to go behind and move it, didn't I, Bobby?" "Yes, ma'am, Miss Zelle," he said, and Nanny said, "but you got to have 'em to set off the little white lights and all yo' other ornaments."

"Well, Mama, you've outdone yourself," Mama said, "I truly mean it, it's the best you've ever done." Nanny frowned, studying the tree like suddenly she wasn't sure. "Course, I rather would a had a fir, but the ones Edgar had were all so small this year he sent me out a spruce instead. He *tried* to sell me a Scotch pine, but I told him if I wanted one a them I could a marched across the road and chopped it down myself . . . the idea. To me there's nothing worse than a Scotch pine, especially all tackied up with tinsel and those big colored bu'bs they use. Myself, I only like the little teeny white ones . . ."

Nanny went on for some time about her decorating views to get some other compliments from us, but her theories were the same as Mama's, which I'd heard, I guess, about twelve hundred times, so I quit listening and snuck a nervous peek at Daddy to see if steam had started coming from his ears. Because the thing was, see, Grody had a Scotch pine in her living room all tinseled up from head to toe and those same colored bulbs on it. I couldn't tell if Nanny knew that and was being mean on purpose, or whether she and Grody were so opposite it just came natural to them to hate everything about the other, even how they trimmed the Christmas tree. Daddy was smiling, but his jaw had that hard line to it, so I could tell he figured he had Nanny's number and was setting up a ambush on his end which he would spring when she shut up, if ever. I was glad when Reed piped up before he could.

"Where's the mouse, Pa?" he asked, and Pa said, "he's up there someplace, honey. Ain't he, Zelle?" Nanny frowned and said, "around the back," and Mama said, "now, Mama, you should put him right up front," and Nanny said, "I'd like to throw that damn thing out—it's shabby, and besides, I don't like rats on my tree." "Don't be mean, Mama," Mama said, "you know he's not a rat. He's a mouse, and he's perfectly dear. Here he is, boys, come look."

She held him out, a old fellow with wire-rimmed spectacles, wearing a vest and knickers and holding out this little-bitty cup. One of his feet was gone so you could see the metal sticking through his fur, which looked like a dried-up cattail. You could tell he came from back in the old days before people really learned to make good toys, when they sort of whipped them up at home and did the best they could. But Mama loved him special, you could tell from how she held him. "This belonged to Pa's daddy, boys," she told us, like maybe we'd forgotten since last year, "from when *he* was little at Rose Hill." She smiled at Pa so you could tell it was something special between the two of them. I think that's why Nanny didn't like that mouse, because Mama was Pa's favorite like Aunt June was hers.

"What's that cup, Mr. Will?" Daddy asked, "is he a beggar?" and Pa said, "nosuh, that's his wassail cup—he's waiting for his Christmas drink, right, honey?" Mama smiled and said, "that's right, Daddy, once a year." "If you ask me," Pa said, "he's looking pretty thirsty." "Then you'd better get the eggnog started," Mama said, and Pa said, "started? Me and Bobby put it in to chill at five o'clock, didn't we, Bob?" and Bobby said, "yes, suh, Mr. Will, right at five." "I'm thinking somebody better take a sample 'fore the folks arrive," Pa said, "see if it's all right," and Nanny said, "sample my foot, you already sampled half a gallon. You stay out of it, hemme?" Pa cut a wink at me and I noticed how his face seemed awful red and shiny and he was cracking jokes and talking more than usual, but I figured maybe he just felt excited on account of Nanny being home and Christmastime and all.

"On second thought, Mama, I do have one *slight* criticism of your tree," Mama said, "your angel."

"My angel? Lawdamercy, May, that was Mama's—I just *love* my angel, don't you? What's wrong with it?"

"I just think she looks a little tired, Mama, is all." She turned to Reed and me with her eyebrows raised and we ran to the car for Nanny's present—we'd rehearsed this part before.

A few weeks earlier, when we were up in Chapel Hill to Christmas shop, Mama took us into this little store on Rosemary Street. There were three angels on a shelf, which Mama made the lady take down and put on the counter so we could look. They were from England, the lady told us, and no two were alike. What was kind of cool to me was that they had real human hair. I asked if it was dead people's hair and she said she didn't think so but she didn't really *know*, so it still could of been. Mama looked at them for a long time and asked me and Reed if we thought Nanny would go for one. We said yes, and Mama asked us which, and we both said, *that middle one*, which was the only one that had blond hair—Mama said that was her favorite, too. I could tell she wanted it about as bad as I wanted that Daisy BB gun from the Sears, Roebuck catalogue or a Barlow pocketknife like Pa's, only when Mama turned the tag and saw the price she bit her bottom lip. "We'd like to think about it," she said, smiling at the lady, who asked if she should hold the angel

for us. "No," said Mama, "thank you, but that won't be necessary."
The lady looked a little sad to have to put them back.

Outside, Mama said it was "simply too expensive" and "out of
the question" and we "couldn't possibly afford it," and we went out
to lunch at the Zoom-Zoom. All the time we ate, Mama had this
little crease between her eyebrows, which meant she was preoccupied, and just picked at her plate. After the waiter came to take our
bill, Mama said, "I've made my mind up, boys. We're going to be
very wicked, and don't you dare tell your daddy. He would have a
fit."

We marched straight back to the shop and had the lady take the
angels down again, and Mama bought the one we liked and had it
wrapped, which made me kind of nervous, like there might not be
enough money left to buy my BB gun or even food to eat. Daddy
was always saying he could barely keep bread on the table with what
Pa paid, and Mama would say that Pa had given us our *house*, for
heaven's sake, what more did Daddy want? Why, we didn't even
have a mortgage. She said Daddy *knew* Pa couldn't play favorites at
work and if Daddy didn't like it, why didn't he change jobs? Then
we could move to Richmond or Atlanta or maybe even New York
City, where Aunt Winnie lived. You could tell that idea excited
Mama because her eyes lit up whenever she talked about the restau-
rants and theaters and shops Aunt Winnie had taken her to. Maybe
Uncle Mark could help Daddy get a job as a reporter, Mama said—
he'd be so good at that, and hadn't he always said he'd like to be a
writer?

Only Daddy would say he'd put in too many years at the Bonanza to flush it down the toilet now, and Mama's eyes would suddenly go dead. "Then just accept it, Jimmy," she would say, and
he'd say, "then why don't you?" only Daddy's eyes did not look
dead, but something worse. It tore me up to see him sad that way,
except that I could also see how mad he was, and when our daddy
got that way he was so big he made the whole house shake. Things
fell off the shelves and broke so you'd want to hide somewhere and
wait till it was over, but he was always sorry afterward and said he
didn't really mean to, only he had always had this, you know, temper.

That wasn't all about those angels, though, because when we started toward the car that day with Nanny's present, Mama still had that little crease between her brows and wasn't talking. Halfway down the street she stopped and said, "boys, we really ought to buy one for Grody, too—do you think she'd like it?" "Sure, Mama," we both said, though Grody was a whole lot harder to predict than Nanny, and back we marched again. Only this time Mama bought both angels so we could have one on the top of our tree, too.

When we came out that time, Mama seemed happy as a lark and we got ice cream cones and ate them sitting on the college lawn, which Mama called "the quad." She told us what the buildings were and how she used to wait for Daddy outside this one or that one and they'd walk home to Ransom Street. They lived in a little-bitty garage apartment and were as poor as church mice only they didn't care because they were so much in love. Sometimes I almost felt I could remember back to then, except I was just a baby not even a year old so I guess I must of only dreamed I could. Anyhow, me and Reed always liked to hear those stories because Mama seemed the happiest then.

So on the night of Nanny's party, we ran to the car and brought the package, and Mama said, "now, Mama, I know you hate opening your presents Christmas Eve, but you have to open this one, and I can't tell you why, but you'll understand as soon as you see what it is." Nanny looked all tickled, like whether it was Christmas or July the Fourth was all the same to her. She put on the reading glasses she wore on a chain around her neck and let our personal Tasmanian Devil, Reed, tear off the paper. The minute she saw what it was she said, "Lawdamercy . . ." and Mama said, real excited, "do you like it, Mama? She's all hand-painted, and her gown is Brussels lace." Nanny dropped her glasses off her nose and her eyes were kind of teary when she said, "if you ain't the worst, May Tilley"—she tended to forget sometimes that Mama was May Madden now. "It's from all of us, Mama, the boys and Jimmy, too," Mama said, reminding her. "Bobby, go git the ladder right this minute," Nanny said, "put her right on top. We'll find another place for Mama's." You could tell Mama was glad she'd spent the money then, because her eyes were teary, too.

Then the doorbell rang, and Nanny jumped out of her chair. "Praise Jesus, here they come and I'm still in my curlers." She took off down the back hall while Mama went to the door. Pretty soon, the house was splitting at the seams from all the people shouting "Merry Christmas!" and clapping backs and making toasts and raising such a furor you could hardly hear what you were thinking. Mama made me and Reed wish everybody Merry Christmas and kiss them on the cheek or shake their hand depending whether it was a lady or a man, except our uncles, both blood and unrelated, also got a kiss, and our Aunt Lucy Brown, who wasn't married and didn't put on make-up, shook as firm as any man. Daddy called her the Sergeant Major, which Mama said was terrible, except she laughed.

I fetched a cup of eggnog for Aunt Mary Landis, and Uncle Johnny asked if I'd been playing any gin. Down at the beach they were our next-door neighbors, and me and Pa and him set up the table in the driveway and played three-hand a lot. "No, sir, Uncle Johnny," I said, "but you better practice up or else next summer I'm gonna take that box of matches off you." Uncle Johnny laughed as though he liked me sassing him. "We'll see 'bout that," he said with a glint in his eye, and Pa said, "you better watch out, boy. It ain't no accident John Landis has the first nickel he ever made in Killdeer. Most everybody else's nickels, too."

Cousin John, their son—he wasn't old enough to be a uncle yet —stopped by with his date before they went on to the club, where the younger crowd was having their own dance. He spent the whole time talking to Daddy like he usually did, because Cousin John was a basketball fanatic and Daddy was a hero to him from when he starred at Killdeer High.

Uncle Herbert Kincannon was waiting in line to get a drink from Bobby, who was pouring with both hands, mopping sweat off his forehead with a soggy paper napkin. You could take one look at Uncle Herbert and tell he wasn't all that big on parties, which Mama told me was because he was a bachelor and the richest man in town from Dixie Bag. She said all the widows would of liked to marry him to get his money, only Nanny asked who would of wanted to. Uncle Herbert looked kind of nervous and severe like he wasn't sure if he should say hello or bite your head off, or maybe he was scared one of those widow ladies might be sneaking up behind him right that minute. He kept tugging his cummerbund and running his finger inside his collar like it pinched. I figured maybe he'd bought his tuxedo in his younger days when he went out more often and wasn't quite so stout. When he finally got his drink I saw him standing by the fire showing Bobby how to stack the next log so it would throw the heat back in the room and not just waste it up the chimney, which I would of bet you money Bobby knew already.

A crowd had gathered around Nanny and Uncle Curly Gower, who was saying, "walked right in on them, in his own damn bed—so help me God, if it was me, I think I would have shot them both right there." Uncle Herbert turned his back on Mr. Hale, our minister, and said, "if you ask me, he should have known what he was getting into when he married her—a divorcée with two children. It was his money. Any fool could have seen what she was after. Not that I'm not sorry for him."

"Herbut, listen to you talk!" said Nanny, taking a big puff on her Old Gold, "what you know about women wouldn't fill a postcard. You never kissed a girl in yo' whole life except yo' mama, and that won't till after you hit thirty-five."

Everybody laughed except for Uncle Herbert, who coughed and turned this kind of purple-red. "I swear to God, Zelle," he said, "if you were mine, I'd thrash you once a week on principle," and Nanny said, "don't you swear at me, Herbut Kincannon. I don't care how many mills you own, I remember you in diapers making mud pies and playing pattycake baker's man. You don't scare me one iota." Then Dr. Watt said, "you better quit while you're ahead, Herbert," and Uncle Herbert said, "while I *have* a head, more like," and they all laughed, which raised his spirits some.

Then Nanny clinked her ring against her glass and said, "and not one damn one a y'all even noticed my new ring," and stuck her hand out, wiggling her finger with that new diamond Pa had bought. "Ain't it cute," she said with a big grin that showed some lipstick on her teeth from where she'd put it on too fast. All the ladies went, "oh, Zelle!" and batted their eyelids, except Aunt Mary Landis, who said, "I'd say you made out like a bandit, sugar." Nanny looked at Pa across the crowd and said, "he's terrible, ain't he?" Pa grinned, too, and turned red to his earlobes—I could tell he would of liked to make a getaway.

Meanwhile Cousin John had Daddy collared discussing Dean Smith's new team at UNC and whether Bobby Lewis or Larry Miller had the finest jump shot, which I could of told them—Larry Miller was the greatest player all around, but nobody ever had a sweeter touch than Bobby L., who could drop them in from thirty feet all night. I watched every game on television, shooting my ball against the doorframe in our den, which was already smudged with fingerprints—every time I passed I had to jump to make sure I could hit it. But if I started dribbling, which made Tawny bark and jump around so that her tail knocked doodads off the coffee table, then Mama would come in and say that if I woke Reed up I was going to be one dead sorry Injun. But sometimes she and Daddy watched with me, and she would yell, *go Heels!* and *beat Duke's sorry butt!* as loud as anyone and get mad at the refs, except she didn't know the rules quite right and mixed up traveling and double-dribbling. If it came down to the wire she'd close her eyes and make you tell her what was happening, so that Daddy and I both laughed to watch her. When the Heels lost, Daddy would cuss and she'd look sad and I'd want to ride off on my bike somewhere and throw rocks at a streetlight. But if they were at the country club and I was by myself I'd cry sometimes if Bob and Larry couldn't pull it out, which I knew was dumb because tomorrow was another day, another game, except I couldn't help it. The Tarheels were my team, I was a Carolina boy.

While they talked, Daddy was glancing kind of nervous over Cousin Johnny's shoulder to where Uncle Sumner Dade had Mama in the corner going on about who they'd bumped into the other day and you'd never guess who So-and-so was marrying. Daddy never liked it much, the way the two of them went on about their old crowd, mostly people Daddy didn't know that well. Especially now he didn't like it, Daddy, because Uncle Sumner had just got divorced from Aunt Molly, which was the biggest news in Killdeer for a year until he moved away to Richmond and took his medical practice with him. They were the first it ever happened to and everyone in town was on Aunt Molly's side except for Mama, who, even if

Aunt Molly was her friend, would stick up for Uncle Sumner when people ran him down too hard behind his back. Because he was her friend since nursery school, where Aunt Molly only came from Greensboro. At least I thought that was the reason why.

But I could also see Daddy's side, watching her get all bubbly at the party, laughing, with that color in her cheeks that made you know why the ladies at Montaldo's asked her all the time to be in fashion shows. Uncle Sumner seemed different, too, lit up and happier around her, which is why it made my daddy nervous, see, and to tell the honest truth it made me nervous, too.

Because the other thing I knew was that when Mama was at Ascension, Uncle Sumner was her beau and escorted her to the debutante party Pa and Nanny threw when she came out—there was a picture of the two of them on the piano. Mama liked to tell the story of that time, about how she had been a Maid of Honor in the May Court and would have been the Queen in her last year except she met my daddy and fell in love and married him and never got to finish. Mama said she'd never regretted it, not even for a single instant, because now she had us, me and Reed, her own two boys. She'd always smile when she said that, except she'd look a little past you like she saw something in the distance she still longed for and knew she couldn't have, and I would try to figure out some way to help her get it, but I never could.

When Mama married Daddy it broke Uncle Sumner's heart, Nanny said, and all you had to do was take one look at how his face lit up whenever Mama walked into a room to tell he had a soft spot for her still. But Mama said that was just foolishness and Nanny should keep her opinions to herself. From the way I saw Daddy looking over Cousin Johnny's shoulder, though, I could tell he didn't think that it was all that foolish.

Daddy didn't just not *like* Uncle Sumner, I'm pretty sure he hated him. Because I heard him say how Uncle Sumner was a rich boy who'd never had to work for anything in his whole life, and when they played basketball together at Killdeer High the only action Sumner Dade ever saw was picking splinters out of his fat butt from where he rode the bench. And once, before the Dades split up and Uncle Sumner moved away to Richmond, they came by to visit us on Ruin Creek one Sunday afternoon. I was in the driveway shooting baskets when Daddy came outside to show Uncle Sumner the new Mustang Mama said we couldn't afford. They took a couple of those old-timey set shots like two cavemen tossing rocks, and Daddy asked if Uncle Sumner was up to play a little one-on-one. Why not, Uncle Sumner said, and they took off their sweaters and rolled up their sleeves, going at it in their penny loafers which you knew damn well they were going to ruin on the asphalt and didn't care one bit. It wasn't what you'd call a friendly game. They tried to smile and act polite, but both of them got red-faced and started throwing hips and elbows right and left when they boxed out. Daddy came down with a rebound and his elbow caught Uncle Sumner in the nose. The sound was like a egg dropped on the kitchen floor, and, boy, I'm telling you, the blood just poured.

Though he was way behind, Uncle Sumner wanted to keep playing even though the front of his white shirt was red. Daddy acted sorry and put his hand on Uncle Sumner's shoulder, only Uncle Sumner jerked away. We went inside, and Mama didn't say a word as she went for a cold compress. Her hands were shaking, though, and I could tell she didn't believe it when Daddy said it was a accident, but I was pretty sure it was. In a way, I was proud of Daddy because he won, but it still made me feel a little sick to watch.

And the thing about it was, Uncle Sumner had gone on to be a doctor like Daddy started out to be, except he only went one year and left, I don't know why. One time I asked Mama and she told me that not everybody is cut out for medicine—it depends on your *temperament*, which means the sort of personality you have. One thing I can say for sure is that just because you aren't a doctor doesn't mean that you aren't smart. Everybody said how smart my daddy was. At Chapel Hill he made straight A's in English and could quote you all about man's first disobedience and the fall of the forbidden fruit, which was from Milton, though his favorite was T. S. Eliot, which sometimes Daddy would come out with at the dinner parties he and Mama gave when everyone had had a lot of Pouilly Fuissé.

They'd all be sitting at the table—Mama, Daddy, Aunt Elise and Uncle Charlie Dawes, our next-door neighbors, and the Dades before they moved away—and Daddy would fill his glass and say, *I am Lazarus, come from the dead, come back to tell you all* in this voice that sent shivers down my spine. Me and Reed could hear him from the den. Then would come the part about the lady turning to the window, throwing off her shawl and saying that wasn't what she meant, that wasn't what she meant at all, and you could tell her saying that had knocked the wind out of this Prufrock fellow's sails. He'd be looking straight at Mama, Daddy would, when he recited that, and it would be so quiet at the table you could hear Ruin Creek whispering along the bottom of our hill.

And I could sort of see all that in Daddy's face as he stared over Cousin Johnny's shoulder at the Christmas party to where Uncle Sumner and Mama were shooting the breeze about some folks they used to know. She had all her color back and seemed happy like she hadn't very often for a while, and I felt especially close to Daddy then. I knew how it must feel to see that little speck of sadness way far back in Mama's eyes, the one you'd want to take away, and worked so hard to make it go, though it was never you who put it there. That speck was present even in the pictures Nanny had of Mama when she was a girl my age, when she'd been fat, like me. I guess that's how she knew that fatness is a stage that you outgrow, only sometimes I got the feeling Mama had forgotten and needed someone to remind her she was beautiful.

The next thing I knew, Daddy had disappeared, and when I went to look, I found him on the front porch smoking a Lucky Strike. "Hey, Daddy, whatcha doing?" I asked, and he smiled and said, "just taking a time-out." "It's freezing out here," I said, "aren't you cold?" He rubbed his hand across my flattop and didn't answer. "Ever see so many stars?" he asked, gazing up in the black sky where millions seemed to tremble, "looks like you could reach right out and grab one, doesn't it?" "Yes, sir, Daddy." He smiled again. "Don't let it fool you, son, it only looks that way," he said, "but maybe you'll have better luck than me." "What do you mean?" I asked, and he said, "nothing, bud, I don't mean anything," and then he laughed, if you could call it that.

"Why don't we go in?" I asked, and he said, "go ahead, I'll be there soon." When I went back, I passed Mama and Uncle Sumner in the library with that yellow scrolled-up paper spread between them on the table. She was telling him about Rose Hill and he was listening with a interested expression the way I guess my daddy never could. I hated Uncle Sumner then, who'd never said a unkind word to me.

About that time, Dee Lou whispered in Pa's ear she needed him to slice more ham for her ham biscuits. He winked at me and said, "come on, boy, let's break for daylight," and we went toward the breakfast room, but Pa stopped on the way to scoop another dipperful of eggnog. He was making me a little nervous then because his eyes were kind of glassy-wild and he was almost shouting when he talked.

"Spread out that newspaper for me, boy." He pointed his carving knife at the *Sentinel* on the sideboard. When I did, he shaved off a slice of ham and threw it down on the front page. "Now tell me, can you read the headlines through that ham?" I tried and said, "no, sir," and he frowned and said, "cain't?" I shook my head and he said, "well, damnit to hell then, it ain't thin enough." He shouted in to the kitchen, "Dee Lou, where's my steel?" and she yelled back, "in the case, Mr. Will, same place it always is." Pa started sharpening, flicking that blade back and forth so fast you thought the sparks were going to fly.

"Now, Joey, son," he said, "what we got here is the left hind leg of a Killdeer County bo'hog, which is the best damn eating you are ever like to find until you die and go to heaven, and, son, there ain't but a couple fellas left who still know how to do the cure. And I don't mean that goddamn sugar cure they do up in Faginia. Salt, boy, that's the secret—you smoke it, pack it in salt and leave it *two* years, not one. And that's why you got to shave it thin, you follow? You cut you off a big old hunk and try to eat that, it'll taste worse than the tread off a old tire, but cut it nice and thin to where you can read the paper through it, stick it inside one a Dee Lou's white bread biscuits with a pat of butter . . . son, I'm telling you, umph, umph, umph. That's the test my daddy used to use."

"You mean Mr. Reed Tilley, Pa?" I asked. "That's right, son, Mr. Reed Tilley who was yo' great-granddaddy. Now when *he* was a little boy our folks still lived out in the country at Rose Hill, and in those days they had their own smokehouse and cured up their own hams and venison. Daddy used to take us out to visit Sundays and he knew all about it and would try to explain to me when I was just about yo' age, only I've forgot the half of what he said and seems like every year I lose a little more. But what I still remember I'mon try to teach you boys so one day when y'all got some children a yo' own you can tell them, too. 'Cause it'll all be gone by then, honey. I know you'd never think it now, but by the time you get as old as Pa the world ain't gonna look a thing like it does now. One day you're a little boy in short britches, the next one you're a grown-up man with children. You blink yo' eyes again and yo' babies got some babies a their own and you got you a buzzard grandson to contend with, and Joey boy, you won't know where it went, it slips up on you, son, in the twinkling of an eye."

Pa had quit cutting and was staring through the window toward the oak tree in the dark back yard like he'd lost his train of thought, and I don't believe I'd ever heard him talk so much at once, which made you know he'd had too much to drink, except I didn't mind, I liked to listen. It made me feel, I don't know, lifted up some way, like me and Pa were part of one big thing that had been there a long time before us and he was searching for the name of it to tell me, except I don't believe he knew. Probably it makes no difference what you call it, it's enough to feel the feeling calm and full inside yourself, which I felt then, and know that it went back to other Christmastimes and other Pas who taught their boys about the ham, that it is done this way and not another. It was a simple thing, but to me a treasure more than gold.

"And I bet you don't know why it's the *left* hind leg either, do you?" he asked. "No, sir, why?" "I'll tell you why," he said, " 'cause a hog sleeps on one side and not the other. Now you think that out and tell me which it is," and I said, "the left?" and Pa said, "nosuh, a bo'hog lays down on his *right* ham ever' single night and that's what makes it tough, so it's the left one that stays nice and tender, follow me?" "Yes, sir, Pa," I said. "Now run this ham to Dee Lou in the kitchen and let's us step outside a minute. Somp'm I wanna show you."

We went through Dee Lou's pantry and down the four back

steps to the garage, where Pa reached in the Cadillac and handed me the keys. "Open up that trunk and see what you can find in there," he said, reaching in the glove compartment for the Seagrams.

Inside the trunk, the light came on, and there it was, a two-piece surf rod in its own case and a jet-black Shakespeare spinning reel. "Durn, Pa, this thing's *cool*," I said. "Think so? Picked it out for this friend a mine and wanted yo' 'pinion whether he might like it." My heart just about hit the floor on that, but I tried not to let it show. "Shoot, yeah, Pa, who wouldn't? Who's it for?" "Wellsuh," he said, "he's a fella 'bout yo' size and build. Fact, he looks a good bit like you, only better-looking." He cut a wink at me and then I got it. "He must be a better fisherman than you to get a rig this good," I said. Pa grinned and said, "he's halfway passable certain days," and then I couldn't stand it anymore. "Come on, Pa, quit fooling." He gave my ear a little tug. "Merry Christmas, buzzard."

I threw my arms around his neck, and he said, "now, I hope you realize that's a trolling rig," and I said, "you mean for in the ocean?" "Yessuh, that's exactly what I mean, fo' in the sea." "What about Mama?" I asked, and he said, "well, I'mon hafta work on her some more, but she knows I bought it so I b'lieve she's gittin' soft and leanin' in our favor." "Durn, Pa, it's the best present I ever got." "Well, hold yo' hosses, honey, there's somp'm else in there." Then I found my brand-new tackle box stocked with every size and shape of sinker, every plug and lure and spoon and size of hook and every pound of test line you could ever need or think of, and when I asked him where he got it, Pa just winked and said, "found it in a mule's track."

Before we went back in, I asked Pa if we could open the secret compartment in the panel of the stairwell, which only me and him and Reed and Grant and Little Will and Daddy knew was there but not Mama or Nanny, and he said yes. Inside, he kept all the knives and swords and bayonets and guns that were his special treasures, and every time we camped in the garage we'd get to take them out real careful wrapped in chamois cloth and pass them one by one around the circle while Pa told the story of what each was and who it had belonged to and how it came to him.

Inside was a rusty dress sword that had belonged to Pa's Granddaddy Mann, a captain in the Civil War who died up in Virginia at a battle called Cold Harbor, where Pa said a quarter of the men in Killdeer County died on that one day inside of half an hour. And there was a ivory-handled German bayonet from the First World War which belonged to Pa's big brother, Andrew, who Pa said was killed by a runaway ambulance someplace in France the day after they signed the Armistice. He could still remember the two men knocking on the door to bring the telegram in the middle of the victory parade. There was a pearl-handled German Luger that Otis Frye brought back from World War II, and others, too. Pa showed them all to us, except for one. In the back of the compartment was a leather gun case he'd never taken out. The one time I asked him, he just shrugged it off, but you could tell from his expression there was something different about that gun. Daddy was the one to tell me what the secret was—it had belonged to Pa's daddy, Mr. Reed, who killed himself.

That Christmas Eve Pa reached in and took it out without me even asking. Unzipping the zipper on the case, he handed it to me— a double-barreled .12-gauge shotgun with sterling triggers and a mounting tooled with vines and leaves. In the silver almost rubbed away you could still read *A. A. Fox & Co., Philadelphia*, which Pa said was the company that made it specially for his daddy, for shooting doves and quail, and that was why, Pa said, the barrels were so short, cut off at twenty-seven inches.

That was all Pa said, and then he sat down on the steps and sipped his Seagrams while I looked at the shotgun. "One day when I'm gone I want each a y'all—you and Reed and Grant and Little Will—to have somp'm outta there," he said, "and since you're the oldest, you git first pick. You don't have to decide right now, you can think it over and let me know." "I don't need to think it over. I want this one, Pa," I said, and he said, "sure?" and I said, "yes, sir, Pa, I'm sure." He nodded. "All right then, honey, 'cept we'll keep it in here till you're older and won't tell yo' mama or yo' nanny, deal?" "Deal," I said, and we shook hands on it. Pa seemed kind of sad about my pick, but why I wanted it was because it meant the most to him.

When I helped pull him up, I noticed the excited shiny light had gone out of his face. Now he looked gray and awful tired. As we climbed the steps, he was limping some on his bad leg and staggered once against the wall so that he had to keep a hand on my shoulder to steady him.

Inside, Nanny shot us a dirty look across the room, and Mama made a beeline toward us. "So, our two delinquents finally decided to return. I swear, Daddy, I don't know which of you is worse." Pa gave me an elbow in the ribs and said, "looks like we're in trouble now, don't it, boy?" and I said, "yes, sir, Pa, looks like." Mama turned on me. "And you, sir, march yourself right upstairs to bed this instant." When I started to say something, she opened her eyes wide that way she would, meaning whatever you were going to say you might as well not waste your breath. "I don't want to hear another word about it," she said, so I kissed Pa good night and left, except I didn't go to bed. I sat down with Reed, who was in his pajamas, spying from the upstairs landing, sucking his thumb and holding Mr. Rex.

They were all creating quite a furor by that time, laughing and yelling and smoking so many cigarettes our eyes burned all the way upstairs. In the foyer mirror, we could see Mr. Hale at the piano with a glass of bourbon and a Camel dangling off his lip. Cracking his knuckles, he tried out some carols, which sounded more like something from a nightclub, with all those jazzy runs he put in them. Before long eight or ten folks had gathered round and started singing, but Pa's voice was twice as loud as anyone's, which made me nervous, especially since he couldn't keep a tune.

"You're supposed to be in bed," I said to Reed because I didn't think he ought to hear such things, but he said, "so are you," which was true, and so I had to punch him in the arm to make him go. He started crying and said he was going straight downstairs to tell, and I had to promise if he wouldn't I'd give him first pick of all the candy in my stocking. I knew he'd take my chocolate coins, which on the outside looked like gold, except he might forget by morning, though, knowing Reed, the chance was slim.

About the time he left, Nanny came out in the foyer, right below where I was spying, and whispered loud to Mama, "I could kill him,

May. I swear to God I could simply kill yo' daddy. He's ruined my whole party." "It's not ruined, Mama," Mama said, and Nanny said, "talk to him, sugar—would you try? I cain't do a thing with him, but to you he just might listen." Mama didn't look too happy, but she headed toward the piano anyway.

"Would you come here a minute, Daddy?" she said real sweet and innocent, "I want to ask you something." Pa was way too smart to fall for that. He stuck his finger up beside his nose, then wagged it back at her. "I won't bawn yesti'd'y," he said, and it was kind of hard to understand him then because his voice was slurred.

Then Uncle John and Dr. Watt came up on either side of Pa and Uncle Johnny said, "come on, old son," and Pa said, " 's'early, John, le's sing s'more carols," and Uncle Johnny said, "I think it's bed for you, my friend." Pa turned to Dr. Watt. "Le's us go git a drink, Watt." Dr. Watt said, "all right, Will," but you could tell he said it just to humor Pa.

"I'll get it, Watt," Uncle Johnny said, taking him by the arm. Pa pulled away. "Jus'a minute, jus'a minute, John," he said, and went over to the tree and from out of all the ornaments took down the mouse that used to be his daddy's and held it in his hand and stared at it for a long time and then let Uncle Johnny lead him off.

"Put him upstairs in the blue room," Nanny said as they went by, and I could tell how mad she was from how her arms were folded tight against her new skinny stomach. I had to get a move on out of there because they were coming straight in my direction, but as I closed the bedroom door behind me I could hear Pa singing "*si-i-lint night*" as they went down the hall. I tiptoed into the bathroom between our room and Pa's and put my eye to the keyhole, one of those old-timey big ones made for a skeleton key, and I could see them pretty good and hear what they were saying, too. I felt kind of bad about it, but I did it anyway.

" 'Member, Johnny?" Pa was saying, " 'member how we used to go, and that ol' one-eyed hoss we had?" and Uncle Johnny said, "that's right, Will, your daddy used to take us carolin' every Christmas Eve," and Pa said, "he did, Johnny, ever' single one. You 'member Daddy, dontcha?" "Course, Will, course I do. He was as fine a gentleman as you could care to meet." "He was, won't he . . . he's gone, John, gone, and Mama, too." Pa made this sound which was kind of like a groan and sighed the air out of his lungs.

"I know, son, I know," said Uncle John, holding Pa's arm tight and easing him down onto the mattress. "What happened to us, Johnny?" Pa said, and Uncle Johnny answered, "I don't know, Will," and loosened Pa's bow tie. "We just got old, I guess."

"How'd we get so old, John?" Uncle Johnny smiled and shook his head. " 'Fwe knew that, we'd know somp'm, wouldn' we, Johnny boy?" Pa said, and Uncle John said, "that we would, Will, that we would." "*Si-i-lint night*," Pa sang again, and Uncle Johnny said, "that's right, Will, lie back now," and took the mouse out of Pa's hand and put it on the bedside table.

Then he got up and I couldn't see him anymore. "He'll be all right tomorrow, sugar," I heard him say, and it was Mama's voice that answered. "Thank you, Uncle Johnny." She came in on her tiptoes and sat down on the bed and kissed the top of Pa's bald head. "I love you, Daddy," she whispered, smoothing down that strand of hair that was poking up from how his hat had sat on it, but it sprung right straight back. Pa opened one eye and grinned at her. "I won't bawn yesti'd'y," he said, "where's ol' mouse?" and she said, "right here on the table, Daddy." "Diddy git his drink?" Pa asked. Mama smiled and nodded. "He got several, I believe." "C'rismus drink, once a year," Pa said, and he was having trouble talking then.

"That's right, Daddy," Mama said, and all of a sudden Pa's face changed. "Oh, Lord, Lord, May," he said, "I'm so sorry, so sorry, May," and she said, "I know, Daddy, I know, it's all right. Everybody loves you." Pa grabbed her arm. "Tell yo' mama, tell her, May, I didn't mean . . . I didn't . . ." "I will, sweetheart," Mama said, "go to sleep now," and she kissed him again and tiptoed out.

I heard him groan one time and then fall quiet, and I stood in the dark bathroom and didn't realize till then how hard my heart was beating, so that it was like to make me feel a little faint and sick inside, except that I did not know why. I only knew that sinking feeling in my gut was back and I felt scared of something I couldn't put a name to, except it was the change, the one I started out by telling you, which makes you feel so small and helpless up beside it.

Mama poked her head into our room. "Come on, boys, it's time to go. Joey, help your brother dress and tie his shoes and hurry please." "I can do it by myself," said Reed. When we got downstairs, Daddy was pulling the car around while Nanny said good night to people in the foyer. Uncle Sumner held Mama's coat for her, and as we walked out on the porch he said, "I think it's fascinating, May. I had no idea they could trace it back that far." "Are we on Charlemagne yet?" Daddy asked as he came up, "who was it that said Southerners are a reasonable people till you get them on the subject of genealogy?" and Mama said, "you just can't stand yourself until you tear it down, can you, Jimmy?" Uncle Sumner looked embarrassed. "Well, what's that joke about how Southerners are like the Chinese?" he asked. Neither Mama nor Daddy even looked at him and he seemed even more embarrassed as he answered, "we both eat rice and worship our ancestors."

"These papers are certified, Jimmy," Mama said, "they were done by a licensed genealogist in Philadelphia," and Daddy said, "come on, May, you think those fellows make a living telling people they're descended from One-Eyed Carl, the miller's son? The court tailor's hardly going to be the one to tell the emperor he's undressed." I saw Uncle Sumner's jaw go tight, and he said, "well, I'll say good night. May, it was wonderful to see you. Thank your mama for me, will you? . . . Jimmy." I could see that little muscle flick in Daddy's jaw as they shook hands.

Uncle Sumner walked off down the driveway toward his parents' house and no one spoke till we got in the car, where suddenly it all exploded.

# NINE

## Joey

"I've never been so embarrassed in my life," Mama said as we turned out of Pa and Nanny's drive, "I'm *mortified* . . . in front of Sumner, too." "Screw Sumner," Daddy said, "who cares what he thinks?" "The insult was to *me*, Jimmy," Mama said, "to me and to my parents." "What insult? Hell, May, I love your Mama and Daddy, you know I do, but, I mean, come on, it's not like they're *aristocrats.*"

"They most certainly are, too—what would you call them then?" she asked. "They're prominent, May, in *Killdeer*," Daddy said, "but that's hardly the same as being an aristocrat. Killdeer's a pretty small pond after all." Mama's face went white the way it did the time I called Dee Lou a nigger. I was scared she might reach out and slap him right across the mouth the way she did that time to me. And she might just as well of, too, for what she said: "I haven't seen *you* making any waves in it." Daddy kept on smiling but his jaw looked like somebody'd carved it from a block of wood, and I knew things were going straight downhill from there.

"Mama's papers are authentic, Jimmy. We have a coat of arms," she said, and Daddy said, "your parents do, you mean—them and twenty or thirty other families here in town. Anybody with the money can order a crest off the back page of *American Heritage* magazine." "Why do you think everybody is a liar and a cheat?" she asked. "You just can't imagine that maybe it's true, that there's something good about anybody, especially my family." "That's not it," he said, "I just wish you'd spend a little more time looking for something good in *ours.*" That was the first thing he said that stumped her some—she didn't answer right away.

If Daddy had just shut up, too, it might of been okay, except he had to add, "all I'm saying, May, you take those twenty coats of arms in Killdeer, multiply them by a thousand—hell, who knows, ten thousand—towns just like it all across the South . . . you think they're all descended from the English aristocracy? Hell, there aren't that many aristocrats in *England.*"

"You really should shut up, Jimmy," Mama said, "you're only displaying your ignorance. Only the eldest son inherited. I suppose you've heard of primogeniture?" "So?" he said. "So," Mama answered, "all the younger brothers—and sisters, too, for that matter —had to go out and make their own way. Meaning that far more left than stayed. And I don't know about a thousand other towns, or even Killdeer, I only know about my family, and our coat of arms is certified, and you won't accept it because you don't know any better, a, and, b, because you can't stand admitting somebody else has something to be proud of that you don't."

That little muscle in Daddy's jaw was going right to town. "You never used to care about this crap." "I never needed to," said Mama. "What's that supposed to mean?" he asked, and Mama said, "it means I'm tired of taking handouts from my parents every month while you go out and buy that brand-new Mustang we can't afford." "I bought that car for you," Daddy said. "Oh, Jimmy, please. Don't make me laugh. I drove it to the store one time and you ran out behind me and looked it over with a magnifying glass. You don't give a damn about anybody but yourself and I don't even think you

give a damn about that either. If you aren't going to make us somebody in this town, I have to do it by myself the best way I know how.
So go ahead and turn your nose up at the Dames, I just have to tell
you I don't give a damn what you think anymore."

Daddy's face was as white as hers by then. He said, "go to hell,
May," and Mama said, "no, thank you, I might run into you."

When we pulled in the drive on Ruin Creek, Mama carried Reed
into the house, then went to her room and closed the door. She was
crying there, I'm pretty sure. Daddy stood out in the driveway in the
pitch-black freezing cold and smoked a cigarette, staring at our
house like he couldn't make his mind up if it was still okay for him
to go inside. I watched him through the window, the way the orange
coal would rise and fall and fade and glow. After a while he
scratched out in the Mustang. I lay awake a long time staring at the
ceiling, waiting for the lights to flash across the wall and the sound
his tires made coming up the drive.

When I woke up the Mustang was still gone. Daddy never did
come home that night—though by then it was already Christmas
morning.

It was barely light, but I could smell the coffee when I got up.
Walking past the double doors that led into the living room, I heard
Daddy cussing and shoving things around in there. Mama was star-
ing out the kitchen window, over the back fence and down the hill
toward the creek. She turned when I came in and wished me Merry
Christmas with sad, apologizing eyes—her face looked puffy.
"Where's your little brother?" "Still asleep," I said. She poured a
cup of coffee. "Take this to your daddy and see if you can help him."

He was sitting in his sock feet Injun-style beneath the Christmas
tree, still in his party clothes—his beard was blue like on "The
Flintstones," his hair all greasy and messed up, and I could see the
veins in his eyes like threads of red lint off the stockings. He had the
instructions to Reed's bike open in his lap, but he wasn't reading
them, just trying to line up two holes on the frame and shove in a
bolt that wouldn't go. "Goddamn piece of shit," he said, and then
looked up and saw me standing in the doorway. "Merry Christmas,
Daddy." He smiled and said, "I think the elves are out on strike."

The whole time we were putting on the training wheels, I was looking around for my BB gun and didn't see it anywhere. Then we heard Reed running down the hall in his foot pajamas and shoved the tools beneath the chair. Mama opened the double doors and held Reed's hand as he grinned in, his black eyes just like hers except that his were bright as stars and hers were two dark wells. "Santa came," he said, and Mama said, "I'm sorry, sugar, he didn't get a chance to wrap the presents." "He was running late and had to get to Buenos Aires," Daddy said, and Mama said, "he left something for you, though." "That's right, it's in the fireplace," Daddy said, "a great big bag of switches and ashes," and Reed said, "nuh-uh, Daddy," and ran right to his bike.

We all went out on the back porch, where you could see your breath, and watched him ride it in the driveway. I saw Daddy reach for Mama's hand, but she made him wait before she gave it. When she did, he smiled, and she did too, only Mama seemed put out. Then Daddy slipped inside and came out with his arm behind his back. "Hey, what's this?" he asked, pulling out my Daisy. "Durn," I said, "all *right.*" It was just like Chuck Connors's Winchester on "The Rifleman." Even Mama smiled.

I filled it from the paper BB tube and fired it over the back fence. "Now, Jimmy," Mama said, and Daddy said, "now, Joey, son . . ." He told me if I ever aimed it at anyone, including Tawny, even if the gun was empty, then it was going straight back to that big home in the sky where BB guns all come from. It would be the last air rifle I would see till I was an old, *old* man, he said, with a long white beard, and was that clear? It was, I said, still blasting at some flying birds. It was getting time to dress for church.

Since we'd spent Christmas Eve at Pa and Nanny's, Christmas Day we went downtown to the First Methodist with Granddaddy and Grody so nobody's feelings would get hurt. They met us on the steps out front and Granddaddy hugged us kind of stiff that way he would, like it embarrassed him, and Grody said, "Law', you precious *things*—come let me show you off."

Aunt Dolly was home from Raleigh and came to church with us. She was a veterinarian's assistant up there and didn't get to Killdeer very much because she couldn't find someone to take care of her cats, is what she said. If you ask me, the real reason was because she and Grody didn't get along too hot. Uncle Sam was back from the U.S.S. *Enterprise*, the ship the Navy put him on to pay his college loan. I hate to say it, but he went to Duke. He didn't go to church with us, and Reed said, "where's Uncle Sammy?" "Still in bed, dear," Grody said, and Reed said, "how come?" and Grody said, "because he doesn't get the chance to sleep late in the Navy. When you're older you'll have the same prerogative." "Oh," said Reed, because he didn't know *prerogative* and couldn't figure out how you could sleep on Christmas Day.

After church Grody entertained us in the living room while Aunt Dolly and Granddaddy made dinner in the kitchen. Through the swinging door I could see Granddaddy standing at the counter wearing Grody's apron which had ruffles on the shoulder straps. He was taking plates down off the shelf and measuring out the butter beans and sweet potatoes in a tablespoon so everybody's portion would be just the same and there would be enough to go around. Grody planned it out that way because waste is a sin, she said, and it was the least they could do, Granddaddy and Aunt Dolly, to serve the plates and wash up after she had slaved and sweated over that hot stove all morning. Granddaddy kept looking at his watch like he wished Christmas would be over so he could go back to the high school, and I saw Daddy also watching with the saddest look before the door swung to.

Reed was mad we had to wait till after lunch to open presents, and he slumped down on the sofa with a peevish look, sucking his thumb and holding Mr. Rex. "Sit up straight, dear," Grody said, "be a big boy and don't suck your thumb—you know what happened to Slovenly Peter, don't you? The Tailor Man came in and snipped those thumbs right off." "For God's sake, Mother," Daddy said, "don't tell him that," and Grody said, "what? Why, Law', that was your favorite storybook when you were small," and Daddy said, "I hated it," and Grody frowned and said, "of course you didn't. That book was Papa's—you used to ask me for it all the time, you've just forgotten." Reed went and sat in Mama's lap, and Daddy said, "yeah right. Well anyway, to set the record straight, it wasn't Slovenly

Peter who had his thumbs cut off. That happened in a different story." "As if I could forget," said Grody, "who do you think read that book to you?" and Daddy said, "so six times eight is forty-six if your old teacher says so? I'm sorry, Mother, I think you've mixed those doctrines up—it's the Pope who's infallible. The word, in your case, is *inflammable.*" "And *infantile* in yours," Grody fired right back at him. It got so quiet I could hear the clock tick on the mantel, and then Daddy said, "touché." "Go touché yourself," said Grody, and for a moment they both grinned like friends.

Then Grody turned to me. "Joey? Run up to your daddy's room and wake Uncle Sam. Tell him it's almost one o'clock, p.m.—and, wait, before you go, can you tell me what 'p.m.' stands for?" "Post meridian?" I said. "That's right, and aren't you smart? When you're rich and famous you'll come back and chauffeur me around in your big limousine, won't you?" I smiled because she always teased that way. "Yes, ma'am, Grody." "Of course you will," she said, "and you'd better hurry up and get one, too, because it looks as though it's going to be a while before your daddy does," which was supposed to be another joke, I think, only this time Daddy didn't smile.

"Don't start, Mother," he said, and Grody said, "start what? All I'm saying is what everybody knows, and the simple truth should never cause offense. You have no business working in a tobacco warehouse. No man in our family has ever done manual labor. I think even May would agree with me on that, wouldn't you, dear?" "I've always thought Jimmy could do anything he put his mind to, Mother Madden," Mama said, "but I also feel he should be free to choose what he enjoys."

Grody kept smiling, but her eyes shot sparks. "Yes, dear, but how much could anyone enjoy lifting those big dusty piles of to-bacco?" "I hardly ever do that sort of lifting anymore," Daddy said, and Grody said, "don't say 'hardly ever,' Jimmy. It's such a coarse expression . . . 'rarely' sounds so much nicer. And, May, please don't think I mean to imply anything disparaging of your father or his business. I have nothing but respect for Will, though I do think his illness should be a lesson to us all. I pray for him every day, dear, every single day. Of course, when it comes to smoking I'm as guilty as the next, but I'm sorry, I just have to say it makes me cringe every time Jimmy lights up one of those awful Lucky Strikes, even after all these years it does. Because I told them all, from the time they were Reed's age and before, 'don't do as I *do*, do as I *say*,' and Jimmy never started till after you were married—not that I blame you. But at least Sam and Dolly have resisted the temptation, thank the Lord, and I suppose two out of three isn't bad. But that you, Jimmy, *you*, my first, should be the one . . . But it's Christmas, the birthday of Our Lord, so let's not fight. For my part, what I say is only meant in love."

Daddy didn't look like he wanted to fight either. I noticed neither he or Mama had taken out their cigarettes, though I could take one look and tell they would of paid a dollar for a puff. There was this kind of creepy-crawly feeling in the room which everybody seemed to notice except Grody. "Run on now, honey," she said, "wake your Uncle Sam."

He was in the twin bed near the wall, stretched out with his face down in the pillow so you couldn't tell how he could breathe. His arms were stretched out to the side like he was in the middle of a swan dive and hadn't hit the water yet. I shook his shoulder once but he didn't stir so I let him catch a few more winks and tiptoed to the chest of drawers where Daddy's trophies were.

I liked to be there by myself sometimes to look at them. My favorite was this silver boy who stood with a bowed head and one arm raised, carrying a crown of leaves. He was naked, with the muscles standing out the same way Daddy's looked in some of his old high school pictures. I hoped one day mine would look that way when I outgrew the stage of being fat, or big as you might say. I would of liked to take that trophy home with us, but when I asked, Daddy said, "we better not," I don't know why.

"Hey, you lizard, get over here and let me give you Chinese torture." Uncle Sam was grinning at me from the bed, and I grinned back and said, "nuh-uh, no way, you must be dreaming. You better hurry and get dressed, Grody said to tell you lunch was almost ready." "She did, did she?" "Yep," I said, and he said, "well, she's a lizard, too." I just howled at that. He jumped out of bed and threw on his plaid robe like the ones we got from Grody last year. "I don't think there's time to take a shower," I said, and he said, "tell Mother

not to wait." "She'll be mad." "Nah," he said, and it was true—
Grody was almost never mad at him the way she got with Daddy.
Maybe that's why Uncle Sam was always cracking jokes and smiling
where Daddy seemed to stay mad half the time when we were there.

Everything went fine at lunch till Grody sent Granddaddy out to
the garage to get the pound cake tin. Grody made the best pound
cake you ever tasted, with a thick chewy crust on top. Pop it in the
toaster with a pat of butter, put a scoop of ice cream on it after it was
warm and it would knock the socks right off your feet—I'm telling
you, no lie, it was about the limit. But you could sooner break into
Fort Knox than get her recipe and she would never cut you more
than a small sliver at the time. Eggs and butter were so expensive,
she said, and she didn't like to bake more often than she had to.
Only, after you finished, Grody would always, *always*, ask you, "will
you have another piece?" What you were *supposed* to answer was
"no, thank you, Grody, I'm full. It was delicious."

So there she was, standing at the cake tin with her knife. "Anyone?" she said, "Sammy, dear?" Uncle Sammy smiled. "No, thank
you, Mother. If I have any more I might come down with the
Dunlop disease like Jimbo's getting here." "What's a Dumlop, Uncle Sam?" Reed asked, and Uncle Sam said, "that's when your gut
lops over your belt like a spare tire, you lizard." "You better wipe
your mustache, Sammy," Daddy said, "you've been drinking too
much milk."

Grody worked her way down through the roll but never called
my name, and I knew why—so did everybody there. I could tell they
were all staring, feeling sorry for me, especially Mama, and then
Granddaddy said, "well, Lilith, it's a shame to let it go to waste. If
no one else is going to eat it . . ." "I'll split it with you, Granddaddy," I piped up, and Grody said, "Thurston, you've had enough,
and Joey, dear, I didn't ask on purpose, because, as you well know,
you're a little overweight. Now May, dear, please don't think I'm
being critical. I know you've done the best you could with him, and
of course it does run in your family. We never had those problems
with our children, thank the Lord, though heredity is nothing to
brag about. I just think a little discipline never hurts, especially with
boys. It's so hard for a man to restrain himself at the table, May, and

certain other places I won't mention, as I'm sure I have no need to tell you. So help me, if I didn't watch Thurston like a hawk, a *hawk*, I don't think you could roll him through that door next week this time. But I'm sorry, I just think it's the most unattractive thing to see a person eat with obvious appetite, don't you?"

Mama didn't answer. No one at the table said a word or looked at anybody else—somehow you couldn't. I don't think Grody even noticed. She went right on chatting as she wrapped the cake in foil and put it back inside the tin, her face excited and lit up the same way Daddy's got sometimes.

"Papa was so lean-waisted right up till the day he died," she said, "but of course he was exceptional and took such pride in his appearance. In summer he changed his shirt three times a day so he'd be fresh for meals. Law', he was such a dresser, Papa, and did I ever tell you, May? He had the first car in Killdeer, the very first one." Mama, whose face was scarlet to her ears, said, "did he? I always heard that that was Mr. Gillam Weeks—you know Mama lived across from them at Seven Oaks."

Grody looked like someone in a happy dream who hates to be waked up. "I think Zelle must be mistaken, May," she said, still smiling but with deadly ray-guns in her eyes. It scared me so that I could hardly breathe to see their hate so clear. "Maybe him and Mr. Weeks bought them at the same time so there were *two* first cars," I said, and Uncle Sam said, "*there* you go, lizard," and Grody said, "well, with Joey, May, I know, and I think you now know, where the problem started. It's all right for the coloreds, but in my opinion no white woman has any business breast-feeding—I'd never even heard of one who wanted to till you and those other girls read that book what-is-it-called and started. I stayed out of it, and then, of course, you had those problems there's no need to mention and learned it for yourself, which is the only way it ever sinks in." "Mother Madden?" Mama said, "I'd truly rather not discuss this with the children here." She was trembling, Mama was, and Grody said, "well, I have had my say."

That was the first I'd ever heard that I was breast-fed and I didn't even know what "problems" Grody meant, but Mama looked at me across the table and her eyes were just so sad it made me want to put my hands around Grody's throat and scream *shut up shut up shut up* and choke her till she stopped. I wanted to tell her it wasn't Mama's fault, because she took me down to Dr. Watt's that time to get my diet, Mama did, and on the way home in the car I felt so happy we were going to start and I would finally at last get through this stage of being fat, or bigness.

I have to tell you honest what occurred: that night at dinner I ate exactly what was typed up on the sheet. Mama cooked it special like Dee Lou did with Nanny's food and everything went fine. But then we all went in the den to watch TV and maybe half an hour or an hour had gone by when Reed or maybe it was Daddy asked Mama for a bowl of ice cream and some Oreos. She went in to get it and I sat there sweating in my chair because I suddenly felt hungry, hungrier I think than I had ever been in my whole life, like the whole inside of me was one big empty hole just crying out for food. I went in after her and said I'd like ice cream, too, and Mama turned around surprised and said, "why don't you have an apple or some celery sticks?" the snack my diet said was okay. "No, Mama," I said, "I want ice cream, I'm hungry, I'm *starving*, it's a stupid diet and it doesn't work and I don't want to do it anymore." Mama looked at me like her heart was breaking, and way down deep inside I think there was a part of me that wanted her to tell me no and make me stop, but I guess she just couldn't. She said, "all right, honey," and took down another bowl and made some ice cream for me, too, and we got no further with that diet, but whose fault was that? I don't give a rip what Grody said, it wasn't Mama's fault.

After all this, Daddy put his hand on my shoulder and smiled at me, but when he looked across at Grody his lips curled like he had a bad taste in his mouth. "Mother," he said, "I love you, but you're so abstemious you're hard to stand sometimes." "Now, Jimmy, that's enough," Granddaddy said, "I won't have you talking to your mother that way," and Grody said, "no, Thurston, that's all right, I know he doesn't mean it." "All I did was state a fact," said Daddy, "the simple truth should never cause offense. Isn't that what you always say, Mother, before you lower the boom?"

Oh, boy, it got icy cold in there in a big hurry, and I was proud of Daddy for standing up to her for us, but it scared me, too, because I didn't know if he could win.

Aunt Dolly got up in a hurry and began to clear the plates. Uncle Sam just sat there smiling and his face was red. "That doesn't even make good sense, Jimmy, what you said—to call someone abstemious is a compliment." "You mean like calling them a stingy tightwad?" Daddy asked, and Uncle Sammy finally lost his smile. "That isn't what it means," he said, "abstemious is more like thrifty, frugal—that's entirely different." "Sorry, bud, no way," said Daddy, "niggardly is closer to it—cheap, tight, parsimonious . . ." and Uncle Sammy said, "how much you want to bet?" "That's enough, boys," Granddaddy said, "I won't have fighting at the table," and they both said at the same time, "we aren't fighting, Daddy." "Go get the dictionary, bud," Daddy said to me, "it's on the shelf above the phone," but I knew where the dictionary was. They got in arguments like that a lot.

When I came back I tried to pass it down to Daddy, only Uncle Sammy nabbed it first and started flipping pages. "I hate to tell you, Jimbo, I *know* I'm right. Abstemious was one of our vocabulary words." He meant the ones he and Daddy had written out on index cards when they were young. They'd kept them in a shoe box on the closet shelf upstairs, and Grody quizzed them all the time so they'd grow up to have a good vocabulary.

"Speaking of which, Sam," Daddy said, "what happened to that shoe box? The last time I checked, it had mysteriously disappeared." Uncle Sammy shrugged. "Gee, Jimbo, I have no idea." "It's in your locker up in Norfolk, Uncle Sam," I said, "I saw it when we came to visit." Uncle Sammy smiled at me. "It is? I guess I forgot I put it there." "Yeah, well, I'd like it back," said Daddy, and Uncle Sammy said, "no way, it's mine."

"All else aside," said Grody, "I think Sam is right about the definition." Daddy laughed. "Gee, Mother, who could have predicted you'd side with him?" "You know that isn't true, Jimmy," she said, "it just isn't. You were the apple of my eye, son, always—not that I loved Sam and Dolly any less, Lord knows that isn't true, but a mother's first is always special, as I'm sure May knows herself."

For a second Daddy's face looked empty and his lips got kind of trembly like he'd lost the heart to fight.

Then Grody said, "but you mustn't overlook the fact that Sammy went to Duke, Jimmy." Daddy's mouth came open and he stared at Mama and then back to Grody. A grin spread on his face like he couldn't believe what he was hearing. "So what, Mother? I mean, so what? I went to Carolina." "Well, of course there's nothing *wrong* with UNC, Jimmy," Grody said, "it has a perfectly respectable reputation in our part of the country, but on a national level Duke is regarded as superior. Of course, with your marks and excellence in sports you could easily have gotten into Duke and probably won a scholarship, but that's water over the dam by now."

"Found it," Uncle Sammy said and looked up smiling, his finger in the book. " '*Abstemious*,' " he read, " 'sparing or moderate in eating and drinking; temperate in diet; characterized by abstinence . . .' Hey, Jimbo, I don't seem to see a single word in here about cheap or niggardly. Want to look?" "No thanks, Sammy," Daddy said, "you hold on to it," and Uncle Sammy laughed. He had that bright lit-up look by then like this was royal fun. "Hey, here's another good one," he said, " '*absterge*'? You should remember that from med school, Jimbo: 'to purge or clean by wiping.' " "While you're at it, Sammy, look one up for me," said Daddy, "*prig*, p-r-i-g." Uncle Sam just grinned and slapped the dictionary shut. "*That* card was one of yours."

Right that second I wished we could leave, and not just Grody's house. I would of liked to move away from Killdeer altogether to some other town like Mama always said we should. Daddy was the one who wouldn't go. I don't know why—I guess he would of missed them all too much.

You wouldn't think that it could get much worse, but after Grody handed out the presents—that year Dad and Uncle Sammy got the robes and me and Reed got slippers—Mama said, "you haven't opened any of your gifts, Mother Madden. Boys, take Grody's package to her."

"Law'!" said Grody, acting real surprised, "aren't you the sweetest things! You shouldn't have bought me anything, May, truly not—having you here is present enough. I do hope you didn't spend a lot on it." Reed was standing by with idle hands, waiting to be called to action, only Grody liked to tear away the wrap herself. She removed the ribbon extra careful and laid it by before she got into the box and started folding back the tissue. All of a sudden she fell quiet, staring down into her lap like she was just too pleased for words or else could not quite figure what she had. "Is it a *doll?*" she asked, and Mama said, real hopeful, "no, ma'am, Grody, it's an angel for your tree," and Grody blinked and fell to studying it again.

I was holding my breath, boy, I can tell you, so was everybody in that room. Finally she let out with, "well, isn't it pretty," and I breathed a sigh that spelled relief. Except when Grody looked up, she had that expression like her coffee cream had turned. "What a shame I'll only be able to use it for two weeks each year." Mama's face just dropped. "If you don't like it, Mother Madden, I'd be more than happy to exchange it." "Oh, no, dear, it's fine," said Grody, "you were sweet to think of me at all." She didn't even bother taking the angel out to show, just tucked the bow inside to use next year on someone else and put the top back on the box. I looked at Mama, knowing how hard it had been for her to spend that money, and she was smiling like she no longer cared.

By then Reed was tired and acting up, wanting to be held in Daddy's lap. When Daddy finally tried to put him down, Reed busted out in tears. "I know what will put the smile back on my sweet boy's face," Grody said, "the other day I went up in the attic and you'll never guess what Grody found . . ."

Reed wiped his sleeve across his runny nose. "What?" "I'll *show* you what," said Grody. She went upstairs and came back with a old-timey cookie tin with a picture of a horse-drawn sleigh on top and something rattling inside. "Come over here and sit with me," she said, and Reed climbed in her lap and helped her pry the lid up—the tin was filled with marbles, every size and color.

Reed didn't look all that impressed with marbles, but Grody said, "do you know whose these were?" and you could tell he started falling for it then. "Nuh-uh, Grody, who?" "I'll tell you whose," she said, "these were your daddy's and your Uncle Sam's when they were just about your age. And, Reed, they were a pair of jaybirds, let me tell you—those two were just the worst!" Reed grinned real wide and said, "what did Daddy do, Grody?" "I'll tell you what," she said, "that old so-and-so won more marbles than anybody else in his whole school, and, Law', he was so proud of them. He kept them in this tin I gave him and wouldn't let another soul touch them. And I bet, I just *bet*, if you ask really nicely, he might show you how to play."

Reed looked across at Daddy, who had this kind of soft expression on his face, and Daddy said, "come here, rascal." They got down on the floor and Daddy showed him all the different kinds and what the name of each one was. Then Uncle Sammy winked at me and we challenged them and had a game of it. That was the first and only time I played marbles in my life because it was a caveman game no kids liked anymore, except I have to tell you it was cooler than you would of thought.

Finally we were having fun but it was starting to get dark outside and time to go. So we broke off and put the marbles back and got our coats and started kissing everyone goodbye and saying thanks again. But when we got out to the porch I happened to look down and Reed had Mr. Rex in one arm and that tin of marbles in the other like he'd just decided they were his and didn't think a thing about it. Grody saw them, too, and it was like some big black cloud went sailing through the sky and threw the shadow on her face.

"Reed, dear, leave the marbles here with Grody," she said, "you can play with them again next time you come." Reed looked up at her with those brown eyes of his like Mama's and his lips began to quiver. "Why don't we just take them home with us, Mother?" Daddy said, "they were mine after all, and nothing's going to happen to them." "They were Sam's, too, Jimmy," Grody said, "don't forget that. And one day he'll have children of his own." "Then let's let Reed and Joey use them till he does," Daddy said, "how about it, Sammy?" and Uncle Sam said, "sure, okay, no problem, Jimbo."

Grody hesitated and you could see the wheels begin to turn like she was struggling to make her mind up what was right. "They have so many toys at home already, Jimmy, more, Lord knows, than any of you children ever had. I just don't think it's right to spoil them so. They need to learn they can't have everything they want if they're to be prepared for life." "They're children, Mother," Daddy said, "can't they wait a while?"

Grody sighed and got down on one knee with Reed. "I'll tell you what, we'll make a compromise," she said, "you show me you're a big boy with nice manners and say, 'Thank you, Grand-mo-ther,' and I'll let you pick your favorite one out of the box. We'll leave the others here so you'll have something fun to do next time you come. Isn't that a good idea?"

Reed looked like he wasn't sure if there might be some trick to it, because when you're a little kid it's kind of hard to figure why it's good to only get one marble when you could of had a boxful. I was telling him, *don't say it, Reed, don't let her make you, it's a trick*, not out loud but in my thoughts I was. Because I remembered too many other times when it was me and I gave in and did something I later wished I hadn't. Sometimes I'd wish I could give back every single pair of slippers and every slice of pound cake and everything Grody ever gave me so she wouldn't have it left to trap me anymore.

But I will give Reed credit. He was pretty cool for a kid his age and not as dumb as you might think. "They aren't yours, they're Daddy's," he told Grody with his lip stuck out that stubborn way he had, and Grody said, "Law', who's acting like a little-bitty baby now?" and Reed said, "you!" Grody climbed up off her knee and said, "you see, that's exactly what I mean and why I didn't want him to have them in the first place."

Reed saw he wasn't going to get them and began to bawl, and Mama took his hand. "Come on, darling, let's go home," she said and picked him up and didn't even say goodbye as they went down the steps.

"Well, he must be tired, poor thing," said Grody. "You'll re-member your manners and be a big boy next time," she called after them, but Reed glared at her with his thumb stuck in his mouth down to the bottom knuckle.

"Goodbye, Mother. Merry Christmas," Daddy said and kissed her cheek, and I did, too. He put his arm around my shoulder and we walked to the Country Squire, and just as we were pulling out,

Grody came back on the porch and waved at us to stop. She ran across the grass and motioned us to roll the window down.

"Here," she said, a little out of breath as she leaned in. When she opened her fist there were two marbles in it. "It's been such a nice Christmas I can't stand for anyone to go home mad." She offered them to Reed, but his mind was made up then. He wouldn't even touch them. "You don't want to hurt your Grody's feelings, do you?" she asked, kind of pitiful, and I could tell Reed was about to cave in over that. "Here, Grody, let me have them," I said, "I'll give them to him later."

Reed glared at me on that like I'd gone against him, too dumb to see that I was really on his side. "Oh, Joey, dear," Grody said, "you remind me so much of your Daddy when he was your age"—she seemed sad when she said that.

As Daddy pulled out onto Raleigh Road, I looked back and saw her standing by the lightpost, waving. No one noticed her but me and I didn't bother waving back because I knew it was too dark already and she wouldn't see me. But in the lamplight I saw Grody —the grass around her feet was all lit up and glittering with frost. I stared down at those two marbles in my hand and noticed what they were—not shooters, which Daddy told us were the best, or puries, which I liked the second, but a pair of cat's eyes glowing in the dark.

"Damn, I could use a cigarette," said Daddy as he turned toward Ruin Creek, grinning at Mama like the weight was lifted off and he was glad to leave. She went for her purse to give him a Pall Mall, but he said, "pop the glove box, mine are in there," and punched the lighter in.

"Don't you think it's just a little bit ridiculous, Jimmy," she said, handing him his pack, "us not smoking there and pretending we don't when she knows full well we do?" and Daddy said, "we don't go that often, May, it's not that big a deal." Mama gazed off through the windshield for a minute with her arms across her stomach. "Well, it is to me." The lighter popped, and no one said a word.

"Come on, May, it wasn't that bad, was it?" Daddy asked her as he lit his Lucky and rolled the window down a crack. He held the lighter out for her, but Mama just stared at him while the orange eye went cold, like maybe he was joking. Only I don't think he was. It wasn't the same for Daddy as it was for us, maybe because he was more used to it from living there so many years when he was young.

"Yes, Jimmy, yes it was," said Mama, "it was every bit that bad, and I have to tell you, I never plan to spend another holiday like that again, never. I can't do it and I won't."

"Look, May, if it was the angel thing," he said, "take my word, next year this time she'll have it right up on her tree and brag to all her friends—you know how she is." "I don't care, Jimmy, I don't care what she does with it," Mama said, "I've never been so hurt in my whole life."

Daddy's face began to change like that dark cloud had passed him, too. "What exactly do you want, May?" he asked, "Mother said she liked it, didn't she?" and Mama said, "yes, and 'what a shame I'll only be able to use it two weeks a year,'" and it was a pretty good imitation Mama did, but Daddy didn't smile.

Mama blew her smoke up to the roof in one big puff. "Every single time she says something halfway nice to you she just can't stand herself until she runs behind and tears it all to pieces. I've just had it, Jimmy, had it up to here."

A blast of freezing air washed in as she tossed out her cigarette. "I'll tell you why poor Sammy sleeps late every Christmas. He's just trying to put off waking up and going down there to that stingy little tree to get a broken heart again."

Daddy's grin was all caved in by then. "It's not exactly as if your parents are perfect either, May." His voice was quiet, but it made the hairs prick up behind my neck. "Well, maybe not," said Mama with a little laugh, "but at least they aren't cheapskates." Daddy said, "yeah, well at least my daddy's not a drunk."

The back of Mama's neck turned red—I could see it by the streetlights as we passed—and when she spoke her voice was shaking. "If it weren't for Daddy we wouldn't have a roof over our heads." "That's right, we wouldn't," Daddy said, "and your family's better than mine, and I'm not good enough for you—isn't that what it always comes down to?"

"You said it, not me," she answered, almost whispering, and Daddy looked like she had slapped his face.

"I guess you should have married Sumner when you had the chance, huh, May? You could have had that big church wedding at Saint Paul's in front of the Colonial Dames and all the assembled hosts." "If anybody wishes that, it's you," said Mama, and Daddy laughed, if you could call it that.

Only then did she turn toward him. "I'm serious," she said, "that way you'd be off the hook, you wouldn't have to think of anybody but yourself. On the other hand, having a family never seemed to make much difference when it came to that."

Daddy put his foot down on the accelerator and the broken yellow line began to blur into a single one, shooting underneath the hood.

"Jimmy, slow the car down," Mama said. "Jimmy, *please.*" Daddy didn't answer, he just took us faster down that icy road.

# TEN

## May

Sumner had nothing to do with it.

For eleven years I'd stayed at home and cooked Jimmy's meals and kept his house and raised our boys, living in the house my parents gave us and taking handouts from Daddy every other month to meet our bills. With Reed finally off in nursery school I didn't want to be there anymore, out in the back yard with Elise taking laundry off the line and trading recipes. It wasn't that I wanted another life from ours but just to open up the one we had, and not just for me, but for all of us, Jimmy, too, though mostly, yes, for me.

I can say that now. Back then it seemed the height of selfishness —wanting something, not for Reed and Joey as their mother, not for Jimmy as his wife, but for myself. If I'd had my choice, I would have gone back to finish school, but we'd left Chapel Hill because of Jimmy and once he settled in with Daddy at the warehouse he didn't

want to leave that either, though Lord knows I'd have done anything this side of murder to get us out of Killdeer, and don't put
murder past me either. If Jimmy had said he wanted to go pan for
gold in the Yukon, I'd have been the first to pack the mule. I'd never
wanted to come back—I knew how it would be right there with both
families breathing down our necks—but men think things like that
are small potatoes and never seem to realize the details are what
make up your life.

Jimmy once told me if I'd really wanted to finish college I could
have found a way, and maybe he was right. I could have divorced
him and left Joey and Reed at Mama's all day for Dee to watch and
feed while I made that hour commute each way and went to class
and rushed back home to make their dinner, cleaning the house and
doing schoolwork in my leisure time, for kicks . . . short of that, I
don't know how I could have managed. School wasn't in the cards,
so I took what was there.

And what was there was Junior League and PTA and Joey's
Scouts; what was there was the Altar Guild at Saint Paul's and my
bridge and garden clubs and doing volunteer work at the hospital. In
Great Books, I read *Anna Karenina* with a group of wives who toler-
ated Tolstoy only for the sake of Culture with a capital C, but in
their hearts felt Anna got exactly what she asked for, wanting too
much out of life and fool enough to think that love was how you got
it. I wept like a baby when she threw herself under that train, and I
wanted to rewrite the ending. It never occurred to me that if Anna
had married Vronsky it might have turned out just as bad. No book
taught me that—I found it out in my own life.

Colonial Dames was one more item in the list, and, yes, it made
me proud when I was asked to join. I wanted Jimmy to be proud for
me as well and was hurt that he wasn't. When he actively stood in
my way, or tried to, I was devastated. Then I just got mad.

When I wanted to hire Otelia you'd have thought I'd asked for
the crown jewels. Eighteen dollars—that's all it cost for three full
mornings—and almost everyone we knew had someone in. "I just
don't see why I should pay someone to take care of our family while
you go practice charity on the indigent hordes in Bagtown," Jimmy
said in that ironic tone of his—*indigent hordes*—as if I'd done any-

thing else since the day I'd married him, "not to mention how you expect me to afford it on what your daddy pays."

That was something else he was always throwing in my face, as though Daddy and I were in cahoots against him when Daddy gave him that job out of the goodness of his heart to keep us from going under after we left Chapel Hill. Never in his wildest dreams, I think, did Daddy expect Jimmy to stay at the Bonanza—I certainly didn't —but Daddy accepted it like a gentleman and never said a word and set out to teach Jimmy the business from the ground up, the same way he'd learned it himself. He paid Jimmy just as much as Otis Frye, who'd been there twenty years and knew the business inside out. But Jimmy didn't want to learn it Daddy's way; he wanted to jump overnight from A to P or Q and was set to run things in a year. Daddy told him it wasn't going to be that way, that at a warehouse there can only be one chief and everybody else has to be an Indian.

Jimmy was always coming up with these fool schemes, like air-conditioning the place—with those twenty-five-foot ceilings, too, and no tobacco warehouse in the world had ever been. Then why not be the first? Jimmy asked. When that old abandoned mill in Lawford Corner came on the market Jimmy wanted Daddy to buy it and set up a second warehouse, the Bonanza Too—that was Jimmy's idea for a name. Of course, he'd run the place for Daddy and make more money than Daddy ever even thought about—we could double our profit, Jimmy said, but Daddy said all we would double was our overhead. The Bonanza Too would draw exactly the same farmers who came to the Bonanza One already, he told Jimmy, only they wouldn't have to drive so far, which would cost him fifty thousand dollars to save a hundred farmers fifty cents in gas.

Well, then, why not buy a truck, Jimmy said, and start a service going out to all the farms to pick up the cured tobacco and haul it in to auction so the farmers wouldn't have to make the trip? But Daddy said, "Jimmy, son, what are you thinking of? The farmers *like* to come to town." It was the one excuse they had, he said, to take a day off work to stock up at the grocery store and stop by the Ford dealer and kick the tires on the new trucks or see a picture show at the Ambassador.

And even if Daddy was too conservative sometimes, it was still his business, wasn't it? That was the thing—instead of going out where he could have put that creativity of his to use, Jimmy stayed where he couldn't and just got mad. The truth is, I think he preferred staying mad, believing everyone was against him, to going out and actually succeeding. *If the way Daddy runs the warehouse doesn't suit you, then stop clinging to his coattails. Go out on your own and be a man*—that's what was in my heart to say to him, but of course I didn't. I probably didn't even feel it then—it's hard to separate the feelings of that time from what came later on . . . I don't think I was angry so much as frustrated and confused. I still loved Jimmy and wanted more than anything to help him, but I just didn't understand the problem.

After Chapel Hill, the understanding had been that Jimmy would work at Daddy's while he looked for something better, but the something better never materialized—the looking hardly started. Twice, Uncle Mark went to the trouble to set up an interview with his editor at the *New York Times*—Jimmy always said he wanted to be a writer. The first time, Jimmy got lost and came an hour late; the second, he got tanked on dry martinis at some fancy restaurant and regaled the group with stories. Uncle Mark said Jimmy had made a hit, but I guess the *Times* wasn't looking for a raconteur, and in any case Jimmy never followed up.

What made it so hard to understand was that in high school he'd just torn the town apart, in sports and school and everything. As an undergrad at Chapel Hill he made Phi Beta Kappa, and even Daddy, who had as good a business head as any in Killdeer, said he'd never met anyone more talented or quicker than Jimmy—you only had to tell him something once. And that imagination of his was just a wonder. To this day I still believe he could have been the president of the New York Stock Exchange or anything else he'd set his mind to. But he was like a runner who came blazing off the start and lapped the field in the first quarter-mile, then something always happened, he'd lose heart or maybe just get bored—more likely he'd start thinking, *why do I have to run this race? what's the point of races? who's the proving for?* The answer he kept coming up with was *for them*, meaning everyone except himself, which was the wrong answer. Jimmy would get resentful, working up to being mad as hell—

at me, at Daddy, at anyone who had the slightest expectation of him
—and all that talent and imagination would get turned into finding
some creative way to blow things up.

From the moment we got married it was as though he turned
into a different person, and we stumbled from catastrophe to catastrophe, a new one every year, each worse than the one before. Many
nights I lay awake wondering if it was my fault—Lilith lost no op-
portunity to make her opinion clear—fretting over what to do to
help him, praying for him and for us. But I've seen it happen too
many times now—marriage is like alcohol, it doesn't change people,
it just brings out what's already there . . . and one day, after everything you've done and all the help you've tried to give, you wake up
and realize nothing's changed and nothing's going to. Things have
got so bad you've lost the luxury of wondering who's to blame and
then you have to learn to help who can be helped—your children
and yourself.

That was it for me, you see . . . that's why I joined the Dames
and Altar Guild and was a candy-striper at the hospital and broke
my nails teaching Joey and the other Cub Scouts in my den to saw
out patterns for their daddies' Christmas tie racks. I made all of it
my job so that we might have something and be someone in our
town, not just May Tilley, Will and Zelle's little girl, and that Madden boy, her husband. There was something driving me, what, I
never stopped to ask. Maybe it was the old debutante trying to
remember who she was, in Mama's phrase. That's what Jimmy
thought, I guess, that I was still attempting to make up for a fall
from grace that everyone but me had long ago forgotten. But it was
less a matter of remembering who I was, I think, than trying to find
out for the first time. It's hard when someone blocks that path for
you, especially when that person is your husband.

To Jimmy, my pride and ambition were like red flags to a bull.
He took them as a personal reproach and punished me. "My mother
never had a maid," he said, "or needed one either, for that matter."
*Why should she when she had four foot servants—you and Sam and Dolly
and your daddy—at her beck and call?* That's what I would have liked
to say to him, but I didn't. I was still at the stage of thinking and
hadn't yet come to saying, which is the beginning of the end. But I

went out and hired Otelia, you can bet on that. I used the money
Granny Tilley left, and if Jimmy and his mother thought it was
because I was too proud to scrub a floor, then let them think.

I don't know what I'd have done without her—stayed home and
scrubbed the enamel off the sink and lost my mind, I guess. That's
what Jimmy really seemed to want, for me to hunker down with him
and be content just getting by. I guess deep down it shamed him that
I wanted more than he was willing to provide. Instead of doing
something on his end, he just belittled and tore down what I tried to
do on mine, and that's what hurt and wore me down the most—
always getting knocked for what I tried to do, as if it were nothing
more than vanity and pretense. There was something in Jimmy that
had to scuttle the boat to test if you'd stay aboard with him and go
down on the ship. God forbid that he should ever succeed at anything—then it was the success you loved, not him. So he made a
career of making sure he never did succeed.

To me it came as a complete surprise. I'd married a boy I loved
and thought I knew and lived with him not quite a year, and then
one day—I mean literally one day—I woke up and he'd turned into
someone I didn't know at all. At first I thought it was a fluke and if I
blinked my eyes he'd change back to who he'd been before. I waited
years for him to show, and there were glimpses, many—when Jimmy
was happy he came out again, but Jimmy was happy less and less as
time went on, and that boy just kept drifting farther and farther off
till I could hardly remember what he looked like, the way it is when
someone dies . . .

Where it started was in Chapel Hill, late spring of that first year,
Joey not even two months old. We were living on Ransom Street at
Mrs. Sneed's, the tiniest little apartment you ever saw, out back over
her garage with outside steps I later lived to curse, going up and
down them twenty times a day with Joey in that stroller, till one
time Jimmy saw me struggling and said, "why don't you leave the
stroller at the bottom?" So help me, it had never even occurred to
me. "You're a genius," I told him and kissed him on the lips. Jimmy
grinned as if the information came as no surprise.

We probably should have looked for something bigger, but it
was so late by the time we started, and we both fell in love with it for

different reasons. Jimmy took one look at the basketball goal in the driveway and said, "I'm sold," without ever going in. For me what did it was the garden. Mrs. Sneed had the most beautiful old English shrub roses I've ever seen; the afternoon we went to look, the perfume from her Empress Josephines filled the whole apartment.

I guess neither of us was very practical, but we were happy there at first—for a long time, really. With all of Granny Tilley's furniture, which Daddy had Otis and the others haul out of storage and drive up in the truck, there was barely room to walk. We had that old Duncan Phyfe sofa with the same chintz I remembered from Granny's living room when I was small, and her Charleston sideboard, and that old harvest table from Rose Hill, so big I could leave out our place settings at one end while Jimmy kept his books spread at the other; in a pinch, I could change Joey in the middle without disturbing the arrangement. To make it fit we had to tuck the long side of the table under the roof slope where the dormers were. Every time Jimmy stood up he banged his head—there was a hole in the plaster in one spot, so help me there was.

One Saturday Elise and Charlie Dawes were over and we were drinking Rob Roys or some godforsaken foolishness Jimmy mixed up out of that *Bartender Bible* he was so fond of. Jimmy was leaning over the recipe, reading the proportions off his finger, and when he stood up to reach for the vermouth he bumped his head again for the umpteenth time and started cussing how he always would. "Are you all right, sugar?" I asked, doing everything I could to keep from laughing, and he stormed outside and disappeared for twenty minutes. When he came back he had a bag from Hudgins Hardware under his arm, and he took out a quart of orange paint and four brushes and passed them out to everyone. LOW CLEARANCE, he wrote and drew a warning stripe. We were all just drunk enough to think it was the funniest thing we'd ever seen and pitched in with him. Someone wrote CAUTION, and another, DANGER. Jimmy started in to write NO HEAD ROOM, but only got the NO HEAD part when he looked at Charlie and they started chuckling that dirty way men do. So help me I had no idea what it meant till Elise told me in the kitchen. I came out and punched his arm. "You do, too," I said, and they laughed twice as hard at me.

We had lots of happy times like that, though it makes me woozy now to think about how much we drank, and nine times out of ten Jimmy was the spark—he was so much fun and everybody just adored him, especially me. As I look back, it seems more like a two-week blowout at the beach than grown-up married life, only it went on for most of that whole year. When I asked, Jimmy always told me things were going fine in school, though I remember sometimes how his eyes would glaze over his books, especially that spring after I came home from the hospital with Joey—that's when we began to feel the pinch of that apartment.

I would come into the den from putting Joey down and he'd be looking down into the garden, smoking a Lucky. I'd ask if he'd like coffee or if I could quiz him on the chapter he'd been reading, and he'd smile at me and say, "maybe later . . . I think I'm going to take a walk." When I straightened up behind him, I'd find it was T. S. Eliot he'd been reading—it was open over his biochemistry text—that one about the footsteps and the garden and the children hidden in the leaves.

Most nights he'd walk around the block and come straight back, but sometimes he'd be gone for hours and come in tight and tell me he'd been at the library, even though he'd left his books at home and smelled of beer and cigarettes. I knew where he'd been: up at the KA house, where he was still a big shot with the underclassmen. What I remember most was the thump of that basketball in the driveway, the way the floor would tremble when it hit the rim. He'd go at it for hours sometimes, even in the bitter cold, late into the night while I tried to sleep. I thought it was just the way he blew off steam, but then he'd oversleep and miss his lab.

Perhaps I should have known, but basically I thought he was so smart he didn't have to study all the time. The way he had of putting things seemed brilliant to me. Daddy, Sumner, Uncle Johnny, all the men and boys I'd grown up around, none of them talked or thought the way Jimmy did; they were like rye grass in the yard, one blade no different from the next, and here where you least expected it, where it wasn't supposed to be, Jimmy sprang up like a bird of paradise, another species altogether.

When he read to me, some poem or passage from a book, it

wasn't how we'd learned to read at Ascension, putting a little check mark in the margin to show we'd finished that one and *knew* it now. Jimmy had a feeling and a gift for language, not just words but for the life words tell, and I thought the gift was part of that something more he had, additional to all the normal things you take for granted in a person. I didn't see then that Jimmy's gift and feeling ran some way counter to, and came at the expense of, all the rest . . .

That's why it seemed okay to me if we went out from time to time, and, yes, I liked it. I liked going to the Little Red Schoolhouse on Saturday night to hear the Hot Nuts or to the Ugly Club where they made you stick your head through that toilet seat before they let you in. I know Mama got on him sometimes about making sure he took me out enough, but Jimmy liked it, too. I don't think there was ever a time I took him from his books when he was studying . . . if anything, I did the opposite. I tried every way I knew to encourage him and give him a comfortable, quiet place to work.

I did all the housework and had dinner on the table every night when he came in, not to mention the hours and hours I spent with Joey in the rocking chair in the bedroom, shushing him in whispers so Jimmy could have the living room to read in peace. If Joey cried at night I was always the one who got up, but I didn't mind any of that, it seemed to be my part, just as the studying was Jimmy's.

I even helped with his assignments—Jimmy hated drawing so I did his anatomy studies for him. I spent hours on those assignments and was so proud when they came back A's—I think they were the only ones he got all term. I could have been a doctor, I know I could, but there was just one chance between the two of us, and Jimmy was the one who got it. Not that I grudged it, I just never dreamed he was in trouble, not so bad and deep as it had gotten. Maybe I didn't want to know—that's probably true—but then who ever does? But if he'd only let me know, if I'd been prepared even a little, at least we could have hoped and worried as a couple. As it was, it came out of the blue—he hid it from me as though I was his judge and enemy, and made it hard for me to act in any other way . . . and, yes, I did feel cheated, of the truth he owed me as his wife. One day, one night—it came that fast.

It was right after his finals. One morning there was an official-looking letter in the mailbox. It was addressed to Jimmy, so I didn't open it, though I saw it was from the dean. When Jimmy came in he read it at the table, then folded it and put it in his pocket. "What's up?" I asked, and he said, "nothing, just a conference. What's for dinner?" He was so casual I figured it was probably something every student had at end of term. "Know what I'm in the mood for?" "No," I said, "but something tells me it's not love." Jimmy laughed. "You're closer than you think, though: a martini. Have you seen my strainer?"

By then I'd begun to notice how, after spending the money for Tanqueray and good vermouth, he'd buy those salad pieces instead of whole olives at the grocery store to save a nickel. That Madden thrift just seemed peculiar then, even amusing in a way, but later on it made me cringe, the way Jimmy would go up to Chapel Hill and come home with ten or fifteen record albums and a case of good French wine and then set a rule that no one in the house could go over three minutes in the shower and had to turn the spray to fine to save hot water.

Jimmy drank a lot that night at dinner and actually seemed quite happy, as if the load of the semester was finally off his back. He dropped off on the sofa, and I put a blanket over him, expecting to find him in bed beside me the next morning. When I got up he was still huddled where I'd left him, with the pillow in his stomach. Relaxed in sleep, his face looked young, the shadows beneath his eyes like those black smudges the boys in football used to paint to play beneath the lights, something you could wash right off.

When I started coffee he woke up and spent a long time dressing. I ironed his shirt and then took Joey in the living room to stay out of his way and watched him going back and forth past the bedroom door wrapped in a towel with a swatch of toilet paper pasted to his Adam's apple with a dot of blood. He brushed his blazer and shined his shoes and knotted his tie several times at the mirror till he liked the knot. Watching all the care he took, I got a feeling, just a hint of something like the coolness of a shadow passing over you for a split second.

"You look nice," I told him when he came out, and he said, "thanks," and smiled, leaning over me to kiss Joey's head. "How did he do last night?" "He only woke up once," I said. "See? If we can get him on a schedule it'll be easier on everyone, especially you." I smiled back. "You may be right." "I am," said Jimmy, all wise and fatherly. "Will you be home for lunch?" "Should be," he said, walking out. "I'll call you."

I listened to him start the car, then opened my nightgown and began to nurse. "We aren't going to put you on any mean old schedule, are we?" I said, "no, we aren't," because it just seemed wrong to me, another kind of stinginess and worse than money. I couldn't bear to leave Joey in his crib to cry the way Jimmy said we should— it was harder listening to that than to get up and give him what he wanted. And it struck me as odd, the way Jimmy had suddenly developed such strong and definite opinions about child rearing—I don't think he had a clue where they came from, but it was clear enough to me. I looked at Lilith—because, of course, that's who I mean— and figured my rule of thumb should be: whatever she says, do the opposite. For that matter, my own mama, too. But I still sometimes felt as though Jimmy wanted to restrict what was between us, Joey and me, because he couldn't share in it, and maybe I even provoked that feeling, though I never meant to.

Sometimes I'd be nursing Joey in the bedroom and look up to find Jimmy in the doorway, and I'd actually blush, as though I'd been caught at something. How long he'd been there I had no idea —I'd been so deeply into it I hadn't even heard him enter—but there'd be this expression on Jimmy's face—not jealousy or anger, but some kind of lost and sad surprise, as though he would have liked to be as close to me and Joey as we were to each other in that moment. But it's just not possible, I think, not between adults; there has to be a child to bring it out.

I was so amazed by the experience myself, the feeling that came over me sometimes in that rocking chair with Joey, a perfect awareness of each other that had no words and was more complete without them . . . there were moments, truly, when I knew him and could feel his essential soul, not as a baby but a presence whose force was equal to my own, a complete little person with a sense of playfulness and humor who felt joy and sadness and knew instantly when

I closed off to him or tried any of those little tricks you sometimes use with children to pretend you're there when really you're distracted, off in your own world. It was absolutely thrilling to me—and even that word doesn't capture it. How do you explain it to your husband? Even in my closest moments with Jimmy, even making love, it was as though we were enclosed in two soap bubbles . . . we could see and hear and touch each other but always through that skin of shimmery soap, so sheer you never even know it's there till suddenly, *poof!* it's gone, and where it was for me was in that rocking chair.

I can't explain, but it was more than just a curious sensation—it was as though the whole earth moved, and I think I'd been waiting since that day at Collie Pond for it to move, only I'd expected it to be through Jimmy—that was the surprise. Perhaps that was my sin against Jimmy, but can you love a child too much? Can you control love, where it goes? I think I never wanted to.

I was off in a new world I couldn't share with him, just as Jimmy couldn't share his world with me. Mine had opened up one morning two months earlier while I was washing the breakfast dishes at the sink. I felt something pouring along my thighs and looked down at my feet, thinking I'd sloshed dishwater, till the contraction reached inside me like a hand and clutched my insides in a fist. When I straightened up, the glass I'd been rinsing was overflowing at the tap, and the water had a pinkish tint. I'd squeezed so hard, I'd broken a big piece off the rim and cut my thumb. *Get a Band-Aid*, I thought, moving toward the bathroom. *Change your dress and underwear, call Dr. Cole, what class is Jimmy in, call Mama, should I drive or call a cab, where are the keys?* A whole long list of things to do popped off like firecrackers on a string, till I tore the Band-Aid wrapper with my teeth and saw my face reflected in the mirror. It was her again, the girl I'd seen that day at Collie Pond gazing up at me out of the water.

*Stop it, just stop it,* I thought, realizing I was doing exactly what I hated so much in Mama, making everything a list, which was supposed to organize your time to free you for the things that really matter, except it never happened. What happened was that every time you checked one item off the back end of the list, a new one got added to the front, till life was nothing but that checklist and you were on a treadmill running to stand still. I didn't want to live that way, but mostly that was what I did. It made me sad to know—but I could change, I made a resolution to—and then the next contraction hit and everything went up in smoke.

I went down on the toilet doubled over, clutching my stomach in both hands, rocking back and forth and groaning in a voice that didn't sound like mine. The pain was like entering a cave guarded by a monster who said, *look me in the eyes and bear it and you'll live; if you look away, you die . . .*

When it passed, I came out in a stillness that was rich and deep and wonderful—the list had stopped. A dogwood branch pressed a crowd of petals against the window screen. I could see a bee crawling at the center of a blossom, so slowly it looked drugged. From Sunday school, I remembered how the pink parts of the petal are where the nails were driven into Jesus' hands. The throbbing from my cut seemed to tie me to that story in a way that wasn't sacrilegious, but commonplace, commonplace in the most wonderful way. And then it hit me—*this is what it is to feel God's love*—not a sweet and tender thing, but a condition of unbearable rigor just like my contraction. Everyone alive had felt it, that was what the crucifixion story meant. Jesus wasn't an exception, he was an example of how that love must be received, and what it promises: dying is the price you have to pay for resurrection and eternal life.

I felt I was dying then, dying to give birth not only to my baby, but to some part of me I'd always known was there behind the mask of every day. I could feel her coming forth like the girl out of the pond, my reflection stepping from the mirror, real, and from now on, I thought, life would always feel as important as it did that moment.

Raw and quivery, I got up and put my lipstick on and took another minute to find the pearl earrings Jimmy had given me for Christmas. I wrote a note for him and left it on the table, and then I walked out to the car. At the bottom of Columbia the light turned red and I knew I wasn't going to make it. I mashed the brakes and dropped my head against the wheel, hugging tight, and barely realized I'd hit the horn.

The next thing I knew, someone was knocking on the window, an elderly man in glasses with white hair and a neat, short-cropped beard. He helped me slide over in the seat and drove me the remaining distance to Memorial. I was already in the wheelchair being taken in before I thought to thank him and to ask his name, but by the time I turned around he was gone. I used to think perhaps he was an angel—maybe I just wanted one.

All that was still so fresh the morning Jimmy left for his appointment. After I put Joey down to take his nap, I started straightening the apartment, and as I emptied the wastepaper basket by the bedroom dresser I noticed a crumpled ball of paper, which I smoothed open before I realized what it was. "In light of your failing grade in biochemistry . . ." it said. I stood and blinked, and read that phrase over and over, hoping I'd misunderstood. The earth shook one more time; I guess you could say that.

Jimmy didn't show for lunch or call me either. In the beginning, I'd stayed home and stewed when he was late, but then he'd show up, looking innocent, and act surprised when I got mad. He'd try to remember to call, but sometimes he forgot, so that day I didn't think that much about it. I must have read that letter fifty times and tried to think it through. They wouldn't kick you out for a single failing grade, would they? Maybe the conference was to decide how he could make it up over the summer. We'd planned to go down to the beach with Mama, but if we had to stay, that wouldn't be so bad— we could still take a few weekends. I had it all worked out and when Joey woke up from his nap I put him in the stroller and went downtown to Fowler's and bought a pot roast, Jimmy's favorite. I peeled the carrots and the onions and the little new potatoes just the way he liked and thought of how, when he walked through the door at dinnertime, he'd smell it and know I did it specially and it would be easier for him to tell me what he had to tell me and easier for me to take it as I should.

Before I knew it, it was six o'clock. The meat thermometer said it was time to take the roast out of the oven, Joey was crying to be fed and Jimmy still wasn't home. I'd started wondering in a more serious way where he might be—not worrying so much as thinking, damnit, he could be a little more considerate. But I wasn't mad—I decided I would give him half an hour more and *then* get mad. I even checked the kitchen clock to make sure I didn't jump the gun.

# ELEVEN

## Jimmy

May was like her daddy in a lot of ways, good and bad, but mainly in the way they both made themselves indispensable to you by playing a supporting role. That self-effacing quality obscured, for me, the size of her ambition at first, and the role she'd assigned me in fulfilling her agenda. It wasn't so much that May looked to me and my career to give us the position she expected for herself and us— she did, of course, but that's the way it was in 1955, and how much has it really changed? No, for May the problem came when I washed out at medicine. For me, the real mistake wasn't leaving school but ever going in the first place—which leaves, of course, the question why.

It wasn't very complicated. I chose medicine because I wanted to be a writer and my parents told me it was impractical, and they were right, and, being young and unsure of myself, I let their rightness matter and decide. And there was Daddy—med school was my last attempt to reach him. I have to tell you it was sweet, for those few months, to see the proud glow on his face, and Mother's, just as it was sweet to see it there on May's. I guess it's always sweet to live for others—till the day you fail. That's when your vision shifts from all the blue wide-open sky outside your window to the grid of iron bars you've been looking through. My family was a cage I thought I'd finally escaped by marrying May; it turned out I'd only stepped into a different one. Where I learned that lesson was in Chapel Hill.

My failure was something May took personally, as if I'd done it against her, with deliberate intent, and though she seemed to take it like a trouper, deep down her attitude toward me changed. That was when that germ of doubt or distrust, whatever it was, first showed up in her eyes. Till then she'd been inclined to see the best. Now she never looked at me without a question brooding back there in the darkness—*when are you going to let me down again?* That's how the whole med school crisis registered, not as my disappointment but as May's, another item in the debit column I had to make up for.

So why do you stay in the cage? There are lots of reasons, I expect—habit, fear; the best is love. However reluctantly I'd entered it, six months after we were married I was far more deeply in love with May than I had been on our wedding day or even back in the first bloom of dating when there'd been nothing but blue sky above our heads. If someone had given me the chance to go back, I'd have made the choice to marry her all over.

Joey was no small part of it. To be honest, I doubt I'd given five minutes' thought to being a father, right up through the pregnancy. But when May came home from the hospital with that little bundle wrapped up in her arms, it was an amazing thing. He had this shriveled-up old man's face like one of those Appalachian apple dolls, and his expression seemed to say *no, I won't, goddamnit, and you can't make me*—my sentiments exactly, a chip off the old block. I could hardly look at him without laughing; for a week I walked around with a sort of rictus grin that wouldn't go away. The first or second morning after they came home I remember waking up to this new cry in the apartment, thinking, *what the hell is that?*

May was so exhausted from her labor, she didn't even stir, so I took him from his crib and walked with him down the steps into the yard. It was barely light, and I remember the wetness of the grass on my bare feet, and the smell—it had just been cut. There wasn't a soul on the street. We went into the rose garden and out the back way to Vance Street, and as we came back up the block the paperboy shot by on his Western Flyer like Joe Crowell, Jr., in *Our Town*. I leaned down and smelled Joey's head with its little furze of hair and it was warm and fragrant, the way the American prairie must have seemed to Lewis and Clark when they came over that rise and saw it stretching out a thousand miles in front of them, a whole new world. Standing there, I felt like God with Adam and whispered all the names of things to him, *bird* and *tree* and *grass*, and Joey opened his eyes and gazed at me solemnly for a moment, as if he recognized me. I felt so moved and happy I was close to tears.

I loved them both that way, May and Joey, so how does it get mauled and broken, love like that? Why isn't it enough? I only know that after we left Chapel Hill and went back home to Killdeer, things began to change. An ugly edge I hadn't seen before cropped up in May. Put a couple drinks in her, and suddenly it was *well,* **my** *family this* and **my** *family that*, this sort of bragging. I tried to tell her it was unattractive, but any license I may have had to criticize the Tilleys had been revoked by then; if I said anything, it was because I was an ingrate and cynical by nature. What got to me about it was that when she said "my family," she didn't mean us—she meant her mama and daddy and her grandparents and all the sacred Tilley ancestors.

Of course she didn't want to live in Killdeer—it wasn't my first choice either—but what else were we going to do? Her brilliant idea was that I should go into the Army. The week after everything blew up in Chapel Hill, without a word to me, she went down to the recruiter's office and he gave her some routine about an intelligence posting in Germany—foreign travel, exotic lands. She came home bubbling over, ready to pack the bags. But what to May was castles on the Rhine was only backpacks in the mud to me. No, the Bonanza made a lot more sense, and it was decent of her father to offer me the job, though it was hardly a sinecure. I worked like a galley slave out there, and Will Tilley was no perfect master either.

The whole first season they didn't even let me weigh in a load without Otis looking at the scales over my shoulder, double-checking to make sure I didn't read the numbers wrong. I lifted bales with Reb and Skeeter, neither one of whom had a fifth-grade education, and if it was slow I grabbed a broom and swept the floor. It was a red-letter day when Mr. Will finally let me take the deposits downtown to Carolina Fidelity and hand them over to John Landis—not to a teller, mind you, but to his cousin, the bank president. That's how they did things, the old-fashioned way, the same way they'd learned in the Depression. Part of it was how they treated a young man coming up: they broke you like a horse, not with cruelty, but with drudgery and toil, jealously guarding their prerogatives and doling out even the smallest responsibility the way a miser parts with gold. The idea was to make you, in the end, like them, a Prudent Man, safe and shrewd and careful.

I don't say the system didn't work, I just think there were other systems that might have worked much better. But the only change they had any interest in was what they could put in their pockets, and you can damn well bet they counted it first before they did. Mr. Will and Landis and Kincannon, that whole group—you had to respect what they'd accomplished as a generation, but they were living in the past and it was time to change the guard. The Depression was over, but they'd never gotten out of it, not mentally—to Will Tilley the bank could always be closed tomorrow morning when you went downtown, and I guess what lay back of it was his daddy's suicide, blowing his head off with that shotgun after they lost everything. That's what formed Will Tilley, selling overalls and leather harness traces to farmers across that dusty countertop at the farm supply to support his mother and his sisters through those years. He'd order suits a half-dozen at the time to remind himself he was rich, but he still saved the rubber band off the morning paper because you never knew when you might need it. Mother was the exact same way, but it wasn't for me. For five years I put up with it and never said a word—by then I could have run that place as well as Mr. Will. To him, though, five years was nothing—he sat there in the office sweating bullets till I came back with the deposit slips.

I had ideas for improvements, good ones—advertising, for one. To Will Tilley, advertising was paying ten dollars for a plank pine

bench and then getting Jap McCurdy, who did our signs, to paint
our name on it—and even then Mr. Will would jew him down from
ten dollars to seven-fifty on the labor. He'd stick that bench in front
of the firehouse or the railroad station or some country store and
stop by twice a day to admire it for a week and then forget he'd put
it there.

My thought was radio. In those days you could hardly drive to
Durham or Raleigh without hearing one of the big auto dealers
doing a remote broadcast from the lot, and I wondered why that
wouldn't work for us. Opening day at the Bonanza, we'd get
WKDH–AM in there, hand out a few door prizes, free soda pop,
maybe even have a band and broadcast the whole thing live. It would
bring farmers in for miles around and blow the Top Dollar right out
of the water. And talk about community relations! I set the whole
thing up, even spoke to Elmo Potts, who said he'd give us a color
TV at cost for the grand door prize in exchange for a few plugs on
the air. So then I take the thing to Mr. Will, and what's he say? *If
they want a goddamn circus, let 'em wait till September when the county
fair rolls in.* Of course, the real reason was the money. He figured
come hell or high water he'd sell forty thousand pounds opening day
—why spend that thousand dollars or whatever it was off the top
when it could go straight into his pocket? When I said it would pay
out tenfold in the long run, he said, "well maybe it will, and then
again maybe it won't"—that was his attitude: why fix what ain't
broke and a bird in the hand . . .

There were a thousand things like that. If he'd listened to me
and bought that strip of land in Lawford Corner when they announced they were putting in the interstate, we'd all have made a
fortune. Maybe then even May would have been happy. But Mr.
Will said, "what if they don't fund it at the legisla'cha, and what if
they do and it's ten years from now?" He wouldn't take the risk or
lend me the money to take it—neither would Landis. To them it was
just a wild-hair eager beaver scheme of mine, and they smiled and
nodded wisely and gave me sage advice: *be patient, boy, you don't have
to git there all at once; Rome won't built in a day; it's the little steps that
git you where you're going* . . . Head down, straight over tackle, a
three-yard gain, time after time—that's how they made their money,

and it's how they expected everybody else to do it, too. They missed the boat and made me miss it. That money was a drop in the ocean to Will Tilley—he could have made that loan to me. Hell yes, I owed him a lot, but maybe there was something he owed me.

And that's exactly what I mean—Mr. Will never saw it from my point of view, neither did May, and Miss Zelle, well, you could just forget it. The same thing that happened with the pregnancy happened again with med school. Nobody said, *poor Jimmy*; everybody said, *poor May, she bet on the wrong horse and now it turns out he isn't worth the bullet it would take to shoot him.*

That whole year in Chapel Hill I was struggling in school. To me, biochemistry was like some foreign language—say, Rumanian— that deep down in my heart I couldn't care enough about to learn. I tried to trick myself into staying interested by personalizing it, regarding May's pregnancy, for example, as an effect of cell mitosis, or, when Joey cried to nurse, thinking of the metabolic pathways of glycolysis and the six-carbon ring. As a strategy, it didn't really work. As far as insight into childbirth went, I would have rather spent the two bits for a paperback copy of *The Rainbow* and read what D. H. Lawrence had to say. The plain fact was that I lacked discipline and didn't really know it. I thought discipline was spending hours working on a fadeaway jumper from the baseline, or doing twice what the professor called for on an English assignment. But that was passion—discipline is something else, consistent application to a task you don't enjoy, and to tell the truth I'd never really needed it. To the extent I had, I'd pulled through on luck and a certain level of raw ability. But luck and raw ability aren't enough for first-year biochemistry.

It took me almost half a semester to realize that, and by the time I did, I was already far behind. A D on midterms put the fear in me, and I tried bearing down, but my heart wasn't in it. I couldn't concentrate—those blocks of text roared by like quotations on a ticker tape and only an occasional fact leaped out and stuck. By Christmas —before that, actually—I was having fantasies about graduate school in English.

But there was May . . . From the time we'd started going out, there'd been the assumption that I was going to be a doctor, with the implied corollary that she was going to be a doctor's wife. It had been sweet to improvise with her on the theme of that shared future, soaking up May's encouragement and praise. How would she react if I switched horses now? Rather than risk disappointing her, not to mention her parents and mine, I just plowed back into my books and didn't talk about my problems.

I couldn't hide my first-semester grades from her, though. With everything I'd done I only managed to pull that D to a D+, and looking back, that's really where that edge of doubt crept in. "School *is* going okay, isn't it?" she began to ask—not exactly an invitation to pour out your misgivings. Occasionally I felt I was in the water struggling to keep my head above the surface while May was on shore, wringing her hands, going, "you aren't drowning, are you? Please don't drown . . ." Even if she didn't say it, I saw it in her face, not concern for me, but worry that I might be letting down the team. That really punched my buttons and brought out my worst; it made me want to shout, *why else am I in the water? I dove in after you, that's why*, something I felt only when I was mad. I was getting mad a lot.

May had started nagging me like Mother. I'd come in exhausted and preoccupied with class, hours of homework still to do, and May would want me to remember to take out the trash. "I do everything else, Jimmy. It's your only job," she'd say "why can't you remember?" After Joey was born, things got worse. Along with all the happiness he brought came other things—sleep deprivation, crying jags, irritability. I was coming up on finals then and time was running out. After they came home from the hospital it was next to impossible to study in the apartment.

I spent hours in a carrel at the library. Once I fell asleep and woke up in the middle of the night with the lights off and the doors all locked—for the first few seconds I thought I'd been pronounced dead by mistake and shut up in the mausoleum—I guess you could say I was in an anxious frame of mind. When I'd go home, half the time there'd be no dinner, no hello-how-are-you. She'd say, "did you remember to buy milk?" She'd asked me at breakfast, fourteen hours earlier, and of course I'd forgotten—I'm sure I did so far too often. Then we'd have tears because I didn't care or take an interest in my family, and that would make me want to shout, *why else do you think I'm out there busting my hump?*

Of course, May was exhausted, too, getting up three and four times a night, but she wouldn't listen when I suggested we try to put Joey on a schedule. To her, a schedule was a deprivation, and she couldn't bear depriving him of anything. Why keep telling someone something when they're going to nod as if they agree, then go behind your back and do the opposite? After a while, I stepped aside and let her handle it, and it was my first clear insight into why Daddy had become the way he was. When your participation is regarded as interference and your forbearance as indifference, it doesn't leave you much room to maneuver in. It was hard to go to school all day and then come home to a hard night of that. Sometimes I needed to get out and be alone to think.

That carrel in the library was my place. Occasionally, in the middle of a review, I'd start to daydream, only to come back to reality with a crash landing. There was desperation at the edges, the sense that an all-out effort on finals might not pull it out. Some games are already lost by the third quarter—maybe this was one of them. The scariest thought was that I might have lost the magic— either that, or my previous success had just been luck and now the streak was all played out. And if you've been magical or lucky all your life and one day you wake up and the spell is broken, who are you?

By then we'd gotten to the head and neck section in anatomy lab. Sometimes I'd look at Phlebas—that's what Whit Thomas and I had christened our cadaver, after the drowned sailor in "The Waste Land."

> *Phlebas the Phoenician, a fortnight dead,*
> *Forgot the cry of gulls, and the deep sea swell*
> *And the profit and loss.*
> > *A current under sea*
> *Picked his bones in whispers. As he rose and fell*
> *He passed the stages of his age and youth*
> *Entering the whirlpool.*

I thought about those lines the first time we saw the bodies—a dozen, there must have been—in that tiled basement room with the big chrome double sinks, under the hum of fluorescent lights, submerged in the pool of hazy yellow formalin, all wearing that identical expression, a composure more vacant than serene. As I say, sometimes that spring I'd look at Phlebas, half his face still intact and vaguely human, the other flayed down to the raw gray underpinnings like something out of one of my old *Monster* comics, and that's how I'd feel, too, as if my face was being stripped away. Looking in the mirror I no longer saw the person I'd believed I was last year, and didn't recognize the one I was becoming, which left the question, who was I today?

It was a whole new ball game, but I'd be lying if I didn't say that there was something interesting about it, because there was. I remember one afternoon staring out the skinny little window in that carrel, like the gun port in castle turret, when a thought occurred to me, a staggering thought . . . Everything I'd ever read, all the greatest writers in all the greatest books—from Shakespeare to the Bible to the Greeks—at bottom, they'd been saying the same thing: *in order to find your life you have to lose your life.* Wasn't that what happened to Hamlet? And Macbeth? And Oedipus? And Job? And Christ? Suddenly I understood, because in my own small way it was happening to me.

Going to med school, becoming a doctor—these things had been built up to me as the crucial step in my life, the key to my whole future. All year I'd been scrabbling to hold on. Suddenly in that carrel the last rotten thread tore loose, and as I watched it slip from my fingers what I felt wasn't loss or sadness or regret . . . I felt free.

I can't exaggerate the effect this had on me. From that musty room in the stacks, I gazed over the sunlit grass where some girls were laughing, sunning their legs, and two boys were running down a dog who'd got their ball, and I suddenly thought, is it worth doing anything—*anything*—in this life that you don't really love?

And I knew it wasn't, I knew that discipline was a crock—what I wanted was only what I'd had before, passion—and I knew this *knowing* and that *passion* were the best and truest things inside me. But they were also the enemies of my purpose to become a doctor, they were the enemies of my purpose to support my wife and child, the enemies of my purpose to live up to all the expectations everybody had of me and which I had, or thought I'd had, of myself. Which was real—the expectations, or the thought the great minds had had, the thought that says you have to lose your life to find it?

I didn't have the answers. May did, though, and so did Mr. Will. The difference between me and them was that they had all the answers without ever having asked any of the questions. Marriage or no marriage, if I hadn't loved May as much as I did, I would have closed my books that day and walked out the door of Wilson Library and never looked back. Except for Joey's birth, that afternoon in the carrel is the one happy moment I remember from that spring. I was twenty-two years old and knew that I was on the verge of losing something major for the first time in my life, and confounding all my fears and expectations, it was the closest I had ever come to experiencing, firsthand, the touch of grace.

Back home on Ransom Street, of course, the feeling didn't last. I made the mistake of trying to share my revelation with my wife. May was in the bedroom changing Joey's diaper as I stood in the doorway opening a beer. When I finished talking, she looked at me as if I'd only confirmed her worst suspicions. "But people have to live, Jimmy," is what she said, as though perhaps I didn't realize that.

By the time I got the letter from the dean, final grades had already been posted. I was waiting for the right moment to tell May —or putting it off, depending on your point of view. So I knew the axe was going to fall and thought I was prepared, but later experience has taught me it's presumptuous to think you can predict your response in such a situation. From the time I walked into the outer office there were things I hadn't anticipated—the presence of two other boys in the same boat as me, for one, the face of a third as he came out of the inner office with a dazed expression, for another. Then there was the secretary, who was too embarrassed or polite to look me in the eye. I wanted to put down my magazine and lean across her desk and say, "hello. *Hello*, it's okay to look. It's not contagious . . . actually, it's a whole lot worse for you than it is for me."

When I went in, the dean was standing at the window and didn't seem to hear me. Outside it was a bright spring morning and you could smell the gardenias blooming everywhere on campus. He had his hands clasped behind his back, and there was something vaguely wistful in his posture that made me think of Daddy for a moment, I don't know why—the office, I suppose, though Daddy'd never had one half so nice, with its rich paneling and leather chair and antique desk.

When he turned around, he glanced at my folder first, then said, "please sit down, James. Nice to see you again." "It's Jimmy, sir." "Yes, of course . . . Jim, I'm sure you can appreciate that this isn't an easy task for me." "Yes, sir," I said, "I'm sure it must be very difficult." He caught it—he wasn't a stupid man. He gave me an appraising look followed by a cool, brief smile. "Yes," he said, "I see your point. I'll tell you what, I'll do my best not to make this any harder than it needs to be, and I'd appreciate it if you'd return the favor."

He was right, of course, and as good as his word. "The problem would seem to be more one of application than ability," he said. In other words, I could have, even if I didn't—always a great consolation. Medicine wasn't the right career for everyone, he said, and there was no shame, certainly, none at all, in finding out you're temperamentally ill-suited to one line of work and changing to another. In fact, it took considerable maturity. And I was young, there would be time, plenty of time. I'd be successful, he felt very sure, not adding what was obvious: at something else.

Far more clearly than anything he said, I remember the sweep hand of the wall clock above his head, the way the needle shuddered faintly as it ticked off each second, like an arrow striking into wood, that and the gardenias—they reminded me of May's perfume.

Having dropped the bomb, he paused a respectful interval to watch the explosion, then asked if I had anything to say. He seemed a little nervous then and I suppose that was the one truly dangerous moment in his routine, the place where the student breaks down and cries, or charges the machine-gun battery, or falls down on his knees

and begs for mercy, whatever may occur to him. Speaking for myself, I had all those impulses, but what I did instead was compose my
face as best I could, and rise, shake his hand and thank him as I left
—for what, I have no idea. Passing back through the outer office, I
didn't meet the last boy's eyes.

Outside on the steps I lit a cigarette and stared across the quad
where people in madras Bermuda shorts were walking barefoot on
the paths, chewing stalks of grass, ready for summer. I felt empty,
and then from out of nowhere an impulse welled in me to jump and
whoop and pump my fist the way we used to when the Southern Star
went thundering down the tracks, whether in victory or rage I didn't
know or care. My heart was thundering like that train, my eyes were
wet. For one moment, one shining moment, I felt free.

Just one moment, though, however shining . . . The moment
after that I had occasion to remember how bound I was and what I
had to do.

I meant to clean my locker out and then go home and face her,
May, and explain there'd been a little change of plan. I meant to,
and I should have—there was really no excuse . . .

Walking down the path, I was sad to think that it was over,
Chapel Hill. For five years, I'd loved it well. As I went along I had
the sense of saying my goodbyes—so long to the Old Well and the
Bell Tower, to the time-mellowed ocher buildings and the ancient
elms now coming back in leaf, so long to the coeds on the grass,
drinking Cokes through straws with their skirts hiked up to sun
their legs, their faces with those youthful roses in them, and no
darkness, no suffering or loss, no knowledge and thus no sex. A year
ago I used to want them; they seemed like children to me now.
Goodbye to them as well.

The tour would not have been complete without a visit to the
KA house; I didn't mean to stay . . .

A few guys were shooting hoops out back when I drove up.

"Maddog!"

"Big Jim!"

"Jay-*bo!*"

"Where the hell you *been?*" they said, pounding the hood of the Bel Air. "You assholes," I said as I climbed out, "don't dent my car."

The ball hit me in the chest. "Go on," they said, and I said, "nah," and Ty Cox said, "come on, Madden, you were never modest —why start now?" So I tossed up a soft hook from the top of the key, my signature shot, and it dropped through.

"Still got the touch, I see," said Ty. I decided I'd stay a while.

We played till lunch—I ended eating there. The place was buzzing, with everybody packing up and getting ready for the party—it was the year-end close-out bash. The Hot Nuts were setting up out back and we talked to Doug Clark and his brother Joe a while. They ended shooting a few baskets with us and before long we were all out on the porch with our feet up on the railings, cracking cold ones, hooting at the line of joyriders backed up at the light, honking out the news: *school's out.* I kept looking at my watch, telling them I ought to get a move on pretty soon, then someone broke the seal on a fifth of Maker's Mark, and after a couple of shots, or maybe three, I felt that mellow whiskey haze drift in, settling in my head like the fine spring weather. Filtered through that golden haze, things didn't seem so bad, and I guess I didn't want to lose that feeling, not quite yet, though I kept looking at my watch, protesting every time they poured another shot, before I drank it.

The next thing I knew, it was eight o'clock, a few early arrivals were coming up the walk, the Hot Nuts were testing in the court-yard, I was still sunk in the rocking chair. All afternoon I'd been feeling no pain, no pain at all. Then something began to change. For one thing, I stopped looking at my watch, but it was more than that. I watched the people milling toward the party—couples you knew would be going to the beach tomorrow, bare-shouldered girls showing off their new spring tans—and I wondered what it was that insulated them and why I'd been singled out. There were guys I knew from med school—I hadn't encountered any evidence they were smarter than I was or better men—yet none of them had been tapped out, like me, for the surprise, the one that takes your life away. And it would never happen either, not to them—by that point in the bottle I could tell by looking. No, life was never going to tap

them on the shoulder and say, *sorry, son, you didn't make the cut; go on
and hit the showers now*. They were protected from what had leveled
me, protected by their family names and their gold signet rings and
the paunches they already sported like their daddies, who they were
growing up to be. Membership in their club passed from father to
son, and if you weren't born inside, you never saw the manor house
except from the back door, standing in your brogans with your hat
in your hands. Oh, they might let you smell the feast, but after you
went out and broke your heart they didn't let you eat—they never
let you eat.

By then that good Kentucky sour mash had made its point—I
saw the maker's mark; it was on me. I swiped a bottle off the bar and
began espousing my philosophy to a group of nervous Chi O girls,
who stared at me with frightened eyes as though Phlebas had sat up
dripping from the pool and started speaking parables. Seeing some
friends across the room, they scattered like a flock of startled birds. I
could see it on my brothers' faces, too—sure I could—the way their
smiles were starting to get tight around the edges, which sent me
back to rush five years before when they had made so clear they
weren't impressed with how I dressed or what my father did. Underneath their firm handshakes and their practiced smiles and their
prep school manners, they were all fuckers; they were fuckers and
they were out to fuck me the way their fathers had fucked my father.
Because I guess that's where it came from—Daddy.

What man in Killdeer had a better mind or higher principles
than his? Who else had devoted his life to public service with that
kind of selflessness? Landis? Will Tilley? Don't make me laugh. And
what did Daddy ever get back from them? A few framed commendations on the wall with his name handwritten in the blanks in
ballpoint pen . . .

The next thing I remember—the memory starts getting jerky
here, like some old bit of damaged filmstrip—several of them had
me by the elbows and were leading me to the front door while I
balked like a mule. They were reminding me how I'd said I needed
to get home earlier. On the porch Ty asked me if I'd like a ride. I
jerked away from him. "Just don't fucking touch me, Ty, okay,

*brother?"* He held his hands up, palms out, and went inside. No, I'm not proud of it.

On the lawn, I turned back toward the house and relieved myself in the boxwoods, pissing on the whole damn thing. Overhead, the stars looked cold and trembly in a spring night black as ink. I felt I could see each one, some rose, some yellow, some with a diamond's blue-white fire. There was a tightness in my throat that made it hard to swallow, but I remember thinking that my life had never felt so real as it did then. What would happen next I didn't know, but whatever it was, it would be something different, something new; there was no way back to where I'd come from—that was something.

Off in the distance toward Carrboro, I could hear a group of boxcars rattling into their couplings. As the whistle blew, I suddenly thought about a summer night in Killdeer long before, sitting in the freight yard under stars as bright as these, listening to Mr. Bones. *There are just two types of people—the fuckers and the fucked; the secret's knowing which you are.* I got in the car and drove back toward the med school, planning again to clean my locker out and then go home to face the music.

My textbooks were probably worth a buck or two—we might need it now—that's what I was thinking as I took them from the shelf and stacked them on the bench. On Monday I would sell them back. But when I passed the hallway trash can the impulse proved too much . . . I dropped them in and brushed my hands—it felt a little bit like lighting your cigar with a hundred-dollar bill, or how I imagine that might be, since I've never tried it personally.

I was halfway up the steps before I realized I could hardly call my tour complete without a last goodbye to Phlebas.

Even in the upstairs classrooms you could smell the formalin, a medicinal perfume that advertised what it was meant to hide. Once you pushed through the door into the lab, it clobbered you like a four-hundred-pound woman in a flowered dress. I always had to pause a minute there and regulate my breathing while I switched realities. There was that sense—the smell was the least of it, though it's true the formalin produced a sort of high that we were warned against because it was so toxic.

Corpses, graveyards, mad scientists performing blasphemous re-animations in secret labs—the first time I went in, I carried those associations with me, but it was really nothing like that. What was monstrous, if anything, was the bland matter-of-factness of it, seeing human beings—parents, husbands, wives—stripped so clean of any poetry or grace or reverence.

I walked over to the tank in the center of the room; it resembled one of those cheap aboveground swimming pools people put in their back yards. The way the light lay on the surface I could see my face more clearly than those beneath, but as I leaned over, Phlebas resolved out of my shadow, submerged on his stainless stretcher like a drowned swimmer at the bottom of a lake. I cranked him up and watched the liquid pour away in torrents, slowing to a steady drip and then an intermittent one. I lit a cigarette.

I hadn't looked at him in a long time—after the first half-dozen labs or so you don't. He was a large bald man with a hooked blade of nose—sixty, sixty-five, about my height or taller, but barrel-chested, with big arms and shoulders like a laborer, and a heavy sack of guts. He'd had a surgical incision in his chest at first, the sutures like tiny black ants crawling in the dark lips of the wound; that was long gone now. His skin was a pasty gray with a shine like wax that came from the body fat—liquefied by the formalin, it covered him like the slime fish secrete. Imposing as he was, there was something helpless about him, about all of them—like Joey in his bassinet waiting for his diaper to be changed. His one remaining eyelid was open slightly, revealing a faintly bluish slice of eye as lusterless as a boiled egg.

Thinking he looked as if he could use a smoke, I doused mine in the tank and placed the butt between his fingers. His hands were huge and calloused, and there'd been crescents of dirt beneath his heavy yellow fingernails at first—they'd long been washed away. You could imagine those hands holding a hammer or a shovel, a glass of beer; see him sitting silent on a barstool, drinking in some working-class joint like Earl's, the sort of man who'd be self-contained and slow to anger—no one would mess with him.

I startled when the ventilation system came on with a tick followed by a *whoosh* of air. My eyes had started burning and pinpricks of cold sweat stood on my brow and upper lip—the telltale signs of formalin toxicity.

I thought suddenly of Daddy. The year I made captain on the JV team I challenged him to play me one-on-one in basketball. What I guess I really wanted was for him to know that I was good and to offer me a little praise, but my request came out as taunting. "Come on, Dad," I said, "don't be chicken. I won't beat you too bad. I'll even stake you a few baskets." The more he put it off, the more I badgered him till he relented and drove me to the gym one Sunday afternoon. As we warmed up, I dribbled between my legs, showing off, then threw a behind-the-back pass that caught him in the stomach, hard. He slammed the ball down and caught it coming up. "I'm sorry, Daddy." "Take it out," he said, handing me the ball with a cold, furious restraint. His eyes were watering behind his glasses—he tried not to let me see that.

On my first out, I faked right and drove left. Taking my feint, Daddy stumbled and fell, ripping the knee of his good Sunday pants as I put in an easy lay-up. He stood there fingering the tear, and when I saw his face—redder than a hydrant that's been pissed on by a dog—I started getting worried, wondering if we should even play. He didn't say a word, just took the ball when I tossed it and put up a set shot from the foul line. It swished clean. "Nice shot," I said, wanting bad to beat him then. My next time out I missed the rim, the backboard, everything, and just that quick, the momentum turned. I started sulking after missed shots, slamming the ball against the court, and as it all went up in flames I looked in Daddy's face and saw he didn't want to win. That game meant nothing to him—he probably would have liked to throw it, but he didn't. It was the same thing as those Number 2 Ticonderogas—I could see the calculation flash across his eyes. He had to teach me the hard lesson, and he did. He went on systematically, shot by shot, destroying me on principle, with only my best interest at heart. After that I never asked him to play again, never asked him to my games. If he took any pride when he read about me in the papers or when we won the title, I never knew it. I was twelve that year, the same age as in that photograph he kept on his desk at Killdeer High.

As I sat near the tank that night, listening to the slow drip of the formalin, a curious unease stole over me. *What if Daddy's dead?* I thought.

It hit me, not as some vague thought or fear, but with the force of certain premonition, and I thought about the stories I'd heard—the voice that whispers to you in a dream at the exact hour of a loved one's death, the ringing telephone in the middle of the night with no one on the other end.

I shoved back through the door and went straight for the pay phone in the hall. I dialed the number. It just rang and rang. I checked my watch—it was almost midnight. They were never, never out that late. It confirmed my fear. I was about to hang up when suddenly I got an answer.

"Hello?"

"Dad?" I said, "Daddy?" and he said, "Jimmy?" "Yes, sir, it's me." "What is it, son? What time is it? Is something wrong?" Behind him I heard Mother say in a groggy voice, "what is it, Thurston? Is that Jimmy?" "Just a minute, Lilith," he said, "what's the matter, son?" "Nothing, Dad. I just called to make sure you were okay." The line went silent till Mother said, "what did he say? Here, give the phone to me." "Have you been drinking?" he asked in a different tone, and Mother said, "oh, Lord." "No, Dad, I was just worried, I'm sorry I woke you, go back to bed." The last thing I heard was Mother saying, "what is it, Thurston? What's he done?" I hung up with a pounding heart, feeling suddenly nauseated.

# TWELVE

## May

The deadline passed and Jimmy didn't show and I got mad, and the sight of my ruined roast just made me madder, the fat congealed around those new potatoes like ice around the boulders in a stream . . . and that had been two hours ago. Since then I'd descended like a diver in a bell, taking Joey with me down past anger into other lightless depths. With him on my shoulder, I kept walking to the kitchen window every thirty seconds to pull back the sheer and check for headlights, but they didn't come.

He was in a state by then, Joey, bless his heart, and I felt terrible because I knew his upset came from me. It was as though I had no right to be unhappy, ever, because of the effect on him, as though my life was not my own. That was the dark side of the bubble—you couldn't escape the intimacy sometimes when you needed to—and it was staggering to me that a tiny baby could cry like that and feel a rage that big. That night it went on for hours, and what made it worse was knowing that it wasn't only my anger at Jimmy that had set him off. We'd been having a pitched battle over feeding, and it wasn't Joey's fault—he'd been doing his part—it was mine. My body simply wouldn't oblige and frustration doesn't start to name the thing I felt.

I'd been having trouble with chapped nipples since the start, but one day at feeding I noticed the left one had turned inward—"inverted" was the word Dr. Cole used. He said it would correct itself and in the meantime just to nurse with my right breast, but then that nipple got so tender it would sometimes crack. That night I looked down and there was blood on Joey's lips—it was the last straw. My own body was against me—even worse, against my child—and if I couldn't even do that, maybe I wasn't fit to be a mother—even animals could breast-feed. That was how it seemed.

I hadn't wanted to give up, but this was just too much on both of us; I was going to have to switch to formula. But tonight . . . what was I going to do tonight? Jimmy had the car, the grocery store was closed, Joey was in conniptions. I tried cow's milk from the fridge, warming a bottle on the stove, but he wasn't having any of it. The second he tasted rubber, he screamed bloody murder, and all I could do was squeeze around my aureolas, expressing a drizzle of gray milk. Joey struggled for all he was worth but couldn't get enough to satisfy himself, and I was powerless to help.

Right or wrong, I blamed it all on Jimmy. The kitchen clock said it was coming up on ten. The night had barely started.

Even though he was screaming, I put Joey in his crib, feeling guiltier than a serial killer for abandoning him, and then I took the step stool and climbed up on the kitchen countertop. On the highest shelf of the highest cabinet was a sack of Mounds bars, which Mama had left. I hadn't touched them in a month, trying to take off the weight I'd gained. Dr. Cole had been on me about it—he'd said a woman had no business gaining more than thirty pounds over a pregnancy. I'd gained close to forty—oh, hell, forty-five—and Mama wasn't any help. She said the whole thing was just cockeyed foolishness, no matter what Dr. Cole said, and Dr. Spock besides.

"Put 'em all together, how many babies have they had? You just tell me that," she said. A pregnant woman *should* let herself go; she should spoil herself rotten and so should everyone around her. It was one of the few perks of an ugly job—that was Mama's view. And if you never got your figure back, well, it had served its purpose— you were married, weren't you? And guilt? You'd better spell that out, I don't believe Miss Zelle was acquainted with the word.

And what she preached she set out practicing on me, bringing those two-pound sacks of Mounds and Almond Joys from Killdeer every Tuesday when she brought Dee Lou to cook and clean. "I wish you wouldn't bring me so much candy, Mama," I'd tell her every week, and every week she'd say, "I don't see it going bad, and, besides, Jimmy has a sweet tooth, too, don't he?" That became my chief excuse for keeping them around—Jimmy liked them, too.

Then one day I looked in the mirror and thought, *oh, God, I'm fat*, and it was as if I'd tumbled down a well and landed in the schoolyard, eight years old again, and could hear the other children saying, *May Tilley, fat and frilly, saw a bug and got the willies.* The nightmare had come back, and I tried to put a stop to it. I hid the candy up on that top shelf, thinking the climb just might dissuade me. One by one my dresses all stopped fitting and I was back in the size tens from my last heavy spell in sophomore year, and more than anything I think I worried about my breasts.

"Look how fat I'm getting," I'd say, wanting Jimmy to contradict me, "will you still love me when you have to roll me through the door?" and Jimmy would just say, "you'll drop it, May"—not exactly what I wanted to hear. Late afternoons were the worst time for me; toward dusk I'd hear them calling me like siren music from that shelf, those bars of evil chocolate, and let me tell you I could climb as fearlessly as any mountain goat. I'd peel the wrapper off the first one at the kitchen table and chew it slowly, taking tiny bites and savoring each one, staring down at Mrs. Sneed's old roses, and the sweetness seemed to sweeten everything, making me feel, I don't know, safe somehow, and then in a strange way I'd just blank out and forget where I was sitting. When I came to, there'd be half a dozen wrappers on the table and past the first bar I wouldn't even remember having eaten them.

And then one day Jimmy came in and caught me at it, and I was so ashamed I turned red as cardinal sin. "I have to stop," I said, "I hate myself for getting fat this way." Jimmy just stood there in the doorway with that muscle going in his jaw. "You don't want to get fat?" He stalked over to my chair and took the piece I was eating. "Watch." He held it up and broke it in two halves, then dropped them on the floor and ground them under his heel and brushed his hands. "You don't want to get fat? Then stop eating like a *fucking pig!*" His shout made me blink and hold my breath, and then he stormed back out, slamming the front door so hard a cup jumped from the dish drain and shattered on the kitchen floor.

I cried for hours, but when he finally came home his arms were full of roses and his eyes teared up as he apologized. Of course, those roses were all stolen from the garden and he was tight, but it seemed small and mean to notice such things then.

The Mounds I ate that night didn't help, but then they never do. Feeling even guiltier, I lifted Joey again and walked him up and down, jogging him and whispering, "shhh, darling, shhh, Mama knows. I love you, hush now, don't cry anymore, it's going to be all right," but all my soothing just made him cry more. "Where is Daddy? Where could Daddy be?" I said, my imagination running off to all the places I least wanted it to go. I saw him with another woman, one who wasn't fat and didn't nag or pressure him, who was always upbeat when he came home, however hard her day had been, who was bathed and fresh and wore a nice dress and perfume and had candles on the dinner table. I stared across the room at the words written on the wall—NO HEAD—and thought she wouldn't hold back there either, this other woman, in the bedroom, even when she felt too tired and had the smell of Joey's diapers on her hands and hadn't had a chance to bathe or put on that nice dress or light those candles or even make him that nice dinner. I blamed myself for taking him for granted, blamed myself for all of it, every-thing, and him for nothing, not even being with that other woman who was less like me and more like who I'd meant to be. And then I thought of that bad curve on Highway 54 and saw him dead among the flashing lights of the patrol cars, and my mind leaped back as if from something hot.

I shifted Joey closer to my hip, away from my sore breasts, and it just tore my heart when he began to bawl, his tiny face puckered and bright red. Unable to bear his crying any longer, I tried one last time to nurse, holding my breath and squinching my eyes closed against the pain, my whole body tensed like a steel spring. But it was no go, and suddenly the whole room started buzzing, as though I could hear the electric current moving through the walls, and the apartment filled with an ugly yellow light, and I wanted to hit him. God help me, for the fraction of a second I could barely stop myself. I had to put him back down on our bed before I did.

"Go to sleep, please go to sleep," I whispered, "leave me alone for just a little, let me get my thoughts, please try for Mama, shhhh." I went out in the living room and lit a cigarette and sucked it deep into my lungs, listening to him wail through the closed door and trying to think what I should do . . . Who could I call—the police? The hospital? The fraternity house occurred to me.

The boy who answered was an underclassman I barely knew, and he was drunk, shouting over the music in the background so I had to hold the receiver away from my ear. "Sorry, I can't hear you," he kept saying, "excuse me, *what?*" Finally I managed to get out of him that Jimmy had left half an hour earlier . . . half an hour—it wasn't a five-minute drive from there to Ransom Street—so where was Jimmy?

I lit a second cigarette with the first and dialed again. Mama answered, and I burst out in tears. "I'm sorry, Mama," I said, and she said, "what is it? What's the matter?" "Jimmy's not home, I don't know where he is. I'm just so sure something's wrong; I don't know what to do." "Oh, Lord, Will, wake up," I heard her say, "it's May, she's all to pieces." "No, Mama, no, don't wake him, please," I said, but she asked, "do you want us to come up there—because we're in the car this minute, this *minute*, hemme?" and then I had to put on brakes. "No, don't. He's probably out drinking with some friends. I'm sure he'll be home soon." "Well, if he's not, you call me back, hear? I don't care what time it is, we're right here by the phone."

After we hung up I tiptoed back into the bedroom and, miracle of miracles, Joey was asleep among the pillows on our bed. I kissed his head, took the blanket from his crib and covered him, then climbed beside him on the mattress. As I closed my eyes I told myself he wouldn't remember any of it—I thanked God for that.

# THIRTEEN

## Jimmy

Outside in the med school lot I checked the car for dents and found one on the quarter panel. "Shit," I said, assessing it with a fingertip; the paint was chipped. If I'd told May once, I'd told her fifty times: park at the *edge* of the lot, away from other cars. Whatever anybody said, I'd loved the Bel Air more than May did. I was the one who washed it twice a week and changed the oil and lay awake at night fretting over dents. People called it "Jimmy's car," and I thought of it as mine, but the falseness of the notion suddenly struck home. The car was May's, and she had married me because I was going to be a doctor—it all seemed crystal clear. Would May have loved me if I hadn't been in med school, if I was going to be, say, a railroad engineer who shoveled coal and had black dust beneath my fingernails like Phlebas? Would she have made my hoecake and buttermilk and packed them in a metal lunch pail and kissed my sooty face at dawn when I came off the graveyard shift?

I laughed and lit a cigarette. There was no point worrying about the Bel Air now; I kicked the son of a bitch myself as I climbed in. May wouldn't want to be married anymore—why should she? This seemed not only possible; as I turned over the ignition, it seemed likely. And as I shoved the gear shift in reverse, it had assumed the status of foregone conclusion. It was over—not just my career in medicine but the whole McGillicuddy. I was going to lose my wife, my little boy, my house, and, yes, my 'fifty-five Bel Air with the chrome rocket on the hood and escutcheons in the hubcaps and a new dent on the quarter panel courtesy of my soon-to-be ex-wife. From ground level, the ramifications of *losing my life to find my life* had a different scale than had been evident from the turret window in my carrel—the difference between a ripple and a tidal wave.

Along with everything else the whiskey clarified, it shed some light on why I'd put off going home.

I went through the streetlight, never even noticing it was red until I saw it gleaming in my rearview mirror like the evil eye. I turned off Columbia into Westwood, banging my head against the roof and cursing as I hit that dip. All of a sudden there was someone in the road in front of me. It appeared to be a woman, standing in the white cone of the streetlight, still a distance off, but coming fast. I squinted, leaning closer to the windshield. She didn't move. I blew the horn and swerved at the last moment, jolting across the curb . . .

I smashed through someone's picket fence and someone else's hedge, listening to the branches scoring down the door and quarter panel as leaves slapped against the windshield like the hands of a riotous green mob. For the first few seconds all I could think was how much it was going to cost; then everything got speeded up and slowed down all at once. A strange light, vaguely green, bloomed over everything. I'd seen that light before, though I didn't know where; something big was happening—it was on the tip of my tongue . . . and then it hit me. *Oh, yeah, I'm going to die. Of course.* That's what the green light was, green for go, and I was going going gone, and I'd never dreamed that it would be so beautiful, that I would feel so free. I saw the stone wall rushing up to meet me, but it was all right, everything was fine, it would be years and years before I hit . . .

When I came to, it was pitch dark around me, except for the watery glow of the radio dial—oddly, it was still on. My heart was galumphing in my chest with soft, sick menace, each beat like a power right hand to the body. My jaw felt unhinged, and when I tried to turn my neck I winced—everything about me ached, down to my teeth. The whole left side of my face was tacky like new paint, only rolled on warm. The blood was already crusting in my lashes, and I could taste it, coppery, on my lips. When I tried to spit, something clicked against the window, which was still rolled up—a piece of broken tooth.

The door gave with a stressed metal creak and spilled me in a heap, squishing on the sodden ground. I beat my pockets for my lighter, clicked the wheel and crawled forward, trying to assess the damage to the car. The whole front end was smashed, compressed to half its normal length. My heart gave me another body punch, one so hard I felt I was going to throw up half my organs. *Man oh man oh man*, I thought, *it's going to cost a lot.*

The flame guttered. I was in the dark.

In the distance, a solitary light winked through the undergrowth and disappeared—a house or possibly a streetlight, it was difficult to tell. There were trees around—I could hear them tossing overhead and just make out the silhouettes of branches moving, black on black, against the sky.

Behind me in the woods a branch snapped with a loud report.

"Is someone there?" I asked. "Hello?"

The wind broke through the leaves like the slow roll of incoming surf, and another branch snapped, closer. My arms went gooseflesh and the hairs crawled on my neck. I was certain there was someone out there. I stood up and began to run, stumbling blind through the woods; branches were whipping, hanging in my clothes—I could hear the fabric tear.

I came out in the open and started hauling along a fence line, through dark back yards with houses on both sides. A dog began to bark. A light came on. A clothesline caught me in the throat and sent me over on my back, my legs kicking out from under me. I lay there a minute, no idea where I was. In the distance I heard the distorted echo of the music from frat row, but it was hard to pinpoint its direction. Turning down a driveway toward the street, I caught my reflection in the side window of a car. I looked like something from a graveyard, the guy who wakes up in the coffin and claws through the dirt with his bare nails.

I looked like Phlebas.

Standing beneath a streetlight, I listened to the instruments die out one by one—guitar, keyboards, saxophone—till there was nothing but the drums, *ba-doom ba-doom ba-doom*, thumping like a heart.

Joe Clark's voice swelled over the mike.

*"The roof,"* he said, *"the roof . . ."*

Five thousand voices joined the chant . . .

"THE ROOF IS ON FI-UH
WE DON'T NEED NO WADDUH
LET THE MOTHUHFUCKUH BURN!
THE ROOF, THE ROOF, THE ROOF IS ON FI-UH . . ."

Listening, I felt an ice-cold zipper opening and closing in my spine—and I knew where I was. Everything was coming from the left.

I went toward it.

# FOURTEEN

## May

When I woke up it was just past dawn, a cast-iron light was coming through the windows—Jimmy wasn't home. I was sure he was dead, and that's how I felt, too: numb and empty. I didn't even bother with a robe, just picked up Joey and walked him in the yard in my bare feet until my nightgown's hem was drenched and heavy with the dew which lay white and uniform across the lawn except in that one place, where I had spoiled it with my footprints going up and down, thousands and thousands of them.

Around me everything was trembly and raw, the houses, trees and cars spilling past their outlines like crayon drawings in a child's coloring book, as though the world was not a solid thing you could trust and count on, but a mirage that might dissolve at any time. As first light touched the redbuds, the new blooms stood out on the branch tips like drops of blood on a pricked finger, and I remembered how in Sunday school they taught us it was called the Judas tree because he'd hanged himself in one. You could always remember, they said, because the dogwood and the redbud bloom at the same time and go together just like Christ and Judas.

I was staring at that tree when a black car sidled to the curb on Vance Street at the far end of our block—Jimmy was careful, but not careful enough. There was a woman driving; all I could really see of her was a shock of straight red hair, shoulder-length and bright. At first I didn't see Jimmy, not until he leaned over from the shotgun seat to kiss her and his face appeared from behind hers like the moon emerging from eclipse . . . a light kiss, lip to lip, lingering just one fraction of a second past all doubt.

Still not having seen me, he stood up on the sidewalk and leaned back inside for a last word. He was smiling but there was something odd about his face—I didn't immediately recognize that it was swollen. He hadn't shaved and still had on the white shirt I'd ironed the day before, though it was crumpled—he was tucking in his tail in back—and all down the front was a brown-red stain that looked like blood. When he dropped his loafers on the pavement they made a sharp, flat sound. He slipped his bare feet into them, stumbling as he cocked one knee behind him, pulling up the stepped-on heel. Then he looked up and saw me.

His face went slack and for an instant he merely seemed surprised, then a hint of panic flashed through his eyes before his jaw hardened, leaving his expression grim. He started to smile but didn't, just lifted his hand in a small wave . . . and if I hadn't been sure before, I was then. I remember how the birdsong in the trees around us seemed suddenly to explode—it sounded like the caterwauling in a locked asylum ward. I felt that hell had come to earth and I was there.

What passed through my mind in that instant? I have no idea— some thought of promises, I expect, broken ones . . . That was the first time, an exception, just as all the times to follow were exceptions, too, until I woke up one morning twelve years later and realized the exceptions had become the rule.

Sumner had nothing to do with it.

# FIFTEEN

## *Jimmy*

The rest of it is a blur . . .

I woke up in a strange house in a strange bed with a tangle of red hair beside me on the pillow. Who she was, where I met her, her name and how we got there—those were mysteries as opaque to me as the Rosetta Stone, the Dead Sea Scrolls and first-year biochemistry. I grabbed my shirt and shoes—my blazer was long gone—and crept away as quietly as possible. On a plaid couch in the den, a small terrier looked up at me with sad, accusing eyes and thumped his tail as I went by.

Outside I looked around—for all I knew, I could have been in Buffalo. I leaned over and threw up in the yard and started running. I ran as fast as I could go, taking lefts and rights, whatever cropped up first, hoping to come out someplace I'd recognize. My sweat, when it broke, smelled like pure grain alcohol and probably was.

About to drop, I came up a small hill and was right back where I'd started. That was the only time I felt like crying.

When I went back inside she was standing at the kitchen table pouring juice. "Hi," I said, and she said, "morning, Roger. Where'd you go?" I had to suppress the impulse to look over my shoulder to see if she meant someone else. "To look for the paper," I said, and she said, "oh, well I don't take." "Listen, I hate to ask, but do you suppose you could give me a ride home?" "What about our picnic?" she asked with a crestfallen face. "I think I'm going to have to take a raincheck." She tilted her head and said, "you don't remember, do you?" "Not too much." "What's my name?" she asked, and I said, "come on." "Tell me and I'll take you." I looked at her and said, "I'm sorry." What else could I do?

It was Grace. And she took me anyway. In the car I noticed that my wedding band wasn't on my finger and was relieved to find it in my pocket. Which leaves, of course, the central mystery: did I sleep with her? I can't be definite on the point. All I can say is that, though my shirt was off when I woke up, my pants were zipped and buckled. It seems unlikely, given my condition, that I could have done much damage. Does it count as infidelity if you don't enjoy it? If you don't even remember what you did? That's a question I leave to the philosophers.

May had her own strong view and a perfect right to it, I guess. When I came up the walk, she didn't ask if I was hurt, alive or dead, or what had happened; she just turned her back and walked into the house. I couldn't blame her—at least not then. Later on, May found out for herself what life is like in a glass house. It's a pity that neither of us was wise enough to mind the adage.

# SIXTEEN

*Joey*

That spring they were going at it all the time, and what it mostly was was money. Daddy would say we couldn't afford Otelia, and Mama would say then how could he afford a car, and Daddy would tell her she should shop on sale and buy chuck beef instead of sirloin, and Mama would say if she did he wouldn't eat it and she was sorry if she couldn't stretch a dollar into five like some, and Daddy would say maybe she should learn.

Sometimes when she and Aunt Elise were folding the laundry in the den, Mama's chin would start to quiver and she'd put both hands over her face. "Elise, I don't know what to do," she'd say, and Aunt Elise would look at me where I was doing homework at the kitchen bar and close the door.

It just made things worse when I brought home my report card with a D in conduct. Till then I'd always got straight A's, but on the playground Eddie Grissom said I had titties like a girl and if I pulled my teeth and grew a mustache he would marry me. I had to fight him over that or else I might as well of not gone back.

I tried to get good grades so Mama wouldn't have to worry—she had enough on her already, with Reed banging his head in the pillow and Daddy slamming doors and scratching out in the new Mustang plus all the poor people in North Killdeer she tried to help in Junior League.

But no matter what I did, they fought, and I didn't see how they could be so hateful to each other over chuck or sirloin or some dead stupid king named Charlemagne. Sometimes I'd get so mad I'd want to scream at them, *shut up shut up shut up! Why can't you behave and treat each other nice like you tell me and Reed we're supposed to?*

I had this dream that there was radiation making everybody sick, like in the movie they showed us at school about the children in Japan, only no one knew where it was coming from. But dreams are only make-believe and don't mean anything. Everybody has bad dreams—I think that's why Reed banged his head, to make them stop, and then I'd wake up, see, and look out the window to see if Daddy's car was home. Sometimes if it was I'd hear them fighting in the bedroom, and one time after they quit yelling the mattress springs began to creak. It gave me that funny feeling in my stomach except I figured it must mean that they still loved each other. The next morning at the breakfast table, though, they looked as mad as ever and hardly spoke.

And one time this woman called our house and I picked up the phone. "Is this Joey?" she asked like she knew me, and I said, "yes, ma'am?" trying to figure out who it might be. "Would you get your daddy, sweetie?" "May I say who's calling?" "Just tell him it's a friend," she said, like she was teasing. If you ask me, she sounded kind of crazy.

That wasn't the only time she called us either. Once Daddy answered and jumped up off the sofa and stretched the cord into the kitchen, where he closed the swinging door and talked in whispers like I'd never heard him do before. And one time Mama talked to her in that Colonial Dames voice she used sometimes, the one that made your flattop stick up without butch-wax. Only I don't think it scared that woman much at all. Mama ended up so furious she was shaking, screaming into the receiver, "don't ever call here anymore!" and then she slammed the phone down in that woman's face.

When Daddy got home that night they had a awful fight, with Mama crying and saying how she felt so humiliated and the whole town knew, and Daddy yelling the kind of yell that made the whole house shake. He said nothing he'd ever done was good enough for her and he was sick and tired of it, and Mama said if that was how he felt then just get out and don't come back. Daddy slammed the door so hard that time it finally broke; there was a crack like a lightning bolt down the top panel. And he left black skid marks on the drive when he tore off.

He was gone two days that time, but when he came home they made up and everything was okay for a while until one morning I got up and saw them in the driveway. Pa was out there, too, and Mama was crying and Daddy was yelling, waving his hands around, and I thought him and Pa were going to fight, but Daddy climbed into the Mustang and drove off. Mama wouldn't tell me what had happened except that Daddy wasn't going to live at home for now, and that was when he quit his job with Pa and went out to the lake to live.

Not long after, we packed the Country Squire and drove down to the beach with Nanny and Dee Lou, and that was where we saw the footprints that I started off by telling you about. We had Mama's thirtieth birthday party at the cottage and Mama cried because she said she felt so old no one would ever want to look at her again, except it wasn't true. The painters who came to paint the cottage looked, and other men did, too, and this was getting worse since Daddy went away.

One night we went to the amusement park at Camelot Pier, where there was this man with greasy hair who ran the Ferris wheel. He had tattoos and big arm muscles with swelled-up veins, and he winked at Mama and told her me and Reed could ride for free, except I didn't want to then. I pulled her hand and made her take us to the shooting gallery so we could fire some guns at those gorillas that pop up at you, and I don't think Mama even understood about that kind of look, because she only smiled back at that greaser like he was a gentleman like Pa or Uncle Johnny who only meant to be polite.

I decided Mama *couldn't* know what men meant when they stared at her that way or else she wouldn't encourage them by smiling back. Because if Mama knew what those looks meant and smiled back anyway, then that would have to mean she liked what those men would of liked to do to her. Only I was pretty sure Mama knew, which was the thing that worried me the most, and I just wished Daddy would hurry and come home, or something bad might happen.

She was getting all emotional on us a lot by then and liked to hug us to her—Reed didn't seem to mind so much but I did. Because sometimes she wasn't careful, Mama—it's hard to think of it I guess when you're emotional—and she would let her bosoms press against me, which made me have that funny feeling like I might get sick or even faint. I didn't like that *any*, and every time she hugged us she'd say how much she loved us, "more than anything in the whole world."

She'd always told us that, and I knew it was only a expression, but I didn't like that either. I remembered a long time ago when Reed wasn't even born and I was even littler than him . . . Mama hadn't joined up with the Dames or Junior League to help the poor and wasn't gone so much. It was just the two of us at home all afternoon, me and Mama, and we'd play and put on records in the living room and she would read me stories like *The Little Prince*, and when she read, it seemed I was the very one the story spoke of and that we agreed on this. And sometimes we would dance and she would try to teach me steps, and we would spread out all my toys across the living room and play with any one I picked, and it was like a party only it was no one's birthday and we would have a treat of ice cream every afternoon and I knew Mama wasn't just pretending to like playing because she was polite and a good mother; she was really happy for herself. I was not a fat child then, I was still thin and had blond hair like my friend Archie's before it changed and got so dark.

Then it would be five o'clock, which was the first time I ever learned to tell, and we'd hear Daddy's tires crunch in the driveway and everything would change. Mama would get nervous and say we had to hurry up and put the toys away, which made me nervous, too, and we'd forgotten all about the dinner. Daddy would come in with a sweaty smell and tobacco dust under his eyes like a raccoon and he'd look at us like he'd caught us doing something wrong that left him out of it, and Mama would see his look and smile and run to kiss him, acting glad and happy, only it wasn't the kind of happiness we'd felt before he came. It was pretend, and I could never tell if Daddy knew the difference. Except I think he did, and I felt bad for him and tried being extra nice the same way Mama did, but somewhere deep inside I wished my Daddy never would come home, and I knew Mama wished it, too. It was this awful secret that we never spoke, but that was why when I got big I hated it so much when she said she loved me "more than anything in the whole world," because I wanted her to love my daddy, too. And maybe if she didn't love me more than anything, which means the most of anyone, then Daddy wouldn't have to be out at the lake with that other woman who'd called our house. Maybe if Mama didn't love me quite so much then things could go back to the way they used to be on Thursday nights at the beach when Mama ran down the steps and threw herself in Daddy's arms and he swung her in a circle with her feet up off the ground.

I wanted things to be that way again or how they were in those old stories I heard Mama telling Aunt Elise from when she was at Ascension. She was still happy then and Daddy was a star. I asked myself why they couldn't be that happy anymore and what had made the change and the only answer I could ever come up with was me. Maybe if I'd never come then Mama could of been the May Queen and Daddy could of been a doctor and even played for Frank Mc-Guire at UNC on the greatest team there ever was—and I would feel so bad for this I'd wish I never had been born.

Only Mama did love Daddy. I know she did because I heard Nanny ask her on the cottage porch one night, "do you still love him, sugar?" "I don't know, Mama," Mama said, "yes, I do. I just don't know if it makes any difference anymore, because I'm not sure love's enough." Nanny was quiet for a long time—I could hear the rockers squeaking on their chairs—then she said, "you're right, honey, it ain't; it's just all there is." I heard Mama crying then, and in my bed that night I was hoping hard for all of us as Reed banged his head over and over, trying to knock the bad dreams out. Only this bad dream of ours was still there the next morning when I woke up and saw those footprints on the porch. They were Mama's.

It was her out there that summer walking up and down till late at night and also early in the morning before the sun came up to burn away that silver dew. Those footprints were there to greet us every morning. They made our porch look like a dance floor, a magic one that could remember all the dancers and the steps they took. Only there was just one person at that ball, and whatever Mama did out there that summer, I don't think it was dancing.

Deep down in my heart I knew those steps were her deciding whether love could be enough, and sometimes I would hear her cry real soft so as not to wake us up, but I was not asleep. I know Reed heard her, too, because he'd tiptoe to the screen and ask her what was wrong, which was another thing he was too young to know— that it's better to pretend sometimes because it makes it harder for your parents when they know their sadness makes you sad. But I was not a little kid like him, so I kept quiet even when Mama came inside and tucked him back in bed and whispered that everything was going to be all right. She'd tell him all the fun things we would do tomorrow, and how much she loved us, him and me—*more than anything in the whole world*—and then she'd sing him "Baa, baa, black sheep, have you any wool," and Reed would stop crying and get still.

And every night before she left our room, Mama would come over to my bed, and whisper my name in her softest voice to see if I was up; she'd rearrange my sheet and kiss my forehead, then tiptoe out into the hall and shut the door. I never answered when she called, though there were times I wanted to. Only I wasn't a little kid like Reed and had to try to help her, even if the only thing I knew to do was close my eyes and make believe I was asleep.

# Part 2

## MEETING THE BEAR

# SEVENTEEN

## Joey

It seemed like fifth grade was never going to end, but finally the spring of 1966 turned into summer. Right before we packed the Country Squire and drove down to the beach, me and Reed went out to visit Daddy at the lake one Saturday in his new house. Only it wasn't a real house, and when we first pulled up I made the bad mistake of calling it a *trailer.* "The actual term is *mobile home,*" said Daddy, "as I'm sure your mother knows," like she'd put me up to it to shame him, but she didn't—I just thought that was the word.

He was two hours late to get us and I think he'd been to Earl's because I smelled beer on his breath and, boy, I'm telling you, the inside of his mobile home was the worst mess you ever saw. I don't think he'd picked up his underpants or washed a single dish since he'd been out there. Every ashtray in the place was overflowing and the worst part was that there were cigarettes in them with lipstick on the filters—Kools, not Daddy's Lucky Strikes—but you could not prove anything from that.

Why it was so messy, Daddy said, was because he'd been busy thinking out the book he planned to write, which was something he'd wished to do since he was young but never found the time. Only now he had nothing *but* time, Daddy said, so why not shoot the moon? If you can tell a halfway decent story, they back up a dump truck full of money and leave it at your doorstep, Daddy said, and I knew he could tell some rippers because I'd heard him lots of times. And maybe this could be his new job, see? Daddy was excited when he talked of it, and it seemed a good plan. When I asked him if he'd read us some, he said he hadn't started putting it on paper yet but was still more in the idea part, and I wished he'd hurry up and get to work so that truck could come and he could move to a real house or come back home to ours.

So then he took us to this dock he had and let us swim, except the water was all brown and mucky and the bottom squished so you wouldn't want to put your foot down if you didn't have to. We went sailing in a leaky rowboat some man loaned him as a special favor, and Daddy seemed to think it was a gas, but Reed's face was white and probably mine was, too, because I was afraid that thing might sink. He had a gun, too, Daddy did, and let us shoot at beer cans in the water after he had drunk them. I'd wanted to shoot a real gun for a while, and Daddy'd always told me no before; to be honest it wasn't that much fun. I think the reason he said yes that afternoon was because he thought he had to let us break the rules he'd made us keep at home or else we might not love him anymore—that's why it wasn't fun.

This gun of Daddy's was a .38 with fake pearl handles which he bought, he said, in case somebody broke into his mobile home or a wild animal walked up in the yard. I was glad he had protection, but the sound scared Reed, who asked if we could go home now. That hurt Daddy's feelings and he said he'd tried to plan a nice time for us all, but we were just so spoiled we didn't know how good we had it. That made us feel bad and we both tried to have more fun, except I would of liked to go home, too, by then I would.

But we had to wait till Daddy felt like taking us, which was a long time. When he dropped us off, his eyes teared up a little and he said how much he'd enjoyed the afternoon. "Did you boys have a nice time, too?" he asked, and we said, "yes, sir, Daddy," but it was like Christmastime at Grody's when you had to thank her for the present that you hated and to tell the honest truth it was about the worst day of my whole life up to then, though later I had several others.

As much as I had hated it and wanted to go home, when we got back to Ruin Creek I felt so mad at Mama I could hardly look at her because she was the one who'd made him leave and have to live that way. But then I thought about those Kools with lipstick on the filters which put me back on Mama's side. Both of them were sad and I felt sorry for them and would of liked to treat them nice, only I *still* felt mad at them. And the worst part was, it seemed like being nice to Mama was the same as being mean to Daddy, while being nice to Daddy was the same as being mean to her, and I didn't know whose side to take or how I was supposed to act. Mostly I kept to myself so I would not hurt anyone. Me and Pa went fishing quite a bit and with him at least I didn't have to worry too much what I said.

Once we got down to the beach I'd look around the dinner table every night at the lit candles and the starched white napkins, and I hated it that we had everything so nice and so much good food on our table while Daddy ate a frozen dinner or pork and beans out of a can. And on Thursday nights when Pa drove down in the Cadillac alone we'd try to make it be the way it used to be when everyone was happy; we'd still have shrimp with Nanny's cocktail sauce and Pa would wink at me before he said *Good bread, good meat, goddamn let's eat*, and Nanny would roar laughing, and Mama would say, "Daddy!" but it wasn't the same. It was like if they had cut away some part of you and you could feel it gone, the hole was right there in the middle of us all and no one ever said a word about it, only everybody felt it. Even Tawny seemed to know.

And then one night the phone rang at the cottage. I answered and a voice I thought I recognized said, "is this Joey?" and I said, "yes, sir?" "Joey, this is Sumner Dade. How are you, son?" "Fine, Uncle Sumner, how are you?" "No serious complaints," he said, "I don't suppose your mama's there?" I got that queasy feeling again and almost told him no, she went somewhere, but I didn't have the nerve. I went to call her and Mama picked the phone up in her bedroom and that bright thing came into her voice. She closed the door but I could hear her laugh, which sounded strange because it was the first I'd heard it in so long. I almost hated her for being happy, which was about as low as you could get.

He was staying at his parents' cottage, Uncle Sumner was, and the next night he came by for cocktails and Mama asked me would I like to pour the drinks, but I said no, I wouldn't. She looked at me surprised and made her eyes get wide that way she would when she was mad at me for being impolite and not remembering who I was. I had a feeling she'd remind me later, but I went outside and let the screen door slam and didn't care what happened.

I climbed the dune to the gazebo, where I watched the plankton lighting up the waves like sparklers up and down the beach, and I remembered Daddy saying once that it was *noctiluca*—he was the only one who knew the name. It means *nightlights*, Daddy said, in Latin, which almost everybody in the whole world used to speak, only something happened and they all forgot and it became a dead tongue only scholars knew. I was thinking that as I sat on the dune that night and watched the waves roll in like thunder, and I don't know why I felt so sad—it was just some stupid language that was dead and gone and which I never even knew except one word my daddy told.

When I came back they all had shiny faces from the dry martinis they were drinking. Uncle Sumner was mixing up a new batch at the bar, which made me wish I'd poured the drinks myself so he couldn't stand there looking so at home—that was Daddy's place or Pa's or mine, not his. "Sumner, I declare this is the best martini I believe I've *ever* tasted," Mama said, which I'd heard her tell Daddy, too, and I wasn't sure if I could trust her anymore. Nanny was warming up and starting to get funny and they were having quite a time of it when Uncle Sumner slapped his thigh and said, "listen, y'all, I just had an inspiration," and looked across at Mama, who laughed and said, "pray tell."

"Why don't we put the top down on my car and drive up to the Beach Club? The Embers are playing and it would be just like the old days." "Oh, Sumner, how sweet of you to ask," said Mama, "but I don't think so." His face fell and, boy, I'm telling you, was I ever glad to see it drop. Then Nanny had to open her fat mouth. "You better not ask me, 'cause I might take you up on it, Sumnuh." Mama laughed and said, "you'd be in big trouble then," and Uncle Sumner took a second wind. "I'd love it. Let's all go, the three of us, and make a night of it. You and me can cut the rug, Miss Zelle, while May sits at the table like a wallflower—we both know she never liked to dance." "Y'all go on and go," Nanny said, "when was the last time you had fun, Maybelle? It ain't like it's against the law," and Mama said, "well, I don't know."

"Come on, May B., just to hear the music and for old times' sake," he said, "how bad could it hurt?" "Dee and me'll feed the boys and git 'em into bed," Nanny said, like she was on his side, and Mama said, "oh, no, Mama, I'm sure we wouldn't be out that late, would we, Sumner?" Uncle Sumner grinned because he knew he had her then. "Your wish is my command. I'll bring you any time you say." Then Mama breathed a little sigh. "Well, I guess I really ought to change and put some lipstick on." "You look dazzling just the way you are," he said, "as always." "If you're going to say things like that, Sumner, I don't think I should go," Mama told him, but she was smiling; that was the sort of compliment she liked the best.

While he went down to fold the top back on his car, Mama turned to me and Reed. "Boys, your Uncle Sumner and I are going out to listen to some music—we won't be more than an hour or two. Behave yourselves and do what Dee and Nanny tell you to," and I said, "he's not our uncle," and Mama looked at me with scary eyes and left without a word.

It was a lie, too—they were gone way more than a hour or even two. I know because I timed it on the kitchen clock till I lost track when Nanny finally made us go to bed. I couldn't sleep and heard them when they pulled up in Uncle Sumner's Thunderbird with the radio up loud. I went to the window and watched as he got out and opened Mama's door. She turned and offered him her hand and Uncle Sumner held it a long time before he leaned to kiss her—it wasn't just a good night kiss either, but on the lips, and Mama let him. I felt even sicker and wanted to scream or get Pa's gun and shoot him dead. When he was gone, Mama came up on the porch and stood a long time in the dark so that you couldn't tell what she was looking at, except I thought that it might be the waves, where you could just make out the sparkle of the *noctiluca*. I heard the first board creak as she began to walk, and a little later Nanny poked her head out the screen door and asked if she'd had fun and how it felt, and Mama said, "I don't know, Mama, it felt strange, not good not bad, just strange is all," and Nanny said, "well, sugah, come on in to bed," and Mama said, "I will in just a little," but she kept walking there for a long time that night.

I know because I laid awake and listened to that board creak over and over and that was when I made my plan I wouldn't live there anymore but with Daddy at the lake. She had Reed and Pa and Nanny and Dee Lou, Mama did, to look after her and help, but who did Daddy have? No one, that's who, except for Grody and Grand-daddy Madden and you couldn't really count them in.

The next morning at breakfast I was so nervous my voice was shaking, but I said it. "Mama, I'm going to go to live at Daddy's house." She stared at me, surprised, and said, "no, you most certainly are *not* either," and I said, "yes, I am, and you can't stop me." "You just watch and see." "No, you can't," I said, "it's against the law to make me stay if I don't want to," and Mama said, "what in the world has gotten into you—have you lost your mind?" "No, *you* have, *you* have, Mama," I said, "I still love Daddy even if you don't. I love him more than you and I'm going there I don't care what you say"—I was screaming then.

Mama looked like I'd slapped her hard across the face. "All right, honey, all right then," she said, "what if we call Daddy on the phone and ask if it's okay for you to pay a visit?" "*Not* a visit. I'm going there to live." Her eyes became so sad I almost told her I was sorry and hadn't really meant it when I said I loved him more, except I knew if I gave in and let her hug me I wouldn't ever go. So I just looked at her and she looked back at me like I'd hurt her worse than anybody, even Daddy, ever did before, but I turned anyway and went to get the telephone and Mama didn't try to stop me; she didn't say a word.

# EIGHTEEN

*Joey*

So what we did was Mama drove us to the bridge in Winton, which was exactly halfway from Killdeer to the beach, and Daddy met us there—Reed, too, because he pitched a fit right after mine and said he wanted to go live with Daddy, too. By then Mama had worked me down to just a one-week visit—"and then we'll go from there," she said, "okay?" I knew that was fair, except I didn't feel like being fair, but on the phone when I told Daddy, he said I could live with him *any time anywhere.* Except right now he also thought a one-week visit might be best—until he got his feet back on the ground. But they at least *agreed* on something.

So Mama turned the Country Squire around and headed east back to the beach as me and Reed went west with Daddy in the Mustang, and it all started pretty good. We stopped at this small roadside place which only Daddy knew about that had a sign of Porky Pig in a chef's hat winking at you—Reed thought was just about the limit. Daddy said their barbecue was the best in the whole state of North Carolina, at least the *eastern* part, he said, because, you know, they make it different in the west. He explained to us about the hot red-pepper sauce they put in the slaw up there toward Lexington, where down east they like it dry. Neither one was better than the other, Daddy said; they were only different, and he liked them both. We had Brunswick stew and hush puppies and chopped barbecue sandwiches on steamed white buns and we were experts on the subject by the time we left there, talking all at once and Reed shouting and jumping up and down in the back seat from all the sugar in the tea.

On the drive we rolled the windows down and me and Reed both stuck our heads out. Daddy lit a Lucky Strike and after while he started humming, and before you knew it we were singing, all of us, so loud that people sitting on their porches or leaving church all grinned and waved, and we waved back, just belting:

> *"One evening as the sun went down*
> *And jungle fires were burning,*
> *Down the tracks a hobo came*
> *And he said, 'Boys, I ain't a-turnin',*
> *I'm headed for a land that's far away*
> *Beside the crystal fountains,*
> *I'll see you all in the coming fall*
> *In the Big Rock Candy Mountains.'"*

"The Singing Madden Boys' Traveling Medicine Show," Daddy said and grinned at us with the wind blowing back his hair so you could see his widow's peak. We went on that way till just around the time we got to Jackson, when suddenly he frowned and shouted, "Shut up! Shut up a minute, damnit!" in that big deep voice of his. Me and Reed quit singing fast and stared at him.

"There's a shortcut right around here someplace and I need you boys to help me look." We turned off the main road onto one that Daddy said looked right and kept on going for a long time way out in the country to a crossroads, where he stopped the car. He stared left, then right, then straight ahead. "This looks like the way," he said, and jerked it to the left. I didn't think it was, but I kept my mouth shut because Daddy had that scary square-jawed look by then, like he might blow his top at any second if you even tried to help.

Finally we pulled over to the shoulder and Daddy walked out in a tobacco field of spindly half-primed stalks and stared up at the sun and then down at his shadow on the ground the way he said they learned to tell directions in Boy Scouts. I don't believe it helped too much because we ended going home through a whole bunch of little towns I'd never even heard the names of, and instead of two hours getting there that shortcut took us four, so it was almost dark when we arrived and that whole time nobody said a word.

But anyone could lose their way and they'd get mad about it; it was the one bad thing that happened that whole day. Once we pulled up at the lake Daddy told us he was sorry he'd yelled except that temper was his curse, you know, and then it was okay again. That night he had a special treat planned out for us, he said, and we all piled back in the car except he wouldn't tell us where we were going till we got there. What it was was a tobacco barn—I'd only seen about a million in my life—except that this was not just any old one, he said. This barn was the old-timey kind where they still cured the leaf with wood instead of barn oil. That meant you couldn't just turn the furnace on and set the thermostat and then go home to bed, no, someone had to sit there all night long and feed the cordwood in the fire. So in the old days, see, they'd have what Daddy called a curing party—a bunch of men would come and keep each other company, and there was one tonight, which Daddy said he wanted us to see before it was all gone.

Daddy pulled off a dirt road and we walked up a rutty tractor path into some woods that were filled with lightning bugs and when the wind blew through the tops it sounded like the ocean, only spooky. It carried down some voices talking low, and then a laugh, which had a kind of low-down ugly sound to it that made me wonder if we should of come. And then we came out in a clearing and could see a bunch of men on logs around a fire, which lit their faces with a orange light against the pitch-black shadows from their hats. They looked like so many jack-o'-lanterns sitting there and just about as scary, too. Their dog sniffed at us and bared its teeth with a low growl and all of them shut up at once and turned their heads to see who'd come, and they didn't look too friendly either, if you want my opinion.

"Evenin', boys," Daddy said, Reed's hand in one of his, the other on my shoulder, "a little chilly tonight, idn' it." One of the men craned his neck, squinting to make us out. "Well, Lord-a-mercy," he said, "look-a-here who come to see us, boys. If it ain't Jimbo Madden." He spat tobacco juice into the fire and grinned at us without a couple of his teeth, then stood up, brushing his hands off on his overalls to shake—I recognized him from one time down at the Bonanza. "What the hale you doin', son, sneakin' up on us that way," he said, "we coulda shot you first and not asked who you was till after." He laughed at that and so did all the rest, including Daddy, only I didn't find it all that funny and Reed didn't either.

"And whozat you got with you, Jim?" he asked, and Daddy said, "Virgil, these here are my two boys, Reed and Joey," and Virgil said, "well, y'all step up and wawm yo'sef whydontcha. We was just about to eat some chicken which y'all are mo' than we'come to set down with us." "That's mighty nice of you to offer, Virg," Daddy said, "but we ate just before we came," and Reed said, "no, we didn't, Daddy." Virgil laughed. "From the mouth of babes, Jim—ain't that what the preacher says?" "I am not no baby," Reed said, and they all laughed, including Daddy, but it wasn't mean. "Nosuh, you're a big boy, ain't you," Virgil said, "and you want you some chicken and we ain't listenin' to yo' daddy on the subjec', this here is the end a the discussion." He reached out and tousled Reed's hair and all of them were smiling like probably they were daddies, too.

And I have to tell you, boy, that chicken was about the best I ever tasted in my life which didn't have a single spice on it or cooking wine like Mama used on hers but just the wood smoke off the fire. The grill they had was just a old scrap piece of chicken wire held up at the corners on green sticks, and everybody ate with their fingers and wiped them on their pants or the wet grass. And that was just the first course. We also had corn on the cob which they cooked up in the green shucks so it let off a puff of steam when you stripped one open, and yams, too, which we tucked down in the coals around the edge. Virgil kicked them with his boots when they were ready and rolled them right across the dirt to you.

By the time we finished I was so full I was about to pop and one man went to sit back on the log and fell and laid there groaning and they laughed at him like they would bust a gut. After that died down they were quiet for a while digesting and then Virgil walked over to the furnace and threw back the door, which turned him solid black against the fire. He threw some logs inside and they began to talk about the cure and when it would be done. Virgil said the damn thing was more trouble than it was worth, doing it this old-timey way and cutting all that wood, and it was probably his last time, and someone else said, "I b'lieve I heard you say the same thing last year, Virg, and the one before that, too," and someone else said, "hell, Virgil, I been knowing you what, twinny-five thurty years, and you been saying it since way back then."

They all laughed and got to talking then about those other years and other crops they made and started telling stories about some other farmers and the wise or foolish things they did. Daddy talked as much as anyone and once he got warmed up he quit saying "ain't" so much and using "won't" for wasn't, and they still laughed just as hard at all his jokes, especially the one about the thermos. Old black Rastus told the reporter from up north it was the greatest invention in the history of the world—it beat out penicillin and the A-bomb and electric lights, and when the reporter asked him why, he said, " 'cause it make de hot stay hot and de co' stay co'." "Why is that so great, Rastus?" the reporter asked, and Rastus said, " 'cause, see, the thang is, how do it *know?*" Yes, sir, they hooted for a long time when my daddy told them that.

Virgil walked over to the trees and brought him back two canning jars with pickled peaches in the bottom which I knew was moonshine brandy—one time Daddy'd brought one home to Mama and they let me taste the peach. As they passed it hand to hand around the circle, off across the fields we heard some coon dogs baying. "Sounds like they got one treed," said Virgil, and I could see flashlights moving jerky in the distance as the hunters ran across the furrows. One of them fell down and said, "shit," which carried all the way across to us as clear as if he spoke it in the circle. "That sounded like your boy, Virg," someone said, and Virgil said, "b'lieve it was," and grinned this big wide grin.

They got off on hunting then and worked back finally to the subject of their daddies and how they used to sit around a fire like this, and you could tell from how those old men talked they missed them still, their daddies. Me, I leaned up close to mine because I was a little cold by then—there was a trace of fall that night—and Daddy put his arm around my shoulder and pulled me up against him, which I liked, and Reed was half asleep there on the other side with Daddy's windbreaker wrapped around him and his arms lost in the sleeves.

Someone went down to the patch and brought a watermelon back all nice and cold with dew trickles running down the sides. As we ate and spit the seeds into the fire I was noticing how the barn didn't seem quite real, but like a magic thing with all the heat waves rising off it, making the air go shivery around the sides, and all the stars were twinkling different there. You could hear the primed leaves rustling inside in the heat and the smell was different from the warehouse, still more sweet and green. I remembered how Daddy told me once the tobacco was alive when it went in the barn and the first heat wasn't meant to kill it but to burn up the stored sugar in the leaves, so what would happen, Daddy said, was it would live out a whole lifetime in a single day, which always made me sad to think about.

The next thing I knew, we were walking back down through those woods and Reed was fast asleep in Daddy's arms. It was all I could do to stay awake myself and keep from bumping into any trees, which is the last thing I remember, but I never will forget that night.

# NINETEEN

*Joey*

I won't forget the next night either. Daddy said he had some business to attend to in town and spent a long time in the bathroom working on his hair to make it stand straight up the way he liked. He came out in a towel with so much bay rum on that Reed held his nose and said, "pee-yuuu, Daddy, you stink." Daddy laughed and said, "the smeller's the feller," and Reed said, "nuh-uh," and Daddy said, "uh-huh, and who's the biggest stinker in the land?" "You," Reed said. Daddy grinned and raised his left eyebrow like Stewart Granger. *"Who?"* *"You!"* Reed shouted and tried to run, only Daddy lunged and caught him on the sofa, tickling him till Reed began to pant. "StopitstopstopDaddystop." When Daddy let go, he bristled his knuckles across my flattop and winked, except I was too mad to smile back. I felt the way I had that night when Mama went with Uncle Sumner to the Beach Club—at least she didn't lie where she was going. But I knew if it was really business, Daddy wouldn't of spent so long on his hair or be in a good mood like that, which Reed was too young to guess.

"Now, listen, boys," Daddy said, taking out his white suede bucks to brush them, "I won't be gone that long and what I'm thinking is the two of you are getting big enough not to need a baby sitter anymore—Joey certainly." "I'm big, too, Daddy," Reed said. "That's right, you are, and you'd mind your brother, wouldn't you, if I left him in charge?" Reed gave me the fisheye over that and pouted out his bottom lip, and Daddy said, "because the other thing we could do is I could drop you off at Grody's house and let her watch you—" "No, sir, Daddy," we both said at the same time, "we'll be fine right here." "You're sure?" he said, slipping his alligator shirt over his head. "We're sure, Daddy." "Good," he said, "because I'm counting on you both," and he gave me a look so I knew who he was mainly counting on.

Before he left he helped us rig a coat hanger on the top of this old TV he had. We hung a tinfoil flag off the end but you could still just get one channel and there was so much snow it looked like you were watching through a shook-up paperweight. We didn't mind too much, though, because it was "Combat" night and we got to watch Vic Morrow taking on the dirty schweinhund Krauts. Reed had this plastic submachine gun I gave him when I got my Daisy and what we did was get our guns and play along with the TV. When it started getting really good I asked Reed if he wanted to make sides —I'd be the Americans and he could be the Germans—but Reed said he'd only play if *he* got to be the Americans, and I said, "*Achtung*, Nazi, time to die!" and shot my brother through the heart.

That was the first time all night I'd pulled the trigger, because, see, it's bad enough to aim at someone but to squeeze the trigger too —well, that's a whole lot worse, even if your gun is empty, and mine was. I knew it was because I always took out all my BB's every afternoon before I brought the Daisy in the house. That was Daddy's rule, and I remembered doing it: there was a picture in my mind of opening the chamber, but I guess that picture was some other day. At least that's what I think occurred. The only thing I know for sure is that a loaded BB makes a different sound from one that you fire empty. That night at Daddy's mobile home the full sound was the one my Daisy made. I couldn't believe my ears and I don't think Reed believed his either.

His mouth fell open as he stared at me and I stared back with my mouth open, too, and then he looked down at his chest and opened his Daffy Duck pajama shirt where right above his nipple was this little bright red spot. Reed touched his finger to it and it came away with one teensy drop of blood and his whole face began to pucker, then he let loose, Reed, with the worst howl you ever heard, like I'd just murdered him.

And, boy, I'm telling you was I in trouble then. I thought to pack my bags and run away and hide down in the woods except I had to help Reed first, who was bawling worse than a stuck hog. "Listen, Reed," I said, "it's not that bad, it hardly broke the skin, it's just one little-bitty drop of blood, it hurts a lot worse than it is, you're going to be okay, it was a accident, I didn't know the gun was loaded." Except it didn't work. The more I talked, the more he cried and at first I thought he was just being spiteful but then I saw he really couldn't stop and I got scared.

I went in the bathroom to look for Band-Aids and Mercurochrome, but the medicine chest was empty except for Daddy's nose-hair clippers, so I took some soap and water to clean Reed up and grabbed the toilet paper off the wall, figuring I could tear a piece to make a little bandage like Daddy used for shaving cuts. Reed wouldn't let me near him, though. He stuck his head down in the sofa cushions and started banging, the first I ever saw him do it when he was awake. I knelt on the floor beside him and kept talking, begging him not to tell because he knew what Daddy would do to me if he found out, except I'm not sure Reed could even hear me. After a long time he fell asleep and I was scared he'd wake up if I tried to move him, so I took the blanket off our bed and covered him and put Mister Rex nearby where Reed would find him if he woke. Then I went to bed myself and prayed when Reed got up he'd be okay again and maybe he wouldn't tell. I didn't think I'd ever fall asleep. I guess I must of though.

One minute I was sound asleep in bed, the next my eyes flew up like window shades and everything was moving in a blur real fast around me and I was flying through the very air. Something had me by the wrist. It was Daddy and I hit the floor with both knees, hard, and then he pulled me after him right down the hall and I felt something give inside the shoulder which he drug me by—*click* it went and that was all. I didn't even shout or cry because I couldn't tell if it was really happening or if I was only dreaming and would wake up soon.

When we got to the living room he dropped me on the carpet in a lump. Reed was sitting straight up on the sofa with eyes as big around as silver dollars and his pajama shirt unbuttoned so that little red mark showed. "What is that, Joey?" Daddy asked, "what is that on your little brother's chest?" and I said, "Daddy, listen—" and he said, "*shut up shut your goddamnmouth boy!*" so loud it made the foil rattle on the aerial, and I did. I didn't say another word. I just hunched down and hoped he wouldn't hit me in the face which I knew Daddy never would except if he was drunk and not himself.

But that night Daddy was—I smelled the whiskey kind of sweet and pukey on his breath, together with the cigarettes and perfume, lady's perfume, not like Mama's but the cheap-smelling flowery kind Marie and Tina wore at the Bonanza. The main way you could always tell was Daddy's eyes, which most times were as green and clear as the ocean when a east wind blows but when he drank turned red, and if he drank a lot his left lid would begin to droop so he'd seem just about to fall asleep on that one side, only the right one stayed wide open with a glassy shine to it like some wild thing that just got loose. That's how Daddy looked that night, and I could tell Reed felt bad for telling on me then, except I couldn't really blame him.

"Answer me this, Joey," Daddy said, real calm like a professor giving me a quiz with that right eye of his about to burn a hole, "I left you here to watch your little brother, did I not?" and I said, "yes, sir, Daddy." He nodded like I'd made a good reply. "And since you're the oldest, you were in charge and it was your responsibility to look after him. Is this correct so far?" and I said, "yes, sir, Daddy, *butsee*—" He cocked his head and held one finger up, smiling in this awful way like he was going to kill me only first he had to prove out scientifically why I deserved my death. "Now am I missing something, am I wrong," he said, "or isn't it an odd way to define *looking after, taking care of* someone, to hold a loaded weapon, aim it at that person, pull the trigger?" "Yes, sir, Daddy, only, see, I didn't know the gun was—" "Shut your mouth," he said, not yelling, just a whisper, "shut your fucking mouth till I tell you to open it again."

He walked over to the corner where I'd laid my BB, picked it up and ran a hand along the barrel the way you'd pet an animal you liked. Then he grabbed hold near the sight bead on the barrel and smacked the stock into his other hand like he was testing it to use it for a club. When he looked at me his jaw was hard as concrete, that little muscle twitching like a pulse.

"You shot your brother, Joey." "But I didn't mean to, Daddy, honest." He smacked the stock a little harder in his palm. "What if you'd hit him in the eye," he said, "he'd be blind right now. What if it had been a real gun, Joey? Your brother would be dead. You hear me? *Dead.*" Reed began to whimper, and Daddy said, "how would you like it if I shot you? Not much, I bet. But maybe I should: that way the punishment would fit the crime." "Daddy, please," Reed said, "don't shoot Joey, he didn't mean to do it," and Daddy said, "you see? You shot him and he defends you." Then, so sudden it was like those sonic booms the Phantom jets from Oceania make down at the beach, Daddy raised the gun above his head and smashed it to the floor. I heard the stock crack open, and then he raised and brought it *whomp* back down again so hard the floor beneath the carpet crunched and started caving in. He didn't stop. I laid there flinching every time it hit, and Reed was screaming at him, "please, Daddy, stop it, please, please stop," but I don't think Daddy even heard. He kept right on till the barrel twisted and the stock flew off, and then he stormed out on the porch and flung the pieces toward the lake as hard and far as he could throw.

He waited till he heard the splash, then turned in the doorway, panting, his face all red, staring at me out of those two different eyes like he couldn't decide if it was over yet. I was thinking which way to run, but he didn't go for me. Instead, he started down the hall toward the bedroom and staggered up against the wall and knocked a picture off and shouted, "shit!" and stomped it with his foot and ground the broken glass beneath the heel of his white buck. When he stumbled through the door he fell facedown in the pillow with

his clothes still on and didn't move again, and I just laid there thinking I'd gotten off pretty easy, considering.

But Reed didn't take it quite so well. I woke up the next morning
to the sound of the TV turned up so loud it made my eardrums
pound. He was slouched in his chair watching "Captain Kangaroo,"
back to sucking his thumb, which he'd stopped doing. He had Mr.
Rex under his arm and was letting his heel bang the chair leg over
and over. "What's the matter, are you crazy? You'll wake Daddy
up," I told him as I turned the volume down. Reed didn't answer or
even look at me; he got up and turned the knob to where it was
before, and I said, "quit it, lizard butt, you'll get us both in trouble,"
and gave him a rabbit punch but not too hard. Reed didn't hit back
or even cry; he just laid down on the dirty carpet and turned his face
toward the sofa with his knees pulled up against his chest, sucking
his thumb and rocking back and forth. I couldn't tell what was
wrong with him or what to do but I was scared to wake up Daddy,
especially for this; no matter what I did, though, Reed wouldn't
speak or budge, so finally I had to.

"What?" Daddy said, startling awake with his hands across his
face like he was having a bad dream. I figured he'd still be mad, but
all he said was, "hey, bud, hey. What time is it?" "I don't know,
Daddy. Ten, I think." "Ten! Good Lord!" He sat up like a shot,
fumbling for his Luckies on the table. "That meeting just dragged
on and on last night." As he inhaled, he touched his temple with his
fingertips like someone'd beaned him there and he was checking out
the egg. Suddenly I realized he didn't remember what had happened, not one single thing, and I didn't know if that was good or
bad, except I wasn't going to tell him.

"Daddy, listen. There's something wrong with Reed, I think."
"Reed?" he said, and two white streams of smoke came pouring
from his nose. "Yes, sir, Daddy, Reed. He's in there laying on the
floor and won't get up." "Lying, Joey, lying on the floor," he said,
"you lay down an object but lie down yourself." "Yes, sir, Daddy,
lying," I said, feeling a little sick to hear him sound so much like
Grody.

"I told him to get up, but he wouldn't even answer me," I said, and Daddy said, "did you do something to him, Joey?" "No, sir, Daddy, honest. I just made him turn the TV down so it wouldn't wake you up, that's all." Daddy stabbed his Lucky out and got up kind of rickety like a old man. "What happened to this picture?" he said in the hall, "did you boys break it? Damnit, Joey, damnit, now I'll have to pay for that." "But we didn't; you knocked it off by accident when you came in," I said, but I don't think Daddy really cared that much or even stayed to listen because he'd seen Reed by then.

"Reed?" he said, shaking his shoulder, "*Reed.* What is it, buddy? Talk to Daddy." He turned to me. "What's the matter with him, Joey? Is he hurt?" "I don't think so, Daddy. I don't know." Daddy picked Reed up and cradled him against his shoulder like you would a baby and Reed began to cry. "There now, there," Daddy said, kissing his head, "what's the matter with my boy? Tell Daddy what the great big problem is . . . Would you like to go downtown and get some breakfast?" Reed shook his head, and Daddy said, "then how about some ice cream—would that make you feel better?" but it was no again.

"I know," said Daddy, "let's all put on our bathing suits and go down swimming in the lake—how would *that* be?" and Reed finally said, "I want to go home." "Home, buddy?" Daddy asked like he wasn't sure what that word meant, "you mean to our house?" Reed nodded. "Is there something there you want? Some toy?" "I don't think he means Ruin Creek, Daddy. I think he means the beach," I said, "I think he wants to be with Mama," and Reed cried till he started hiccupping, which made me know I'd hit it right.

"But why?" Daddy asked, "what's the matter? Aren't we having fun?" He looked at me and I said, "yes, sir, Daddy, only I think maybe he's too young for it." I tried to keep my voice down, only Reed still heard me. "No, I'm not!" he said and just cried harder. Daddy put him down and lit another cigarette, pacing like he wasn't sure what he should do.

"Maybe if we called Mama," I said, "she could meet us halfway like before." Daddy stopped dead still. "Jesus, boys—*Jesus*—we can't tell Mother. What would she think?" "I don't mean Grody, Daddy, I mean *our* mama." He looked confused. "Of course, of course—

what did I say?" "You said *Mother,*" I told him, and he said, "I meant *your* mother, May. What did you think I meant?" We'd never called her *Mother* in our life like they did Grody, but I guess I was a little mixed up, too.

"What will *May* think?" he said, taking a deep puff on his Lucky. It almost seemed like he was scared of her, only he couldn't be, I figured, or else he wouldn't yell at her the way he did and stomp and slam the door and scratch out of the driveway.

"She's been so mad at Daddy lately, boys," he said, wiping his eye, which had a little mist in it, with the back of the same hand that held his cigarette. "I'm afraid she doesn't love me anymore." His lips were trembling and I was about to cry myself, I felt so terrible for this, and I was mad at Mama for not loving him, except I knew she did. "But she does love you, Daddy," I said, "I heard her telling Nanny." "She did?" "Yes, sir," I said, and he stabbed out his Lucky. "What else did she say?"

The second he asked, that feeling in my stomach came on strong again, like maybe it was wrong of me to tell, unfair some way to Mama. I thought maybe he'd tricked me into it, except one look at Daddy's face was all it took to know he truly meant it when he said he loved her. Then I began to think about that other woman who called our house and filled his ashtrays with her cigarettes—right that minute I could smell stale menthol smoke in Daddy's hair and clothes when he got close. *What of her?* I wanted to ask, *why if you love Mama so much do you see her?* I wanted to scream this question at my daddy but I knew it would hurt his feelings and also probably make him mad, and God knows what he'd break this time. "That's okay, bud," he said, "you don't have to tell me if you'd rather not, I understand." He seemed so nice about it I felt bad and almost told him what I knew. I didn't, though.

"Okay, then," he said, "I guess there's nothing else for it but to make the call. Joey, I think it might be best for you to talk to her. You wouldn't mind that, would you?" "No, sir, Daddy, I don't mind." "And, son . . ." he said. "Sir?" "Let's just say we all had a nice time together only Reed felt ready to come home, and leave it at that, okay? I can't see any point in bringing something up that might upset her, can you?" "No, sir, Daddy, I won't say anything." "Good," he said, and handed me the phone.

So we met back at the Winton bridge. Mama and Daddy both had their dark glasses on and Reed ran straight to Mama, who picked him up and then he seemed okay again. "Hello, May," Daddy said, leaning against the Mustang puffing a Lucky, and Mama said, "hello, Jimmy." All you had to do was take one look to see she was the maddest, which made me think maybe Daddy was right and the fault was mostly hers. He smiled at her so sad and tender, Daddy did, and Mama only frowned at him like she knew something bad had happened we weren't going to tell about except that she'd expected it before we even went.

I carried Reed's suitcase to the station wagon while Daddy waited, and after Mama put Reed in and closed the door, she lifted her dark glasses and knelt and took my hands. "Joey, are you sure you wouldn't rather come with us?" she asked, "you don't have to stay, you know." Right up to that second I hadn't decided what to do, and then I knew. "No, ma'am, I want to stay," I said and felt so mad at her, I don't know why, because of that sad look I guess, and because there was a part of me that wanted to go with her, to climb in the Country Squire and drive back to the beach where there were fresh sheets on my bed and everything was clean, only I couldn't. I hadn't even been at Daddy's three whole days or helped him much at all, and Mama made it seem okay and far too easy to give up, but I couldn't, not this time, not on my Daddy I could not.

"All right then, honey," she said, "but remember, I'm only a phone call away, and so is Pa. You know his number at the warehouse, and if you change your mind and want to come home early, you can ride with him on Thursday night, all right?"

"I won't change my mind," I said, and Mama sighed and kissed my brow and pulled her glasses back down on her eyes. Only as she climbed back in the car did I feel something flutter deep inside, which made me want to call her back. It passed, and I just waved goodbye as they drove off, thinking that to visit for a week might be enough, and maybe Daddy wouldn't need me there to live with him forever.

# TWENTY

## May

There is a point you pass from wanting to live forever to being grateful you don't have to. That year was it for me.

The winter had hardly been a picnic, but once the warmer weather hit—I don't know what it was—but suddenly it was flying so thick and fast you couldn't stay dry under an umbrella. And it was my favorite season, too, the spring, it always had been, with the little new green shoots and buds, the crocus and narcissus, then the jonquils and my favorite of all, the dogwoods. The hill above our creek was full of them, more even than Mama and Daddy had, so you'd look out some mornings and it would be like the inside of that paperweight on Mama's desk; you'd think that it had snowed. Everything was bursting up out of the ground, and there was something rising in us, too, particularly in Jimmy. But whatever it was, that bad sap, it was rising in me, too. That year a little of my feeling for it died; I've never seen the spring with quite the same fresh eyes.

The sort of thing that usually hits you every year or two was happening every month, it seemed, then week by week, pounding down on us like giant rollers in a northeast blow, shuddering the ground beneath our feet, till I felt like one of those poor souls you see in newsreels, wandering in shock after a hurricane. First there was the episode with What's-her-name, which was in April, right around the time of Joey's birthday. Apparently everybody in the whole town knew but me—I was so ashamed. And would you like to know how I found out? I'll tell you how.

I'd made an appointment at Lorraine's to have my hair done for Joey's party and had to switch—something had come up, I forget what—from the afternoon to the following morning, and I guess Betty didn't tell Lorraine I'd called. So I go in first thing and there's no one in the shop but Lorraine's niece, little Edie Perkins—that's how I still thought of her, Little Edie Perkins, though she was already married and divorced by then, all of twenty-two. Edie gives me my shampoo, then sits me up and starts to comb me out. I'm sitting there reading *Redbook* or one of those, not a thought in my head, and Edie says, "you know, you have such pretty hair, Miz Madden, I always did think so." I smile at her in the mirror. "Thank you, sweetie. I found a gray one in it the other day." "There aren't too many, though," says Edie, which was the first I realized there was more than one. I couldn't help noticing, either, how she'd blossomed, though her reputation was a little overripe, if what I heard was true—not that it was any particular concern of mine what Edie Perkins did or who she did it with. Or so I thought . . .

Well, I just gave her a cool stare and went back to my magazine, and not two minutes later here comes Lorraine in the back door almost running, lugging that big purse of hers and fighting the chin strap of that plastic rain thing she wore even when there wasn't a cloud within a hundred miles. She was all red-faced and flustered, trying to hide it with a smile. "Edie, sugar, I have a few things in the car," she said, "could you come help me, please?" "Just a minute, Aunt Lorraine, I'm almost done," Edie said, and Lorraine said, *"now"*—Lorraine, as mild and Christian as they come. *"Now,"* she said, like that. So they go out in the parking lot and I hear voices raised, and then Lorraine comes in alone. "Oh, Miz Madden, I'm so sorry," she says, "Betty didn't tell me you'd switched times or else I never would of had her here, never in this world, I'm just so sorry I don't know what to do. I'm going to give you a free set."

You want to know how I found out? That's how. I was so ashamed—and mad? Let me tell you, I was fit to be tied. I went straight to the Bonanza and caught him on the loading dock out back with Skeeter. "Skeeter, would you run inside a minute, I need to speak to my husband." I was trying to be casual, only I must have scared him half to death, because Skeeter started stuttering the way he hardly ever did, "yuh-yuh-yuh-hes, ma'am, Muh-muh-muh-hiss Muh-hay." Poor thing. I lit into Jimmy like a house afire, and you know what he said? He denied the whole thing to my face, so help me Jesus, he never even blinked, said he and Charlie had been out at Earl's having a beer after the softball game, and she—Little Edie Perkins, that is—started making eyes at him. She was drunk, he said, throwing herself at everything in pants, strutting it up one side and down the other, and "just to get her off his back"—that was his exact expression—he danced with her one time. "One time" was what he said at first and then he changed his mind and said, "or maybe it was twice." Either way, that was it, the whole ball of wax, he said, and if I didn't believe him I could just ask Charlie Dawes, and believe you me, I would have if I'd thought it would have done me any good.

The worst thing about it, thinking back, was how he lied, looking me dead straight in the face, those green eyes of his as mild and clear as Collie Pond on a sunny day. "I've never been unfaithful to you, May," he said, so help me, just like Honest Abe. It knocked the wind out of my sails, it truly did. There's something scary about a person who can lie that way, as though it's a contest and whoever holds his version tighter wins, and never mind the truth. He'd learned it from a master, though—it was Lilith Madden through and through. He never did confess it either. Jimmy came clean on certain other things, worse things even, but not about that girl. I don't know whether it was shame or shamelessness—but if shame, why didn't he just stop? From time to time a person stumbles or a person falls—Jimmy, he just seemed to dive.

That day out there I ended up apologizing to *him*, and Jimmy let me, which burns me up to think about even now, and that she touched me, that little whore, that she had the gall to stand behind my chair and bat those big blue eyes and wash my hair, it makes my skin just crawl. And if he had to do it, why did he pick her? For the life of me I couldn't understand—why couldn't he at least pick someone nice? Because you can't help taking it as a reflection on you personally—if you've been there, you know what I mean. I'd almost rather Jimmy had picked one of my *friends*, for heaven's sake, some-one I could look at and see the qualities I lacked and understand why he might want her. But Edie Perkins? The only qualities I could discern in her were ill-breeding, coarseness and poor speech. On her best day, the most you could say for Edie was that she was young and she was pretty, in a common sort of way.

It wasn't obvious to me back then, as it is now, that Jimmy'd set out *not* to improve on what he had, *not* to find someone who bet-tered what few good qualities I might possess. No, his purpose was to find the opposite, a woman whose opinion of herself was so low she'd ask for nothing and be thrilled at anything she got, who'd look at him as a big spender if he flipped her a nickel for the drink machine.

Big and strong and full of energy as Jimmy was, there was some-thing oversensitive and even delicate in him, something that felt life —just normal everyday life, I mean—as an unbearable pressure, the way a breeze feels on the skin of someone who's feverish or has been out too long in the sun. And he was too much in the sun, my young handsome husband was. I hardly know what makes me dredge up that old saw, or even what I mean by it, except it was the same thing his mother had, the pain Lilith carried and seemed intent on making everyone around her carry, whatever good it did her—company in misery, I guess is what it was. The difference was that Jimmy fought much harder than she ever did not to let himself become a monster. Whatever he did to me, whatever I might take from him, I won't take that. I saw that struggle back behind his eyes and bled for him.

I guess a part of me still does, a part that I don't let myself feel often because it makes me remember what it's easy to forget from such a distance as we've come, that I loved Jimmy Madden once upon a time and wanted to grow old with him and lie beside him in the plots we bought at Laurel Ridge. It was sometime that spring that he first took me out to show me where they were. We stood there in the quiet with the blooming world around us and stared down at the little squares of grass we'd bought on time, as time was running out, and he reached out and held my hand—I had forgotten that. Oh, I still loved him then—God help me, right or wrong, I did. Twelve years into it, I still believed there was a chance for us, and I still think there was. If Edie Perkins had been all it was . . .

But then the next wave hit, you see, and by the time I fought back to the surface such a world of water separated us that all the good will in the world could not have helped us bridge it, and there was precious little good will left by then.

# TWENTY-ONE

## *Jimmy*

How did it happen? Who knows? It happened how it always happens—I just wanted it too much. And then there was the booze—that was part of it, maybe the biggest part, and I kept winning, hand after hand. Sometimes bad luck wears that disguise.

Every Friday night Tommy Janklow ran a poker game downstairs in the pro shop at the club, and once or twice a month I'd stop by, mostly with Charlie, sometimes not. The group tended to be the same, the younger crowd. We all knew each other, though occasionally you might bring along a friend from out of town. Hopgood was his name, this fellow, Hop, a running mate of Tommy's, some minor figure on the tour. He'd hardly opened his mouth before he started dropping names. Arnie and Gary—he called Palmer and Player by their first names as if they were famous pals of his and told an anecdote or two—who knows, maybe they were true. With that haircut and the manicure and his hundred-dollar shoes he was a pretty slick customer, though not as slick as he appeared to think he was. I took a strong dislike to him right off, but in poker that's just sauce. I figured if Tommy knew him he was probably okay.

I didn't have that much to lose anyway—I never took any serious money out there. That night I'd just cashed my paycheck, but most of it was locked up in the glove box of the Mustang in my wallet—all I carried in was a couple of loose twenties. I won the first hand with two pair, kings over threes, and it was just one of those nights—you know how it is—everything seemed to go my way. Before I knew it I was up four hundred dollars, most of it Hopgood's. He was sitting there with that black telltale look, the little dyspeptic smile frozen on his lips, while behind his eyes he fumed. By that point he'd stopped dropping names. I admit I liked taking his money, dishing out a little of what I mostly seemed to take. Oh, yes, it did my heart a world of good.

And back then four hundred bucks was serious money—to me, it was. I was drinking, as I said, but the booze only seemed to sharpen my perceptions—I could read him like a book. He might have shot a scratch game in golf, but he was no poker player. When his cards were good, he sat back quiet and scanned the table with a gloating eagle look; when they weren't, he pushed back in his chair, swilling his drink as if he didn't give a good goddamn about the game or anything. He was so obvious you might have been suspicious, except that it was only Tommy Janklow's Friday game—I'd played out there a hundred times—and I didn't think Tommy would bring some ringer in.

I couldn't tell you to this day whether he was very goddamn good and played me like a fiddle or only very goddamn lucky, but Hop was making all the classic errors. The more he lost, the more he wanted to raise the stakes. I won five hundred dollars in a single hand—one hand: heady stuff—and then he wanted to go double or nothing on a cut of the cards. "Come on, you guys," Tommy kept saying, "this is just a friendly game. Let's keep it that way, okay?"— no one was listening. Everyone else had pretty much dropped out by then except for Hop and me, and I knew I had no business playing for those stakes, but I was in the rhythm of it, what can I say, all lit up inside. I had the blood scent in my nostrils. I won it, too, that cut.

I never looked back after that. By eleven o'clock I had two thousand in cash in my pocket, by eleven-thirty I had Hopgood's IOU for twelve hundred more. I can't tell you the effect it had on me.

The whiskey was going down like water—I could barely taste it —and I could see all the things I was going to do with that money. I'd take May someplace, Hawaii maybe, like that National Geographic special we'd seen on TV . . . We'd stay in an old hotel like something from a Conrad novel and comb the beach for shells, her favorite pastime. I'd hire a glass-bottomed boat and take her out across the reefs to see the brain coral and the brightly colored tropical fish we'd never seen before. We'd watch frigate birds wheeling off the cliffs, trek through rain forests and walk the lip of live volcanoes, staring down into the magma where the world was being made, the newest place on earth. And maybe it could all be new for us as well—that's what I was thinking—maybe there was some way back to where we used to be when May's eyes still had that melting look of love in them. I thought it could be that way again. That was all I wanted.

I could see it in my mind so clearly, too . . . driving home toward Ruin Creek, first light, the dew on everything, the pine needles sparkling like jewels. May would search my face as I came in, her eyes all grave and dark that way they got, set to be disappointed one more time and warming to her role. Only this time I'd say "baby, look," and turn my pockets out, tumbling all those bills onto the breakfast table like washed lettuce leaves. I'd grin and tell her, "count it," and she'd say, "Jimmy, what on earth . . ." at a loss for once, "there's five thousand dollars here!" That was the magic number I'd fixed on in my mind by then, you see. Why five? Who knows; it had a nice round sound. "Pack your bags, we're leaving for two weeks"—maybe I'd say a month—hell, two months, why not? We had the money, didn't we? When I walked into that game a hundred dollars was more than I could afford to risk; two hours later, maybe three, my appetite—hell, the size of my whole life—had expanded to the point where five grand seemed a middling sum. If I was drunk, it was less on booze than on winning—it had been a long dry spell since I'd won much of anything, a long dry spell indeed.

How do you explain to someone else that once upon a time when you looked in the mirror you saw someone with more luck than trouble in his life, a person you admired and even liked, and then, and then . . . then something happened, something slipped away or got misplaced. You had to live on faith that it was real, that brightness you possessed, though year by year it grew more distant, till you wondered if it was a dream. But the day you stop believing is the day you die.

Sitting at that poker table I felt it coming back. I remembered what it had felt like once upon a time when I believed it was my nature and my fate to win. I saw how it had brought out all my joy in life and made me better, not just to myself but to everyone around me. It could be that way again—this one break was all I needed to recover my patience and my sense of humor with May and with the boys. It didn't feel like luck; hell, no, it felt like the rightful recovery and unfolding of my own true nature. Should I fall down on my knees and thank God for giving back what had been stolen from me, what was mine to start with? To do well and be happy—didn't I have a right to it? Don't we all? I felt magical, you see, magical on booze and cards the way I'd once felt without the aid of either. In my weakest moment I felt strong and mistook everything.

I should have walked away, only by then I'd already been to Hawaii and come home, you see, and there were still these other pressures—the car loan to pay off, the addition to the house we badly needed—if only I could get them off my back, one clean boilermaker, the K.O. punch.

The long and short of it was I got drunk and I got greedy and I stayed too long. Toward midnight we were playing thousand-dollar hands. It was Hopgood's deal; I picked up two jacks and drew a third and was already reaching for the pot when Hopgood laid his cards down one by one, assembling a full house. I just can't tell you; it was like getting coldcocked by the Lord. That was the first moment I felt simply drunk and not immortal. I could still have walked away with twice what I made at the Bonanza in a month—that was the hell of it. But I had to get it back. I threw away another thousand trying to win back the first. It went straight downhill from there.

I signed my first IOU and started doing just those things that had seemed pathetic two hours earlier when Hopgood did them. It happened the way it always happens; there's no originality involved in fucking up your life. When we totaled up, I'd lost as much as I'd hoped to win—five grand, or close. How could I afford to walk away? It was at that point that Hopgood finally said, "you're good for this, I hope," and I said, "don't worry, you'll get your money— ask Tommy, ask anybody here." Tommy didn't say a word or so much as blink his eyes, no one did, until Hop said, "maybe we should wrap it up."

It wasn't until that moment that I thought about the house. We owned it outright, May and I, and though it's true it had come from her parents, it was in both our names. Something in me slipped its mooring; I just snapped—I put it up against the loss. To tell the truth, by that point I'm not even sure the chance of winning was what moved me. It was as if I couldn't rest while there was some- thing left. I had to lose the last thing, too, in order to complete the losing process and arrive where I was bound to go. Sure, I was drunk —but does anybody ever get that drunk? I don't know; maybe it's no accident—this thought took me years—no accident that the last thing I felt compelled to lose was the house the Tilleys gave us where I'd lived twelve years without ever feeling once that it was mine.

Maybe that was why I did it, maybe not. A thing like that you think about for a long time—I have—you come up with a hundred explanations and hypotheses, but in the end you never know. Your heart remains as dark and as unfathomable to you as to the ones you loved and hurt by what you did—there are no words to tell them that. Maybe I just wanted to know if May still loved me, or ever had, or had the slightest idea who I was—that's only one more guess.

We went double or nothing on a single cut, Hop and I—my suggestion that time. He cut first and turned up the nine of dia- monds, leaving me four tens and sixteen faces, twenty ways to win. I turned up the six of spades . . . Just that quick, five thousand turned to ten. The room was silent as a tomb till I said, "how about one more?" I wanted to keep playing even then. "I don't think so," Hop said, taking mercy on me, I suppose.

Outside in the parking lot the stars burned cold and pure in the spring sky. I don't believe I'd seen them quite so clear since that night outside the KA house in Chapel Hill after I flunked med school—diamond writing on the black wall of the universe, spelling out once more the thought: *to find your life you have to lose your life.* The woods were full of insect sounds and I could see the clubhouse night-light gleaming on the black skin of the pond. I stood there thinking of George Bailey on the bridge in Bedford Falls, remembering how the group of us who used to caddy sometimes vied to see who could stay down the longest. No one ever beat me at that game.

# TWENTY-TWO

## May

That night when he didn't come home was like Chapel Hill revisited, everything the same, except not really—really, nothing was. I wasn't that starry-eyed Ascension girl who wore a hat to church and little white gloves that buttoned at the wrist, the girl who saw a life ahead of her like a fairy tale, filled with adventure and romance. Mama and Daddy's life, the life I'd known growing up—I'd taken for granted Jimmy and I would also have that one day, only we'd improve it with a poetry our parents never knew. But by that spring it had finally dawned on me that for every dimension Jimmy had that Daddy didn't, he lacked one Daddy had. I'd started out by seeing just the *more*, but I was not her anymore, that girl who wrapped her party shoes in tissue and wanted nothing more than to be Queen of the Spring Ball—the stars had left my eyes . . .

And Jimmy had changed, too, as much or more than me. The boy who stood beside me at the altar and said "I do" had streaked like a comet through our town, the apple of his teachers' and his coaches' eyes, with that easy smile and open disposition and sunshine on the path ahead, which stretched like a straight road through a fertile plain, there for him to claim and take, as much as he could find it in himself to want. That was where the problem came, you see, somewhere in the wanting part. It's hard for me to put my finger on it even now . . .

But year by year I watched the dark clouds gather and begin to roll, and twilight came. Something happened to the boy I loved and married, my sweet prince. I dropped his hand or he dropped mine; we got separated and came to live in different worlds, his a darker and more frightening one than mine. Even if he'd escaped our marriage, Jimmy would have run into himself some other way. You don't escape, not that, not anyone . . . That's what this life is, the forest we're lost in, where no path is an accident and all lead just one place, straight or turning, short or long, back to yourself—that's what I think. And what I know is that I watched him step by step descending his into that other world I can describe for you only through the effect I saw it have on him. It was a hotter place, I think, where gravity was more intense and people didn't work for their prosperity and happiness; they slaved for tyrant kings, and there was no love there, no justice and never any rest. I saw it in the way he began to sleep with a loaded pistol underneath the pillow, and how he jumped when you walked into the room where he sat brooding. I saw it in the conspiracies and slights he saw in the innocent remarks of others and in the way he slew them one by one with that brilliant, cruel wit of his behind their backs, people who never even knew they were his enemies. Even Daddy, who broke his heart so many times trying to understand and help, was just another evil king to Jimmy, out to pay as little as he could to take as much as he could get.

No, Jimmy wasn't really with us anymore, not by then. You could no longer talk or reason with him—I couldn't, at least—or reach him in any way down in that world where he had gone.

That's where we'd arrived when that spring came. We, who'd sworn we'd be different from our parents, with their compromised marriages and the angry truces they'd learned to keep, had become just like them, sitting by the watch fires in our own armed camps, studying the riddles of the scars and humps we had acquired. And so that second sleepless night, whatever its superficial resemblance to the first, was vastly different, twelve years different. The second time around, I wasn't frantic, I didn't fret and pace. I didn't even realize Jimmy wasn't home till I woke up in the middle of the night and checked the alarm beside the bed—it was already after two by then, but there'd been many nights that winter when I'd gone to bed alone while Jimmy was wherever it was he went those days, doing whatever it was he did. By mutual agreement, we'd stopped arguing about it—I was so fed up and tired of it I hardly had the strength to care.

I got up and checked on the boys, then tried to sleep again and couldn't, so I took up my book from the night table. After while the wind picked up, tossing the boughs. A few drops of rain pelted the house, streaking down the panes. I stared at those twisty little rivulets, reminded for some reason of that day in Watt Pound's office when I got the news, lying on the examination table as he and Daddy talked of Philadelphia in the other room. I wondered what it would have been, the other life I might have had if I'd climbed aboard that northbound train. Now Joey had just turned eleven . . .

I did not regret my life or what I'd made my mind up to that day at Collie Pond—not that night, not ever—because you can't. There is a place you have to stand and hold something sacred in your love and pay the price for it and not regret what you gave up. If there was any difference between me and Jimmy, that was all it was, I think. Smart as he was—smarter than me in many ways—he never really learned that, which I think I always knew.

That night for the first time I thought of a life without him, not so much desiring it—not yet, not then—as trying to imagine the shape that life might take. It seemed like a sentence then . . . to be thirty years old, a divorcée with two children—I thought no one could want me carrying that. To be alone forever, to be punished in that way—for what, I didn't know—made me angry; but more than angry, I was terrified. For myself, I was at the point of risking it, or close. It was the thought of Reed and Joey growing up without a father that still held me like an iron chain—what would it mean for them? Could I be so selfish as to put myself ahead of them? What frightened me most, I think, was finding that perhaps I could.

That night I sat listening to the creek, which sounded fretful, too, tossing in its bed, and watched the dogwood petals falling past my window in the dark like large flakes of snow—in the morning the hill was carpeted with them and Ruin Creek was white. As I made coffee, I watched them wash away downstream, the last of spring, and when I heard the car turn in I thought it must be Jimmy, till the Cadillac nosed around the house. Daddy was limping when he climbed out and there was still a patch of lather below his ear that he'd missed shaving, not much whiter than his face—I can't remember ever seeing him more grim. He'd hardly begun to tell me about Uncle Johnny's call from downtown at the bank when Jimmy pulled up in the drive, already talking before he got out of the car.

# TWENTY-THREE

## *Jimmy*

I woke up in the back seat of the Mustang, sicker than a dog, still in the club lot. The sprinklers were watering the greens, and I sat there watching them fan rainbows back and forth, a country gentleman and man of leisure surveying his demesne. I hardly cared that I'd lost everything I'd worked for for twelve years; it was having to tell May, to see her disappointment again, that made me wish I'd drowned myself when I still had the chance and never seen the sunshine of that day.

I drove up Country Club past the Tilleys' on the hill, then turned on Raleigh Road and passed my parents' house, first Sodom, then Gomorrah, pulling in at Lonnie Ruffin's Shell, where I'd bought my first pack of Luckies all those years ago. I went into the dingy bathroom and splashed cold water on my face and stared at my reflection. The cracked mirror put my eyes at two different levels like a flounder, a bottom dweller, or an accident victim who hadn't been sewn together right. And not all the king's horses or all the king's men either, brother, let me tell you . . . Then Humpty Dumpty knelt down on the concrete floor and vomited till I felt I was bringing my intestines up. It was about the roughest morning I remember—I say that as a veteran of several notable campaigns.

Resting there with the cool porcelain against my cheek, I fell asleep and came to gasping, hugging the bowl like a life ring. Suddenly I was afraid to go outside, I wanted to stay there, huddled on the floor of that windowless cell like that flounder on the bottom of the ocean. I felt safe there, with the smell of industrial-strength floral disinfectant and the smudges of black axle grease on the sink and the single dim bulb. I listened to the tank refilling, raising the float until the valve shut off, and just as quickly as it had come, the panic went away.

I walked outside and lit a cigarette, the last one in my pack, and stared up at Lonnie's sign, the scallop, badge of Saint James, patron of pilgrims and wanderers. As I smoked, I realized I should have followed my impulse that night twelve years before and run away and had some other life; almost any would have done. I should have left the pilgrims on the ship—they'd have all been better off without me—and taken a tramp steamer to Malaya or the Belgian Congo and lived up some nameless river in a grass hut with a brown barebreasted woman who didn't ask too much, only a few shells and beads. I could have been Lord Jim, and it wasn't too late even then, I still had a buck and a quarter in my pocket and half a tank of gas. That morning was the low point of my life—how do you tell that to your wife and children? I'm thinking maybe you don't have to. I'm thinking they don't really have a right to know—not them, not anyone. That morning was between me and my maker—let him judge, who made this stinking world.

As I was standing there, up the empty road in that black boat of a Chrysler, along came Daddy on his way to work, staring straight ahead, oblivious of everything. He passed not fifteen feet away and, so help me, never so much as turned his head, sitting there with his back straight, his eyes focused in the distance, that look that always made me think he must be pondering matters of great import.

That was when my inspiration hit me: rather than surrender title on the house, why not just take out a mortgage? I could use the lump sum to settle with Hopgood, then pay the bank off by the month. A mortgage was hardly the end of the world—Charlie and Elise had one; so did almost everyone. The fact that it would take us thirty years to get back where we'd been the previous night seemed almost inconsequential beside the possibility of squaring what I'd done. And I wouldn't have to crawl to May or her daddy with my tail between my legs—that was the best part—I wouldn't have to ask the Tilleys for a dime.

In this light, you see, what I'd done seemed regrettable, but not a damnable offense, not irredeemable. And my name was on the title, after all. With luck I might even pull it off so May would never have to know.

I went down to the Piggly Wiggly and bought a razor and a pack of blades and shaved with soap and cold water in Lonnie's bathroom. I combed my hair and splashed on some bay rum from the bottle I kept in the glove box, then put on my jacket from the night before to hide the wrinkles in my shirt. I called the warehouse and told Mrs. Weems I'd be a little late, and then I drove down to the bank and waited till Landis strolled up Commerce Street from breakfast at the Scuppernong, jangling the keys.

I called him Uncle Johnny the way May always said I should. "If you'll just be nice to him, he could do so much for us, Jimmy," was how she'd put it, meaning so much for me. I told him we'd been feeling a little cramped since Reed was born and had discussed the idea of an addition. "I wouldn't want this to get around—except, of course, you're family, Uncle Johnny—but we've been thinking about another child. If we added on a master bed and bath, then, see, we could move Reed and Joey to our room and put the baby in theirs."

It went off like a charm, too. Landis—Uncle Johnny—said he couldn't be more delighted, he was glad we'd worked out our differences. It was only when I said I needed the funds as soon as possible that he took a beat. "Jasper Johnson has a bid in on another project," I told him. "If we don't pin him down, I'm afraid it'll be late fall or winter before we can line him up again"—that just came to me, who knows from where. "Well, if that's all it is," Uncle Johnny said, "Jasper's a friend a mine, we been doing business a lot a years, and I'd be glad to talk to 'im for y'all . . . What sort of ballpark figure y'all been discussin' anyhow?"

When I said ten thousand, Landis arched his eyebrows and his eyes went cool. "Jimmy, son, y'all could put in gold commodes, and it wouldn't cost ten thousand for a bed and bath. If Jasper Johnson put that notion in yo' head, I'mon talk to 'im right enough."

I felt sweat begin to bead along my hairline then, seeing the cross connections, how wide and deep they ran, and all the ways it could go wrong. "I'd prefer to handle the negotiating end of it myself, Uncle Johnny," I told him, "meaning no disrespect. That figure would include some renovation, too, and ten thousand wouldn't be out of line on a mortgage, would it, considering the value of the house?" "No, I don't 'spect it would," he said, "but there's the monthly note to consider, too—I'd hate to see y'all bite off mo'n you could chew. Now if Will was to cosign . . ."

"That's the thing, though, Uncle Johnny," I told him, "I'd like to do this on my own." "I see," he said, nodding at me over the steeple of his fingers. He let me hang a while and then said, "I 'spect that's natural, a young man wantin' to be independent. We'd hafta git a little mo' specific on the details, but in principle I cain't see a problem. Tell you what, you and Miss May plan to come in and see me sometime next week—I'll see cain't we have something ready for y'all to sign."

Until that moment I'd thought I was home free. "I wanted to make this a surprise," I said. "Well, son, it's only a fo'mality, a course, but her name's on the title, too, ain't it?—I b'lieve I'm re-callin' how it is—and we got to stick to the legalities, see."

This had not occurred to me. Hardly thinking, I said, "maybe I could pick the papers up when they're ready and take them home to her." I was prepared to forge her signature if it came down to it—apparently it had.

Landis looked me over closely. "Tell you what I'll do; minute they're ready, I'll bring 'em over to the house myself on my way home. It ain't far out my way and I hadn' been out there to visit y'all in I cain't even remember when. That'd suit you, wouldn't it?"

I saw then it was never going to fly and started mobilizing for retreat. "You know, Uncle Johnny," I said, "as I sit here thinking, it strikes me May's going to find out soon enough anyway—it's probably foolish trying to keep it a surprise. Why don't I just go ahead and tell her tonight when I get home? I'll get back to you on it first thing tomorrow."

I could always call and say we'd talked it over and decided against it. "All right, son," he said, "you handle it how you think best." "I appreciate you taking the time, Uncle Johnny," I said as I got up, and he said, "my pleasure, son, any time a'tall," and we shook hands.

I walked out in the morning traffic on Commerce Street as drenched and lightheaded as if I'd spent the weekend in a Turkish bath. I couldn't tell if Landis had suspected anything—he'd been pleasant enough, but as I replayed the conversation it seemed that once or twice I'd seen him measuring me with that old mule trader's look like Mr. Will's, the one that made you feel they could read your name written in indelible ink in the back collar of your shirt. The only thing I knew for sure was that I was walking the edge of an abyss, and the only thing between me and the fall was May.

I thought of her at home, not knowing where I'd been all night. I could see her face, how it would be as I came in, that hurt look she'd turn on me, the one that tore me all to pieces every time. Standing in the middle of the sidewalk in a reverie, I suddenly thought, *what if I just tell her? What if I come clean?* However much I dreaded it, deep down I wanted to. In my heart of hearts I wanted nothing more than to confess and ask her to stand by me. She'd say yes—I knew she would. At worst, she'd say yes because she'd loved me once, even if she didn't love me anymore. I told myself I'd find some way to make it up to her.

And maybe I'd set the whole thing up for no other reason than just that, to ask May one last time to see me as I was, to see my worst and lowest and accept it together with my highest and my best, to see if she could still love me, knowing everything. All my life I think I'd wanted nothing else than to be known and loved that way by just one person—doesn't everyone?—the way our parents never can. And if you ever find that love, the one that can look into your darkness without fear or judgment, if you should ever be so lucky, then doesn't it free you up to give your lover something other than your worst and lowest, to give your best and highest, too?

I think that's why I did it—I do now, though at the time it wasn't clear. If you're looking for hypotheses, that's the one I favor.

I didn't go to work; I climbed back in the car and headed home toward Ruin Creek. The scenarios I ran through as I drove were various but all had happy outcomes, and in my heart, though I was desperate, I felt liberated. At last I was going to have the chance to do what I'd wanted to all along, to come clean with May and with myself, not because I'd been forced—though if you care to look at it that way, I suppose I had been forced—but because I wanted to.

Of all the endings I'd imagined, the real one I was walking into was the only one I missed . . . By the time I pulled into the drive-way, the Cadillac was already there; Landis's phone call had caught Mr. Will on his way out the door to work, so he beat me home.

# TWENTY-FOUR

## May

That's what I remember, Jimmy talking, the desperate rush of it, far more than what he said, as though, if he stopped for even a second, we'd have time to annihilate him with the condemnation he was so sure we'd prepared. After the first minute I wanted to tell him, *stop, just stop it,* less for me than him, the way you want to put a suffering animal out of its misery. I guess Jimmy thought he could talk his way out of anything, even that. If he could just keep going long enough, eventually he'd come up with the right combination of words to make it be what it was not and not be what it was. He was freshly shaved and had red exhausted eyes, and it was there that you could see that other world I talked about, in Jimmy's eyes. They stared back at you from there, no longer clear as when I'd married him, and he had aged in other ways—that morning I could see him like a person you've known well who's been away for a long time and come back changed.

He wasn't himself, he said; he'd had too much to drink and had lost so much by then, you see . . . It wasn't because he was enjoying it or wanted to keep gambling—he swore he never would again—it was the thought of all the bills he had to pay and his responsibilities . . .

"I just wanted to get back what I'd lost," he said. The anguish in his face was almost more than I could stand. It wasn't that I didn't feel for him, or that Daddy didn't—but what Jimmy had done struck at the core of everything, our very life and the preservation of that life, mine and the children's. It had come down to that, you see, down to us or him, down to me or you, and when you reach that point, in the twisted roots and the black dirt, love is not the issue anymore—you can't let it be. Whatever anybody says, real love is a fragile flower that grows only on the highest slopes and mountaintops of human life; real love is rare, not common; it's the crown, not the foundation; love is the last thing, not the first. We were down to far more basic things that day—surviving—that's as basic as it gets.

"Do this for me, May," Jimmy said, "I'll never ask for anything again." Daddy answered him before I had a chance: "She ain't gonna sign those papers, son; you best make up yo' mind to it right now." Jimmy turned on him. "I expect May can answer for herself, Mr. Will," he said, "and maybe you'd best let us work this out between ourselves—it's really not your business." "Whether it is or idn', I ain't gonna stand by and watch her jeopa'dize her future and the children's. I'll lend you the money, son, I'll *give* you the goddamn money, but so help me, Jimmy, it's the last thing I'm gonna do—I mean it, son, the last." Jimmy's jaw went hard as he stood weighing Daddy's offer. "If that's what you want to do I won't say no," he finally said. "I'll pay you back with interest. Just so you understand one thing: I'm not asking—I didn't come to you."

Daddy narrowed his eyes as if Jimmy had become some faraway object he couldn't quite make out. "You ain't askin'," he repeated, his chin trembling. He shook his head and spat down in the dirt like some old country man—and then he lost it. "Son, you are the damnedest piece of work I ever run across. What choice have you left me, Jimmy? To stand by and watch them all git thrown out in the street? But you ain't askin', no sir, you ain't askin' and it ain't my business. Lemme ask you, when a dog messes in the middle of yo' rug and you're the one has to go behind and clean it up, don't that make it yo' business? Don't this make it mine? If it don't, I don't know what does."

"Daddy," I said, "Jimmy . . . both of you, just stop right there." "I can't talk to you with him here, May," Jimmy said, "one of us has got to go," and I said, "what is there to talk about, Jimmy? You've pretty much covered it, it seems to me," and Jimmy said, "that's it? Don't let that be it, May." "I didn't, Jimmy, don't put that on me, I'm not the one." His eyes misted over, those red exhausted eyes . . . "Go ahead and say it then." "I think you should go," I said. "You're sure that's what you want?" he asked, and I said, "I think so." I didn't say "for now"—that morning there was no "for now" inside me, not the shadow of one, anywhere. Jimmy started nodding and kept nodding; then without another word he turned around and climbed back in the car and drove away. It was a relief to watch him go—that morning.

There were other mornings, though . . .

# TWENTY-FIVE

## *Jimmy*

O<sub>h</sub>, I came clean all right, only not in the beautiful releasing way I'd imagined—for it's one thing to confess before you're caught, and another thing again to be surprised by the police as you stand over the body clutching the bloody knife. Then, even if you meant to come forward on your own, no one is inclined to believe you when you tell them so, or even to really give a damn what your intentions were; they just don't care. Then, what it looks like is simply what it is—I couldn't even blame them all that much.

All things considered, I guess it could have gone a whole lot worse: there was no public scandal; I didn't have to go to jail or face down any bohunks armed with baseball bats; I got to keep my knee-caps, such as they were; they let me keep the Mustang, too, which was pretty generous, considering . . . I only lost my job, my home, my wife, my family, my life, everything except my sons. They didn't take my boys from me; I did that to myself and blamed myself the

most for losing them. So tell me if you can, when the day comes—
and it always does—when your sons come to you, solemn-faced, and
look you in the eye the way you tried to teach them a man should
and does, when they put their question to you—*what happened,
Daddy?*—how do you explain?

# TWENTY-SIX

## Joey

After dropping Reed with Mama we were quiet for a long time on that drive till Daddy asked if there was something special I'd like to do before I left. I thought it over and asked if maybe we could play some basketball and work on my left hook—I didn't have it straight about my pivot foot—and he said, yeah, he thought we could accomplish that, and grinned for the first time.

The next day after dinner we drove to the high school gym. Granddaddy Madden had them leave it open evenings in the summer to give the youth of Killdeer *a constructive outlet for their energy*, which is how he talked to the Jaycees, but it just meant to keep the boys from Bagtown off the street. Daddy put on his old black-and-orange letter jacket, with STATE CHAMPIONS across the back, and tucked a towel in his collar the way you could tell they must of in his day. He showed me how he did it and also helped me tie my Converse so the laces didn't make an X but went beneath the tongue and made straight lines, which was fairly cool to know even if the towel thing was kind of dumb.

There was a ton more guys than I expected playing on the two small courts with wooden backboards that ran crossways to the big one that had glass. The first game was for high school guys and older, the second mostly kids from junior high. They were older but I knew a lot of them from Midget football—I probably wouldn't of gone in if I'd been by myself but with Daddy there it was okay. Before we went, I turned to him and said, "gee, Dad, it's kind of hot in here," and ditched the towel.

The problem was, there wasn't really any place to practice. We just stood around under the main floor backboard and took a couple shots while the guys were at the other end. When they came downcourt on fast break we had to hightail it out of there, and once or twice we dropped the ball and got some dirty looks. We decided it wasn't worth it; we'd just wait till closing time. Being the son and grandson of the principal, we could stay. Daddy went to find the janitor, Bill Hughes, his old friend.

So I just hung around, you know, and watched the guys from junior high to see if they were any good. Roy Duvall was sitting on the floor with several others. He used to be the fullback on the Demon Deacons the year me and Archie joined the Tarheels. Archie's brother Wade was the Deacon quarterback, and the night of our first game, he kept handing off to Roy, sending him through my hole—Wade knew I wasn't all that good; it was a dirty trick if you ask me. Only I could beat Wade or Archie either one at basketball because however fast they were, they were both kind of stiff and awkward in their shoulders and couldn't dribble good or shoot like me—I guess I got that from my dad.

I didn't know if Roy remembered that or knew my name until he said, "hey, aren't you Joey Madden?" "Yeah, hey Roy." "Listen, we've got winners, wanna play?" I thought that was pretty nice of him except I was a little scared I might not be as good as them, so I said, "thanks, but I'm just watching." "Come on, man, we need one more," he said, which was the real reason why he asked, and I said, "nah, I came to practice with my dad." "What a weenie," said a boy I didn't know, "forget it, Roy, he probably sucks." "Who cares?"

said Roy, "we don't have to pass to him; we'll lose our turn if we don't get a fifth," and the other kid said, "we'll find somebody off the losers." They didn't speak or even look at me again like I'd just disappeared. I was pretty used to stuff like that from older guys; what made it bad was when I turned around—there was Daddy standing in the door. He'd heard every word they said; I saw it on his face before he smiled.

"Hey, bud," he said, "I'm thirsty—how about you? Wanna get a soda?"

We went out to the public entry and got two Cokes from the machine and sat down on the stairs. All the teams that ever played for Killdeer had their pictures on the wall out there, and in the trophy case was the game ball from that old conference final against Durham. Whenever I went to a game I stopped to look, but I think Daddy had forgotten it was there, or maybe it was just so long ago he didn't care.

"You didn't feel like playing with those boys?" he asked, and I said, "nah, Dad, I'd rather wait till we can practice." Daddy smiled and sipped his Coke. Through the open doors we saw a freight train, crawling slow down Depot Street—it blew its whistle once but didn't stop.

"It's okay to be scared, you know," he said, watching as the train moved off, which took me by surprise. "I wasn't *scared*, Daddy. I'd just rather play with you." He looked at me this way like he could see right through me, not to judge but kind of soft and gentle like he understood. "I know, bud. I know. I'm only saying it's okay . . . because I'm scared myself, son, lots of times. Even out there on that court where I was probably more at home than any other place I ever was, I was still scared sometimes, Joey. And you know the most afraid I ever was?" I blinked my eyes and shook my head. "That Durham game." Daddy nodded toward the trophy case with the game ball—he hadn't forgotten after all.

"And in that game," he said, "the scariest thing was when Red Wells bounced me the ball down in the lane. The crowd was chanting *ten, nine, eight,* and on the count of seven he hit me with the pass, which came this close, Joey, this close to going out of bounds, except it didn't. My back was to the goal, I faked left, used my right foot as a pivot and threw it up without even looking at the glass. The second it left my fingertips I knew it was going to drop—you know that feeling? I just knew, but right up to that second I was scared, son, as scared as I believe I ever was in my whole life. And the next second they stood up in the stands and cheered . . . and all I'm saying is those two moments went together just like this." Daddy held his index fingers so they touched. "Just like this," he said. "So it's okay to be scared, Joey. Everybody is. But you still have to go out there and do your best—to win you have to play. I know you can, I always have—remember that, okay?"

"Okay, Dad," I said, and he reached out and laid that great big hand beside my cheek this way I can't remember he ever touched me any other time. "So can you, Daddy," I told him, "you can still win, too." I don't know why I said it, I guess because it seemed he was giving something up to me, like that crown of leaves the silver boy held in the trophy on his old chest of drawers—he'd once had it in his fingers, Daddy, only he'd let go and it had slipped away. More than anything in the whole world I would of liked one of my own, to carry it and have some people cheer, but not if it meant taking it from him so he would have to go without, not that way I wouldn't. But I still have to tell you in that moment I loved him so much I felt my insides split apart, pouring out this kind of light that made it hard to breathe, and what I couldn't understand was why it had to hurt so much and feel so sad to love someone that way.

Daddy looked at me for a long time and that little muscle flicked along his jaw like what I said had hurt his feelings, only he knew it wasn't meant that way and he said, "sure, bud," and gave my cheek a little pat with that big hand which could palm a ball. "Sure," he said, "I know. Now stand up here." And then he showed me how to do the move from the low post—fake left, pivot off the right foot, release from the left hand. We did it a few times without the ball till I began to get the hang of it, and when he said, "ready to go back?" I answered, "ready." We went side by side through those big double doors with Daddy's arm around my shoulder, and when people turned to look I felt real proud because they knew that he was Jimmy Madden, the best who ever came from there, and that I was his son.

I think Dad enjoyed it too, because on the drive home he said how good it felt to get some exercise, he ought to do it more and get in shape again because he'd been blowing pretty hard out there toward the end. What we ought to do, he said, was set us up a workout schedule, train together till I left and then keep going, each man on his own.

"Interested in trying that?" "Shoot, yeah, Dad," I said. "What if we get up tomorrow morning at the crack and take a run around the lake?" "Sure, okay," I said. "Deal?" "Deal," I said, and we shook hands on it.

About that time we happened to pass Earl's and Daddy said, "would a cold one hurt us much?" I smiled and shook my head and he pulled up. Inside, he ordered a Pabst tall boy and a Sun Drop for me and we went in back to shoot some pool. "You know something else we ought to do," he said as he was chalking up, "or *I* should?" "What, Dad?" I asked, racking the balls. "Get to work on my story," he said, "it's time to quit procrastinating." "If you want, we could work on it tonight when we go home, and I could help you think of stuff." Daddy got this serious expression that made him look like he was mad except he wasn't.

"Let's go," he said real sudden, "let's go right now before another minute passes," and he laid his cue stick down and we walked off and left those balls racked up for someone else to break. I felt excited then, like everything could change and we were setting off on a adventure, just the two of us. We stopped next door at Mr. Hanlon's grocery store and Daddy bought a spiral notebook and a pack of Number 2 lead pencils which he loved the name of, Daddy said, *Ticonderoga*, and the smell especially, from when Granddaddy Madden used to bring him free ones from the high school. But as we were getting in the Mustang he sent me back to Earl's to buy a six-pack for the road, and he'd already finished one and started on the second by the time we got back to the mobile home.

Inside, we made a few bologna sandwiches and Daddy turned on the TV to catch the Yankees game and popped another beer, and I was scared we might get sidetracked. Daddy said he only wanted to

see Maris's at-bat, who was his favorite player, don't ask me why—
he had a nervous, sweaty look I didn't think the Home Run King
should have and hadn't been the same since he hit sixty-one. Everyone loved Mickey Mantle more, including me, because he smiled
and made it look like fun, and maybe that's why Daddy pulled for
Roger. But he struck out again that time the way he had all spring,
and Daddy said, "shit," and stalked off to the kitchen. I joined him
at the table and ripped the cellophane off the pencil pack for him.
"Damnit!" Daddy said, "we should have bought a pencil sharpener
—how could I forget that?" "We could use a knife," I said and
found one in the kitchen drawer. It worked okay, but Daddy's mood
kept getting worse. He leaned across the notebook with his arm
across the top and started writing like it was a test at school and he
was scared I might cheat off his paper. He erased, wrote something
else and drew a line through that—his jaw had started hopping.
"Damn!" He slapped the pencil down, pushed back his chair and
got another beer.

"What's the matter, Daddy?" He just glared at me, and I
couldn't see what I had done. "Look," he said, "there's no point in
you just sitting there staring at me. Go on in and watch the game
and call me if anything happens." That left eyelid of his was looking
kind of heavy—I noticed it as I got up to leave, and he was on his
fourth or fifth Blue Ribbon.

I sat on the sofa listening to the scratching sound his pencil made
and then the paper tearing, getting crumpled in a ball, and then his
beer can getting crumpled, too, and ringing in the metal garbage
can. The refrigerator opened again, and Daddy went into the bedroom and closed the door. I heard him talking on the phone, laughing every now and then, and after maybe half an hour he came out.
"Well, bud," he said, "it's been a long day and I guess the basketball
took more out of me than I expected. I think I'm going to hit the
hay. Good night."

"Night, Daddy." He rubbed his hand across my flattop and
started down the hall. "Maybe we can work on it some more tomorrow after we go running," I called after him, but he didn't answer or
even turn around. I just heard the crunch of glass when he stepped

on that broken picture, which was laying there from yesterday—or lying, I forget. The game was still going but I switched it off—it was the bottom of the ninth and the Yankees had already lost.

Before I went to sleep I opened the spiral notebook on the kitchen table to see how much he'd written, only it was blank. I fished in the garbage can, took out the crumpled pages and smoothed them open. There were three.

The first said, "Once upon a time"

The next said, "Twice upon a t"

The last said, "Thrice upon a dime"

And that was all.

Washing up in the bathroom, I studied my reflection while the water ran and tried to see if I was handsome like Mama said, except I couldn't really tell. When I reached for the soap there wasn't any, so I opened the drawer to look for a new bar. Inside, was a foil coin like the chocolate ones we got for Christmas, only in it was a Trojan like Stevie Poe stole from his daddy and showed us in the woods one day. Looking at it, I thought of Archie and his daddy's medal which he won in World War II.

Back when we first moved to Ruin Creek the year I started school, Wade and Archie brought that medal to my house one day to show. Archie told me how it proved his daddy was a hero and got wounded in the line of duty, and I didn't know if it was true, it seemed like bragging, so I said, "my daddy is a hero, too."

"I bet he doesn't have a medal," Archie said, and I said, "yes, he does. It's in the house," trying to think fast, and Archie said, "then bring it out to show." "Daddy doesn't let me 'cause it might get lost," I said, and he said, "why don't we go in and look?" "Mama isn't home and doesn't like me bringing strangers in." "So, you don't have to tell her, do you?" he asked, and I said, "but the door's locked; she always locks it when she goes out grocery shopping." Archie pointed to the station wagon in the drive. "There's your car right there. How did she go shopping, did she walk?" "No," I said, "I guess she rode with Aunt Elise," and Archie looked at me and said, "I think you're a lying chickenshit." "Takes one to know one,"

I told him, and he said, "so let us see your daddy's medal, *if* he has one," and I said, "you just wait, I will," and he said, "when?" and I said, "well, some other time."

Not long after that they brought the medal by again, and that day they were fighting over whose turn it was to carry it—Wade and Archie were always fighting over something and Wade was two years older and the biggest so it wasn't fair. "Look, you two," I said, "just let me carry it for you; my shirt has a button flap and everything." I didn't have a plan, I only said it so Archie wouldn't have to take another whipping. They didn't look too sure at first, but Wade said, "okay, but if you lose it, Joey, your ass is grass and I am going to mow."

They were going to take me up into the woods that day to see their camp, but first I had to use the bathroom, so I said, "wait here, I'll be right back." While I was standing there to take my leak, I reached in my pocket for the medal, and as I held it I can't say what happened, only it was kind of like I went into a dream or I got hypnotized or something. I thought, *what if I dropped it? What if it fell down the commode? Or what if I just said it did?* Nobody in the world would ever know for sure what really happened—only me. The medal could be mine if I told Wade and Archie this, you see—and then it got to seem I *needed* it.

I tiptoed in and hid it in my daddy's drawer and went back on the porch. I guess I'd been gone a little longer than I thought, because they already looked like they knew I was up to something.

"Where's Daddy's medal?" Wade asked, and I said, "oh, boy, y'all, am I ever sorry . . . it was a accident. I was standing there doing my business and the durn thing slipped out of my hand right when I flushed the handle. I reached in to get it but it went *right* down the hole before I could, and I am *reallyreally* sorry, y'all, but I have to go inside now because I have to help my mother do some stuff and we can see your camp another day *okaysobye.*"

Wade and Archie dropped their jaws like I'd just landed from a spaceship. "You little turd," Wade said, "you're hiding it in there, I know you are," and I said, "honest, Wade, I'm not, I swear to God I'm not." Wade's eyes got bulgy then, the way they would before he went for Archie and smacked him up beside the head, so I went in real quick and closed the door on them and didn't answer when they pressed the bell.

Only they kept on and on like no one ever taught them any manners in their life and finally Mama heard and came to see. "Miz Madden! Miz Madden!" Archie said, "Joey stole our daddy's medal and won't give it back." Mama looked at me. "No, I didn't, Mama, I swear to God I didn't." "Yes, he did," they said, "did, too, Miz Madden!"

"Joey?" Mama said, and I said, "ma'am?" shaking in my boots. "Why would they lie, son?" "Because, Mama, they took it out and lost it somewhere and their daddy's going to whip them when he comes home and now they want to blame it all on me so I'll be the one to get in trouble." Wade and Archie looked like they were going cross-eyed and were going to choke, was how mad they were. Mama studied me for a long time, then them, then me again. I could tell her heart was torn over taking my one word against their two, except I was her son and they were boys she hardly knew, and so she did. "You boys go home and don't come back until you learn how to behave," she said, but when she shut the door on them she gave me this look like I'd better not be lying, except I think maybe she already knew.

Then their mama called, Francine, but when Mama said, in that polite Ascension voice of hers that made my flattop stand up without butch-wax, "I believe you must be mistaken, Mrs. Cobb," that was the end of poor Francine.

And boy oh boy, I knew what I had done by then. That medal that was going to make my life complete, now I just wished I could dig a hole back in the woods someplace and stick it in and let it rust away to dust. One thing I knew for sure, Daddy's drawer wasn't safe and it could not stay anywhere in our whole house—Mama had a way of finding things.

That afternoon we went to Nanny's and when they left the room I lifted the sofa cushion where Nanny always sat and stuck the medal way down in the crack and figured I would leave it there for a few years like maybe ten until the heat died down. I didn't know about rotating cushions, something ladies do to keep their chintz from wearing too much on one side, but they all knew, Mama, Nanny and Dee Lou. Dee happened to rotate that very afternoon. We'd hardly walked back in the house before the phone rang. "May," said Nanny, "Dee just found the strangest thing . . ."

And boy oh boy oh boy oh boy, we couldn't even wait till the next day. Mama left the meatloaf in the oven and marched me straight out to the Country Squire and drove me back to Nanny's, screeching tires at every stop sign. She waited while I went inside to get it, and Nanny said, "I'm sorry, sugah pie, I didn't mean to git you in hot water." Mama was so mad she couldn't even talk till we got back to Ruin Creek, where she braked at the bottom of the Cobbs' driveway. "Joey, I've never been so disappointed, *never*. I'm simply mortified. Now you just march up there and give it back and apologize to Mr. and Mrs. Cobb and don't come home until you do."

She roared off up the street toward our house and I considered ducking back behind a tree and counting one-one thousand two-one thousand to a hundred and then going home, except I knew it wouldn't work, so I took a deep breath and knocked on the screen door. They were all sitting down to dinner saying grace and passing a plate of sliced Merita white bread which they preferred to dinner rolls like Mama served at home. "Here's your medal, Mr. Cobb," I said, "I'm sorry." He reached out for it and never said a word to me, only his eyes were kind of gentle so I knew he wasn't all that mad. Then Francine got up from the table and said, "Joey, won't you have some supper?" which I thought was just as fine as anything they could of taught you at Ascension or Colonial Dames. I sat down and ate a hamburger with them which the Cobbs liked cooked till there was no pink left inside, and in a pan not on the grill, but it was good their way with a slice of Kraft cheese from a plastic wrapper on the top. It's kind of funny but Archie was my best friend for a long time after that and even sometimes let me hold the medal, though I didn't want to so much anymore.

Standing in the bathroom of Daddy's mobile home that night with the foil coin, I thought of that, I don't know why. I wished I had blond hair like Archie and could run fast enough to play the backfield like he did instead of only being tackle and getting creamed on every play. Daddy always told me I did great and that it's better being smart, but his eyes still lit up some different way when he shook hands with Archie after we played. I understood it, too, because whatever anybody says, when it comes to being smart or being fast and scoring touchdowns, everybody knows down in their hearts which wins.

I decided I did not look very handsome after all, and turned the water off and went to bed.

# TWENTY-SEVEN

## Joey

When I woke up the next morning the thought of going for that run just made me want to groan and roll back over. The idea had seemed fairly cool the night before, when it was far away, only now up close I wondered if I couldn't think up some excuse like how my knee felt stiff from all that, you know, ball.

When I lifted the shade it was overcast and drizzly outside and there were mist devils rising off the lake in twisty ribbons. It was kind of cold out, too, like fall, which made me think of going back to school, though it was still two weeks away. If you figured twelve weeks to a summer, that meant a sixth, or one whole slice of pie, was left, which was a lot, except it didn't seem like much, I don't know why.

To tell the truth, I expected Daddy to be the one to roust me out of bed since it was his idea to run. But before I even pulled the covers off I knew he wasn't up, because I'd of smelled the coffee if he was and heard the water in the percolator. The radio would be on, too, for the news and farm report. But everything was still, so still I heard the drizzle ticking on the metal roof. Listening to that, I changed my mind about the run, I don't know why. It just suddenly seemed important we should keep our deal.

So I got up and laced my Converse and found my Carolina sweatshirt, tucking a towel in the collar so Daddy wouldn't get the idea I was ashamed of what he showed me. I splashed water on my face and banged around in a few kitchen drawers, whistling loud and hoping Daddy would get up by himself so I wouldn't have to go and wake him which might start things off on the wrong foot.

I waited half an hour and at ten to eight I started coffee. I wasn't sure how many spoons you need, so I filled the whole thing to the top and poured a cup which looked about like when you change your motor oil. Daddy was sleeping in his clothes again with no sheets on the mattress, just a blanket pulled on top, another habit he was getting into since he left home except at least that time he took his shoes off first.

"Wake up, Dad," I said, "it's time to go," and I pulled up the shade. Daddy groaned and raised his head, shading his eyes and squinting at me out of one. "What is it? What's the matter, son?" "Nothing, Daddy, we just need to take our run before it gets too late." He looked at the alarm clock on the table but it had run down because he never wound it up. "What time is it?" "Eight o'clock," I said. His jaw flinched then. "Look," I said, "I made your coffee." I tried to hand him the cup before he could get mad, but he didn't even notice it; he just glared till I dropped my eyes. "I was sound asleep," he said, "we have all day to run." I put the cup down on the table. "I know, Daddy, but we said the crack, the crack of dawn, and it's already after that."

Something changed behind his eyes; they got that soft look from the night before like he could see into my heart again and what he saw there made him sad. "Listen, bud, I'll tell you what. Right now my bad knee feels a little stiff from all that ball we played last night, but let me sleep another hour or so and we'll see then—fair?" I looked at him and felt like I would scream or start to cry, but I couldn't. All I could do was not to say it back, "fair," because it wasn't. I turned around without a word and went out on the steps, and I guess it must of been five minutes later when he came out, a towel tucked into his collar and his Converse laced, carrying that cup of coffee. "Jesus, Joey, this stuff would singe the whiskers off the Frito Bandito." He grinned and knuckled me across my flattop. Then we went.

We headed off along this path into the trees and everything was cold and drippy in the woods and all the dead leaves squished beneath your sneakers like soggy Raisin Bran. The only other times I'd tried to run on purpose was wind sprints at the end of football practice or else when Coach made us do laps around the field for goofing off.

So, see, we hadn't gone too far before I started puffing pretty bad and got this raw feeling in my chest like someone scraped my lungs with razorblades. Daddy was coughing with a bubbly sound and hocked him up a couple of the grossest-looking oysters you ever saw from all those Lucky Strikes. We stopped to catch our breath and bent over, hands on knees, just heaving there. I figured we'd run a mile or two at least but when we checked the watch, we hadn't even gone five minutes. If Daddy had wanted to call it quits I probably would of said okay, only his jaw was tight like he was mad about it now and not about to give up yet, and I guess I'd asked for it.

While we were standing there something rustled in the woods behind us. It sounded really close and really big and I can tell you, boy, we lit out as fast as we could go, crashing through the brush until we came out on the beach, if you could call it that. Daddy looked at me with big round eyes so I couldn't help laughing, and he laughed too, which made us want to run some more.

It was kind of rocky there but not so bad if you were careful where you put your foot, and there was like this sort of steam inside my clothes that made me feel all loose and good like I could keep on going. I think Daddy felt it, too, because he said, "I'll race you to that dead tree over there," and he took off, boy, eating up the dirt with those long legs. I gave it all I had, but Daddy pulled away from me like I was standing still. It was worth it, though, getting beat, to watch him go.

He was almost to the tree with quite a lead when he turned and rowed his arm like he was hauling in a fish. "Come on," he called. I heard the echo slap flat off the lake and at that moment Daddy's foot turned on a rock and he went down. I heard his grunt—*uhhnnn*—all the way to where I was.

"Daddy?" I called but he just laid there, flat on his back, and didn't answer. For a second right around my heart I got this awful feeling like a mule had kicked me there.

By the time I reached him I was panting hard and scared, but Daddy wasn't dead or knocked out cold or anything. His eyes were both wide open toward the sky like there was a whole picture show up there.

"What's the matter?" I asked, but he just closed his eyes and pressed his lips together as a teardrop rolled across his temple. "Is it your knee?" Daddy shook his head so I couldn't tell if it was that or if he maybe didn't know where he was hurt. Then he took a deep breath and finally looked at me. "I'm okay, son," he said, "I might have sprained my ankle but it isn't bad." It was a relief to hear that's all it was, I'm telling you. "Does it hurt a lot?" I knew it must to make him cry, but he said, "no, not bad." "Can you walk on it?" "I don't know," he said, and I said, "maybe if you put your arm around my neck and lean, we can make it to the house and call someone."

Daddy didn't answer right away and when he finally got around to it all he said was, "I don't think so, son." "Huh? How come?" I asked. "I just think I'm going to lie here for a while," he said, and kind of laughed, if you could call it that. "I think that's what I'm going to do."

I felt the raindrops in my lashes as I blinked and tried to figure what was wrong and what to do. Finally I said, "you can't stay here," and he said, "why?" "Because it's wet and you'll get soaked and catch a cold." He just laughed, like catching cold was not a big concern of his. "It isn't funny, Daddy." "No, I guess it isn't, is it?" he said. "No, it's not." "I guess I haven't been a real great dad lately, have I, bud?" he said, and I said, "yes, you have, you've been just fine." Daddy smiled and shook his head like he knew I was lying. "No, bud, I don't think so, and I want you to know, Joey, I'm sorry if I hurt you and your brother." "I know, I know that, Dad," I said, "but please, just get up and come home with me, okay?"

Daddy only blinked up at the sky. "You know, till lately I always thought I was a better father to you boys than my dad was to me. Suddenly it's looking like I turned out worse and I'm not sure what happened." "No, you're not, you're twice as good as him," I said, and Daddy smiled again like I was only saying it so he'd feel better, but I wasn't.

"Not that I blamed him, Joey," Daddy said. "Granddaddy was just wrapped up so tight inside himself and scared of something . . . For the longest time I never knew what it was, I didn't even know it was fear, but now I do. Daddy held himself so straight because he was afraid if he let go just once, even for a second, he'd fall down on the ground and never get back up and never want to. The whole world would come crashing down around him—that's what he believed, and so did I—except it doesn't. Look at me, here I am flat on my back, and you know what?"

I shook my head with that hot feeling in my eyes like they were going to cry on me no matter if I wanted to or not and I did not, but he was smiling, Daddy was. "It's really not that bad down here," he said. "Goddamnit, Joey, I'm amazed, I really am . . . I thought the difference would be so enormous, life and death, but all it is, one minute you're standing up, the next you're lying down. If there's a difference, it's so slight you'd need an instrument to measure it." Daddy looked back off into the sky again. "To find your life you have to lose your life," he said, "I used to know that—how did I forget?" and then he turned to me like I might know the answer.

I just stood there with tears rolling down my cheeks, hoping Daddy couldn't tell them from the rain. I didn't know if he was so smart he'd figured out something no one in the whole world knew or if he talked that way because he hurt so much that something had gone wrong and made him sick inside. I guess at least I wanted him not to love it so, because I think he did, my daddy, falling, which was maybe why he kept on doing it because the moment right before he hit the ground seemed to him like flying, the only time he ever felt like he was free.

"You still can't stay out here, no matter what you say," I told him, the only thing I knew, and he said, "come here, bud." He raised his hand like he was going to let me help him up, only when I took it Daddy pulled me down to him. "Sit here with me a while," he said, "just hold my hand." "No," I said, and tried to pull away, but Daddy held me tight, still smiling, and I started sobbing then. I couldn't help it, I just couldn't.

"It's going to be okay, Joey," Daddy said. "You may not believe me now, but it really is, son, I've never been so sure, especially for you . . . Sometimes I worry about Reed, but you know, son, ever since you were a little baby I've always known—and I think your mom has too—we didn't need to worry about you. Whatever happened you would be okay. And you will be, Joey, everything will turn out fine, believe me."

I didn't. I didn't believe my daddy when he said it or want him to believe it either. I wanted him to know it wasn't fair to do these things like make me sit there in the rain and hold his hand while he gave up and let the whole world fall apart and smile and say it was okay.

"Now listen, bud," he said, "dry your eyes and go back to the house and wait for me, okay? I'd like to be alone a while and when I'm finished I'll come back," and I said, "how will you get there?" "I'll walk, and if I can't do that I'll crawl." "Why can't I just call an ambulance?" I asked, and he said, "no." "What if I did it anyway?" Daddy's jaw flinched once.

"I'd rather you didn't, Joey, but if you feel you need to—not for me, but for yourself—I'll understand. You do what you have to, so will I, and right now what I have to do is lie here for a while." "Why, Daddy, why?" I asked, and he said, "because it took so long to get here, Joey. I've been traveling so long and never even saw where I was going . . . now that I'm here I want to stop and look around and see where I've arrived."

Except I could of told him, and I would of liked to. Where you are is lying, Daddy, *lying* on the mucky shore of a brown mucky lake out back behind a run-down rusty trailer not a mobile home, a *trailer* is the honest word for where you live. You're out here with a twisted ankle talking crazy in the rain and it's up to me to get you home only I don't know how and you aren't helping. That's where, Daddy, that's where you've arrived and so have I—you took me with you.

That's what I would of liked to tell him, but all I said was, "well, would you at least like a drink of water or anything?" Daddy smiled. "That would be nice." As I started off, he said, "and son?" I turned back. "One more thing," he said, "while you're up there, look under my pillow and bring my gun when you come back, okay?" I stood with water dripping down my face and that bad feeling in my gut again, the worst I'd ever felt. Daddy just kept smiling with that soft look on his face. "Just in case whatever we heard in the woods up there comes back," he said, and I said, "okay, Daddy," and walked away real slow until I turned a corner in the trees where Daddy couldn't see me anymore. Then I ran as fast as I could go back to the mobile home and did the one thing I could think to do which was to pick the phone up and call Pa.

# TWENTY-EIGHT

## Joey

It seemed to take forever till Pa came. I sat on the steps, dreading any minute I'd look up and see Daddy at the entrance to the path, mad as hell because I disobeyed and ready to do me the way he did my Daisy. I felt bad about his glass of water, only if I took it he'd ask about the gun, and I decided I'd rather break both promises and take a whipping than have Daddy shoot himself if that was what he meant to do. I just hoped it was a deer we'd heard before and not a pack of wild dogs or a bear or anything that bites, but mainly I was praying Pa would hurry up.

And then he came. The minute I saw the Cadillac I jumped up and ran to meet him, and I guess I must of been telling it too fast at first because Pa said, "whoa, there, boy, where's the fire? Slow down." He put his hand on my shoulder like I might fly off, and I took a deep breath which felt like the first good one I'd had all week.

"Took a run . . . umm-hmm," Pa said. "Fell down? I see . . . just like to lay there for a while he said . . . umm-hmm, umm-hmm." Pa listened, nodding, with that clear-eyed look he gave the farmers as they told their problems on the porches, but I wasn't sure if I should tell about the gun except it just, you know, slipped out. Pa quit talking then; he didn't nod or say "umm-hmm," just stood there still. "But it was in case a animal came from the woods, Pa," I told him. "That's what Daddy said—we heard one, too, we really did."

"Where is it," Pa asked, "the gun?" "Under Daddy's pillow," I said, and went inside with him, wondering if I should of told. Pa stood near the door and looked around at the filled ashtrays. There were only Luckies in them now and not those Kools with lipstick on the filters—I was glad of that. He scanned the kitchen table stacked with dirty plates, and then I followed him across the broken picture back to Daddy's bedroom, stepping over scattered shirts and dirty underpants. I was used to it by then and hardly noticed, only Pa, he noticed—*his* jaw was flinching, going right to town.

"Well, the two a y'all ain't gonna score too many points on housekeeping," he said, trying to make a joke of it. "Don't be mad, Pa, okay?" "It ain't you I'm mad at, honey." "Or Daddy, either," I said, and Pa gave me a look like it was a hard promise I was asking him to make. "You don't hate him, do you, Pa?" I asked. He sighed like he'd been holding his breath, stared at his shoes and shook his head. "I love yo' daddy, son. We've had our diff'ences, but I love him and I always have." "Then don't yell at him, okay?" "I didn't come out here to yell, Joey. If I thought it would do any good I might, but I don't, so I won't." "He's just sad, Pa," I said, "Daddy's just so sad." I started blubbering again like a stupid kid and Pa pulled me close. "I know, son, I know." As he patted my back, I could smell his Chesterfields and Aqua Velva. "Dry yo' eyes now, let's go see if we cain't find him." Before we left, I saw Pa slip the gun into his pocket.

Daddy hadn't moved a muscle from before except to spread his arms like Jesus, and I was glad no animals had got him. When he saw who I'd brought with me, though, Daddy stared at me like I was Judas who'd sold him out for thirty silver dollars only he still loved me anyway, and that was worse than the glass belt, if you ask me.

"Hey, boy," Pa said with his hands in his pockets, rain dripping off his hat brim and making the shoulders of his gray suit black. Daddy just said, "Mr. Will . . ." and gazed the other way. "Taking you a breather?" Pa asked, and this hot look flashed through Daddy's eyes like he was expecting to get yelled at and here Pa was being nice and it wouldn't take too much niceness to make him cry, Daddy. His jaw flinched, trying not to. "I guess you could call it that —yes, sir." "Mind some comp'ny?" Pa asked. Daddy shook his head and Pa took out his pocket square and spread it on the dirt before he sat, not that it did much good. "Joey, son," he said over his shoulder, "how 'bout you lemme and yo' Daddy talk a minute to ourself if you don't mind." "Okay, Pa," I said, but I did mind. "I'll go get your glass of water, Daddy—you still want it?" "Sure, that would be fine," he said, like his mind was occupied with several things right then and a drink of water wasn't high up on the list.

I ran as fast as I could go because I didn't want to miss too much of what they said, though I wasn't sure they'd let me listen. When I got back, Pa was talking and I stood waiting till he finished. I was right out in the open on the path—either of them could of seen me if they'd turned to look, but neither did.

"I don't know, Mr. Will," Daddy was saying, "I wish I did," and Pa said, "well, give it a shot, whydontcha." "What it is, Mr. Will, I just feel tired is all, real real tired . . . I don't know if you've ever felt that way." Pa waited to see if there was more, but Daddy'd stopped. "Jimmy, son," he said, "I wake up tired every morning and go to bed the same, so does every man I know. The only time I ain't tired is when I'm working, fishing, with the grandchildren or drunk, and gittin' drunk just makes it that much harder gittin' out of bed the next time . . . that's a fact I've known since I was yo' age and before." Pa reached in his side pocket, took out a pint of Seagrams and unscrewed the cap. "Every other week since then I been meaning to go on the wagon," he said, " 'cept those thirty years slipped by so fast I never got around to it." He took a sip and winced and wiped his sleeve across his mouth. "The only thing I know today I didn't know back then is just one thing: how fast it goes—that's all I want to tell you." He held the bottle out and Daddy took it, sitting up like Pa had his attention.

I was also listening close because I'd never heard Pa mention this before, about his drinking, much less admit that he got drunk, and it was kind of . . . I don't know, just not as scary as you would of thought.

"But, son," Pa said, "and don't take this wrong 'cause I don't mean it critical, Jimmy. Speaking for myself, I'd rather dig ditches for a living than lay around counting up my past mistakes, wondering if I'd just of changed this or that part, see, then everything would all be different now . . . Fretting over what cain't be changed is a thankless job, long hours and low pay. Seems to me it takes less effort just to get up off yo' back and put yo' shoulder to the wheel again. Life's tiresome enough business, Jimmy, just the real part, without piling a whole bunch of foolishness on top."

Pa took the bottle and had another sip, offering it back. This time Daddy didn't take it. "Well, I understand your feelings, Mr. Will," he said, "but the questions are real, too, or they sure seem that way to me. Whether you like it or not, there are certain times you have to stop and ask." "Maybe so, Jimmy, maybe so," Pa said, "but there's certain other times you maybe hafta not, times you have to *not* stop and *not* ask but just keep going and hold tight to what you got or lose it."

"I can't live blind like that," Daddy said, "sometimes I wish I could, but it just never worked for me. To tell the truth I don't see how anybody but a coward could stand a life like that." "Well, son," Pa said, "between a hero laying on his back asking questions everybody since the time of Adam tried and no one found the answer to 'em yet and a coward who quit asking and got up off his backside and did some useful work for someone else besides himself—well, I'm sorry, but I'll take the coward every time and hold him tight and never let him go, 'cause that kind of coward's rarer than a hen's tooth, Jimmy, and heroes are a nickel to the gross."

They were looking right dead square in each other's eyes, breathing kind of funny. "Don't get me wrong, Mr. Will," Daddy said, "you've done a lot for me over the years and there was never anything I appreciated more than when you covered what I lost at Tommy Janklow's. I know you did it more for May and the boys than me, and I intend to pay you back, but it still meant the world. I did a goddamn foolish thing and you stood by me, but Mr. Will, that doesn't change the fact that I've sweated blood for you twelve years at the Bonanza; I gave up a better future I had every reason to expect so I could marry May—not that I regret it or blame you. I'm just tired of everybody acting like she was the only one who ever made a sacrifice and that everything that ever went wrong was my fault. Can you see that? There've been times I've loved you as much as my own father and cared to know how your life felt to you, from inside. But in all this time I never felt you returned the favor or tried to see my side, and maybe all the ways you helped, financially and otherwise, just meant you never had to try."

Pa didn't answer right away. "All right, Jimmy, son," he said, "maybe you're right, and let's just leave the money out of it—that water's passed the bridge in any case. If I don't understand yo' point of view, then why don't you just come straight out and tell me— what is it with you, son, that you have to come out here and live this way? Even if you don't respect yourself enough to give a damn, how you could stand to do it to yo' child is beyond me."

"Joey asked to come," Daddy said. "Course he did, course he did," Pa said, "you're his daddy, where else would he wanna be 'cept here with you? That ain't the part's confusing me, Jimmy. What I don't git is why it has to be like this." "Like what? You mean my living in a mobile home? What if I do? What makes you think you have the right to judge—your money?" Pa kind of laughed, if you could call it that. "I've known sharecroppers with patches on their knees, Jimmy, who even if it was the only pair of overalls they owned they washed 'em out at night and hung 'em on the line to dry so they'd be clean the next morning when they went back to the fields, and if they lived on a dirt floor it was *swept* dirt. My whole life I've felt nothing but respect for that kind of pride, so don't fool yourself, son; this here between us ain't got a thing to do with money, though if that's what you wanna talk about I wish you'd explain to me one time why it is a man with yo' education and talent cain't go out and make enough to meet his family's needs and satisfy himself."

"I'd think you of all people might have some insight into that," Daddy said, and Pa said, "I b'lieve I always paid you a fair wage and more than fair and if it won't enough and if you didn't wanna stay and wait yo' turn, I never tried to keep you. Hell, Jimmy, nobody was ever more surprised than me when you stayed on at the warehouse, unless it was May. Now, whatever you might think, I ain't saying she's blameless in this matter and I never have, but you act like there's something wrong in her wanting more out of life than y'all have got so far. I know you've worked hard, but ain't she spent the last twelve years cooking yo' meals and keeping yo' house clean and raising those two boys? It ain't like she sat around eating cream puffs all that time, and I'm sorry, but it just don't seem to me it's all that much she's asking. But you act like it's some kind of plot and she's out to suck yo' blood . . . but, son, that's what it's all about—working hard for what you want and once you git it to enjoy it and share it with the folks you love. If there's some other secret to life, I ain't run across it yet and I'm sixty-one years old—nosuh, that's the whole damn thing right there."

"I guess you never had a dream," Daddy said, and Pa said, "a dream? What dream is this?" and Daddy said, "that's what I mean—all these years we've known each other and you never asked—weren't you even curious?" "Well, if I won't, I am now," Pa said. "Ever since I was in college," Daddy said, "hell, before that, way before, since I was almost Joey's age—I've loved books and wanted to be a writer." "So what stopped you?" "I'll tell you," Daddy said, "what stopped me was getting married when I was twenty-one and having to go to work to support my family. What stopped me was getting up every day and putting my shoulder to the wheel the way you said and coming home dead tired at night and never stopping to ask the questions. Maybe I fell short according to May's standards, maybe someone else could have done a better job, but I still did the best I could, and you know what, Mr. Will? Somewhere in there a funny thing happened—working all these years to meet my obligations to everybody else, somehow I forgot my obligation to myself and my dream slipped away. So I don't need you to tell me how fast it goes, Mr. Will. Thanks, but I already know."

"I see," said Pa. "Well, son, I'm glad I asked and sorry I never did before 'cause you just taught me something. But I 'spect there's a couple things about me you don't know either, and one of 'em is I am on yo' side, I always have been and I am right now and so is May and so are yo' two boys—that's something you don't seem to know or appear to of forgot. And another thing is I have had a dream myself, Jimmy, in my time, quite a few in fact, and some of 'em came true, some didn't. Most mornings when I wake up tired, it's the ones that didn't I'm wrestlin' with and what gits me out of bed is hoping they still might. Whether you believe me or not, one of those dreams is for you, son, you and May and the boys, and the other is for June and hers. A lot of other dreams, they came and went, but those stayed on and they're the big ones for me now, Jimmy. That's why I know whatever dream you have, however fine and brave it is, you cain't turn yo' back on yo' responsibilities and the people who love you to go chasin' after it—that's the one thing you cain't do." "What if that was your only chance, Mr. Will?" Daddy asked, and left the question there to hang.

"What if you knew," he went on, "in your whole life you were only going to get one shot at what you wanted, one shot to realize your dream, and the cost, Mr. Will, the price you had to pay was turning your back on everyone you loved and all their expectations —what would you do then?" Pa didn't answer, and Daddy said, "see, that's the kind of question I had to stop to ask."

Pa took a drink of whiskey and stared out at the misty lake. "Well, son, maybe there's a lot about you I don't know, but one thing I do know and believe down in my heart is that you're man enough to pick the right side of that question even if the boy in you still has to ask." "Maybe being a man has more than one definition, Mr. Will." "Not in my book," Pa said, and Daddy said, "maybe the book I'm in is one you never read."

Neither of them spoke another word; they held each other's eyes a few more seconds before they looked away like there was nothing else to say. Of the two of them Pa seemed the saddest, where Daddy just looked mainly hurt and mad.

"Listen to me, Jimmy." Daddy glanced down at his arm where Pa had laid his hand. "One way and another I been trying to tell you this ever since I've known you, so let me say it one last time and then be done. A dream's a fine thing, son; life ain't worth a damn without one, especially if you're Joey's age when one day you're gonna grow up and be president and the next you're gonna be a football hero or a soldier or God knows what-all. But one day you grow up and have to pick one thing and go after it with all you got, 'cause just like dreaming's part of what it is to be a boy, once you git to be a man it switches on you, son—then the job is making it come true. And, Jimmy, hard as that may be, it would be easy if that's all there was to it, but it ain't, 'cause sometimes it don't happen, son. Sometimes the cards are stacked against a man, or he gits a few tough breaks, maybe he ain't smart enough or maybe he's too smart, and then there's the ones who got it all right at their fingertips but instead of grabbing hold they just keep cutting off their hands. There's as many reasons as there are different people in the world, but whatever the reason, if you gave it yo' best shot and couldn't make it happen, then you got to let go of that dream and walk away —that's the hardest part of being a man, Jimmy, but you got to learn it, son. 'Cause if you don't, if you hold it past its time, a dream that don't come true will make you stay a boy forever and a funny thing happens, Jimmy, I've seen it many times. The dream that made life seem worth living turns on you and poisons the real life that's still possible. I'm talking family, Jimmy, I'm talking about a wife and children and a job and friends and a home, all the things that matter, son, all the things you got. You can throw it all away for a dream's sake and think you're being brave and honest, Jimmy, but I got to tell you, son, every horse's ass since Adam probably thought so, too. To me it's just a sin.

"I know because I saw it happen to my daddy, Jimmy, and it cost me half my life to pick up all the pieces of the broken dream he left behind. I was almost forty-five years old before I got back what I had the day I was nineteen, shaving in the bathroom mirror at the Deke house, when Johnny Landis knocked and said my Uncle Burke was there. Jimmy, I still had lather on one side and the other was shaved clean when I walked out in the hall with my straight razor open and there he was, Burke, with his hat in his hand, leaning up against the wall. 'Oh, Lord, Lord, Will,' he said, 'yo' daddy's dead, he's done shot himself, Will. You got to come home, son, you got to come home now with me.' That's what he told me, Jimmy, and I wiped my face and went.

"There's a day life grabs you, Jimmy, it grabs you like a bear and starts to squeeze. I saw it git you, son. You were twenty-one which was too damn young and goddamn rotten luck and I never felt so sorry for anybody in my life as I did for you that day unless it was May standing right beside you at that altar, just eighteen. Me, I was nineteen like I told you when Daddy went in the library and locked the door and blew his goddamn head off with a shotgun—that was the day the bear got me. I tried every way I knew to break out of the grip, I turned and twisted and I hollered and I yelled, but one day, son, you got to turn to the bear and start squeezing back, you got to look him in the eye and say, 'now I've got you, you furry son of a bitch, see how you like it.' And that's the day it changes, Jimmy. That's the day.

"I don't know what else to tell you, son. I tried to help you the best way I knew how—maybe I made a mess of it, and if I did I'm sorry. I know you're mad as hell inside and so was I. I hated my daddy, Jimmy, just like maybe you hate yours and maybe you hate me. But the day I squeezed the bear, son, I stopped hating. The day you make yo' life, that's the day the past stops mattering.

"I know you've got dreams. Some of 'em are way over my head, but I got to tell you, Jimmy, I got to say about the hardest thing to you I ever said to anybody in my life: if a man tells me he's got a dream and quits his job for it and the next time I run into him he's got a sparkle in his eye and a new spring in his step, I'm gonna figure whatever he's up to it agrees with him. But, Jimmy, if I go to that man's house and he's still in bed at noon and there's no sheets on the mattress and dirty dishes in the sink and if he looks at me with muddy eyes like he's working on a two-week hangover and when he trips and falls down on the ground he cain't find the strength to climb back on his feet and come in out the goddamn rain . . . if I ask a man in that condition what he's doing and he tells me he's following a dream, I got to b'lieve he's either lying to me or he's a goddamn fool who's lying to himself—now tell me, Jimmy, which are you? From where I'm at it looks like you're busting up and letting yourself go all to pieces and so ashamed you're calling it a dream, but, son, nobody yet ever sold me shit for apple butter or piss for lemonade, and I'm here to tell you you ain't gonna be the first."

Daddy stared out at the lake with eyes as sad and dull as lead, then squared his shoulders and turned to Pa. "What gives you the right to say that to me?" "Prob'ly nothing, son," Pa said, " 'cept I love you." "You don't know what's in my heart." "So you keep on telling me," Pa said, "and why I keep on sitting here is trying to find out. All I know is what it looks like, son, and what it looks like is you're in a hole and digging deeper and for the life of me I just cain't figure what you're after, is it gold or maybe you're just waiting to hit bottom. Jimmy, son, there ain't no bottom to this hole you're in. A man just either up and quits one day or he goes all the way. I'm tellin' you lay down yo' shovel and climb out, and if you ain't gonna listen to me or someone, well, then, here . . ."

He took out the .38, Pa did, and slapped it into Daddy's hand. "You may's well go 'head on and git it over with," he said, " 'cause if it's what you mean to do ain't no one gonna stop you. At least be man enough to git up off yo' ass and git the gun yourself instead of askin' yo' son to fetch it for you." "That's not why I asked for it," Daddy said, and Pa said, "it ain't? Well, I'm right glad to hear it." "I don't want to kill myself," Daddy said. "Then what exactly is it you *do* want, son?" It got so quiet I could hear the drizzle rustling the leaves, and I felt cold. "I don't know, Mr. Will," Daddy finally said, and his voice was close to breaking.

Pa put his hand on Daddy's shoulder and when he spoke his voice was different, too. "Then lemme ask you this—are you through with this marriage?" Daddy shook his head. "I still love her, Mr. Will." "Then why don't y'all try to patch it up?" Pa asked, and Daddy said, "I don't know if we can, I don't know if May even wants to." "Well, if it was me, I reckon I'd make damn sure I found out before I let my marriage go." "She doesn't want me down there, Mr. Will," Daddy said, and Pa said, "I know she don't want you cheatin' on her with another woman. Beyond that I don't know *what*

May wants and I ain't real sure May knows herself, so you don't either, son, and you ain't gonna find out too much setting here on yo' rear end with her down there.

"Tell you what . . ." Pa stood up slow and picked up his white handkerchief, squeezing out some water and brushing off his pants. "Tomorrow's Thursday," he said. "Come six o'clock I'm leaving from the warehouse same as always and taking Joey with me. If you want a ride, there's room for three." When Daddy didn't answer, Pa just nodded and said, "think it over, son," and turned around and walked away, limping some on his bad leg. When he got into the woods, he reached in his coat pocket for his Chesterfields and as he lit one up I saw how bad his hands were shaking.

After he disappeared up the path, I turned back to Daddy, who was sitting there looking at the .38. It seemed little in his open palm. In a while he put it down and bowed his head and covered his eyes with that same big hand. His shoulders started shaking then, but Daddy's crying made no sound, if that was what it was.

# TWENTY-NINE

## Joey

Around five o'clock we set off for Grody's house to have a meatloaf dinner—to be honest I wasn't all that hungry and Daddy didn't look that keen to go himself. I don't believe he'd said five words all afternoon, which made me think he was still mad at me for calling Pa, except he didn't look that mad. After a nap he washed the dishes and I swept the carpet and emptied all the ashtrays. Then he took a real long shower and shaved and combed his hair and put some fresh clothes on, and by the time we left there was a clear look to his eyes and skin I hadn't seen there in a while, but he still didn't say too much.

"Lord, you're early," Grody said when we walked in. "I had bridge club today and the girls just left. I declare, they're all so finicky they run me ragged—one wants coffee, one wants Sanka, another wants a Coca-Cola. You'd think they'd be considerate enough to ask for the same thing, wouldn't you, and be grateful to get it, too. I certainly am at *their* homes, but do they reciprocate, no, sir, you'd think their parents never taught them any manners. But, Law', I haven't had a chance to even *think* of dinner yet."

"Well, we could come back later," Daddy said, "I've got a couple of errands I can run downtown," and Grody said, "no, since you're here I may as well put you to work so you can earn your board." She winked at me to show that was a joke. "Can you tell me what *board* means, Joey?" "Isn't it like food?" "Law'," she said, "isn't he the smartest *thing!* Food is right. Come here, precious, and give your grandmother a great big kiss.

"Now, Jimmy," she said, "if you don't mind, run up to the store and bring me back a quart of milk. I was going to call your daddy, but you can save him the trip." "Sure, Mother. Come on, bud." "No, no," Grody said, "leave Joey here with me. He can fold the card table and put away the chairs and keep me company while I start dinner—wouldn't you like that, sweetie? You can entertain your grandmother, and if you're hungry, here, please have some nuts; the girls ate all my cashew pieces but there are still some peanuts." She handed me the dish the ladies had picked through. "But not too many or you'll spoil your supper. Now where's my purse?"

"That's okay, Mother," Daddy said, and she said, "no, no, Jimmy, I know how short you are." "I don't think a quart of milk is going to break me." "Every nickel counts," she said, "particularly when you're out of work, and I just have to say I think it's so unfair for you to lose your job after all you've done for him down there—I thought Will Tilley had more character than that." "He didn't fire me, Mother—you know that—I left on my own." "It's so like you to defend him," she said, "but let's not talk of it; we're going to have a pleasant evening. I just want you to know, son, I'm on your side and I'll defend you to the death." Grody handed him a quarter from her change purse and Daddy said, "thank you, Mother." His jaw was going like a fighter jumping rope.

"Oh, yes," she said, "and dear?"—Daddy turned back from the door—"while you're out, if you'd run by the power company for me . . . They're open for another twenty minutes—the check's right here, and please make sure they stamp it paid." "For God's sake,

Mother," Daddy said, "just put a stamp on it and put it in the box—it only costs a nickel." Grody opened her eyes wide like it surprised her when he raised his voice. "I just thought since you were going out and it was on your way . . ." "On my way?" Daddy said, "it's halfway across town."

"Never mind then, Jimmy, I have to go out tomorrow morning anyway," she said, giving him her curdled-milk expression. "I'm serious, Mother. If it saved money I could understand it, but it ends up costing more in gas for me to drive than just to let the mailman take it—let me treat you to the stamp, okay? It would be my pleasure." Daddy grinned like he thought that was pretty good, only Grody wasn't grinning; her chin had started trembling like it always did when she was going to cry and tell you how you broke her, you know, heart.

"What is it, son? Is something wrong?" Daddy answered, "no, Mother, everything's fine," and he'd stopped grinning. "Is it money, Jimmy? Do you need some?" she asked, and he said, "no, Mother, I'm all right—really." Grody emptied all the pens and pencils from the Duke Blue Devil mug that rested on the dictionary and took some money out, which was the first I ever knew she hid it there. "Here." She pressed a bill into his hand. "No, no, that's your grocery money. I don't need it, Mother," he said, trying to push her hand away. "Take it, honey, I want you to." She hurried through the swinging door into the kitchen before he could refuse again. Daddy didn't meet my eyes, just walked to the front door and slammed it as he left.

I started folding chairs and Grody came back from the kitchen sniffling and patting her eyes with a paper napkin. "Is he gone?" "Yes, ma'am," I said, and she peeked through the curtain to make sure. "Where do you want these?" I asked. "You're so dear—here, let me help you." She lit a Raleigh and walked ahead of me upstairs to open doors while I carried two chairs in either arm. I stacked them in the second bedroom closet under the roof slope where she kept her winter clothes, and as I started down to get the table, Grody grabbed my arm and pulled me down beside her on the bed, which took me by surprise and kind of scared me for a second. Her eyes were red and tears were rolling down her cheeks and she was looking at me, Grody, some way nobody in my whole life ever did before, which scared me even more.

"What is it, Grody? What's the matter?" She just said, "oh, Joey, Joey," and stared at me with those deep scary eyes like she was the most unhappy person in the world, or else the way a monster might before it ate you. One part of me wanted to help her, but another part wanted to run away as fast as I could go.

"Oh, Joey, Joey," she said again with more tears rolling, and I said, "what, Grody, *what?*" because I couldn't stand her staring in that awful way without telling me what the matter was. "Just hold me, darling." She put her arms around my neck and let her head drop on my shoulder so I could feel her tears trickling lukewarm against my neck and smell the Raleigh smoke and stale perfume and something else like aerosol coming off her hair and clothes and skin, and all of it together made me kind of dizzy, like I might throw up, especially the sour smell rising from the sheets.

I'd never in my life had that radiation feeling in my stomach so strong as then, but a hug was all it was, I told myself, and why was that so bad, except it felt like something different, something much, much worse I didn't know the name of or if they even had one in the dictionary. But maybe that was just my imagination and part of what was wrong with me: that I could think a thing like that of my own grandmother who told me all the time how much she loved me and just felt sad right now and wanted to be hugged. So I sat there stiff, thinking I must be pretty mean and heartless to look at it that way, except I couldn't help myself. I just wished she'd hurry up and finish and get off me.

"I just don't know what to do about your daddy," she finally said, wiping her sleeve across her eyes and looking up again. She took my hand in both of hers and put it in her lap. "He's not himself. He hasn't been in the longest time. He was never like this growing up, Joey, *never.* The boy I raised would never be so disrespectful as to scream at his own mother about a postage stamp. I just don't understand it. We gave these children everything, *everything*, and Jimmy most of all. But, Joey, one day your daddy walked in through that door downstairs and told us he was getting married and from that day to this, from that hour, he's never been the same."

Grody was still crying but her eyes turned hard as she said that. "Oh, Joey, I don't mean to blame your mother," she went on, and I knew where she was going then and would of liked to scream at her to stop before it was too late. I wanted everything to stay the same as it had always been, with her and Mama hating one another secretly because of how each blamed the other for the way my daddy was, but never saying it aloud, see, only thinking it and showing it through things like Grody turning up her nose at Mama's Christmas angel—you could live with that. But if Grody said this next thing, if she tried to make me side with her against my mother, then I'd have to hate her, and I didn't want to. More than anything in the whole world I didn't want to have to hate her.

"I've tried so hard to see May through Jimmy's eyes and love her as a daughter, just as I do Dolly. All those years the children were growing up we were happy in this house, we never had unpleasant words, but from the day your daddy married her it seems we can't discuss the smallest thing without it turning to a fight. What am I to think? What would anyone? She turned his heart against me, Joey, against his own mother. If I blame her for anything, it's that.

"And if only she'd known how to help him, Joey, if she'd made him happy, I could have accepted it. But from the time your daddy turned against me and against the way he was brought up, nothing has gone right for him, not one single thing. Ever since that year in Chapel Hill—Jimmy simply wasn't used to that sort of life, keeping those late hours, and particularly the drinking . . . If May had held the reins a little tighter and looked over his shoulder and made sure he did his lessons the way I always did when he was growing up, if she'd known how to be a proper wife to him and love him the way I loved him as a mother, Jimmy would have made it. Joey, your daddy would be a doctor today and everything would be so different, so so different. But she wasn't right for him. I knew it from the start and had a premonition it would turn out badly. I tried to tell him, but he wouldn't listen, he just wouldn't listen—"

"Tried to tell me what?" Daddy said and we both turned around and saw him standing in the doorway, holding a brown paper bag.

"Oh, Jimmy." Grody dropped my hand like a hot potato, putting on a great big smile. "I didn't hear you come in, honey." "Apparently not," he said. Those clear green eyes of his had a smile in them for me—"hello, bud," he said—but when he looked back at Grody they were flashing lightning, Daddy's eyes.

"Joey and I were having us a little private chat," she said, "weren't we, sugar?" I didn't answer, and Daddy said, "were you really—what about?" "We aren't going to tell him, are we, Joey—that old so-and-so can just mind his own beeswax, can't he?" "If you have something to say about May," Daddy said, "you say it to me, not Joey—I won't have you talking to him behind my back." "I wasn't, was I, Joey?" Grody said. I didn't say a word to save her; I got up and went to him.

"I heard you, Mother," Daddy said, putting his arm around my shoulder. Grody's face changed. "Well, you should be ashamed for eavesdropping," she told him, not smiling or pretending anymore. "If you did, I'm sorry, but maybe it's time you finally heard the truth. Everything I said to Joey I said out of love for you, Jimmy, whether you can see it or not. I said it so he'll see the story has another side from what they're telling him down there, May and Zelle, filling his head with lies to make him hate us. All I ever wanted was what was best for you, and I still do—in your heart I think you know that." Daddy said, "no, Mother, in my heart I actually don't. I wish I did, but in my heart it seems to me that what you mainly wanted was what was best for you."

"How can you say that to me?" Grody asked, "I gave you children everything, I sacrificed my life for you," and Daddy said, "no, Mother, you only think you sacrificed your life for us. In reality we sacrificed for you. You're so selfish you even seem to think what's happening in my marriage is about you, how much you're suffering, how hard it is for you—but this isn't your pain, Mother, it's mine and May's and Reed's and Joey's, *our* family's pain. You aren't concerned with it, and you should be ashamed for taking advantage of a child who's in the middle. If you aren't, then I'm ashamed for you, and I won't have it, Mother, do you hear? I won't. It sickens me.

"Now come on, bud," he said, "I don't know about you, but I feel hungry. Let's get a bite and go home to our trailer." "Okay, Dad," I said. "What about dinner?" Grody asked, "your daddy will be here any minute—what will I tell him?" "I don't know, Mother,"

Daddy said, "maybe you should try telling him you love him—who knows what might happen . . . And by the way, here's your milk. I'm sure you want it back." As we left I saw the silver trophy on the chest of drawers in Daddy's room and felt as happy then as if we'd won that crown of leaves ourselves, me and Dad. It seemed like everything might be all right again. I truly thought that it could be that easy for the world to change.

# THIRTY

## Joey

That night we had a greasy cheeseburger and fries at Earl's and Daddy let me sip the head off his Blue Ribbon while Earl winked and grinned with his bad teeth before he looked the other way. After that we went out to the softball field and watched a game under the lights and all the grown men called out, "Jimbo, where you been?" and walked over to shake hands like they were glad to see him. Daddy kept one arm around my shoulder as he said hello and told each one, "this is my boy, Joey," and someone knocked a home run over the left-field wall so high it sailed out of the lights and seemed to disappear among the stars.

The next day as I packed my suitcase at the trailer it was real strong on my mind whether Dad was going to the beach with Pa and me. I was almost scared to ask, except he seemed in a good mood and was whistling a tune, so I finally did. "Think I should?" he asked with a big grin. "Yes, sir, Daddy, I sure do." He pursed his lips and nodded. "Well, bud, so do I." I don't believe I ever felt much happier in my life than I did then.

That afternoon as we were riding into town a song came on the radio that made us start moving in our seats, and Daddy said, "shh, shh, I want to hear this." We didn't catch the title, but the DJ said the singer's name, Aretha Franklin, which was the first I ever heard of her, and Daddy said, "I've got to get that tune." Later on the drive we started up ourselves—to sing, I mean—the same song as the day I first came down, which was his favorite one, my Dad's:

> *"In the Big Rock Candy Mountains*
> *There's a land that's fair and bright,*
> *Where the handouts grow on bushes*
> *And you sleep out every night,*
> *Where the boxcars are all empty*
> *And the sun shines every day,*
> *Oh, the birds and the bees and the cigarettes trees,*
> *And the lemonade springs where the bluebird sings*
> *In the Big Rock Candy Mountains."*

By the time we got to the Bonanza it was close to three o'clock. I thought he meant to come inside with me, but as we pulled into the lot, Daddy said, "listen, bud, I have a couple of things I need to do before we leave. You go on in and find your pa, tell him I'll be back by four, four-thirty at the latest." "Can't I come with you?" He smiled and rubbed his hand across my flattop. "No, son, this is something I have to do myself." I just said okay and went in by myself.

Inside, there was a auction going on and Pa let me walk the aisles with him and turn the tags on the sold piles. I said hello to Otis at the scales out back and then to Mrs. Weems and Tina and Marie in the front office. Over by the drink machine, Skeeter tried to ask me how Daddy was except he started stuttering so bad he couldn't get it out, but I knew what he meant and that the others felt the same. Skeeter was the only one who could come straight out with it, being simple like he was. It seemed a long time since I'd been there and I was glad to see them all, even Reb, who didn't tell me any lies that day.

By that time it was after four, and then four-thirty came, and five, and then the others left, and finally at six o'clock Pa locked the doors and we went out in the lot to wait. We sat there in the Cadillac with the windows down and watched the Southern Star streak through at 6:26 on its way from Richmond to Atlanta—the conductor blew the whistle, but it didn't stop in Killdeer anymore.

We left pretty shortly after that and I made Pa drive by the trailer on the way, but Daddy wasn't there. I knew by then he wasn't coming and had a pretty good idea where he might be, but maybe he just went to say goodbye to her—at least that's what I hoped.

I think Pa felt about as bad as me because he hardly spoke a word for the first hour or so, but then he said, "thought we might do us some fishing this weekend at the Inlet if the weather holds. Howzat sound by you?" "Okay, Pa." "Maybe troll for mackerel," he said, "break in that new pole a yo's . . ." "You mean in the ocean?" I asked, and Pa said, "yessuh, I mean in the sea." "What about Mama?" "B'lieve we finally wo' her down," Pa said and grinned for the first time. I tried hard to smile for him, but even the thought of offshore fishing, which I'd waited for so long, didn't cheer me up too much that night. Right about that time we crossed the Winton bridge.

Later on Pa took out the Seagrams and asked me if I'd sing a song for him and I knew what he wanted was "The Wabash Cannon Ball" which always put him in that peaceful mood. But that night all I felt like singing was "The Big Rock Candy Mountain," and I tried, except I couldn't make the verses rhyme.

# Part 3

## LABOR DAY

# THIRTY-ONE

## Joey

So me and Pa grilled T-bones in the drive that night the same as always, only Daddy's stayed upstairs in the refrigerator still wrapped in the white butcher paper from the Piggly Wiggly. It was pretty nippy out there, another thing that made that Thursday night seem different from the way it always was before and how it was supposed to be. Pa said it was just high pressure coming down from Canada, which meant fine fishing weather for the morning, but to me it meant another summer day I'd never see again. To me it meant fall coming closer, bringing on that change whose name I didn't know except that I could see it in the way the stars stood out above our heads, sharp and clear, the way they never are in summertime, which makes the sky feel bigger over you. It's real pretty, that kind of autumn night, though there's something sad in it that makes you feel alone under those cold burning stars. I moved a little closer to the fire and to my pa—him, mainly.

On the stroke of ten we all sat down and Pa said grace like always. Mama didn't even bother pretending to be shocked; she only smiled like she appreciated him for trying even if it didn't do much good. Nanny said, "Will, sugah, we got to see cain't we find you a new blessin'. After thirty years I b'lieve that one a yo's is just about wo' out." "What the hell is wrong with y'all?" Pa asked, "it ain't a fun'ral, is it? Nobody that I know of died." He seemed mad at us for not acting like we were supposed to on a Thursday night, and then Reed said, "when's Daddy coming, Mama?" and everyone shut up.

"I don't know, sugar," Mama told him with a sad expression, her answer every time. It made me want to throw my napkin down and shout, "he's not! Not ever!" so Reed wouldn't have to keep on asking, only I knew it would just hurt Mama more and make that sad look sadder.

"Please excuse me everyone," she said, standing up with her clean napkin, "I don't feel very hungry. I believe I'll take a walk." "You have to eat, May," Nanny said, and Mama said, "I'll get something later, Mama." They had the exact same conversation every night and then again at breakfast every morning, only I don't think Mama ever did get something later—she was getting skinny as a rail, like she'd been to the Rice House, too.

Even in the short time I'd been gone you could see the difference in her cheekbones, which had shadows under them from her not eating much and all that walking she did on the porch at night. As soon as it got light those footprints trailed down the front steps and disappeared across the sand. She'd be out there many days till suppertime, Mama would, just walking on the beach, up past Camelot Pier, north to where the houses stopped and the dunes grew wild again, on and on toward Virginia, till she was tanned darker than a hickory nut and had reddish sun streaks in her hair which she didn't bother putting in a French twist anymore but let the ocean wind blow wild around her face till it looked like a mane.

Now she was threading her napkin through the ring when suddenly headlights flashed across the wall. Tawny raised her head with her ears pricked and thumped out a slow drumbeat on the floor. We heard the sound of tires crunching over loose sand in the driveway and Reed stood up real sudden so his chair legs skidded on the floor. "It's Daddy!" "Oh, no, darling, I don't think so," Mama said, like her heart was broken that he'd get his hopes up just to have them dashed again.

Except it was. Tawny cut loose, barking and turning circles by the door. And suddenly there he was, all six-foot-six of him, framed in the screen with his arms full of flowers, those orange ones Nanny called "outhouse lilies" which Mama always made us stop to pick along the road. I guess Daddy also must of known she liked them, because it looked like he'd cleaned out a field full, and there was champagne pinned beneath his elbow together with a Whitman's Sampler box, the big size that has two or three of everything including chocolate-covered cherries, Mama's favorite kind.

He just stood there, Daddy, looking like he wasn't sure if he could come in anymore or had to wait to be invited. "Speakin' a You-know-who," Nanny said, taking the glass chimney off the candle to light a cigarette, and Pa said, "Lord a mercy, look what the cat drug in," with a big grin. "Looks like I caught y'all eating," said Daddy, acting polite the way you would with strangers, and Mama put her napkin down. "Hello, Jimmy," she said in a quiet, nervous voice, and he said, "hello, May," the same, except that he was smiling, Daddy, where Mama looked dead serious like she had doubts if this surprise was good and she was scared of finding out.

"Well, come *in*, Daddy," Reed said and took off toward him like a shot. Before he got there, though, Tawny crouched on her front legs and sprung straight in the air like someone fired her from a cannon. Daddy flinched and reared back on his heels and then he dropped it all, champagne and flowers, candy, everything, and caught her up against his chest. Tawny licked his cheek and sat there with a doggy grin, and we were howling, let me tell you, boy, everyone around that table, Mama, too, and suddenly it was Thursday night again.

"Dee Lou, fetch me that other steak out here," Pa called into the kitchen, "them coals should still be hot enough, I reckon." "No, no, Mr. Will, I ate on the way down," Daddy said, and Pa said, "ate my foot. You'll just have to eat again, won't he, boys?" and me and Reed both said, "yes, sir, Pa." "Really, y'all," Daddy said, "I don't want to impose." " 'Impose'?" Pa said, like it made him mad, that word, "what you talking 'bout 'impose'?" We all looked at Mama, who needed to say something then. "Don't be silly, Jimmy, of course you'll eat." She spoke in that Ascension voice which made it hard to tell whether she said it just to be polite or really meant it from her heart, and it was strange to see them act that way, all careful with each other, like two people who'd just met.

Daddy shouldered open the screen and dropped Tawny on the porch before he picked up Reed, who reached out on the sly and pushed the door back open for Tawny to come in again. "What in the world . . ." Daddy said when he felt her rub against his legs. When we laughed, Reed grinned and hid his face in Daddy's chest. Mama knelt and started gathering the lilies with her skirt spread on the floor, and Daddy put Reed down. "Here, May, let me get those for you." "No, no, it's all right, I've got them," she said, "Joey, sugar, run ask Dee Lou for a vase and put some water in it," and I said, "yes, ma'am, Mama . . . What *happened* to you, Daddy? You said you'd be back by four . . . We waited and waited."

"I know you did. I'm sorry, bud, and you, too, Mr. Will. You'll never guess what happened . . . Remember that song we heard on the radio?" When I nodded, he said, "well, I went down to Alston's to see if I could find it, and of course they didn't have it, but I was pretty stuck on the idea by then. So I tried Lawford Corner and couldn't find it there and ended driving all the way to Chapel Hill. I thought I could make it back in time, which is why I didn't call, but on the way home I ran into a jackknifed tractor-trailer and had to back up half a mile and take a bunch of dirt roads to get around. By the time I made it to the warehouse it was right at seven-thirty on the station clock. When I didn't see you in the lot I just kept coming, hoping I might catch you on the way, but I guess I didn't. It was quite an adventure . . ."

"Sounds like it," Mama said, and Nanny blew a smoke ring and said, "mmmm . . ." with slitty eyes, and Pa just shook his head and threw in, "umph, umph, umph." They'd had a few adventures of their own with Daddy and knew all about them. I did, too, and to tell the truth I was just as glad I missed this one. Sometimes it seemed Daddy made things more of a adventure than they had to be.

"Well, did you get it?" I asked, reminding him. Daddy blinked those clear green eyes at me. "Get what, bud?" "The *record*," I said, and he said, "yeah," and grinned, "yeah, I did, actually." "So what's it called?" I asked, and Daddy said, " 'Respect.' " Nanny smirked. "No wonder you had trouble finding it." I saw Daddy's jaw flinch once but he kept smiling. "Sometimes old dogs can learn new tricks, Miss Zelle." "It ain't the tricks so much as whether you can get rid of the fleas," Nanny said, and Mama said, "Mama . . ." like Nanny should butt out and shut her trap. I thought so, too. But Daddy said, "no, May, I know what your mama's thinking and she has a certain point." "You have no more idea than a hoot owl what I'm thinking, Jimmy Madden," Nanny said, "if you did, yo' brains would curdle up and run out of yo' ears." "Nanny, *yuck*," Reed said, and Pa said, "well, y'all quit yappin', whydontcha, and put the damn thing on so we can hear it. We could use some music around this place to cheer up all these sourpusses."

"Run get it for me, bud," Daddy said, "it's on the front seat." I was halfway down the steps when Mama called, "Joey," and I remembered the vase she'd asked me to go get. I turned back, but all she said was, "please don't slam the door. I won't have you running through this house like a wild Indian." She went off to fetch the vase herself, and I felt pretty bad, I truly did, only I figured Daddy needed my help more.

"Well, it ain't Tommy Dorsey," Nanny said when the forty-five dropped on the platter of the Dumont, "but it ain't half bad either." Her legs were crossed, with one shoe dangling off her heel, and that espadrille was hopping as she worked the beat, tapping her diamond ring against the arm rail of the chair. Daddy grinned and said, "come on, Miss Zelle, let's cut the rug," and she grinned back for the first time like she was softening up. "Naw, I'm too old for such foolishness." "That'll be the day," Daddy said, and it was good to see them back to their old tricks. "And anyway," Nanny said, "I ain't the one you should be askin'."

We all turned to Mama, who looked up from arranging flowers. "What? Oh, no, y'all, really . . . let's all sit down and eat before it gets too cold." "Come *on*, Mama," Reed said, and she said, "well, all right, sugar, come over here and Mama will dance a little bit with you," like that was what he meant, only Reed was way too smart to fall for anything that feeble. "No, with *Daddy*," he said, and even with her hickory tan she flushed so you could see the red come through. They looked at each other kind of shy and Daddy held his hand out, smiling. She pretty much had to take it then, with us all watching, wanting her to.

Dee Lou came out of the kitchen and leaned against the door to watch. "Ain't they cute," Nanny said, and Dee said, "yes, ma'am, Miss Zelle, sho is," beaming at them. "Come on, you two buzzards," Pa said, looking happy but a little bit embarrassed, "let's slap that other T-bone on before the fire dies out," and Reed and me both said, "yes, sir," but neither one of us was very quick to follow. "Like it?" Daddy asked her, grinning, and Mama said, "mmmm . . . the music, yes," and right then came the part where Aretha says,

> *Ooo, yo' kiss is*
> *sweetuh than honey,*
> *and, guess what,*
> *so is my money . . .*

Daddy did his Stewart Granger eyebrow and Mama laughed, which got his courage up to swing her underneath his arm. Reed clapped and I whistled with my fingers in my mouth, and Mama flushed down to her shoulders and really cut loose for a minute so Daddy had a hard time keeping up. As he held her hand and tried to guess which way she was going, he had a soft smile in his eyes like he was proud she danced so well, and Mama smiled back, too, a real smile now, not the kind they teach you at Ascension which you can never really tell about. She slowed down just enough for him to catch the beat, and I have to tell you they looked pretty smooth out there—for their age, they did.

We trooped down to cook the steak then, me and Pa and Reed, and we weren't in the driveway long before they came out on the porch where Mama leaned across the rail. "Daddy, boys," she said, "y'all go ahead and eat, don't wait for us. We're going to sit in the gazebo for a while and talk," and Reed said, "can I come, too?" and Mama said, "no, sugar, you eat your dinner while it's warm. I'll be back in time to tuck you in." "Daddy, too?" Reed asked, and Daddy said, "yeah, bud, me too." He twisted the wire off the champagne and shot the cork over our heads, and Tawny pricked her ears and took off after it, her claws skittering across the concrete, like someone shot a duck for her to fetch, though I doubt she'd ever seen one in her life except if it was flying south. At the bottom of the steps Mama toed her shoes off and left them on the driveway as she and Daddy stepped into the sand and walked out of the light.

They stayed up there for the longest kind of time, all through dinner and way past it, too, till even the pots were clean—they came last in Dee Lou's washing order. All you could see of them was the glow of their white clothes against the dark which made them look like ghosts, Mama and Daddy, and the orange coals of their cigarettes getting brighter, then dimming off again. At first they were across from each other on opposite benches, but later they moved to the same side, and it was right around that time that Nanny said we had to go to bed. "Mama told us she was going to tuck us in," Reed said with that pouty lip like he was set to stomp and whine, "she promised." "Now listen," Nanny said, "if y'all want to he'p, the best thing you can do is just behave yo'self and let yo' mamindaddy have a little time alone, hemme?" Reed looked at me and I nodded like even if it was a trick it was still true, what Nanny said, and he went quiet then; we both did.

After we'd washed up Reed asked if he could get in bed with me, and though we hadn't done that in a while, that night I said it was okay. Once he'd dropped off, I laid there listening to him breathe and smelling that green pea smell of his. Having him beside me made me think about the old days, how it used to be before Pa got sick and Nanny went off to the Rice House, before Mama and Daddy got so mad and started fighting all the time. Then, real soft and slow, Reed started banging his head into the pillow. I closed my eyes and said a prayer. I asked God to let it all go back and be the way it was before, to give back what was ours when we were all still happy and hardly even knew.

Later I woke up to the creaking of that loose board on the porch. At first I thought it was Mama out there by herself again, only then I heard the whispers, his mixed up with hers, and I remembered Daddy had come home. "Smell that breeze," he said in a clear, happy voice, and Mama said, "mmmm, the wind just shifted, didn't it?" "Know what that reminds me of?" he asked, and she said, "hmmm?" "A fresh start," Daddy told her, and when she didn't answer right away he said, "to me it does."

"We've had so many, Jimmy," she said at last, "I wish I could understand why it always seems to end up the same way for us." "It can be different this time, May, I know it can." "You've said that before," Mama said, "and so have I," and Daddy said, "I know, I know we have, but something's changed for me, if I could just make you believe that." "I'd like to, Jimmy," Mama said, "there's nothing I'd like more." "But?" "If there's a but," she said, "it's only that it can't just be the words. You're so good with those, honey, you always were and I've always been so ready to believe you, but this time I have to see, I have to see it with my own two eyes . . . Oh, God, that sounds so selfish, as though I'm deciding all of it for both of us, and I don't want to. You may not believe it, but that's the last thing in the world I want, Jimmy, to decide for you and Reed and Joey, when I can hardly manage for myself." "Then let me help you," Daddy said, and she said, "please don't say that," and he said, "why?" "Because I want to believe you mean it and I'm too afraid you don't." "All I'm asking is a chance to prove it to you, May, one more chance," he said. "Don't give up on me, okay?"

"Jimmy," Mama said, "oh, Jimmy, Jimmy," and Daddy said, "come here." There was a muffled sound like she was crying up against his chest, and Daddy just kept saying, "shhh, shhh, it's okay," and Mama sniffed and sighed.

They fell quiet for a long time after that, till finally Mama said, "well, it's getting chilly out here. We probably ought to go in now." "I'll get my things and put them in the downstairs bedroom," Daddy said, and she said, "no, honey, I don't want you to," and Daddy said, "you don't?" and she said, "no," which was the last word they spoke. After that the only thing I heard was the floorboard creak out in the hall as they snuck in, then the latch—*click*—as they shut the bedroom door. I drifted off to sleep again, feeling warm and safe inside the way I used to feel a lot before this whole thing started the morning I woke up and found those footprints on the porch.

# THIRTY-TWO

## Joey

When I got up Friday morning Mama and Daddy were still in bed and Nanny was all smiles, shushing us and making everybody walk on tiptoe. When A. Jenrette came over from his cottage, I was just as glad to go outside with him, though I didn't like him too much anymore since that time in Durham when he said I looked like the Shoney Big Boy. He had a pack of dirty playing cards he'd lifted off his daddy and we looked through those a while, but to tell the truth A.'s weren't as good as some that Stevie Poe showed me and Archie in the woods one day, and I wasn't very interested. When Uncle Johnny asked us to help set up the card table for gin rummy in the driveway, A. went over but I cut out alone.

Underneath the Jenrettes' house there was a place we used to play when we were kids, though mostly Reed and his bunch used it now. It was always cool and dark down there, and grownups never bothered you because you had to crawl to get there. I'd always liked how, if you looked out into the sunlight, you could see everything that happened but people looking in could not see you, and that was where I went.

I hadn't been there long when Mama and Nanny came down in the driveway in their flip-flops heading for the beach. They called me several times, but I didn't feel like hauling the umbrella over the hot sand so I didn't answer, and Reed, wherever he was hiding, didn't either.

Tawny poked her nose between the lattice slats and whined at me, wanting to play fetch. She wriggled beneath the bottom board, dropped her stick in my lap and bothered me until she caught the scent of a sand fiddler and went on the attack, barking and paddling till her head and front legs disappeared into the hole. Out with the wet sand tumbled one of my old Matchbox cars, a Chevy Bel Air like the one we used to have. Daddy had given it to me and it was my favorite toy for quite a while, though I'd lost it so long ago I'd practically forgotten. As I picked it up and tried to wipe away the crud, I thought of how we used to go to ride on summer nights before Reed came, me sitting in the middle or in Daddy's lap to steer—he'd let me blow the horn sometimes, my favorite thing to do. It was dusk and we'd be somewhere in the country with hay smells drifting through the window and lightning bugs across the fields. Mama would point to grazing cows and say, "what does the cow say?" and I'd say, "moo," and sometimes Daddy would say, "wuff," or "cockadoodle-doo," which made me laugh—that was the first joke I ever understood. Then Mama would begin to sing, "Baa, baa, black sheep, have you any wool," and I'd drift off and wake up back at home in my own bed and we were happy then.

When the Bel Air finally died and Daddy sold it off for parts, he found a Matchbox the same color and gave it to me, knowing how much I'd loved that car. One day out playing I'd lost it somewhere and cried myself to sleep that night, but since that day I hadn't thought about it once until it rolled out between Tawny's spread hind paws, all gritty and crusted up with rust. As I turned it over in my hand that morning, thinking maybe I could clean it up and make it bright again, I heard tires crunching up the driveway and a radio blaring loud enough to wake the dead.

I stared through the boards as the front end of Uncle Sumner's Thunderbird rolled to a stop with the rag top down and the chrome hubcaps gleaming like two mirrors. He was behind the wheel in what looked like a straw sombrero with the string pulled tight against that little double chin of his. He stumbled when he hopped the side, not bothering with the door—it was hard to tell if he was drinking or just trying to act younger than he was, but I noticed he was pretty spiffed in leather deck shoes with no socks and madras Bermudas and a crisp pink oxford shirt with the sleeves rolled to the elbows. I got a real bad feeling, seeing him there. He kind of hesitated when he saw the Mustang, like it was the first he'd realized Daddy had come down, but then he leaned in the back seat and took out a thermos and a brown paper bag and trotted up the boardwalk to the dune, and I had to move around to the east side to keep a eye on him.

Once he reached the gazebo he put his stuff down on the bench and waved and cupped his hands to call, and he rang the dinner bell we had up there. Mama appeared over the dune in her dark glasses, smiling and breathing hard, and just about that time the door of our house slammed and I moved back around to where I was before. Daddy had come out on the porch and was watching them, too, real quiet, with a dark look and that square set to his jaw, the first I'd seen it since he'd come. When Mama saw him she waved and started down the hill with Uncle Sumner close behind. Daddy didn't bother waving back.

"Hello, Jimbo," Uncle Sumner said, sounding friendly, "I didn't realize you were here." "Look, Jimmy," Mama said, "Sumner's made a pitcher of margaritas. Why don't you slip on your suit and come down on the beach with us and let's all have one. The little boys are probably ready to go swimming anyway and you know I feel better with you there." "Sumner could watch them," Daddy said, "you wouldn't mind, would you, Sumner?" and Uncle Sumner seemed a little flustered, like he wasn't sure how he should answer. "I understand you've been doing that anyway," Daddy said, "keeping an eye on things for me since I've been gone, and I probably ought to thank you for being so conscientious and concerned." "Hey, Jimmy, listen . . ." "No, really, Sumner, I mean it," Daddy interrupted, "from the bottom of my heart, I do. You've always been a gentleman and I'd expect no less."

Uncle Sumner looked at Mama then. "Maybe I should go," he said, taking off his sombrero, and Mama told him, looking straight at Daddy with a face as set as his, "no, Sumner, I want you to stay right here and have a drink since you were nice enough to fix them." He squeezed her arm and said, "another time," and threw his hat in the back seat as he got in, going through the door this time.

"Thank you so much for that, Jimmy," Mama said as Uncle Sumner backed out the T-bird. "Don't mention it." "Why?" she asked, "I'd be so grateful if you'd explain to me why you felt it necessary to do that." "Do what?" he said, and she said, "hurt Sumner's feelings and humiliate him that way." Daddy shrugged and smirked a little. "It's not that complicated, May. If you think hard I'm sure you can come up with the answer."

"Sumner is a dear childhood friend of mine, Jimmy." "Come on, May," Daddy said, "I know you've been seeing him—it's all over town." Mama didn't answer; she just stared at him. I couldn't even breathe.

# THIRTY-THREE

*Jimmy*

Molly filled me in on things. I ran into her, the former Mrs. Sumner Dade, one afternoon at the Piggly Wiggly down on Commerce Street. She was in the frozen meat aisle peering at a boneless breast as if she couldn't quite make up her mind—I had a feeling she'd been there a while.

To tell the truth, I was a little shocked at her appearance—her hair was frazzled and her eyes had a glassy focus that didn't seem directed on that chicken or on me or anything in the present moment. I had to say her name three times before she came out of her trance. Seeing who it was, she latched on to me like a comrade in arms and told me someone she knew had seen May and Sumner at the Beach Club one night dancing. Molly retailed the story with a disconcerting little smile, as though she took some perverse delectation in it and naturally assumed I'd feel the same. I didn't. The information caught me by surprise, and leaving aside the question of rights and whether I still had any, it hurt me a good bit.

Molly didn't seem to notice. She was like a connoisseur whose specialty had become betrayal—the crueler the detail, the more she seemed to relish it. And I don't mean cruel to me—no, that was just a sideline—she was the star victim in the tale she told. Yes, I was shocked and not just by her looks. That was my first encounter with divorce, with the toll that first year or two can take even on a charming and attractive woman. Molly had been both; now she was like a vengeful wraith, thinner than a razor and as dangerous, mainly to herself.

Having brought me up to speed, she tilted her head in a musing way and fixed her gaze on me. "Why don't you come by for dinner sometime, Jimmy? We have a lot to talk about, I'd say." "Sure, Molly, we really should," I said, and she said, "how about tonight?" It's possible I mistook her intention, but I don't think so—it was a come-hither look straight out of hell.

When I didn't answer right away, she said, with that same odd smile, "you're blushing," and I said, "sorry," and she said, "what for? I don't think we owe them anything—do you?" "I don't know, Molly, probably not, but unfortunately I've got plans." "Oh, yes, I'm sure you do," she said, "I've heard about that, too. Well, if you change your mind, you know where I live."

The way she said it sounded almost like a threat. Maybe in a way it was—because I have to tell you, for a fraction of a second the possibility of taking her up on it passed through my mind, I couldn't even tell you why. I guess I was a little crazy, too; we all were by that time, including May and Sumner. Being crazy, though, is not much of an explanation. Getting revenge would be a stronger possibility— maybe that's what Molly had in mind. But I don't think that's what the impulse was for me, and certainly pleasure didn't have a lot to do with it. No, I just think deep down I had an instinct to do what women asked me to and give them what they wanted if I could. A shrink could probably come up with a nuanced explanation, but the core of it, I think, was simple pain, just that. I had a radar for that in a woman—sensing it triggered an alarm that made me want to reach out and do something to relieve that pain. Considering how much I've caused, it's almost funny.

But that was it, you see. Because if you can't heal that pain, if what you do or try to do is never enough, what then? For me that was always where the window bars came back into focus against the sky of everything I'd wanted love to be, including what I wished to give.

I've wandered off the point of Molly, though, who was back to gazing at that chicken in the freezer like Cassandra into her own private crystal ball.

All of which leads up to Edie Perkins, I suppose, and what exactly can I say? I didn't go out looking for it; it found me. It happens sometimes, and things at home were bad by then. May never looked at me without that mote of distrust in her eyes, the foregone conclusion that I was going to fail and disappoint her one more time. With Edie it was different. She listened with real interest when I talked and wasn't predisposed to judge. The fact that I'd been to college impressed her; so did my position at the warehouse—I was still there then—and what I knew about the business. Strange as it may seem, she looked up to me, and I think that had more to do with it than sex, though sex was also part of it—the bedroom had pretty much shut down back home on Ruin Creek. I know she was just a kid, but she'd been around the block and she was plenty bright. Being with her made me feel like, hey, when you got down to it, what exactly was my failure, what had I done wrong? By some people's standards I'd done well, respectably by almost anyone's. Edie didn't want the moon and stars like May or Mother.

What did Edie want? Just laughs at first, I think, like me, a little tenderness. But as things went along that spring those little innuendoes crept into her conversation. She began to ask me how I saw the future, what I wanted from it, what I hoped—questions that weren't really questions but disguised instructions on Edie's hopes and dreams, attempts to catechize me on their rightness and attractiveness. I was supposed to express enthusiasm for the part she'd assigned me in that future which suddenly was no longer mine, but ours and, far more deeply, hers. Sometimes I'd writhe while Edie, thinking her true motives were opaque, went on blithely showing me the Golden Land our wagon train was rapidly approaching.

I don't blame her—I didn't then. She was a twenty-two-year-old kid with a kid of her own and no husband, no education to speak of and a part-time job in her aunt's beauty parlor. I guess I looked pretty good to her. It went from laughs to wanting to be loved, to wanting to be healed of all the pain—Edie had her share, like anyone. It went the way it always goes, the very same—having gone to her for respite and some laughs, I ended shackled with a second unofficial wife riding me as hard for disappointing her as May had ever done.

Even before May kicked me out, I was trying to find a gentle way to call it off with Edie—another fond illusion. Somebody once said a soft cut leaves a stinking wound—truer words were never spoken. I didn't want to hurt her—being nice, I stayed too long and hurt her worse.

One of the last nights we spent together I took her to the Angus Barn in Durham. The little dinner theater was doing *Our Town* with some halfway famous actor in the lead as the Stage Manager—I can't recall his name right now.

Edie came dressed to the nines in a low-cut dress, too tight for her by half, and blinked around the restaurant with a face as somber as the little match girl's brought in from the snow. I don't mean to give the wrong impression—deference wasn't Edie's style, she wasn't the sort of woman who gave you occasion, or permission, to feel sorry for her often, but when I saw her watching me over her salad, waiting to see which fork to use, it almost broke my heart. I always think of that and how she sat there as I talked about the play, impressed because I knew the names of all the characters and who had written it, listening reverently, as if everything I said came out of *Bartlett's Familiar Quotations*. For a moment—only one—she reminded me of May, who'd once listened that way, too.

George and Emily's wedding had a powerful effect on me that night. I hadn't come expecting it, but as I listened to that halfway famous actor reciting the same speech I'd said in senior play, something struck home in the lines the way it hadn't when I'd said them on the stage at Killdeer High . . .

*I've married over two hundred people in my day.*
*Do I believe in it? I don't know.*
*The cottage, the go-cart, the Sunday afternoon drives*
*in the Ford . . . The first rheumatism, the grandchildren,*
*the second rheumatism, the deathbed,*
*the reading of the will . . .*

At just that moment Edie leaned across and put her hand on mine. "What's the matter, sugar?" she whispered, "you look sad."

I squeezed back and put my finger to my lips, never moving my eyes off the stage.

*Once in a thousand times it's interesting.*

*Yes*, I thought, *yes, but only once*. As much as anything in my whole life, I guess the difference in the way I'd come to understand those lines measured all the miles I'd come with May. That night I heard something I'd missed when I was seventeen and had the world before me and thought I'd have oysters and champagne for breakfast and light my cigars with hundred-dollar bills. I heard the great and terrible despair of being human and loving someone else. I was comforted to know that someone else had felt it, too.

Edie stands as a regret, a mild one as they go. A far greater one is May. May is the great regret of my whole life as she was also the great love. Why didn't I come clean about Edie? The answer is, I don't really know. Having denied it the first time May asked, that day at the Bonanza, I was afraid to change my story—that was part of it.

At bottom, though, I think I was ashamed—not of Edie, not because she wasn't good enough for me. No, because she wasn't good enough for May.

# THIRTY-FOUR

## May

After Jimmy moved out to the lake that spring, I began to second-guess myself and the decision I'd made, asking him to leave. By summer, when I left for Nags Head with Mama and the boys, I'd changed my mind a hundred times, a hundred times a day and every hour of the day, rehashing what I thought and felt and wanted, along with what I didn't want. That's what spurred those endless walks I took down at the beach. One minute I'd be at the bottom of the cottage steps taking off my shoes, the next I'd look up and be someplace I didn't even recognize, ten miles from home, and morning would have turned to afternoon. That's what that summer was—the memory is like a fitful dream that vanishes on waking, leaving an unease that you can't shake. Waking from it took me years.

And then my birthday came . . . I didn't want a party—I had to fight Mama tooth and nail about it, but she still had Dee Lou bake a chocolate cake and counted out those thirty candles one by one. Her love was like that; I'd been fighting it, kicking and screaming, since the day I was born. I was somewhere up in Kitty Hawk that afternoon, not quite to the pier, when I turned back and came out of my reverie long enough to see where I'd arrived. There wasn't a single bather on that beach as far as I could see, not an umbrella or a chair, not a seagull, not a dog, just a thousand miles of blue, wide-open space. I stood there underneath that soaring sky alone in all that beauty and realized everything I'd built had crumbled, everything I'd made was gone. I was thirty years old and not a single dream I'd had at eighteen had come true, and I was desperate to put something back into that empty landscape to replace what I had lost; I didn't want to be alone there. I think that's why it happened . . .

Shortly after my birthday, a face and form materialized out of the blue emptiness I'd seen that afternoon, a figure from my past: Sumner. But it wasn't because of him—I still say that. And it wasn't a wave, not nearly so big and terrible as that, but just a gentle swell that lifted me and set me lightly back down on the beach, a place I recognized, with solid ground beneath my feet.

I don't believe it would have occurred to me to call him, but I was glad when he called me, and I did not say no. He was staying at his parents' cottage north of us and came by for a drink—as I recall he made martinis, and somewhere along about the second one he suddenly remembered the Embers were playing at the Beach Club and asked us if we'd like to go, being oh so gallant and including Mama in his invitation. She almost shoved me out the door. Neither of them would hear excuses—I suddenly had a list that ran to several pages . . . I couldn't have been more nervous if he'd asked me to take off my clothes—I suppose the two things didn't seem that far apart. But Sumner was so easy and disarming—"just for old times' sake, May B.," he said, and underneath the thousand noes, down in the bottom of the chest, I found a single yes, like the last item in Pandora's box. I felt that's what I was opening, and if you want to know, the spark of hope the prospect of a date aroused was scarier to me than all the screeching black-winged reasons I gave myself for staying home. The blackest and most terrible of all was Joey's look as we went out the door—that was the first time I remember seeing it—as if I was sporting off with some rich yachtsman in a speedboat and leaving him and Reed aboard a sinking ship to go down with the captain.

It seemed we picked up right where we'd left off, Sumner and I, all those years before, as though we hadn't aged, two arrested teenagers, only lighter on our feet than we had been and wise to many things that had tripped us up before, free of all that desperate heat and urgency. It took an hour and a third martini for him to get me on the dance floor, but once I went I didn't want to stop, not even when the band knocked off at one o'clock. I couldn't believe it was so late. We'd been up there four hours and, after the first, the weight had lifted and I hadn't thought of Jimmy once—it felt like the first clean breath of air I'd taken in six months, and Sumner was so good to me in just the way I needed him to be. All night long he opened doors for me and lit my cigarettes, standing when I came back from the ladies' room and pulling out my chair. He told me several times how beautiful I looked, and I had not felt beautiful in years—somewhere along the way, my shine had flickered out, as I'd seen it pass from Ellie Sims to Lisa all those years before, but that night it rekindled and gave off a glow I know was grateful, however dim it may have been. I'd forgotten how that felt—to be appreciated and attended to; I wasn't used to it. All of which is just a way of saying I had fun, I guess, and what's sad is realizing what an astounding concept it had become by then, fun, a simple thing like that . . .

We closed the place that night, and still neither of us was ready to go home. I hesitated when he suggested we go for a walk; the notion gave me a twinge—not so much the thought of being alone with him as facing it again, the beach, my adversary. But it was different, softer beneath the moon, a different kind of walking than I'd done. He rolled up his trouser legs and I took off my shoes and trailed them off a finger, and we set out southward, watching the plankton light each breaking wave like white teeth shining through a smile. It didn't seem forced or risky when he took my hand, more brotherly and sisterly than anything, the way it was when we were small and Catherine made him take my hand to cross the road up to the club. If Sumner felt different, he didn't really tip his hand—the attentions he showed were all consistent, in my mind at least, with what you might expect from an old friend escorting you for a night out on the town.

We eventually sat down in someone's gazebo to stretch our legs and take in the salt air. We lit two cigarettes and smoked, listening to the waves, as the Big Dipper twinkled in the wet dark overhead. After a silence, Sumner said, "you want to know a secret, May B.?" and I said, "what?" "I've been carrying the torch for you for years," he said, throwing it out in that loose joking way. "Sumner Dade, you're drunk." He smiled and shook his head. "I'm not, not that drunk anyhow . . . I've loved you lo these many years, so help me, May, I have—I don't believe I ever really stopped." "Stop, I mean it now," I said, but he went on, "Molly knew it, too—every time we came to dinner at your house we'd fight when we got home. One thing or another always set it off, but underneath it was the same . . . I think women sense those things a whole lot better than we do."

I realized he wasn't joking then and I could hardly have been more surprised—when you've sunk to where I was it's hard to imagine there's still someone out there who might want you. My Aunt Lucy used to have a filly that always startled when you raised your hand to stroke her—she'd been mistreated by the man who owned her first—and that's what I was like . . . Sumner saying that to me just made me want to bolt. I almost did. "I'm flattered, Sumner," I told him, bland as bland. "I don't know what to say"—worse still. "Don't say anything," he said, "nothing is required. I'm not asking you for anything, and it's okay not to know what you feel about it now or even not to feel anything at all. I'm just happy here tonight, happier than I've been in longer than I want to think about, and you're the reason why and I wanted you to know."

Suddenly I was grateful for the dark because my eyes had filled right up. What those tears were I hardly knew, except that I was moved and put at ease by him and didn't feel the need or the desire to run. "Nothing further ever has to come of it," he said, "come on now, let me take you home."

But I couldn't forget. That night I didn't sleep, and the next morning at breakfast I'd hardly left my room when Joey hit me with that look again, and I mean hit—it had all the impact of a fist and the physical intention of one, too, I think. Overnight it had darkened and acquired a conviction I can only call fanatical. "What's the matter, sugar?" I asked him in alarm, and he glared and let me hang. Finally he said, "you know," handing me my own heart on a platter, already carved in bite-sized pieces.

I don't think it was really Sumner, even, but all of it, the whole accumulated tension of that year. The image of his face is etched in acid on my heart; it staggered me to see where all the turmoil in my life and Jimmy's had brought him. He and Reed were my whole happiness; my single thought had been to keep them safe. Yet somehow, despite my vigilance, life had crept in through the hidden seams of the walls my love had built and touched them with a pain as great as mine.

Joey's look sentenced me without appeal, and at that moment there was little I wouldn't have given to undo what had been done to bring us to that pass—including Sumner. There I stood, a grown woman, on the verge of crumbling before a little boy—I don't know what prevented me; maybe I'd just crumbled once too often—but with the slap still stinging I stepped back and took a breath and resigned myself to what I thought could never happen, to let my own child condemn me. Crumbling would not have changed it. And when he said he wanted to go live with Jimmy, twisting the knife a final time, I didn't even try to spare him that.

Joey had to go, but so did I—that was all it was for me . . . You have to let them, hoping half a life from now they'll understand and see a glimmer of the way it looked through your eyes then. Our sins as parents are so obvious, but no one ever says what tyrants children are.

It was while he and Reed were visiting Jimmy back in Killdeer that Sumner and I went away. His first plan was to visit Richmond so that I could see the house he'd bought and was restoring on the James. Big Sumner had died the year before, and Sumner and Ann had both come into what Mama delicately referred to as "a nice piece of money." Much as I'd have liked it, I had nightmares about running into half the world up there. Daddy's sister, Aunt Julia, lived not far from him, and even if I'd been divorced and free—which I was not, as we well know—I wouldn't have stayed with Sumner at his house under any circumstances whatsoever. I'd tried throwing caution to the winds before, and look where it had got me. Twelve years of marriage had made me more conservative, I guess, but it's just like that expression of Mama's: *Remember who you are.* In the end I don't think there's much choice; there's something that remembers for you.

Conservative or not, I still went away with Sumner—with Miss Zelle Tilley's blessing, too, I did, though Daddy never knew. In the end we picked Virginia Beach as neutral ground—it was close and no one knew us there. It started well, a crystal day with wind, and Sumner put the top down on his Thunderbird, which made it hard to talk above the roar—that was fine by me. I was in what you might call a ruminative mood. He seemed happy and excited, not bubbling over like a boy, but in a subtler way, with some spine in it, the way you want a man to be. I felt I was beginning to get to know him in the present tense, in a way that had eluded us those years at home as friends.

Sumner didn't take the route Jimmy and I had always used—up 168 through Chesapeake, that way—but drove back just this side of Elizabeth City before he turned north and took us through mile after mile of farmland with an occasional patch of swamp or forest. "I love this drive," he said, almost shouting to be heard, and I could see the little recognitions flash across his face as we passed some landmark, or a new view opened up, things I could only guess at, not having that shared history mapped out inside. That history was his and Molly's—that was the only time I really thought of her.

I can't tell you where we were exactly—I'm pretty sure we'd crossed the line into Virginia, though—when we passed a sign that advertised an auction. Miracle of miracles, Sumner said, "we aren't in any hurry, are we? Want to take a look?" He got tens on all the judges' cards with that, believe you me, and best of all, he didn't even know he'd scored. Not that I was testing him, but the second time around you notice certain things that slipped by you before.

While I'm on the subject, though, I probably ought to say I liked him more and more, the person Sumner had turned into. He'd taken on a kind of solidness, an assured and reassuring weight that reminded me of Daddy in a way—I liked the smooth way things seemed to flow around him like the airstream over a well-made wing. With Jimmy, everything was fraught with some exhausting and unnecessary extra effort that familiarity had made invisible to me. Now, contrast made it clear. He'd turned out pretty well, I thought, Sumner had, and independent of anything between the two of us, I was pleased and proud of that for him. My thoughts were starting to range free and far afield, farther than I probably should have let them go, but to tell the truth I didn't have the energy to rein them in and was in no position—so I felt, at any rate—and certainly in no mood, to play coy.

So we followed the arrows on the signs, turning up a half-mile drive lined wall-to-wall with pink crape myrtles, all in gorgeous bloom. There was a roan horse grazing in a field beside a still black pond, and from the moment we turned onto the property I had a curious sense of recognition, which deepened as the house, a white Greek Revival, came in view. It was considerably the worse for wear, but you took one look and knew that some impressive life had been lived there once. I wondered if someone important had owned it and I'd seen a picture, but I don't think it was that. Under the spell the afternoon had cast, as I was coming up for air from my own life for the first time in twelve years, I think I saw the house I'd always wanted and dreamed I'd have; it was like opening an old yearbook and having a pressed flower fall into my lap.

Later, as I milled through the dark, high-ceilinged rooms where the auction lots were laid out for review, I paused over a woman's photograph in a tarnished silver frame. She appeared to have been about my age when the shot was taken—sometime in the twenties or thirties I guessed, judging by her hair and clothes. She was lovely, dark-complexioned with a finely drawn mouth and trusting eyes I liked.

An elderly lady beside me at the table told me who the woman in the portrait was. She'd owned the house, and they'd been school-mates long before. It seemed strange to think of them as contemporaries, the beautiful young woman in the photograph and the frail, white-haired lady at my side, her face crisscrossed with lines as fine as the cracks in the glaze of an old china cup. "You should buy that frame, dear," she told me, smiling as she strolled away, "you can't find that heavy sterling anymore."

I did buy it—not for the frame, though. Later, when I unpacked at the hotel, I put the picture on my bedside table.

Sumner had reserved a suite with two adjoining rooms—close enough, but with retreat still possible—which struck me as evidence of a nice tact, if also perhaps a little smooth, as though he weren't without experience in these matters, which I expect he wasn't. I didn't grudge him that—it piqued my interest, and amused me some, to think that he'd turned out a ladies' man—perhaps he always had been, but somehow I'd never got past the boy next door who rang the doorbell Friday nights after the football games with his leather jacket and his mooning, soulful face, moping after my big sister.

I drew a bath and steeped for half an hour, feeling the tension starting to dissolve, rising in a shimmer off my limbs like the water's heat. Leaning my head back on the rim of the old clawfoot tub, I closed my eyes and flirted with sleep, more seductive than the thought of sex by half. When I climbed out, pink and languid, it was a struggle not to fall naked into those fresh sheets and watch dusk drift in off the ocean through my window, a settling blue smoke. I was afraid, though, if I closed my eyes I might not open them again for twenty years. Instead I put on the blue cocktail dress Mama bought after the Rice House and never wore, and met Sumner on the porch. He'd shaved a second time and put on a dinner jacket. We sat in the deep cushions of the wicker chaises and drank old-fashioneds and watched the sunset, listening to the little orchestra play foxtrots in the dining room. Later on he ordered oysters Rockefeller and a bottle of champagne, and we took our shoes off and walked down to the water's edge, drinking from the bottle, neither of us feeling any pain.

During dinner—we'd ordered and were in the middle of our she-crab soup—we heard the first rumblings of thunder. It sounded far off, as if it might miss us, and then, just that quick, the way it does that time of year, the storm was right on top of us. The curtains bloused full and then flew sideways as the waiters dashed to close the windows. The air changed suddenly, turning wet with a stronger tang of ocean salt. Everyone stopped eating and watched the black cloud sailing toward us from the east with lightning pouring out of it like gold jewelry from a burglar's ruptured sack. Then a terrific crack exploded nearby with a splintering sound—there was a queer, fresh smell in the air and all the lights went out. For a moment everything went still, and then the sky opened and the rain began to pour like water off a tarp. Bedlam erupted as waiters rushed to bring hurricane lamps to all the tables. Sumner lit his lighter—"there you are," he said, "what do you think?" "It's wonderful," I said, excited by the storm and general discombobulation. "Dinner could be hours now," he said, and I said, "let's don't wait— we can take the rest of the champagne upstairs and watch from the balcony."

Sumner's lighter blew out on the creaky staircase and he bumped me from behind. "Sorry." "Why are you whispering?" I asked, and he said, "I don't know"—and there was a slight hitch in his voice. As I turned, his breath misted over my face like cobweb, warmer than the air and smelling of champagne, and then his arm circled my lower back and pulled me tight until my breasts crushed flat against his chest and I could feel his body's warmth and staggered pulse through the cool film of our clothes. He kissed me, and I kissed him back; and neither of us said a word until we reached my room.

There was a fire laid in the grate, white birch logs that we decided were probably ornamental, but we lit them anyway and opened the French doors and stepped out. The wind was streaming so hard I had to narrow my eyes and grip the iron railing for fear it might strip me off—the sensation was like riding something very big and very fast. Both of us were instantly drenched, but it was wonderfully invigorating to be out there, as if all that electricity in the air kindled something in the cells to higher wakefulness. The ocean was a pale, luminous white, rolling and pitching in the dark, and there were smaller flecks of white riding above it, foam, perhaps, or birds.

I didn't realize how cold I was till we came in and closed the door. "Your lips are blue," Sumner said, and he got a towel from the bathroom and gently patted dry my face and hair. The weather had brought a shine to his eyes and skin, and when we kissed again I could taste the ocean in his mouth. "You should change," he said. "Into something more comfortable?" He smiled. "Something dry at least." "Promise you won't look," I said as I slipped off a stocking. "I promise," Sumner said, "but I wouldn't put much stock in it if I were you." "It isn't as if you haven't seen it before, Sumner," I reminded him, "of course, there's more of me to go around these days." "There couldn't be too much," he said. I laughed and let my dress drop to the floor. Stepping out of it, I took off my slip and underthings and wrapped the plush towel around my shoulders.

When I sat down before the fire, I could feel the smooth bricks already warm beneath me, and I liked that feeling. My teeth were chattering slightly, and in the mirror above the mantel I could see Sumner undressing behind me, taking off his jacket and folding it carefully with the lining out, the same way Daddy always did. He tucked his towel around his waist, joined me at the fire and put his arm around me, pulling me close for warmth. I lifted my towel open, wrapping it a turn around his shoulders so that we were naked underneath. I felt my left breast slide over his bare chest and his hand moving to touch it, lifting . . . The towel dropped on the bricks and I lay back on it and pulled him onto me. The firelight cast shadows and orange highlights, playing tricks with his face.

Downstairs, the band had recovered. So close to the floor, I could hear it suddenly, particularly the bass—it sounded like a waltz, and when I closed my eyes I could see the dancers, the men in dinner jackets, the women in cocktail gowns, whirling in the candlelight beneath the great dark crystal chandelier, a stately music playing just above the storm, rattling the old shutters against the side of the hotel, whistling in the flue as the fire roared. Swept up in all of it, I didn't want that storm to end, but to carry me away and drop me in some other life.

Perhaps that's what it did . . . I wasn't aware the lights had come back on till I opened my eyes and saw the bedside table lamp shining on the photograph. There was a wetness in my lashes, though I wasn't really crying; if I was, I could not have said what for. But as I stared at the portrait over Sumner's shoulder, my attraction to that unknown woman suddenly came clear—she was who I might have been and in some deep sense had been supposed to be. If I'd been born a generation earlier and had the life Mama brought me up to want and to expect, I might have lived in a house like hers and had that unguarded look in my eyes, too. That was the very moment when I realized it would never come to pass, that dream, because a dream was all it was.

If at that moment God had offered me the chance to go back and undo everything that had happened, I might have taken it and stayed with Sumner and never gone home again—there was a part of me that would have liked just that, but it was the smallest part. Lying there in my old lover's arms, I saw it so clearly: *this is not my life.* It wasn't mine any more than the road Sumner had brought me on that afternoon was my road. I was in someone else's life with him in that hotel, I don't know whose. Perhaps it was the life I might have had if I'd made the choice to go to Philadelphia. I only knew it wasn't mine. My road with Jimmy wasn't finished . . .

There's only one, you know, one road that's your true life—you don't know that when you're young. Much as I enjoyed the different road that Sumner showed me, which was as beautiful and fast as the one I knew, what was missing was the shimmer of all the history I'd made with Jimmy along ours, where every mile recalled the memory of a dozen earlier trips and what had happened there: the flat tire, the wildflowers we'd stopped to pick. As we passed, I saw the ghosts of all the former selves I'd been, reminding me of who I was; for better or for worse, I couldn't give it up. The grief I felt was knowing how much was missing between us even as I recalled, for the first time in months, that something wasn't. I didn't know if it could still be salvaged—very possibly it couldn't—but I had to wait until I did know.

As we lay there afterward, I asked Sumner whether he ever thought of Molly. He didn't answer right away. He first lit two cigarettes and handed one to me. Then, in a soft voice I can still hear, he said, "it's hard to change, May, isn't it?" and I said, "is it? I think change would be a snap, I really do—the hard part's wanting to." There was a little flight of pain in his eyes even as he smiled and let his gaze drift to the ceiling. I think he understood.

# THIRTY-FIVE

*Joey*

"All right," Mama said to Daddy as Uncle Sumner's Thunderbird backed down the drive and pulled away, "so what if I've been seeing him? What if we did go away?" and Daddy said, "you went away with Sumner?" Mama sighed. "That's not the point." "Where?" asked Daddy.

"I'm not sure that's any of your business, Jimmy." "I'd say it is," he answered, "I'd say it's very goddamn much my business, May." Mama shook her head. "No, Jimmy, listen, please. The point is I could be with Sumner if I wanted to, except I'm not, I'm here. That's the point. Please try not to miss it this time, please try hard." "I'd say the point was whether you've been fucking him and if you mean to keep on doing it," Daddy said, "I'd say the point is that Sumner's in love with you and you damn well know it—he is now and he always has been; some things never change."

"You're so right, Jimmy, some things never do." Her voice sud-

denly seemed tired. "What's that supposed to mean?" he asked, and
she said, even more quietly, "I think you know." Daddy laughed a
little bit, if you could call it that. "You're right," he said, "Dade was
a wuss in high school and he still is," and Mama said, "at least he
took the trouble to grow up, Jimmy. You're the one who never
changed."

"Come on, May, what the hell do you expect when he comes
sniffing around here that way?" With a look that seemed to gather
all the confidence he'd lost, she answered, "I'll tell you, Jimmy. I
expect you to behave civilly to my friends. That's what Sumner is,
my friend—and yours, in case you've forgotten. Whether you believe that or not, whether you like him or despise him, I expect you
to treat him decently because of me—and that's the least of what I
expect."

"Damnit, May, I mean *goddamnit*," Daddy said, "just what exactly the hell do you want? I'm trying here, I'm busting my hump to
make this work. I wanted more than anything for this weekend to be
a new start for us, but you've got to meet me halfway."

"Haven't I, Jimmy? Haven't I? I didn't realize meeting you halfway meant hurting Sumner to satisfy your childish pride. I didn't ask
him over here this morning—did that dawn on you? Apparently it
didn't, or the fact that I also had high hopes for this weekend. I'm
such a fool. I should have known it was going to be this way. How
can we start over? We can't just close our eyes and wish away twelve
years. Last night it was flowers and champagne; today we're right
back at each other's throats. I've been on this roller coaster with you
for so long, honey, so very long . . . From one day to the next I
never know which it's going to be. I used to love the champagne
well enough to make the other worth it, but I don't know if I can do
it anymore—I'm sorry but I just don't know . . ."

Mama's face crinkled like a sheet of paper balled in someone's
fist. She raised her hand to cover it, and Daddy said, "May, listen—"
and she said, "no, you listen, Jimmy. What simply staggers me is
that you can crucify me like this over Sumner and never breathe a
word about that Perkins girl. What about that? I went away with
Sumner for a weekend; you've been seeing her for months, haven't
you? Isn't that the truth?"

Daddy didn't answer right away—he looked scared and mad at once. "You asked me that before," he told her in a voice so low that I could hardly hear, and Mama said, "you told me nothing happened."

When he still didn't speak, she said, "well?" His eyes flicked away across the dune toward the ocean. "Nothing did," he said, and, watching from my hiding place beneath the Jenrettes' house, I thought about those Kools with lipstick on the filters and knew it was a lie.

When I looked for Mama, she was gone—there was nothing left but tracks.

# THIRTY-SIX

*Joey*

Daddy followed Mama to the beach and they were gone all afternoon and came back together in the dusk like two explorers who've
crossed through a hard mountain pass on foot and come home halfway dead and needing rest. They were holding hands, but I couldn't
tell if they'd made up for real or if it was just a truce. That night at
dinner Daddy seemed real careful what he said and did, like his
words and hands were china and might break if they touched anything too hard. Mama didn't speak at all, or eat. When Nanny asked
her if she wanted something else, she just blinked and said, "I'm
sorry, Mother, what?" like she was coming back from some far
place. I didn't eat much either.

   In bed I listened to the water running in the pipes as Mama
washed up in the bathroom. When she finished and went out,
Daddy tapped softly at the bedroom door and Mama said, "come
in." I lay awake a long time waiting to see if he'd stay. I think he did

—at least I never heard him leave—and I felt better then, like maybe it was only one more argument out of all the ones they'd had and it was over now.

When I woke up Saturday morning it was still dark outside, but the bedroom door was open with the hall light on, and Pa was standing there with his hands in his pockets, already shaved and dressed in his white fishing outfit—canvas ducks, a short-sleeved shirt open at the throat to show his undershirt, and that Panama with the dark band. The brim threw a shadow on his face from the light above him, but I could tell he was smiling, Pa, that special way that hardly showed up on his lips but more in the set of his whole face. It was always clearest early in the morning, that smile, which I believe was Pa's happiest hour, when things were starting up and there was time for all of it.

"Morning, son," he said. "Morning, Pa." "Ready to go give them fish what-for?" "I don't think they're up yet," I told him, wiping sleep out of my eyes. Pa laughed real soft. "I 'spect we better wake 'em then."

I pulled on my bathing suit and the old Converse I'd cut to low-tops after they wore out—you needed shoes at the Inlet launch because of all the broken glass and oyster shells on the bottom. Thursday night when I'd come in, Mama had made me throw my Tarheel T-shirt in the laundry—I'd had it on all week at Daddy's and I guess it kind of stunk, though it's hard to smell yourself—but I needed it for luck, and Mama was asleep, so I figured what she didn't know wouldn't hurt her, and I dug it out of the hamper.

In the kitchen Pa was pouring coffee into the big plaid thermos and fixing sandwiches from last night's steak, spreading mayonnaise on one side of the bread with a butcher knife and A.1. on the other. "Should I go wake Daddy up?" I asked, and Pa said, "I 'spect we better let 'em sleep, honey—we'll all go another time." I guess I knew that's what he'd say even before I asked, and it was probably best, considering, only I'd always thought he'd be there, Daddy, my first time in the ocean, and I felt let down it wasn't going to be that way.

When Pa hit the light it seemed strange to see the porch without the footprints, just the silver dew rolled on like a fresh coat of paint still wet or snow when you're the first to leave your tracks. Well, that day I was. As Pa turned on the headlights of the Cadillac, easing the boat from the garage, the screen door slammed upstairs and here comes Daddy with his shirt flying open, hopping on one leg to get into his pants.

"Hold on, y'all, hold on," he called, trying to yell and keep his voice down all at once, "you weren't gonna leave without me, were you?" "Thought you were catchin' up yo' beauty sleep," Pa said. "Hell, Mr. Will, I'm beautiful enough, don't you figure?" Pa laughed at that. "Beautiful as you're gonna git, at any rate . . . Now zip yo' fly whydontcha and hop in here so we can git gone sometime 'fore Christmas." After we pulled out on the beach road Daddy turned to me in the back seat. He was all red-eyed and stub-bly, with his hair sticking up funny on one side. "Morning, rascal," he said with a wide grin, brushing a hand across my flattop, and I said, "morning, Daddy," not sure I should trust his happiness and almost scared to hope.

No one talked much on the drive. Pa turned the radio dial to find the weather; Daddy smoked a Lucky with his elbow on the open window, letting the wind blow through his hair. The moon was still up in the west, close to full and bright when we set out. By the time we got to Whalebone Junction, though, and crossed over onto Park Service land, it had melted like a ice cube in a glass of water till there was nothing but the outline left. It was so pale it seemed like you could see the sky behind it, and in the east the light was coming up and starting to put color back in things. As far as you could see, the marsh grass spread around us turning a straw color now which was all green before. It was so still at first it didn't seem quite real but like a picture someone took of the same thing. Then way off in the distance a puff of wind moved over it coming toward us, bending down the stalks, which stood up straight again and shook themselves when it was gone. It stirred up some butterflies, big golden ones, which fluttered up and drifted down again real slow —I'd never seen so many at one time and wondered what they were.

Before long the bridge reared up ahead of us, looking more than ever like a brontosaurus skeleton bending over half a mile of open water to graze the scrub pines of Pea Island. The neck still didn't reach, though they'd hooked up a few more bones since the last time I was there. Closer to us, the outriggers of the charter boats bristled up like spears in the marina. Most of them were still at mooring, loading ice and groceries for the trip out to the Gulf Stream, churning the water white inside the harbor and filling the air with diesel fumes so strong they almost turned my stomach as we passed. Once we got down to the launch, though, the air turned fresh again and the roar of radios and engines died away so you could hear the whooshing of the current as it slid along the sandbar and, farther off, the echo of waves breaking on the ocean beach.

I helped Daddy lift the big net from the boat and carry it down the beach, where we unrolled it on the sand to check for holes. Wading through the shallows to seine for bait, we had to watch for stumps—they were left from back before the ocean pushed the Inlet through, Daddy told me, when there were ancient forests that had been covered up by sand. The sound was warm, much warmer than the ocean, honey gold and clear around your ankles, though if you looked out a ways it clouded up with all the silt and turned a murky brown. You could see where it dropped off sharp to the channel, which ran like a dark streak through lighter water a quarter-mile from shore. Daddy sank his end pole in the sand while I dragged mine around him in a semicircle, drawing a faint line across the bottom that got erased before I hardly passed. That was one sign how strong the current was out there—another was the way it scooped the sand from underneath your feet the way the ocean does when it sucks back a wave.

"Y'all watch out now," Pa called from shore, where he was drinking coffee from the thermos cup; a sunbeam was flashing in his glasses and lighting his white hat. "Joey, son, don't git too deep. Remember what I told you." "I know, Pa, the twinkling of an eye," I said, grinning at Daddy, who winked at me like it was one we had on Pa. "And y'all can wipe them smirks right off yo' faces, too," he said, " 'cause I'm just as serious as a heart attack, hemme?" "Yes, sir," we both said. Pa nodded. "Good, you better. Now I'mon run up to the tackle shop and see cain't I find out what's bitin'. Meet y'all at the car."

After two sweeps, the bottom of the cooler was filled with finger mullet down among the ice cubes, which had melted clear already and were tinkling like a cocktail stirred by all those squirming minnows. "That should be enough," said Daddy, "wait here while I go rinse off," and I said, "can I go, too?" "Sorry, Charlie, your pa would shoot us both." "Come on, Daddy, that's not fair," I said. "Go get your life preserver then." "It's way back at the boat," I said, and he said, "Joey, son, we're in a hurry. Just don't start, okay?" "How come I have to wear one and you don't?" "Because I'm your father; I'm responsible for you." "Yeah, right, sure," I said, "since when." And everything just stopped.

Daddy's jaw squared and his eyes went shiny like I'd stabbed him through the heart, and something in me turned to jelly. "I'm sorry, Daddy." He just said, real soft, "start carrying things back to the car," then turned his back and waded out before he dove. I stood there feeling like the most cruel and selfish person ever born, wishing I'd never said it—I didn't really mean it anyhow. I was just mad and it slipped out. But as I watched him pull away with that long-armed lifeguard crawl he learned at Camp Blue Moon, something happened, I don't know what it was, I suddenly realized I did, I suddenly realized I did mean it, and to know I meant it felt so bad I wanted to bend down in the sand and vomit up my heart.

I lugged the seine up by myself, and when I came back I found Daddy sitting on the beach with his legs drawn up, staring toward the ocean where the sun was rising between the pylons of the bridge. "I don't think I can carry this," I said, trying the handle of the cooler. He looked back at me over his shoulder. "I'll help . . . come sit here with me a minute first." He patted the spot beside him on the sand, shook a Lucky from his pack and lit it as I joined him. "Look," he said, breathing his smoke in deep and pointing with the coal. The sun looked like a giant red balloon floating over the horizon in slow motion, bobbing on the water for several seconds before it lifted clear. As it climbed, the daylight seemed to fall toward us like a drawbridge, and the ocean, which was midnight blue before, lit up and turned a orange gold like lava that had started boiling and caught fire.

"Some show," he said. "Yeah, it's nice." "Nice?" Daddy laughed this way that made me wish I'd picked another word. "How many times in your whole life do you see something like that?" "I don't know, Daddy." "Not many, Joey, take my word for it," he said, "not nearly enough. And you know the saddest part?" "Nuh-uh, what?" I asked. "It happens every day," he said, "every single one." I wasn't sure why that made him sad, but when he said, "do you know what I mean?" I said, "I think so," and Daddy smiled like that pleased him, which was mainly all I wanted even if my answer wasn't true.

He nodded east. "Look out there and tell me what you see." "There's the bridge," I said, not sure what he was pointing to. "What else?" "The ocean." "What else?" "I don't know, Daddy, the sun?" "Look harder, Joey, right out there," he said, "there's something swimming in the water—see it?" I shaded my eyes and squinted. "Nuh-uh, where?" I asked, "all I see is reflection of the sun."

"Know what I see?" he asked. "What?" "A golden dragon," Daddy said, and blew his smoke out of his nose like one. "Oh," I said, a little disappointed—for a minute there I'd thought he meant something real, a whale or porpoises, but Daddy smiled like this was better. "Every day it swims around the whole world once," he said, "wherever the sun is rising, that's where it is and everything is magic there, but only for that single moment. If you happen to be in exactly the right spot to catch it as it passes, you get to make a wish. Today we are—I know what mine is. Do you?"

I started to answer but he shook his head. "No, don't tell me—if you speak a wish aloud it won't come true, right?" "Right, I guess so, Daddy." "I can say this much, though," he said, "I feel better this morning than I have in a long time, Joey. There's a part of me missing when I'm not with you boys and your mom. I don't know how I forgot that, but I did, and if anything good came out of it, I guess it's remembering how much you all mean to me . . . I missed being here with you this year. I lost a summer—we all did, I suppose. I just hope a summer's all." I knew what Daddy's wish was then: it was the same as mine.

"Look again and see if you can see the dragon now." "Sure, Dad, yeah, I can," I said, wondering why he always had to make things bigger and more special than they really were, why the sunrise couldn't just be nice instead of the most beautiful one that ever was. And even that was not enough for Daddy—it had to be a golden dragon that could make your wish come true. Pa never saw that kind of stuff, and I wondered if the reason was because he didn't need a magic dragon anymore.

By the time we walked back up, Pa had already backed the trailer down the ramp and was leaning against the grille. "All set?" He threw down his Chesterfield and ground it underfoot. "Good," he said before we even answered—he was ready to get going. While the boat was still on land he made me climb in and put my life preserver on—I hated that, but when I tried to argue, Daddy said, "you listen to your pa," so it was no use trying.

Standing in waist-deep water at the bottom of the launch, Daddy caught the stern as Pa cranked the boat down over the trailer's rubber rollers. When I unclipped the winch line, the current swung the bow around so fast that Daddy shouted, "whoa there, Nellie," and leaned back, digging his heels into the bottom to anchor us. Pa spun the wheels getting up the ramp, leaving wet tire marks across the parking lot and limping like Festus on "Gunsmoke" as he ran back down.

"Let 'er rip," he said, puffing as he flopped over the side. Daddy let go then, hitching a ride on the still propeller as the current swept us out. He let his feet drift back in the wake, in no hurry to get aboard. Then we bumped the first channel marker, scaring off a pelican and turning sideways to the current, and I said, "come on, Daddy," just as Pa called, "damnit, boy, quit foolin'." Daddy grinned at us and ducked under—the water slicked his hair back from his widow's peak—and then worked hand over hand around the side, dipping us so low we took on water as he hoisted himself in. He had to yank the cord a half-dozen times before the engine finally caught, spinning the propeller to a blur and shooting white bubbles back into the wake as the bow slowly lifted.

Out in front of us a parade of charter boats was heading off around the breakwater, all white and spaced out in a line. The nearest turned south toward the Inlet, the captain up top at the wheel looking brown and calm like he belonged there, the party down below on deck looking white and like they didn't. They all had on orange life preservers, too, I noticed.

Daddy cut in line and we followed around the point and headed east. As we drew near, the bridge grew bigger and bigger till you had to crane your neck to see where a few workers were standing at the rail, looking over, not much bigger than plastic Army men. The roadbed threw down a wide band of shadow that rested perfectly still on the rippling water. It felt a little cooler as we crossed—and then we were in the Inlet, where I'd never been before.

A dredge was working in the channel, shooting out a rooster tail of sand, which rained on one end of a low silt island, the other thick with jostling birds. Between the noise of the dredge and the gulls' racket, we couldn't hear each other shout and had to point to things.

Toward the mouth of the Inlet, the channel narrowed and ran between two sandbars not much more than twenty yards apart. Waves were breaking on either side of us, little muddy ones on the sound side and giant green ones crashing down like thunder on the ocean bar, making white explosions and drenching us with spray as we went gliding down the middle over silky water just deep enough that you could see the bottom.

Once we cleared it, everything changed. Swells started rolling underneath us from the east, and I said, "are we in the ocean now?" because I thought we must be, only Pa said, "not quite yet." It wasn't two minutes after that when we came up to this line running through the water, not straight but wavy like a curtain hanging from the surface down as far as you could see. On one side the water was still that muddy brown, on the other, blue-green and crystal clear. A cool breeze lifted off the surface as we crossed and the smell changed, too. Pa looked back at me from the bow. "Now," he said, and I got butterflies, especially when I gazed back to shore; the marina buildings had shrunk down smaller than Monopoly hotels and the bridge looked like something made of Tinkertoys.

Pa baited the rigs and passed the poles to me, watching as I played them one by one into the wake. "Ho!" he called each time when it was far enough. When I flipped the bail, the line drew tight, shaking off a few bright drops. As I set each rod in its mount, it leaned slowly back and stopped at the same angle as the others. "Look, they silently agree," said Daddy, and me and Pa both smiled, knowing what he meant. Daddy slowed to trolling speed, then turned us north along the beach. No one did much talking; we just squinted out across the water, taking big deep breaths from time to time and going, "ahhh." It felt pretty good to be there after all. A flock of terns raced along with us for a good ways all in a straight line, piping as they flew, and there were two big pelicans gliding together, now one leading, now the other, sailing up over the crests and dropping into the troughs always a foot above the water and never flapping their wings once the whole time I watched.

After twenty minutes Pa got a strike and stood to reel in a good-sized Spanish mackerel, which came up in the wake all silvery green with zebra stripes along his sides. He took one look at us and ran back hard with the drag singing on Pa's reel like a forty-foot-long zipper. Pa was grinning so wide as he worked him, you could almost see the fillings gleaming in his teeth, but he still said, "here, boy, bring 'im in while I git the net." "Nuh-uh, Pa," I said, "I want to catch my own," because I couldn't take his fish, though if he'd asked me twice I might of, but he didn't.

When Pa jerked him in across the transom, Daddy had to duck to keep from getting tail-slapped. The mackerel dropped between the thwarts, where we all watched him flipping for a minute. "He's a game one, ain't he," Pa said, and took the pliers out of his tackle box and jerked the spoon out of his gullet, spurting blood across my arm. For an hour after that you could hear him thrashing in the icebox, beating himself to death against the walls, slower and slower till he finally stopped. When I looked in, that bright ocean color had tarnished to a dull lead gray and his eyes had clouded up and didn't look too interested anymore. I felt kind of bad about it then, the way I always did, and would of liked to ask if Pa or Daddy ever felt that way, except I was afraid they might say no.

I still wanted to catch one just as bad though, only it was a good while before my first strike came. Daddy was turning us back south in a wide slow circle, careful not to cross the lines. On the beach, a woman was cantering bareback through the swash on a big chestnut horse; I was watching her when something hit my spoon and I mean hard. My rod whipped over so far the top eye touched the water—it would of snapped for sure, I think, except the line broke first. That rod came flying back at me like a bow string when you let the arrow go, and left a hank of green line coiling in my lap. We all stared at each other, blinking like our eyes had sun in them.

Pa said it might of been a turtle, one of those green loggerheads that lay their eggs in spring. Daddy said he bet it was a shark. Whatever it was, it was big, that much I could tell you. I could feel it in my hands for half an hour, throbbing from the shock. It kind of changed the mood, too, and made me think of what might be down there gliding underneath and not be quite so quick to trail my hand along the side, and whatever luck we had—if one fish counts for luck —ran out. We didn't catch another thing all morning or even get a single bite.

At lunchtime we dropped anchor close to shore and Pa passed out the sandwiches and let me use the church key on his Barlow to open a can of beanie-weenies. Later, we tried bottom fishing for a while but had no better luck, and about one o'clock the wind picked up from the southwest and a few clouds appeared, those giant white ones you see a lot that time of year which look like Conestoga wagons. As we started south, whitecaps were feathering the water off the bow and leaving lace trails to the stern, and the same trip that took us forty minutes coming out took over three hours getting back. It was after four o'clock by the time we saw the waves breaking on the Inlet sandbar. By then the chop had beat us half to death and we were soaked and burned and looking pretty grim around the mouth.

I expect we would of gone straight in if Pa hadn't wanted so bad for me to catch something my first time so I'd remember it, you know, that way. If he'd of asked, I would of said I didn't care, because I didn't, not by then. The only thing I cared about was going home and having Mama rub some Solarcaine across my shoulders and putting on dry clothes. Pa didn't ask me though.

It all happened pretty fast. I remember watching a white boat come toward us through the pylons of the bridge, admiring how she rode and squinting to make out if she was rigged for marlin. The next thing I knew Pa said, "son of a bitch," and knelt forward on the bow thwart, peering straight down in the water. "Son of a bitch," he said again and suddenly stood up and pointed ahead of us. "Look, y'all, look." He moved his arm, tracking something in the water I couldn't see. "Where, Pa?" I asked. "There," he said, "right *there*," jabbing his finger. "See 'em? . . . See 'em now?" And then I did.

Against the white flank of the sandbar six feet down I saw a shape blur by so fast I couldn't make out what it was except the color, red, like a blood trail in the water, then a second one, then two more.

"I'll be goddamned," Pa said, "I'll be a goddamn monkey's uncle if it ain't," and he was laughing, his face lit up like it was five A.M. again. Me and Daddy both called out at once, "what is it, Pa?" "what is it, Mr. Will?" Above the engine and the wind, above the noise the waves made crashing on the outside bar, Pa shouted, "it's the drum! It's the red drum, boys!" I only knew the name and that it was a fish, but from the way Pa looked and said it, I could tell it was important and not just to him—important to me, too, because of what it meant to Pa.

"Jimmy, hit the throttle," he said, "Joey . . ." Pa turned to me. "Yes, sir?" "Git yo' pole," he said, and we took off hell for leather after them, leapfrogging the swells with the engine revving to a crazy whine each time the propeller cleared the water. Spray was flying everywhere and Pa stood in the bow with his knees propped against the thwart and the painter line wrapped a turn around his wrist while he took turns with his free hand pointing where to go and holding down his hat. Leaning around him, I could just make out the fish, four shadows gliding and darting under the glitter on the surface. They seemed to be pulling away, swimming faster than the boat could go, and suddenly they veered right and streaked away like lightning toward the shallows.

"Stand up, boy!" Pa said, "stand up now!" As I did, he dropped into his seat and grabbed two fistfuls of cloth in the waistband of my bathing suit. "I got you, son," he said, "go 'head." "What, Pa? What am I supposed to do?" "Throw the goddamn thing," he said, "cast ahead of 'em where they can see the splash," and I said, "don't I need to bait it?" "Goddamnit, Joey, *now*," he said, "just use what you got." I dropped the rod over my shoulder and whipped it out, watching the spoon sparkle as it caught the light and sailed over the top. As it started falling toward the water, the wind bellied under my line and held the arc a minute till the white splash came when everything collapsed. It was too far left.

"Haul back," Pa said, "haul back and try again," and I cranked so hard the muscles in my forearm burned. I was scared it was going to be too late because already I'd lost sight of them and figured by the time I made my second cast they'd be long gone—only I never got to make one. That was when I got the strike. My pole whip-sawed double with a whirring sound like a green willow branch if you've ever swung one, and I'm telling you I thought I'd hooked me a torpedo. I started to reel in, but the crank arm-wrestled me the other way. "No, boy, let him run with it," Pa said, "the line's too light, he'll break it like a thread—that fish is thirty pounds at least!" To me it felt more like a hundred. I was holding on for everything I had and couldn't free a hand to ease the drag, so Pa reached around my middle and did it for me. Then the pressure eased, the rod tip lifted and the line went spooling out, going *weeeeeeeeeeeeee* like children screaming down a sliding board, as it ran away from us through the water.

"Chase it," Pa called back to Daddy, "he'p 'im make up line." "It's getting mighty shallow, Mr. Will." "I know," Pa said, "just slow down and go like I point." We turned out of the channel and followed the fish into shoal water, where you could see the bottom rushing by, little sand dunes like a desert from the window of a plane and here and there some grass that flattened down as we went over it. "I think I lost him, Pa," I said, reeling slack as hard as I could go, "there's nothing on here." "Keep at it, honey, you just ain't caught up yet." And then I did; the fish tugged back. Pa grinned and said, "hello again."

"Should I let him run some more?" I asked, and Pa said, "does he want to?" I took my hand off the crank: this time the line didn't whirr out like before; the drag went *tick . . . tick . . . tiiiiiiick* like each inch was a mile. "There's yo' answer, boy," Pa said, "he's digging in his heels to fight. Cut the engine, Jimmy."

When he did, the current seized back in, turning the boat in a slow pinwheel as we drifted east again, toward the ocean. I followed the line around the boat, lifting it over Daddy's head and turning a circle in Pa's arms like we were dancing. Most times you know you're going to win against a fish and only wish there was some way to make it last. Not this time. That drum felt like a cinder block on the end of a wire coat hanger, and I didn't know if I could get him to the boat or in it if I did.

I stuck the cork grip of the rod into my stomach and fought for every turn till my arms and legs were shaking. Sweat ran down my face and stung my eyes till things began to blur; I couldn't free a hand to wipe it. When that fish finally came up in the wake, though, it didn't matter anymore; the second I laid eyes on him I got this kind of twinkly feeling over my whole body, and for a second the air was filled with strange white sparkles that winked and swarmed around my face. They went away when I remembered to start breathing.

He was a big, blunt-headed fish, thick around the middle and streaked red along his sides like he had war paint on. As I yanked him, he yanked back, wagging his head like Tawny with a slipper, trying to shake that hook out of his lip. After a flurry he'd stop to rest and just tread water, whisking his tail real slow from side to side and staring up at us out of the water like he was curious to see what had him. Then his gills flared and the ridgy stuff turned brighter red inside as he shot off again.

"Look at him," Pa said, "look at that sombitch," and Daddy said, "Jesus, that's a fish." "He's forty pounds if he's a ounce," Pa said. Daddy whistled. "You think?" "I been catching puppy drum half my life," Pa said, "but I never saw a full-grown red that big but once before and that was forty years ago—hell, fifty's closer . . . I won't much older'n you are, Joey, out here with my Uncle Burke and, lemme see . . . Andrew, I b'lieve—yes it was, my brother Andrew, Jesus, Lord, right before he went away to France . . . and Daddy, Daddy, too . . ." When Pa spoke again his voice was different. "Lord have mercy, I'd forgotten that . . . they were all still here, and that was the last time . . . we didn't catch one either, just got a look as they went by."

Suddenly the boat lurched like we'd hit a speed bump going fifty miles an hour in reverse. Everyone pitched forward as a wave slid beneath the beam and spread in front of us with a white *whoosh*, melting back into the water. "Shit," said Daddy, and Pa said, "what the—" He locked his arms around my waist—that was the only thing that kept me in the boat—and when we rocked the other way, I fell over backward on top of him and dropped the pole. It didn't go overboard but thumped against the bottom, and I reached out over my head, watching upside down as it clattered away toward the stern, slow at first, then faster and faster till suddenly it hung up on a eye ring and stopped dead.

"Let go, Pa! Let go!" I wrestled free and crawled after it, banging my knees, as it seesawed on the transom, the small end tipping toward the water as the heavy reel end tipped up in the air, pausing at the top like it was making up its mind if it should come back down. It didn't; it slid slowly into the water so quiet it didn't even make a splash. I lunged for it and missed, then lunged again, plunging in up to my waist while Pa and Daddy grabbed my legs and kept me in the boat. Opening my eyes under water, I watched my pole drop down and down till it became a shadow, then just part of all the other water—I missed it that time, too.

At least I thought I had till I felt the faintest tickle in my hand and came up blowing. "Pa!" I shouted, "Pa! Daddy! Look, I got it! I caught the line!" I grinned over my shoulder, trying to show them, but just at the surface the slack drew taut and pulled my arm back under water, where the tickle turned to something else, something more like razor wire sliding ice-cold through my palm. I made a fist but that only turned the wire red-hot and didn't even slow it down, so I wrapped a twist around my hand. It cinched up so tight it made me suck air through my teeth.

"Pa . . ." I said, "Pa!" "We got you, honey. Try to git it in here on the cleat," he said, "we might can save it." "I don't think I can," I said, wrestling my hand out of the water. The tips of my fingers had turned dark blue and I watched a red bead slip out of my fist, and then a second, sliding down the line like pearls on a thread, faster and faster, till they became a stream and made a red cloud in the water. Pa stretched over the stern and gripped my forearm with both hands to help me pull, his face so close I felt his stubble as he turned his head. "Just a few mo' inches, son. I almost got you, hold it." "It hurts, Pa, I can't," I said, and he said, "try." "Daddy?

*Daddy?*" "I'm right here, son," I heard him say. Across my shoulder I could see him sitting on the middle thwart, his hands folded in his lap, looking calm except his eyes, which were red and wet. "Help me, Daddy," I said, and he said, "it's okay, Joey, let it go." I blinked my eyes one time and did.

For a second it was a relief, and then the second after that it seemed as though a curse had fallen down on things and sucked the life from them. Everything stopped mattering, even that red drum, which had meant the world to me one minute and the next meant nothing. Pa felt it too, I could see it in his face. He'd lost that five A.M. expression and turned grayer than the mackerel in the icebox. "Lemme have a look at that," he said, reaching for my hand as he took his handkerchief from his back pocket. "I'm sorry, Pa," I said as he tied the ends and pulled them tight. "Lissen here," he said, "nothin' to be sorry for, you did yo' best—there're plenty mo' poles where that one came from and they'll be plenty other days to fight." He smiled at me but that smile seemed tired and old some way that made me want to cry more than the pain or even losing. Then Daddy said, "Joey, it was just a fish," and I stared at him, hard, but his face had that soft look you couldn't hate, so I turned away before he saw what I was feeling.

That was when I saw the boat, a fifty-foot white Hatteras riding down the channel with her nose way in the air and her stern sunk low, pushing out a giant cresting wake that broke from one end of the sandbar to the other in a line like dominoes; that was the first I knew what hit us. She wasn't rigged for game fish either, just a pleasure boat out for a spin.

"Son of a bitch," Pa said, "son of a goddamn bitch." We all yelled and shook our fists but, up top at the wheel, the captain never turned his head. As the yacht passed, though, the party on deck looked up and cheered us, raising their cocktails in a toast. They thought we were waving.

*4 Ava*, said the name across the stern. "For Ava and for always, too," said Daddy, laughing, "world without end. Amen."

# THIRTY-SEVEN

*Joey*

As we headed back the sun was just as high as it had been at ten A.M., but in the west now not the east, which changes it some way, the light, so it doesn't seem so fresh and hopeful anymore but brings out deeper blues and golds you never see in morning. In the distance a few ducks were heading south; you could tell them by how straight they flew and the fierce way they beat their wings, like the one thing they could think about was getting there, wherever they were going —home, I guess.

At the launch we idled in the current, waiting as another group went first, one of them a kid about my age down in the water with the older men, heaving at the stern to get their boat up on the trailer. From the back he looked a little bit like Archie, blond and lean like that—he didn't have a life preserver on.

"Howzat hand?" Pa asked, and I said, "fine," though it was throbbing pretty bad. "I 'spect we better git some antiseptic on it, don't you, Jim?" "I bet they have a first-aid kit at the tackle shop," Daddy said, "as soon as we dock I'll run up and see." "It's okay, y'all, it doesn't hurt," I said, hating all the fuss they made. "If you get fish poisoning you'll sing a different tune, budd-roe," said Daddy, and Pa said, "why don't you go 'head on, Jimmy—we got to wait fo' this bunch anyhow . . . Throw a clove hitch 'rounnat pole and we'll wait here till you git back."

Daddy tied us to a pylon and vaulted over into chest-deep water and waded up the ramp, where he stopped a minute to help the others push before he trotted up the road in squishy shoes. We raised the outboard, Pa and me, and started gathering things together in the boat until the other group had cleared. "No sense wastin' time," Pa said, "I'mon run on up and git the car—wanna go?" "That's okay, Pa, I'll just stay here." "All right, honey, you can keep an eye on things. Be right back." He climbed over the bow real careful and pulled himself hand over hand up the line, then used the side wall of the ramp as a railing. At the top, he turned. "Stay in the boat now, hemme?" I stared back mad until he nodded and moved off, not just limping but hobbling worse than I'd ever seen before—I figured his bad leg had stiffened up from being in the boat all day, but he looked like a old, old man.

While I was sitting there, that blond boy from the first group came down from the parking lot and walked out on the stone breakwater, stretching his arms for balance like a tightrope walker. "How's it going?" he shouted, "catch any?" "Yeah," I said, "a few," thinking one would count, so it wasn't a lie. "We caught a *bunch* of trout," he said, "my dad got one that must of weighed ten pounds." "Yeah?" I said, "well, we hooked a red drum." He opened his eyes wide and dropped his voice. "You did?" "Yep," I said. "How big?" "Forty pounds, at least—maybe fifty." "Can I see it?" he asked. "My dad took it to the tackle shop to get it weighed." "Come on, let's go look at it," he said, and I said, "can't. I have to stay and watch the boat." Right then his father called him from the car. "Shoot, I gotta go," he said, "see ya later." "See ya." I watched him run off, hating him because he had blond hair and I'd lied to make him like me, but hating myself more for doing it and wondering why I always did. I'd thought I was all through with that, but I guess I wasn't, and maybe

I never would be—maybe I'd always be the sort who let the big one get away, then made up stories afterward, just like Daddy. I didn't want to be, I didn't want to be like him, not anymore, which made me want to cry or kick somebody's dog, about that mean and hateful.

While I was sitting there, one of those big golden butterflies we'd been seeing all day long—Pa said they were monarchs—dropped from out of nowhere and fluttered around the boat. I reached up to touch it but the wind blew it away across the dark blue water. As I watched it disappear I slipped out of my life jacket, which was soaked and chafing at my sunburn, and glanced toward the tackle shop for Daddy and toward the car for Pa. The coast was clear and, I don't know, I just felt hot and mad and pretty well fed up, I guess, and tired of always doing what they said, so I thought to hell with it and eased over the stern. And it was no big deal either. I could feel the current tugging but no worse than I'd swum in many times, and besides, the water felt real nice, so I just held the propeller and floated, rinsing off and getting cool.

Pa didn't see me till he'd backed the trailer down and started climbing out. I pulled up on the stern and grinned. "Hey, Pa." "Damnit, boy, did you hemme what I said? How many times have I tol' you—" "I know, Pa, but I was hot," I said, "and anyway it's no big deal." "It's gonna be a big deal when I git my hands on yo' behin'. Come on up here now this minute." "Come on, Pa," I said, "we don't need Daddy, I can help you with the boat." "I ain't fooling, Joey—*now*." "Okay," I said, and ducked under to rinse off one last time and also show him that, even if I did it, I was not the sort to jump. When I pulled back up, my hand, the hurt one, hit wrong on the transom; I opened it to change my grip and when I closed it there was nothing there.

I came up blinking, watching the stern drift forward in slow motion, leaving me behind as I stood still in the current, reaching out as the water crept slowly up my neck and touched my chin and didn't stop. "Pa?" I said, and my mouth filled with water. "Joey?" My name was the last thing I heard before the water filled my ears. And it was like Pa always told me, in the twinkling of an eye . . .

As I went under, everything turned quiet; the surface drifted off above me all shimmery and billowing. Then my foot touched bottom and I pushed off, shooting up again and through into the sound. I heard Pa calling, *"Joey, Joey,"* much louder now. As I broke the surface, I saw him wading from the bottom of the ramp, stumbling, reaching both arms toward me, his glasses crooked on his nose and his face all choked and terrible. "Lord, O Lord, he'p us," he cried, "somebody he'p us, please," but there was no one there to hear. I felt bad to see Pa so upset—it didn't seem that serious to me. I didn't feel like I was drowning; I was only floating backward in the current a little ways from shore. The water wasn't very deep and I wasn't all that scared, not even when I tried to right myself to swim and felt my shoes like two lead weights pulling down my legs. *Just untie them*, I thought, *easy*, remembering to take a gulp of air as I went down the second time, pulling my knee up to my chest to reach the laces.

When I pulled the string, though, the bow shrank to a hard little knot, and I sank down and down trying to untie it till my air was gone. I looked back toward the surface, and it was farther than I ever could of thought, like when we used to dive down in the deep end at the club, playing cross-pool . . . Sometimes you'd touch the drain and hold the grate to see how long your bubbles took to rise until you couldn't stand the pressure in your ears. It was like that, but farther, twice or three times more.

I pushed off again but got only halfway up before my speed dropped off to nothing and I started drifting sideways and then slowly down. I went crazy, clawing at the water, trying to climb it like a wall that wasn't there. I kicked my legs so hard that in only seconds my stomach muscles burned worse than after the tenth wind sprint at football practice. I stretched my neck and lips to drink the air, watching the shimmering come closer, closer, thinking, *almost . . . almost . . . now*, except I breathed too soon and swallowed a whole mouthful of water, which went down my windpipe not my throat and exploded like peroxide in my nose. When my head finally broke the surface I was coughing so I couldn't stop to take a breath and there was something in my mouth that burned like vinegar.

But it was worse than that, a whole lot worse, because when I looked, the shore had disappeared. I don't mean it was far away; I mean it wasn't there at all. In front of me there was nothing but wide water as far as I could see and it was like a awful dream. One minute I was in Oregon Inlet, helping dock the boat, and now I was a thousand miles to sea or God knows where, and how this could be so did not make any difference: I was there. Then over my left shoulder I glimpsed the bridge, which had been on my right before, and when I turned I saw it there, the shore, behind me, sixty yards away . . .

By then I'd drifted down the beach to where we'd seined for minnows in the morning, me and Daddy. There were people from the campground lying out on towels or building sand-drip castles. I was almost too tired to lift my arm to wave, except a voice said, *hold on, Joey, don't give up, keep fighting, son.* It sounded like Pa, but I couldn't tell if he was calling from the beach or if it was inside me, something I remembered. "HELP PLEASE HELP ME!" I called as loud as I could, waving so they'd see . . . A woman in a straw hat reading in a fold-up chair dropped her magazine and peered over her dark glasses, searching side to side like she couldn't tell where the sound had come from. As the water crept back up my neck I saw her stand and point, and several people turned their heads and pointed, too, and I went down.

In the silence I could hear my voice still screaming. It seemed to echo off the bottom, and come back, but it was getting weaker, and that other voice, the one of Pa's that said, *don't give up, son, hold on,* was getting weaker too. I wanted to keep fighting, only when I tried to swim my arms seemed to have no bones left; they waved in the current limp and willowy like the sea grass on the bottom. I realized it was going to let me down again, my body, but I couldn't hate it anymore or even feel that mad. It hardly seemed like mine and it was easier to forgive it now that it did not belong to me than all that time before when I believed it did.

This was like a kind of sleep I drifted into when something snapped me out of it—the cold, I think . . . When I woke up, the light around me had begun to turn to shadows and I could see how deep I'd sunk. I was scared, except I thought it might be a dream and if I tried hard I could wake up and Mama would be sitting beside me on the bed and everything would be all right . . . But then another voice came to me in the water, not hers or Pa's, but Daddy's this time—*it's okay, Joey, just let go*—and I started crying down there where it made no sound or any difference, sadder than I'd ever been before, not because it was a lie like I first thought when Daddy said it in the boat, another lie to go with all the others he had told, no, because it wasn't, that was why. As I sank down to where the lights began to fade I realized he was right, Daddy, more right than Pa, and had been all along, and just as sudden as it came the sadness went away . . . Something shivery and warm shot through me like electric current and I realized something good was happening to me, a wonderful surprise . . . I was going to have him back again, my daddy, the way we were before the change, and not just him but everything we used to have and lost . . . It was all down there on the bottom waiting for me. I could stop fighting for it now, it was returning by itself and I could listen to the whisper telling me, *give up*, and trust to close my eyes and breathe the water in, and that was what I did . . .

When I opened them again everything had changed. The shadows had disappeared and the bottom was lit with a brilliant light as green as emeralds, so beautiful it made me want to laugh. The sea grass spread around me like the marshes we'd passed at dawn, the stalks all leaning one way in the current as it moved through like the wind and I could hear it now, *whsssssssssh*, that wind, *whsssssssssh*, it said. As it passed, it stirred up golden butterflies which, when I looked closer, turned to tiny shrimp and sea horses, a whole herd that spooked and stampeded when they saw me. When I moved to take a step, I bounded off the bottom like a trampoline and landed fifty feet away. My toe scored the bottom, sending up a trail of sand, each grain winking in the light like gold dust . . .

I felt so light and free I could of run like that forever but there were things to look at on the way . . . I saw the cogwheel of a engine buried like a rusty starfish in the sand among the broken oyster shells whose ridgy backs looked like they had some old-timey writing on them, like the little birds and animals the Egyptians used instead of letters, which in school had made me feel like I could almost understand what those old scribes had meant to say, only right before I got it it had slipped away . . . When I moved again I found my lost pole and Shakespeare reel lying at my feet, not broken but oiled and perfect like it came from the box on Christmas Eve . . .

All around as far as I could see, the ocean floor was glittering with objects, millions of them, as though a fleet of Spanish galleons sank and spilled their treasure chests; it seemed like everything that anybody ever lost or wanted was there to find and have again . . . I would of liked to take my time to look, but then I noticed everything was moving like slow tumbleweeds pulled by something, some force, sucking them all in one direction where the current flowed and made the grasses bow . . . the same force was pulling me, and though the motion seemed so slow it wasn't . . . I knew there would not be time to gaze at all the sunken treasures and felt more sad for this, I think, than dying, which I knew that I was going to then except I didn't really mind . . . It was just a word that frightened people because they didn't really know the meaning, once you did it wasn't scary anymore, and I could see that meaning like Egyptian writing on the backs of the old oysters who left their poems behind and I could read them now . . .

The only thing I was sorry for was my family—I wished that I could tell them this, that what was happening to me was not a sad or painful thing but far more beautiful than words could ever say . . . and then, as though something heard my wish and granted it, I rose back through the water with no effort where none could help me swim before and found them all there waiting for me on the beach . . . Mama was holding Reed, pointing where to wave goodbye, and they were younger, from the time before our trouble came, the way I wanted to remember them . . . The same jeweled light that lit up everything below the water shone on them, and each appeared to me as their own true self . . . above them in the sky the sun was green . . .

Everyone was there but Pa, for some reason he was not . . . in his place I saw a tall lean boy with long dark hair who looked familiar, a little bit like Daddy in his high school pictures, but I couldn't think where I had seen him if I ever had . . . He stood apart from the others and seemed upset and angry over something, and as I went back down into the underlight I realized he was me, the person I would of grown up to become, and I was just as glad I wouldn't have to now, as much for him as me . . .

As I drifted down for the last time, something on the bottom winked and caught my eye . . . I thought it was a gold doubloon half-buried in the sand, but when I picked it up it was a medal like the one I stole from Archie's dad—not his, though: this was mine . . .

When I came to I was on the beach, coughing up a great hiccup of salty water that washed over my cheek and burned like acid as it ran into my ear. Something powerful had me pinned. At first I saw nothing but a huge dark shape, its mouth locked over mine, clicking teeth with me as it sucked out my breath and put it back. Even when it pulled back far enough for me to see that it was Daddy, I felt scared. Everything was wheeling, and in the sky above his head was a swarm of butterflies . . . For a moment a little of the magic light still clung to him and made the line of clear snot running from his nostril sparkle like a crystal thread. Even the purple smudges under his eyes seemed beautiful, but most of all it was his eyes themselves. I could not stop looking—they had the color of the underlight in them, which there isn't any name for, but as I watched, that light began to fade the way the mackerel faded in the boat, and the swarm of butterflies tumbling in the air above his head turned to lightning bugs, then flying sparks and finally into nothing, and I began to cry harder than I ever had before.

Daddy raised me to his chest and rocked me. "It's okay now. I know it was scary, son, but I've got you now and it's all right." "It's not, it's not, Daddy," I said, sobbing and sobbing. "Shhh, bud, shhh, don't try to talk." I had to tell them, though. "You don't understand," I said, "you don't," and he said, "what, son? What don't I understand?" "It was beautiful, Daddy, *beautiful*," I said and he stopped rocking me. "He must still be in shock," he said to Pa.

"But I'm not. I'm not, Pa," I said, hoping he would understand, "it was beautiful." Pa's face seemed darker than I'd ever seen it and his lips were trembling. Suddenly the lenses of his glasses flashed, and he reached out and slapped me hard across the mouth.

I stopped crying then and watched him turn his back and walk away. He propped both hands on the hood of the Cadillac and stood with his head bowed. For a minute I felt confused and scared, like maybe they were right and it was just a dream. Then I felt it pressing there, the medal, real and solid in my fist. Only when I opened it to look, there was nothing but a quarter.

# THIRTY-EIGHT

## Joey

Mama and Nanny were both real quiet, listening to the story with expressions that were halfway scared and halfway mad as hell. I could tell they would of liked to jump all over someone for what had happened at the Inlet and that Daddy would of been their favorite pick, only he'd saved my life and I almost had not come home, so there was no one to get mad at. Later on, after they'd stopped hugging me and asking if I was all right, they perked up and wanted the details, so everybody told their side, starting off with Pa. When it came to me I just said I'd blacked out and couldn't remember much and let the other go. After the way Pa took it, I decided it was better not to tell what I had seen, like if you went off on a long trip and knew nobody would believe you if you told them where and it was better not to even try or else they might think there was something wrong with you and probably they'd be right. Because how could it feel good if you were dying and I was?

Mainly I held my peace and let Daddy tell it, which was just as well because his story was the best, about like you'd expect. I didn't even mind when he made up some things that never happened because for once the main part of it was true—that he dove in the water and pulled me out when I was drowning and was a honest hero. Mama and Nanny made a fuss about how brave he was, which made Daddy beam so bright you probably could of seen him out to sea a couple miles. He drank a few too many Pabst Blue Ribbon talls and after while began to call me Jonah and the Ancient Mariner and Phlebas the Phoenician, which got a laugh from them. I knew it was just in fun and didn't mind too much. After Pa had said *Good bread good meat*, Daddy said, "Mr. Will, if you don't mind, I'd like to add a word tonight," and smiled around the table.

"Things haven't been too clear lately, at least for me," he said. "I don't know, I guess my thinking got mixed up, but I want to tell you all today when I looked out there and saw an empty boat and open water where Joey was supposed to be, everything got real clear in a big hurry. All I could think was, God, just let me find him, let me find my boy, and I understood more clearly than I ever have in my whole life what matters, what's important, what I love, and it's all right here. It's you, Joey, and Reed, and you, May. It's you, Miss Zelle and Mr. Will, each and every one of you, my family . . . I can't tell you all how rich and blessed I feel to be here tonight, especially when I think how close I came to losing it . . ."

His face puckered and he shook his head. "I'm sorry, y'all, I . . ." "There, there, son," Pa said, "that's all right. We know, we all know how you feel."

I don't know what it was, but my heart wasn't in it somehow, even then. They kept saying how lucky I was to be there and it was a miracle I was still alive and I should thank my lucky stars, and I knew all of it was true but I felt separated off, not a part of all their joy. They seemed like ghosts that you could pass your hand right through who'd come back from some other world or lifetime you were once a part of, or else the ghost was me.

Part of it, I think, was how things stood with me and Pa. I saw him staring at me over dinner several times, but we hardly said two words all evening except good night, and then we just shook hands.

Usually afterward I'd hug him round the neck, and I could tell he wished I would, but I just couldn't somehow, not because I felt that mad at him for slapping me but more ashamed because what I'd said earlier made him ashamed of me. For the second night in a row I hardly felt like eating, though Dee Lou served spoonbread with Log Cabin syrup. Mainly I just wished I could go to bed and be alone and sleep for a long time and maybe when I woke up things would be back like they were before.

After lunch on Sunday as I walked down to the beach to take a swim everything seemed strange and different at the edges. Reed was working on a sand castle and I helped him for a while. We were on our knees in the swash, scooping sea fleas into a green plastic bucket, when I looked up and saw Mama returning from her walk. She'd been gone when I woke up that morning and was still way up past the Croatan Hotel when I caught sight of her, nothing but a black speck on the beach among a lot of others, but even from that distance I knew it was her, I don't know how, I could just tell. Something made me wish she'd stay a speck out there instead of getting bigger and more real with every step, bringing something back with her I didn't want to know about.

"Hey, Mama," Reed called and ran off to meet her. She raised her glasses and waved, her hair all tossed and curly from the ocean breeze and her eyes a little more direct and clear than normal. It made me nervous when she turned that look on me, like she was calculating things and sad the way the sums came out. She picked Reed up and carried him to the umbrella while I rinsed my hands. Stretching on my towel, I closed my eyes and didn't speak to her.

"How far'd you walk?" Reed asked, and she said, "I don't know, sugar, a long way." "Past the pier?" "Past the pier," she said. "You missed lunch." "I'm sorry, that wasn't very nice of me, was it." "That's okay," Reed said, "Dee Lou left you a sam'ich in the fidgerator." "Where is everyone?" she asked. "I think Pa and Uncle Johnny went to ride," he said, "and Daddy's at the house." "Hello, Joey," she said, and I said, "hi." I could feel her watching like she couldn't tell if I was mad or why I might be—she didn't know I'd heard their fight the day before.

"Where's Nanny?" she asked, and Reed said, "taking a nap." "That sounds like a good idea, doesn't it?" "Nuh-uh, I'm not tired," Reed said. "Well, maybe now you aren't, but by tonight you'll wish you had. Why don't you try to sleep a little while? It probably wouldn't hurt your brother either." I didn't bother answering.

"I will if I can sleep down here," Reed said. "Well, if you'll really try . . ." He grinned to get his way and nestled into her. When I opened my eyes she was stroking his hair, gazing straight at me.

"Mama?" Reed said after while. "What, sugar pie?" "Is Daddy going to come back home to live with us now?" "I don't know, honey," she answered softly. "Don't you love him anymore?" I heard her breath go ragged and all funny like Reed's question caught her by surprise. "Of course, of course I do," she said when she could finally answer, "I'll always love your daddy and care what happens and want the best for him, *always.*" "Then how come, Mama," Reed said, "how come if you do, he can't come home?" "I didn't say he couldn't. I said I didn't know." "But, why, Mama? Why don't you know?" When she realized he wasn't going to let her off, she answered. "It's just that sometimes two people, even if they love each other very much, still can't be happy together, Reed. When they've tried their best, there comes a point they have to stop hurting each other and learn to live apart." Mama's words made me think back to early summer when the footprints first appeared, how I'd heard Nanny ask her on the porch one night if love could be enough. I realized in the meantime she'd found her answer, Mama had. In the moment she first spoke those words I hated her for everything that answer took away.

"But if that happens, Reed," she went on, "I want you to know it's not because of you or Joey, not in any way, never think it." I knew she said that as much for me as him, aware that I was listening in however hard I tried pretending. "And the other thing I want to tell you both is that, whatever happens, your daddy will always be your daddy and love you every bit as much as he does now, just as I'll always be your mommy and love you too, and I hope you'll love me—none of that will ever change. The only difference is we won't be married anymore. He won't be my husband and I won't be his wife and we'll live in different places . . ."

When she said that I couldn't stand it anymore. I got up and ran down to the water and when I saw the sand castle I kicked the tower down and smashed the wall and stomped the thing to pieces, which was a mean and stupid thing to do, I know.

Mama followed me and took my arm and tried to pull me to her, but I shouted, "let me alone, you hear?" and pushed her harder than I should of or ever had before. "Joey, please," she said, "please listen," but I said, "I don't care what you say, Daddy saved my life and he's a hero, a *hero*, do you hear? And nothing you do can ever take that away from him, not *ever*." I could see she was on the verge of crying, which made me feel so bad for her I wanted to reach out and almost did except I knew that if I let her touch me, if I let her pull me to her like when I was small, that would be the end for me.

"Joey, darling, the last thing I ever want is to take that from your daddy," she said. "I'm so grateful to him in my heart for what he did, because he saved you, and I know how much you love him. A boy's father should be his hero and I'm glad you have that, but, darling, there are things Mama needs, things I have to have that don't have anything to do with that. Can you try to understand that? I know it's hard; it is for me too. Only try as best you can, okay? Please try for Mama." But I couldn't try for her or anyone and didn't even want to. I only screamed, "I hate you," and turned my back on her and ran into the sea.

# THIRTY-NINE

## Joey

That afternoon the footprints on the beach were mine. I found them there still headed out as I turned back for home. Everyone had left the beach by then and it was getting late, that time of afternoon we'd started for the launch the day before, and those same clouds, the giant white ones, had come back out from whatever hiding place they kept for mornings. They seemed to be a thing of afternoons, those clouds, and fall, that long blue light it gets, and there were fleets and fleets of them like clipper ships, a whole armada heeling with a trailing wind as they sailed off to the northeast, away toward England.

When I crossed the dune Pa was standing at the corner of the cottage, shading his eyes with a Blue Ribbon in his hand as he examined the blank wall. He seemed so interested in something, I thought I might make it past, but he turned quickly like he'd felt my eyes, and then we had to speak.

"Hey, Pa," I said, and he said, "hey, boy, whatcha know," and I said, "not too much." "We got somp'm in common then—reckon we can still be friends?" "I guess," I told him, and he said, "you guess? Well, that's somp'm, ain't it. Leastways, it's better'n a kick in the head." "We're still friends, Pa," I said, "you know we are," and he gave me that tickled grin of his and held his hand out and we shook on it, and it was put behind us, what had happened yesterday, like that.

"Whatcha doing here anyway?" I asked, because that side of the house was one you didn't go to much except to throw away the bacon grease or bury fish bones. "See here?" He pointed with his beer. "Seems to me we've sunk a little in the northeast corner." His finger traced the sag the row of shingles made beneath the kitchen window. "B'lieve the wood has rotted underneath. Noticed it last year, but looks to me it's gotten worse. Next thing you know we'll be setting down to supper and the damn thing'll come right down around our ears—that wouldn't be much fun, now, would it." "No, sir, Pa." He frowned and took a sip of beer. "Nosuh, it would not . . . 'spect we're gonna have to pay a call on Carl and see if he cain't git this place back shipshape." Carl Wembley was the carpenter who'd built the cottage.

Pa put his beer on the windowsill and raised his hat to mop his brow. "Don't reckon I could talk you into riding with me to Mann's Harbor? I could use the comp'ny." "Sure, Pa, I'll go." "Good," he said, "I was thinking we might stop by Whalebone Junction on the way, look in at the tackle shop. Seems to me I know me a young fella needs him a new fishing pole." He cut a wink at me. "I just wish I had my old one back," I said. "That's something I cain't he'p you with, honey." "I know, Pa, I know you can't, it's gone." As he tucked his handkerchief back in his pocket and began to put his hat back on, one of those gold monarch butterflies lit on the crown and sat there, opening and closing its wings.

"Well, I'll be dogged," Pa said, smiling, "would you take a look at that—he must be all tired out." "From what?" "Migrating, I s'pose," he said, "it's this time every year they go," and I said, "where?"

Pa reached for his Blue Ribbon. "Seems to me I heard one time there's this place way down in Mexico," he said, "a hill they all go back to in the wintertime, every single one of 'em the whole world over right to that same spot . . . You'd never think it, would you, a little-bitty thing with paper wings like this could make it all that way? Must be several thousand miles."

"How do they find it?" I asked. "Well, Joey, that's something I don't rightly know as I can tell you, son. I reckon way down deep inside a butterfly remembers where he came from same way a person does and every once in a while he's got to go back for a visit just to see the place again—it ain't that different when you come to think of it . . . Me, I know sometimes I git a hankering and hop in the car and head out to Rose Hill to go see Mama and Daddy where they are . . . One a these days I 'spect you boys'll have a place like that, you and Reed and yo' two cousins, a place you'll remember special where a lot of good things happened to you and some bad ones, too. Funny thing about the bad ones, they make you love it every bit as much as the good ones do and maybe more. Never did know why that's so 'cept it is . . . Maybe it'll be right here, you never know.

" 'Cept if we don't shore this northeast corner up, there might be nothing left for y'all to come back to and that'd be right pitiful, now, wouldn't it?" "Yes, sir, Pa, we better get it fixed," I said, and he said, "come on then, let's go pay Carl a visit," and he held his hat up to his lips and blew away the butterfly, which seemed to wake up as the breeze caught its wings and tumbled it across the dune in the same direction all the clouds were going, out to sea.

It was dusk by the time we left the tackle shop, and everything below had turned that kind of ashy gray it gets, though way up high the sky was blue. I was happy with my rig, a Shakespeare like the one I had before, and threw my arms around Pa's neck and said how much I liked it. But I knew I'd never love it like the one I lost, which was my first, and I think Pa knew, too.

Carl Wembley lived off by himself in a pine wood a mile or two outside Mann's Harbor. The road to his house was carpeted with needles, which made the tires go whisper-soft so you could hear the forest sounds around you. He came out barefoot on the porch as we pulled up, a man about Pa's age as thin and tall as Pa was short and round, squinting at us in a way that didn't strike me as that friendly till Pa called, "whatcha know, young fella." "That you, Mr. Will?" he said as we got out, and Pa said, "what's lefta me," and Carl said, "I'll be damned," and Pa said, "that's a bet I'd take." They both grinned, and Carl hurried to offer a hand as Pa grabbed the railing and struggled up the steps onto the porch.

"Look at me here all broke down," Pa said as they shook hands, "and you ain't hardly aged a day since I last saw you." "Bad knee?" Carl asked. "Something like, Carl, something like." Carl shook his head. "The worst misery's on the inside, Mr. Will." "Lord, ain't it the truth," Pa said, "you remember my grandson Joey, don't you?" "Sure I do," said Carl, "that's some pole you got there, son—looks new." "Yes, sir, thanks, it is." "Want to try it out, there's some right nice bass down in the creek."

We took a path to this little dock he had with a rotty skiff tied to the pole, and Carl kicked over a log and grabbed a cricket from the soft black dirt and helped me bait my rig. He and Pa stood by a while, quiet as I flicked it out; then Pa said, "how 'bout a beer, Carl? Got a six-pack cooling in the car," and Carl said, "no, thanks, but I'll have a real drink with you if y'all'll come up to the house."

Pa asked me if I wanted to go with them, but I said no and stayed and practiced casting, listening to their voices getting louder on the porch and laughing more, but listening mainly to the woods—the tree frogs and the crickets and cicadas. The sounds seemed strange because you didn't hear them out where we were on the beach; all summer long you never would. They made me think of Ruin Creek and Killdeer, going home and starting school again, how it was almost time.

"Well, that's one thing taken care of anyhow," Pa said as we climbed back in the car. "I don't know 'bout you but I feel a little better." As he backed up and started out, I stared at him and then away through the windshield and felt his mood come right back down to mine.

"Ah, well," he said, "there's some problems you can solve, honey, and some you cain't. I wish it was another way but there's nothing me or anybody else can do 'bout that." "Mama could," I said, "she could change it if she wanted to," which I probably would not of said except that I could tell he was a little drunk. "That's asking a whole lot, son, ain't it?" Pa asked, "for one to make the change for two?"—not quite as drunk as I had thought. "I seen a few attempt it, more'n you'd expect, but none I know of ever yet pulled it off. Seems to me yo' daddy's done as much or mo' to put the situation where it is."

"I know you all think that," I said, "I know you think it's Daddy's fault." "I wouldn't be so quick deciding what other people think if I was you, Joey . . . Most times it's so much everybody's fault it's just about the same to say it's no one's, which is hard, son, real hard when you're busted up inside and mad as hell and there's no one you can blame." "If it's no one's fault, how could it happen, Pa?" I asked, "you tell me how it could," and he was quiet for a long time before he spoke.

"I don't know as I should say this to you, honey. I been contemplating on it for a while and if I'm wrong I'm sorry, but seems to me if you're old enough to have to deal with something, you're old enough to know the thing you're dealing with . . .

"Yo' daddy he's a good boy, son, and a good daddy to you boys in many ways. He's got a big heart and he means well and he's awful smart and talented, but he's a grasshopper, Joey. He's like that one in the story I know yo' mama read you, who sang and fiddled while the ants all worked. Everybody loves a grasshopper, Joey, and I love 'im, too, I love yo' daddy just as much as anyone, but when you're a grown man with a fam'ly to take care of, you got to learn to be a ant sometimes. It ain't just you then, Joey; there's other people counting on you, and when it comes down to the pinch, to sing and fiddle don't feed hungry babies and it ain't so charming then, you see . . . Then that kind of charm becomes a selfishness which to me is one of the worst faults a grown man can have. When he does, it don't leave room inside his life for anybody else, Joey, and even if he can fiddle the moon down from the sky that still don't change it, son.

"I know this ain't a easy thing to hear, because it never is when it's got to do with fam'ly, and the worst of all, I guess, is when you have to hear it on yo' daddy. Believe me, son, I know . . . 'cause my daddy was a grasshopper too, Joey, and I loved him more'n I loved 'most anything in my whole life just like I think you love yo' daddy, but I reckon it's also why yo' pa became a ant.

"As clear as I can see it, that's the truth, son. I'm telling you man to man, and it's nothing I ain't said to Jimmy's face mo' times than one. He cain't hear me, Joey. Maybe you can."

Pa glanced once at me and then away through the windshield while I sat knotted up inside, feeling like I might explode. What he'd said was only what I'd told myself a thousand times in secret, only in the end it always seemed it was in me, the selfishness Pa spoke of, not in Daddy, that I could think such things of him. But here he was saying it aloud, my pa, who'd never lied to me, and the strange thing was it scared me more to think it might be true, what I'd known all along, than to blame myself for everything like I had done before. That way scared me less, to blame and hate myself for everything, than to blame Daddy and risk that I might have to hate him. What I wanted more than anything was to go back, but Pa stood in the road and blocked my way.

"He can still change, Pa," I said, "he's trying," and Pa said, "he can and could of any time these last twelve years, Joey. People can always change, that's one true thing, but another is they mostly don't. I'm sixty-one years old, son, and I've never had to learn a sadder lesson than this one I'm telling you right now—it's the last thing I'mon say . . . You cain't he'p someone who won't be he'ped, Joey, however bad you want to and however hard you try. Whatever it is inside yo' daddy that keeps making him mess up and hurt everyone around him, either he don't want to find out what it is and change or else he cain't, and in the end it comes to the same thing—if they won't they won't, and you just got to face it, son, you got to look the truth right dead square in the eye and not blink, Joey, 'cause it's when you blink it gits you. There's certain people in this world you got to learn to let go of, son, or else they're gonna take you with 'em, and yo' daddy's one. If you don't remember anything I ever said to you, remember this—to love someone don't mean you have to go down on their ship. Nosuh, Joey, you point 'em where the life preservers are, you wait till the last minute and git down on yo' knees and beg 'em if you have to, but when the last minute comes and they're still fiddling away or standing there saluting the flag or whatever it may be, you jump, son, you jump and swim for yo' life and don't look back, 'cause whatever you owe anybody in this world, Joey, it ain't that, son, not yo' life, not even to yo' fam'ly."

We'd reached the house by then and Pa pulled into the drive.

"I hope I won't wrong to say this to you, son," he said, turning toward me in the seat after we'd parked. "It's been on my mind since out there at the lake that day and if I'm wrong, God forgive me —either way it's done." I saw it scared him a little, too, to say what he had said. "You aren't perfect either, Pa," I told him, and he stared at me dead sober for what seemed like fifteen minutes, though I doubt five seconds passed. I was quaking like a leaf inside though I made myself keep looking in his eyes, and then I watched that grin of his spread right across his face. "And all this time I thought I was," he said, and laughed, and for a instant somewhere deep inside something I'd never felt before just soared like Pa had set me free.

# FORTY

## Joey

Upstairs everything was gearing up. In the kitchen Daddy had the steaks laid out on the countertops, banging them with a ball-peen hammer while Dee Lou watched, her arms akimbo, as the clean dish towels he'd wrapped the T-bones in turned red. Pa took one look and said, "Lord have mercy, boy, whatcha doing to my meat?" Daddy looked up grinning. "Tenderizing, Mr. Will," he said, wiping a trickle of perspiration from his forehead on the shoulder of his shirt. "That meat's tender as a baby's behind," Pa said, and Daddy said, "wait till I get through with it, it'll melt in your mouth, not in your hands."

Pa shook his head. "Well, lemme go see 'bout the fire then." "Already lit," said Daddy, but Pa went back out anyway, heading down toward the garage.

"Daddy, please don't let the screen door slam," Mama called

after him. When he didn't answer, I saw her look that way and frown.

She and Nanny had both slipped into dresses and done their hair and put their jewelry and their make-up on, though as Mama set the table I noticed she was still in her bare feet. She was putting new white candles in the hurricane chimneys, which sparkled like Dee Lou had been at them that afternoon, while Nanny fiddled with her cocktail sauce, tapping her toe while Aretha, her new favorite, belted from the Dumont.

"Joey, try this for me, sugah, see is it hot enough." She grabbed my arm as I went by and made me taste it off her finger. "Well?" "Mmm-mmm, Nanny." "Hot?" she asked. "It made my hair sweat." She frowned like she didn't trust me on the subject. "It still ain't right," she said, and dumped in another tablespoon of horse-radish.

A little later Mama took me aside. "Joey, run see about your Pa," she said under her breath like she didn't want Nanny to hear. She was watching us, though, Nanny, with a eagle eye, and when Mama realized, she raised her voice again. "Tell him to come upstairs and join us." She tried to hide it, but I could tell she had suspicions.

She was right, too. When I went downstairs I found him by the glow of his cigarette coal in the garage. He was sitting in the dark on the wheel well of the boat trailer, smoking a Chesterfield and sipping a pint of Seagrams.

"Want me to turn the light on, Pa?" "Leave it," he said, real short, which took me back. "You okay?" "Fine," he said, and sighed. "Just taking me a little breather from the race." "Oh," I said, "well, Mama said why don't you come upstairs and join us." "Awright, honey, you tell'uh I'll be up inna minute." That was the first I noticed his voice was getting slurred. "Want anything?" "Thanks, b'lieve I'm set." As I started off, though, he called after me, "you could brimme down a beer out the icebox if you're coming back," and I said, "okay, Pa."

"Just where do you think you're going with that?" Mama asked when I brought a tall boy from the kitchen. "Pa asked for one." "Joey, please don't sneak him anything to drink behind my back," she said. "I wasn't sneaking, Mama." She sighed and took the can just as the door slammed again and everybody turned around.

As Pa crossed the sill he caught his toe and reached for the lamp table which was all that kept him on his feet. "I'm awright, I'm awright." Mama rushed to take his arm, and Nanny said, "Will Tilley, damn yo' time. What'd you promise me?" "Now lissen heah," he said, "y'all jus' go right 'head on 'bout yo' business 'n lemme tend to mine." I was surprised how much worse his voice had become. "Oh, Daddy," Mama said, giving him her disappointed look. "Donchoo Daddy me, May Tilley," he said, "you ain't so big yet I cain't still putcha cross my knee, hemme?" "Come on, sugar," she said, "come lie down and try to close your eyes for a few minutes before dinner."

Pa pulled his arm away and called across the room, "what say, boys? She mus' think h'ol' daddy jus' fell off the turnip truck." He grinned at us. "B'lieve she's gotta 'nother think comin', don't she? Will Tilley won't bawn yesti'd'y . . . won't bawn day 'fore that neither . . . That right? That right what I said, boys?" I called back, "yes, sir, Pa," because he was looking straight at me and I don't think Reed could answer anyway—his eyes were big around as jar lids. "Tha'sit, tha'sit," Pa said, nodding, " 'attaboy, you tell'uh, you tell'uh, son . . . See there, Maybelle? You sha'lissen, sh'lissen to yo' boy . . . he's a smart'n . . . crackerjack . . . run gitcho' Pa a beer, honey." "Daddy, I don't want you asking them to do that," Mama said, "I mean it now," and Pa said, "wouldn' hafta if you'd git me one yo'sef . . . that right? That right, boy?" and suddenly he dropped down backward into a chair.

"You boys go help your daddy cook the steaks," Mama said, and when neither of us was quick to move, she widened her eyes that way. "Right *now*. Don't make me tell you twice." As we went past, Pa cut a wink at me and laid his finger up beside his nose, except he wasn't grinning anymore.

While we were downstairs cooking we heard voices raised above the record player, and when we came up with the steaks the stack of records had all dropped and were turning kind of seasick on the platter with that scratchy noise they make. Pa's door was cracked and I could see him lying down in there—nothing but his shoes sticking up at the foot of the bed. Mama pulled the door to as she turned the Dumont off, and Nanny came out of the bathroom. She'd been crying; I could tell because her make-up was a mess— most of it was on the balled-up wad of Kleenex she brought to the table and dropped into her shrimp-peel dish.

"Idn' Pa eating dinner?" Reed asked, and Mama said, "your pa's a little tired and idn' feeling well." "He's polluted, idn' he?" "Reed Madden, where did you pick up such a word?" Mama asked. Reed said, "from Nanny," and Nanny laughed and sniffed at the same time. "Come gimme a kiss, you precious thing," she said to him that way she never used to do before the Rice House, and you could tell Reed didn't like it much because he said, "I have to eat my dinner first, but I will later, Nanny."

Mama tried to keep the conversation up, complimenting Daddy's steaks, and he pitched in and did his Stewart Granger eyebrow to help out, but whatever anybody tried, it didn't make much difference. It was a pretty quiet dinner.

We were almost through when the bedroom door creaked open.

"Mr. Will," Daddy said, and we all turned as Pa came out in pj's, still wearing his black socks and wingtips.

"Y'all go 'head, go 'head and eat, don't lemme interruptcha," he said in a low voice, looking kind of meek and ill. "Would you like to try to eat something now, Daddy?" Mama asked, "I could fix your plate." "Naw, naw, set still. Jus' a glass a water's all, and I'mon g'on back to bed." He looked at Nanny then. "You mad at me?" "Madder'n a rattlesnake," she said, and he said, "I'm sorry, Zelle . . . All a y'all, I'm awful sorry if I spawled yo' supper," and we said, "that's okay, Pa," except for Nanny. "Go 'head and say it then," he told her and she glared a minute more, then called into the kitchen, "Dee Lou, bring the aspirin bottle, and the saltines while you're at it." Pa grinned ear to ear.

"I see you eyeing it," she said, pushing the steak platter toward him with the fat trimmings lined around the edge, "we ain't been married this long for nothing." "Tha's right," Pa said, "tha's right, she can read me like a book, always could. This ol' gal won't bawn yesti'd'y neither," and Nanny blushed as he leaned down and kissed her cheek. "G'on, g'on," she said, and Pa said, "well, maybe one." He took his place at the head of the table, picked up a carving knife and spread a thick pat of butter on his cracker before he dropped the fat curl on it.

"Lord have mercy, umph, umph, umph," he said, shaking his head and smiling as he chewed, "who wants to try one?" "I do, Pa," Reed said, and Pa said, "climb on up here then," and pushed back from the table so Reed could get into his lap. "How 'bout you, boy? Want one?" he asked me. "Sure, Pa," I said, and leaned to let him put it in my mouth. "Howzat? Zat good?" "Mmm-mmm," I answered, nodding with my mouth full, and Reed said, "it's the best, Pa," and Pa said, "tha's right, tha's right, boy, best you'll ever find."

"It's eleven o'clock now, Reed and Joey," Mama said, "kiss everyone good night and go wash up for bed." I worked down the line, saving Pa for last, and when I kissed him I said, "Pa?" "What, honey?" "Can we go fishing in the morning?" I asked, and he said, "if the weather holds, you bet." "I wanna try out my new pole," I said, and he said, "we gon' git 'im, too, this time, ain't we, boy? This time we gon' git that sombitchin' drum." "Yes, sir, Pa, he'll wish he never messed with us," I said, and I remember how he pulled us both up close a minute, me and Reed, so I could feel the whiskers on his cheek and smell his Aqua Velva and his Chesterfields. Then he said, "now you two buzzards git on outta here," and let us go.

# FORTY-ONE

*Joey*

That night I dreamed I found a hidden staircase in the cottage and climbed up to a attic room that Carl, I think, or else some other carpenter had built when he was there to fix the house. It was like a lookout tower; the walls were solid glass on all four sides and you could see for miles. I felt excited to discover this and wanted to tell everyone there was another story in the house, but as I looked out to sea I saw a black shape coming toward us, like a wave but not a wave —I could not tell what it was—but coming faster than you could believe.

I woke up with a start, the sheets all twisted and damp around me. It seemed I'd barely closed my eyes, but I'd slept longer than I thought because Pa was already up, standing in the door in his white fishing clothes. His hands were in his pockets and he smiled that little morning smile at me and I could see his face real clear, except I couldn't tell exactly where the light was coming from—the hall light wasn't on; I figured it must be the moonlight coming in. "Hey, Pa, is it time to go?" I asked him, sitting up to rub my eyes. "Not just yet, honey, you sleep on a while," he said, "I'll wake you when it's time." As I lay down and closed my eyes again, he stood beside the bed a while and I felt safe and calm to have him keeping watch.

The sun was pretty far off the horizon when I finally got up Monday morning, Labor Day. I jumped out of bed and ran to the big room in my pajamas, mad that no one had come to get me earlier—now we were going to miss the tide. Nanny was eating her half-grapefruit at the table in her robe. "Morning, sugah, want some demi-pamplemousse?" Most times that joke would make me smile, but I just said, "morning, Nanny, I'm not hungry," and went past her to the kitchen, where Mama was frying sausage at the stove.

"Where's Pa, Mama?" I asked like she'd hidden him somewhere, "they didn't leave already, did they?" She shot me a look over her shoulder. "Good *morning*, Joey." "Morning, did they?" "Sweetie," she said, "I don't think you're going fishing today. I'd be real surprised." "But Pa said we were, he promised." "Joey, please don't whine," she said, "I know you planned on it last night, but I don't think he's feeling well today and we should probably let him sleep."

"But he's already up," I said, "he came to my room all dressed and everything." She put the lid on the frying pan and wiped her face and turned around. "When, honey? When did he do that?" "Just a little while ago," I said, "he told me we were going and he'd wake me up when it was time and now he didn't and we've missed the tide."

Mama looked a little stumped on that. "Well, he must have checked the weather and gone back to bed. Maybe the wind is wrong or something." "But it's not," I said, "it's light onshore and the barometer's on thirty, see? Fair." I pointed to the weather station on the wall so that she could read the evidence herself. "It's high pressure down from Canada; that's *good* weather, Mama." "Well, I don't know what to tell you, honey," she said, exasperated now, "I thought he was asleep, but maybe he went out somewhere. Let me take these sausages out and I'll go see."

She took off her apron and wiped her hands and I followed as she tiptoed to the bedroom door and knocked real soft and opened it. "Daddy?" she whispered, poking her head in and blinking as she looked around.

"He's sound asleep, sugar," she whispered, pulling the door to behind her. "Maybe you dreamed it. Why don't you go out and play? I'll call you when the eggs are ready." I was so ticked off I let the screen door slam on purpose.

Outside it was warm and everyone was barefoot like the day before, wearing shorts and swimming in the ocean, throwing sticks for dogs, but it was fall, no more denying it. All you had to do was take one look to know that it had settled in for good and wasn't going away again. Even when you breathed, the air seemed different and more clean and left a empty ache inside your lungs that made you long for something, and the sunlight spangles on the water had a different shine.

I sat in the gazebo for a while and watched the people playing on the beach, but the horizon seemed to call my eye out past them, way, way out to where a white ship was passing, a ocean liner steaming north with blue smoke from the smokestacks trailing south like thoughts of where it left. It was beautiful, that ship, like one I saw once in a bottle, but watching it go by made me feel sad and restless and a little lost up there. I can't explain but it was like the sky had gotten bigger since the day before, like a crystal bowl somebody had turned upside down and emptied out. It made me want to turn it right-side up again and fill it back, but what would you put in a bowl that big . . . It would take a brand-new world, I guess, and I still wanted back the one I had and didn't know where I would start.

To tell the truth, I didn't want to think of it, so I just cleaned the reels. I cleaned them all, even the old-timey brass ones Pa had from way back in his daddy's day which no one ever used. They were corroded green and all locked up, but I went after them the best I could. I took them off their rods and ran buckets of fresh water to soak the salt off and towel-dried each one and started taking them apart as far down as I dared till I began to get a little foggy on the order of the parts and where the little screws and washers went.

Then I dripped some 3-In-One down in the works and put them back together.

I was spread out all across the floor of the garage when Mama came down in her gardening clothes, a pair of blue jeans rolled to just below her knees and one of my white T-shirts. Her gloves were tucked in the back pocket and she had a giant glass of tea just the way she liked it, with a candy-cane-striped straw and a sprig of mint and saccharine to watch her figure. She was on her way to plant some fall bulbs Aunt Mary'd brought her down from Killdeer, when she saw me going at it there. "Good heavens, what got into you?" she asked, and I said, "I don't know, I just felt like it." "Won't your Pa be pleased." "Some of them still don't work too good." I held one up to show her what I meant, and she said, "but I bet they all feel so much better," and I said, "ha ha," trying not to smile, except she knew she got me and smiled back with her lips pursed, getting lipstick on her straw.

By the time I finished I'd killed about an hour. Upstairs Nanny was working on her jigsaw puzzle, a picture of a boulevard in Paris with snow and horse-drawn wagons and little Frenchmen in berets walking toward the Eiffel Tower. She'd start it every June as soon as we came down, then get distracted playing bridge. Before you knew it, it was almost Labor Day and she'd get in a state and not bother getting dressed but sit down in her bathrobe first thing every morning and stay till late at night, filling ashtray after ashtray with Old Golds and hardly answering when you spoke to her. Some years she got further than others, but she never finished, and the last official act of the whole summer would always be to break it up again.

Daddy also seemed to catch the mood; he was washing the Mustang in the driveway. As Mama wiped her arm across her face and took a sip of tea, I saw her glance at him, and just as clear as if she spoke the words aloud I heard her think, *why don't you wash the station wagon, too?* I could see how it escaped her that he wouldn't think of this as natural as breathing the same way she would think of it for him, and how much she was frustrated by this, but wouldn't mention it because it would just cause another fight and not do any good. For one split second, the same thing I'd watched I guess a hundred thousand times before seemed all lit up, like someone threw a spotlight on the two of them. He glanced up and saw her, and Mama only smiled a tense, mad smile and turned back to her gardening, and I saw how Daddy's jaw went tight as he smiled back and how, when he began to soap the windshield, that smile changed to a kind of brooding frown, like he knew he was in the wrong again but not what for. That was always when my heart went out to him and took his side of things, because somewhere deep down I guess I knew my daddy wasn't really grown-up in the same way Mama was or Pa or even me, but that day it did not; if it went out at all, it went in equal parts to both of them and mainly I just saw it clear and understood.

I didn't really want to hang around, so finally I knocked on the Landises' door and asked Uncle Johnny if he was up to play some gin. He seemed in the same predicament as me, so we set up the chairs and table in the driveway and had at it. After while, A. Jenrette came by again and we played three-hand for a penny a point, except instead of money we used the box of Blue Diamond matches Aunt Mary kept upstairs on her stove.

When Uncle Johnny went inside to pee—he had some condition that made him go a lot—A. took out that dirty deck and we switched cards, filling Uncle Johnny's hand with naked ladies. So out he comes, with that relieved expression he'd get, and reached for his cards. "Well, now," he said, kind of chipper, "let's see here what we got." Then he fanned them out and under that thick wave of silver hair his face turned stop-sign red. He kind of coughed and cleared his throat, but all he said was, "well, I reckon it was bound to come eventually . . ."

"I reckon it was bound to come eventually"—I don't know why, but I remember it so clear, and how the second after that the screen door slammed at our house. Like when you start counting off the seconds from a lightning flash until the thunder sounds, I waited to hear Mama say, *please don't slam the door,* and if one time the thunder didn't come, you'd be surprised and wonder why, and, see, that was the thing that made me glance up over Uncle Johnny's shoulder and see that it was her this time . . . this time Mama was the one who slammed the door, and I don't know, I don't know, but right that very second some voice inside me said, *oh, no* . . .

She stood there moving her lips like she was talking to herself, and then her hand went to her mouth and covered it, and then it flew away like her lips were scalding hot . . . She began to shake them then, both hands, this way I never saw her do before, not her or anyone, but like a nurse with a thermometer, shaking down the mercury, only both at once like something terrible had touched them and she was trying to shake it off, and then she broke and started running toward the steps.

I saw it all in one split second and I remember it so clear, how I said, "Mama?" underneath my breath, knocking my chair over on the concrete as I stood . . . Uncle Johnny said, "whoa, there, where's the fire?" and I said it aloud this time: *"Mama?"* I shouted it as loud as I could shout and I remember the change in Uncle Johnny's face, the way it froze as I began to run.

I reached the bottom of the stairs just as she was coming down and Mama never even looked at me; she just reached out and stiff-armed me aside. I blinked and watched her go, stunned how hard she hit my shoulder, and she didn't run five steps before she turned and came right back to where I was and knelt in front of me and took my hands in both of hers and looked at me like she didn't remember pushing me or even seeing me till then.

"Joey, listen very carefully," she said, "run and find your daddy, run and bring him back as quick as ever you can." "What is it, Mama, what's the matter?" "Just go, darling, go," she said, "and fly." At that moment it was like some muddy stream between the two of us ran clear again the same as I remembered it from long before, and all I wanted was to help her and to keep her safe who had helped me and would of run through fire to try.

I've never run so hard as I did then, cursing the sand at every step, the way it caved beneath my feet and my own legs for being fat because they couldn't carry me as fast as Archie ran. As I struggled up the last few feet of dune I prayed Daddy would be there when I looked. Across the top, the east wind off the ocean chilled my sweat and filled my shirt like a balloon. I saw the big umbrella, and his towel stretched beside it and his indentation pressed into it like a wet footprint. His dark glasses and his lighter and his pack of Lucky Strikes were there, but Daddy wasn't. I looked north and south but didn't see him anywhere and it was like that moment at the Inlet when I came up and the shore had disappeared and there was nothing there but me alone in a wide world of empty water and even time is now your enemy. For just a second I had a scary feeling of something alive, watching me from back behind the sky, and I did not know who or what it was but there was goose flesh up my neck and arms . . .

And then out in the water where I'd looked before, but farther, way, way out, a movement drew my eye. A sleek dark head appeared and then a long white arm, first one and then the other, pulling slow and graceful through the water like the paddle wheel on a old Mississippi steamboat, and I would of known it anywhere, that lifeguard stroke of Daddy's which he'd learned at Camp Blue Moon . . . I ran down to the water's edge and shouted for him, jumping up and down and waving both arms overhead, but he didn't hear and just kept on, not toward me or away but parallel to shore. I ran in the same direction till he stopped to rest and started treading water . . .

"Daddy!" I shouted. "Daddy!" When he noticed me I saw the white flash of his grin across that distance as he whooped and waved me out to join him. "Hey, the water's great," he called, and I screamed back, "come in! Come in!" I could see him cup his hand around his ear. "What?" he said, "what's that?" I stumbled out chest-deep and just kept shouting, over and over, "COME IN . . . COME . . . IN . . ." till he began to swim toward me, faster now.

He came up from the swash slicking his hair back with both hands from his widow's peak, the water sheeting off him everywhere. That happy-go-lucky grin was gone. You could already see in his face something scared and all tensed up, scary, too, to me.

"What is it, Joey? What's the matter, son?" he asked, and I said, "hurry, Daddy, something's wrong up at the house. Mama said for you to come." He opened his mouth as though to say something more or ask a question, then didn't, and like that he was gone, pulling up the hill away from me with those long strides.

When I got back to the house Dee Lou was on the porch kneeling next to Reed, who was clinging to her, his eyes big around and scared and solemn. As I went past, she reached out to try to hold me, too, but I pulled away and pushed through the screen door . . .

At the far end of the room Uncle Johnny was holding Nanny's hand, trying to, as she pulled back from him. "Don't you say it . . . Don't you tell me that, John Landis, you hemme?" she was saying in that gravelly old voice like she was furious at him, and when he heard the door, Uncle Johnny looked across at me with eyes the same as Reed's.

The next second after that I looked left toward Pa and Nanny's bedroom . . . The door was open all the way against the wall and Mama was pressed back against the door not ten feet from where I stood. She didn't look at me, not even when I slammed the screen; her eyes were fixed on something else and I looked where they looked . . .

At the end of the twin bed, where I'd seen Pa's wingtip sticking up the night before, I now saw his bare foot, just that. The door-frame cut out all the rest . . . There was something in the color or the way it lay, I can't say which, that made the hair rise on my neck. Next to Pa's there was another foot, pointing down as Pa's foot pointed up, and they were moving, both of them at once, riding up and down together with a rhythm that made the bedsprings creak. What I was seeing I could not explain, except that it was Pa's leg pointing up, and the other one was Daddy's . . .

I started forward, but Mama suddenly turned to me with flashing eyes. "Joey, don't come in," she said, and there was something in her voice that stopped me cold. But I was close enough already to see Daddy lying facedown on the bed on top of Pa, with their mouths pressed together like a kiss . . . He was out of breath and sobbing as he gasped, "come on, come on, goddamnit, breathe, God, God, *breathe*," and as he turned his head to listen to Pa's chest, I saw his eyes were red and terrible and in despair . . . Mama leaned against the door as though trying to back away from this as far as she could get, and the look in her dark eyes was still more terrible to me. I can't say whether it was pity or disgust, except to see it there made me know this was the end not just of one thing but much more . . .

"Stop it, Jimmy," she said finally, "stop it. Daddy's dead." And after the lightning flash, the thunder finally came.

Trailing the covers in his fist, Daddy slid to the floor beside the bed, first on his knees, then back with a heavy thump onto his seat. Covering his face with his big hands, he sat cross-legged, a damp stain spreading under him from his wet trunks, and wept this way that would of torn your heart in two if you could feel, but I could not. My heart had frozen colder than a stone . . . Behind me I heard Nanny: "Oh, Lord, May, Lord, Lord, no, he ain't, I know he ain't . . . Where's Dee? *Dee Lou?*" Nanny yelled for Dee like she was set to go to pieces, and Mama stepped out of the bedroom. "Mama," she said, real soft and calm, "Mama," just that and nothing more, two times, and I can't say what it was, but everybody in that room turned to look at her, at my mama, every single eye. I don't think she even knew, but it was like in battle if the standard-bearer fell. I watched as clear as anything the very moment of her life when Mama stepped to catch the weight that Pa had carried on his shoulders all of his and raised the flag before it hit the ground and we all turned to follow who would lead us now . . . My heart was numb but for a moment it swelled up inside my chest, and I remember thinking this was something fine—that and how much she looked like Pa.

# FORTY-TWO

## Joey

We marched downstairs like soldiers then, or sleepwalkers, Reed and me, to Dee Lou's room, where I sat quiet on the bed with my hands folded in my lap while Reed took out his coloring books and colored on the floor, careful not to go outside the lines. I felt a kind of stillness creeping in, drop by drop, like one by one each thing in the world was coming to a stop and pretty soon nothing would be moving anymore. I couldn't tell exactly what I felt, but it seemed strange and some way impolite that the sun outside should still be shining and the sky should still be blue. I felt as if now dark should fall for us to be a kindness and wished that it would hurry up and come, and I was sad the world outside in that fall light remained as beautiful as it had been that morning.

It didn't seem right to play like Reed, but after while I began to think of my new fishing pole—I couldn't remember where I'd put it and was suddenly afraid it might be lost, so I went to look and found it leaning against the wall in the garage exactly where I'd always leaned the old one. I took it back to Dee's room, not to play with but so I could keep a eye on it, and I just sat there holding it.

When Mama came, she'd dressed and put her make-up on, and her perfume smelled too strong the way it always did when she first sprayed it. "Come here, boys, come to me," she said, sitting down on Dee Lou's bed with her arms spread for us. Her eyes were bright like she'd been crying earlier, but she was smiling now and she seemed two or three times more alive than I remember any other time, the way a tree you've seen a thousand times in your back yard will seem all fresh and new, drenched black after a rain. "Where's Pa, Mama?" Reed asked as he nestled close, and she said, "that's what I want to talk to you about, darling. Your pa has gone to heaven, he's gone to be with God." I wasn't very happy with this story and couldn't tell if she believed it either, only I could see from Mama's eyes she told us this because she wanted us to have more comfort than she had, and even if the words felt wrong I couldn't blame her. "When will he come back?" Reed asked, and she said, "he won't, baby." Reed said, "oh," and Mama said, "but one day you'll see Pa again, we all will." "Is Pa dead?" Reed asked, and I could tell it was hard for Mama to have to say it clear that way, but she said, "yes, baby, yes, he is." She kissed us then. "I want you both to go upstairs now while I talk to Dee . . . Nanny wants to speak to you."

I could already hear Nanny at the bottom of the stairs, not crying but speaking in a trembly voice to someone—I thought Aunt Mary had come over from next door. But as we reached the porch, before going in through the screen door, I caught a glimpse of her through the bedroom window . . . Nanny was sitting on the bed beside Pa, holding his hand and smiling as she spoke, and her cheeks were streaming tears. I could see him, too, my pa . . . His eyes were closed and his face looked peaceful, relaxed and younger than I ever knew. With her other hand Nanny was smoothing down that strand of hair, which even then would not lie flat. On the bedside table I saw his glasses with the gold frames as thin as wire. They were turned upside down, and the sun was flashing in the lenses.

When Nanny came out she had on a black dress and her silver

hair was brushed. Her eyes were washed with tears, but even so they had that spark you always saw in them when she said, *Remember who you are*. She called us to her and kissed us both and gave Reed Pa's felt hat with the smell of him in the silk lining. Then she pressed his Barlow knife into my hand. "You remember 'im, hemme?" she said. "Y'all remember Pa." And she could not say any more.

We took these awful treasures and went outside, where the other children looked at us with solemn eyes like we were famous now. "Our pa is dead," Reed told them, bragging over it like it was something to be proud of, and I turned on him and said, "shut up, stupid, shut up, don't say that, don't *ever* say that again." His lips began to tremble and the look in his black eyes reminded me too late he was my brother and still too small to know. When I tried to tell him I was sorry, he wouldn't let me near.

I went away from everyone and hid beneath the Jenrettes' house, in our old place, where it felt safe. Through the lattice boards I watched the neighbors come and go, dressed up and somber and polite. The ambulance came up the drive with the light flashing, but no siren. Later, Daddy came down with the first suitcase and Dee Lou with a box of linens. On and on it went, until the light began to change and the great cloud ships appeared and the blueness in the sky shed away its hurtful brightness and turned the very color that I felt, and dusk fell like a soothing peace. As dark came on, the orange light kept turning on the ambulance, splashing on our wall and in the windows and on Daddy's face and each one as they passed like a slow procession, carrying boxes and suitcases, so that it seemed as if a great fire was burning and by its flickering light we were all gathering what we could to take away.

I watched two attendants wheel the stretcher out and lift it down the steps as Mama and Daddy and Nanny stood on the porch and watched, too. As they rolled it across the concrete, the wheels made a crunching sound in the loose sand that made me think of Thursday nights and waiting for the Cadillac to turn into the drive and there would be no more of this . . . The men collapsed the legs and rolled the stretcher into the ambulance and I could see his shape beneath the sheet, my pa's, until they closed the doors, and that was the last time I saw him.

They sat in the cab and waited then, those two men, smoking cigarettes. It was dark when Mama called and I knew it was time to go. I reached out for the knife I'd laid beside me in the sand, and suddenly it wasn't there. I looked on the other side and then traced back the path of everywhere I'd been but couldn't find it anywhere. "Joey!" they were calling then, "Joey!" I crawled under the bottom board and ran to Mama in the driveway. "I can't find it, Mama, I can't find Pa's knife, you have to wait," I told her, and Mama said, "the men are set to go, Joey. Run back one more time and look." Reed came to help and Tawny, too, but even the great digger couldn't find it. Maybe it's still down there in the sand with my Matchbox Bel Air, like buried treasure from a ancient kingdom which fell down the day we lost our king.

# FORTY-THREE

## *Joey*

It was full dark as we pulled out, following the turning orange light ahead of us, across the three-mile bridge, past Mann's Harbor, back where you could hear the tree frogs and the crickets and cicadas sing again. Uncle Johnny and Aunt Mary came behind us with Dee Lou, and Daddy drove the Country Squire with Mama next to him and Nanny, too, in the front seat while I sat in back with Reed and Tawny. Up front they talked softly for a long time and then Mama whispered, "shhh, shhh, she's asleep," and everyone fell quiet.

It did not seem right to me to sleep, except I did. I don't know how long or where we were when I woke up. Reed was curled up close beside me, sucking his thumb and holding Mr. Rex tucked to his stomach, while up front Mama's head had drifted onto Daddy's shoulder and her mouth was open.

Daddy had his window down and his elbow propped outside. He seemed calm and quiet as he smoked a Lucky, the night wind riffling his hair, and close behind him Tawny sat like she could never tire of this, to ride with him no matter where, and it was their watch now. I watched Daddy's cigarette as he flicked it out, the way the coal streaked past the window like a shooting star and bounced away across the asphalt, breaking up behind us. Sitting up, I put my hand on his shoulder and he smiled in the rearview mirror. "You up?" he asked. "Yes, sir." He was quiet for a while before he said, "I was thinking all the thousand times we made this drive, and how Pa loved to listen to the radio." We sat then, both of us, remembering, and Daddy was the one to start but I was thinking of it, too.

"Here's to Daddy Claxton," he sang in that clear baritone, but softly so we wouldn't wake the others. On the second line I joined him:

> *"May his name forever stand*
> *As a symbol of the justice*
> *In the courts throughout the land.*
> *When his final race is over*
> *And the curtain on him falls*
> *We'll carry him back to Dixie*
> *On the Wabash Cannon Ball . . ."*

And we went speeding on like that locomotive through the dark, the last night of summer and the first of fall, heading home to Ruin Creek. You could smell mown hay blowing green across the fields, and I caught a glimpse of fire as someone threw open the furnace door of an old wood-fired barn where they were curing out the cutter now, the last, best leaf. The woods were all lit up with lightning bugs strung like Christmas lights in the branches of the trees, and I felt lifted up somehow way high. As Daddy sang, it almost seemed to me, against all hope, that we might come out with a happy ending after all; it almost seemed like maybe I'd just dreamed that look in Mama's eyes and the hard words they spoke . . . but deep inside I knew this was another made-up story and a lie, the same as telling yourself being fat is just a stage. It's not—I was fat. It isn't the same as being big and strong and not a stage, and if I was ever going to change, I couldn't listen anymore to lies but say the honest truth of it aloud to my own heart. That night was when I did, and also said another truth I knew: that Daddy wasn't coming home. I hated what I knew, I hated it so much . . . but the truth I hated even more was that it was probably better if he didn't. He'd still be my daddy and I'd keep on loving him even if Mama had to stop, but our old life, the one we used to have before the footprints, that was gone and never coming back. That was the hardest truth of all.

And what was left . . . Just that, I guess, the truth, which in a way was Pa's last gift to me and more than all the fishing poles and Barlow knives there ever were, even if that night beside the loss of him it didn't seem like much. As we drove, I realized even if Pa was gone, my love for him was not. I still had that, and I could feel it there inside me deep and strong. It bound me to him like the fisherman's knot, which you can cut in a split second but not untie; if you hitch it fast and right, nothing in this world can ever make it come undone, not even the tidal wave the day it comes. I had my love for him and each of them—for Nanny and for Reed and Mama and for Daddy, Daddy, too—mine for them and theirs for me, and even if love wasn't strong enough to hold our world together, it still made the broken pieces shine.

*The author is grateful to a number of people who helped along the way: Leslie Alexander, Sally Alston, Larry Kessenich, Roland Merullo, Wendell Minor, Charles Rose, Amy Williams, Renée Zuckerbrot; with special thanks to Frances Apt, David Gernert, Ned Leavitt and Bob Wyatt; and, above all, to Stacy Huntington.*